LORD OF THE WARRIORS

BY

RIVER WOLF

Other Novels by River Wolf
Available from Amazon

Teenage Anarchist

Disarmed

My Dark Side

Guy Slimy

The Black Group

Secrets and Demons

LORD OF THE WARRIORS

BY

RIVER WOLF

DEITIES OF SIONIA:

Dirotalo: deceased dragon god

Hermateio: god of the arts

I'magee: god of magic

Lazox: god of animals

Majatee: goddess of the mountains

Nadix: god of the jungle

Phalaetus: goddess of agriculture

Qiami: goddess of war

Rahn: god of fire

Shilotey: goddess of weather

Silotious: queen of the gods and goddesses

Zadeezey: goddess of water

Zadohkoo: god of death

GLOSSARY:

Alontae: holy book for the deities

Basbahti: a northern town which is known for dragons

Blood and Bull: Krull's gang on Bounty Hunter Island

Bounty Hunter Island: an island ruled by the mob in southern Sionia

Dadeaka: a farming community on a plateau

Dadokoh Square: a large plaza in Santalonia located outside of the palace

Danjia: a grassland territory in north-western Sionia

Eftalous Lake: the largest lake in Sionia

Fordonchi: a town on the north-east coast of Sionia

Frosher Volcano: a dead volcano outside of O'Jahnteh

Gogalyta: a mountain town in eastern Sionia

Gradit: a south-eastern town in Sionia

Joandosya: a right-wing political party

Laleaka: a rich town on the east coast of Sionia

Naflit Bayou: a swampy region in south-eastern Sionia

O'Jahnteh: the third largest city in Sionia

Paleeshii: a gang from Xatica

Patassy: the most northern town in Sionia

Post 17: individuals who do not physically age after 17 due to a curse

Raroaka: a town on the west coast

Rognanakh Highlands: a grassy mountainous region in north-eastern Sionia

Santalonia: the capital and largest city in Sionia

Sionia: the country which this story takes place in
Sixalix: a southern coastal town with massive beaches

Stodaneatoo: the second largest city in Sionia

Tathika: a humanistic race of dragons which Wes is part of

Thoolithay: a disease which Bashar gets

Thithaleeth: oil which can burn for a long time even when wetted with water

Vadonty: a mountain village outside of Stodaneatoo

Valushia: Krull's hometown

Vigilum: a member of the police force

Vindadong: Keifer's ship

Wadassy: Jason's tribe

Wadonshea: the Sionian communist party

Xatica: a lawless territory sandwiched between rivers and mountains

Yefhati: a cave buried beneath Naflit Bayou where apocalypse rituals were held by past death magic cults

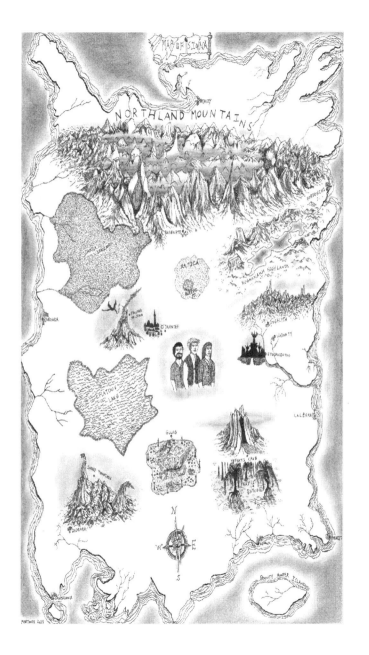

BOOK I:

LIVING WITH A REVOLUTION

I sat on my magic carpet and drifted toward the sky. Going for a ride on my magic carpet usually eased my anxiety. Carrying my sword next to me also calmed me down. With all the turmoil that had recently erupted in the land, it seemed wise to carry a weapon at hand.

I flew my magic carpet to the east. Heading deep into the jungle would help me escape from the chaos which was brewing in my hometown O'Jahnteh, the third largest city in the kingdom of Sionia, a continent surrounded by an endless ocean.

When I sought escape, I often imagined that I was the peoples' hero: the Lord of the Warriors. I would punish thieves who robbed the defenseless, slaughter serial killers, and vanquish politicians who were societal criminals. I loved seeing myself as a champion who destroyed evil with swords and magic. If I had my way, I would become a superhero.

I firmly believed that everyone should help one another. As people, we had a responsibility to ensure that others were healthy, smart, happy, and taken care of in times of distress. If the government wanted you to support their system, then they had to take care of you. I didn't believe that one could be a patriot if the government was making things hard for you.

Sadly, my boyhood fantasies were becoming less entertaining and more rooted in the darkness which was getting harder to ignore.

Protests were being held outside government offices daily. All too often, the protestors were being silenced and arrested by security troops. Those who weren't protesting were joining the vigilum forces. Since thousands of government workers had been laid off, these unemployed folks needed jobs. The government was pouring money into defense forces, so many people were signing up to join the military or the vigilums forces. All salaries and social benefits for joining security forces had risen to attract more recruits.

I was glad that my dad had no plans of joining the vigilums. Up until a month ago, he'd been a crew leader of the city garbage force. After twenty years of hauling waste, he'd been laid off. The settlement he received was only the equivalent to two weeks of pay.

My mom ran a small shop outside of our house. Selling tea, beer, sweets, and household products wasn't bringing in enough cash to keep our four-person family afloat, so my dad awoke early every morning and headed out to the jungle to pick wild fruit which was sold out of the store.

Flying about on my magic carpet didn't clear my mind of these ailing thoughts as much as I'd hoped. After an hour of cruising, I stopped by my friend Marco's house.

Marco's mom had died of malaria a few years back. His brother had turned to gang life, and no one was sure of what he'd been up to since his disappearance some seasons back. Marco's dad was a prison guard and an executioner. When mine and Marco's school had closed, Marco's dad had told him to find work, ignoring Marco's plans to study botany at university. Unlike many other citizens, Marco's dad agreed with King Rex's new policies of increasing the security forces. A larger force of vigilums meant more criminals which meant more work for dungeon keepers and executioners.

I invited myself into the clay-brick bungalow which housed what was left of Marco's family. I heard a familiar laughter coming from the room Marco shared with his brother.

"Yo Don, what's going on, you crazy son of a bitch?" our friend Robin said.

Robin was sprawled on the floor with a bottle of wine.

"Same old," I said. "What about you clowns? Have you been partying or banging any chicks I might know?"

"The nosy man has no understanding of privacy," Marco said.

"I'm hoping for the best among my friends," I said.

"I won't tell cuz it will make you jealous," Robin laughed.

"In that case I'd like a hit from that bottle of wine," I said.

"You got to pay me eight pieces of eight if you want some," Robin smirked, "make that sixty-four."

"You capitalistic twat," I said.

Robin passed me the bottle. For the past few generations, Robin's family had owned the largest chariot-building company in Sionia. As tycoons, his family paid no taxes and enjoyed all the wealth money could buy. They supported King Rex's new economic policies of eliminating government funding toward schools, healthcare, recreation, and road construction. Many laid-off government workers were now flooding into chariot factories. Robin's parents figured that they could open more factories since many people were desperate to work for minimum wage, a wage so stingy that it would have been illegal under past governments.

"Much better," Marco spoke. "In my house we show our guests hospitality and treat them with snacks."

Robin's bottle of port was expensive but too sweet for me. At least once a week, Robin stole a bottle from his parents' large collection of spirits. As long as Robin didn't steal an overly prized bottle which was being saved for a special occasion, his folks never took notice of his thieving. My parents didn't have any money for booze, and Marco's dad would empty a bottle before resting it on the table. As fifteen-year-olds, it would be another three years until any of us could legally buy booze.

"So, what are you guys going to do on the weekend?" Marco asked.

"Isn't everyday a weekend for all of us now that we don't have to go to school anymore?" I said.

"I guess you're right," Marco said, "still, I kind of miss school."

"You need to learn how to entertain yourself man," Robin said. "Quit being a boring turd."

Since all schools had become private, Marco and I were playing hooky since our parents couldn't afford tuition. Like schools, libraries had also become privatized. Many books had been sold off while some branches had been bought up by businessmen. Instead of borrowing books for free, you now had to rent them. Fewer and fewer people were going to the library.

"I will need credentials from a school if I want to get into university or find a scientist job," Marco said.

"I'm supposed to apply to a new academy this weekend," Robin said. "How about you audition for me?"

Marco and I had been friends since we were little, but we hadn't met Robin until about a year ago. He'd been expelled from every private academy in town for everything from attacking teachers, to getting drunk, to pissing in the headmaster's rose bushes. As a last resort, Robin's dad sent him to the same public school which Marco and I had gone to. With the cancellation of the public school system, more private academies were opening. Robin's dad had his fingers crossed that one of the new prep schools would accept his son. Previous headmasters had red flagged Robin's name, and Robin's dad had a feeling that bribery would be the only method of getting his son back in class.

"I'd be happy to go to any academy, but I know that there is no way your dad would ever sponsor me," Marco said.

"If you decided to focus on business or engineering instead of biology, he might just do that," Robin said. "My old man hates to admit it, but he knows I have no interest in designing new chariots or running the company."

"That's cuz you'd run it into the ground," Marco laughed.

Although I thought it was a crime against humanity to shut down all social services, I didn't miss school. I'd been mediocre at academics. Team sports didn't interest me. I'd never been artsy-farty or a tradesman. I'd always been unsure of where my career path would take me.

I liked sword fighting, but my greatest passion was genie magic.

In ancient times, there were no genies. Then one day, the god of magic, I'magee, decided to create his own army. I'magee rounded up a legion of men and women, all humans. He didn't invite any ogres or cyclops to join his army due to his prejudices. However, I'magee did round up both black and white folks, and my gang was proof of this since Marco is black while Robin and I are white.

I'magee presented each of his chosen humans with a ring. Through these rings, the humans became genies. Genies can control magic carpets and manipulate them into aviation vehicles. More importantly, genies can use these rings to control magic. Through intense training, a genie's ring gains a wide range of magical powers as well as more longevity toward spell craft.

After a genie woman gives birth, her baby is taken to one of I'magee's temples. During a baptism ceremony, the genie baby is given it's ring. A genie cannot command magic without wearing their individual ring.

Control of magic was my greatest strength. Teachers had always told me that I was a magical prodigy, and that I could become a truly gifted practitioner of magic. I had taken my studies with magic very seriously, and I could perform a lot of spells which others couldn't. Due to my strengthened ability with magic, I could fly my magic carpet for a long time without needing a rest. I could also easily manipulate fire, wind, and water. Within the last year, I had learned to control lightning bolts, something which few genies ever attempted.

I kept hoping that one day my magical energy would get so strong that I would be able to use magical powers to fix all the political problems in the Sionian government.

"Hey guys, I got an idea for something we can do this weekend," I said.

"Do you want to sneak into the all-girls school again?" Robin laughed.

"That was your idea asshole," I said, "and we wouldn't have been chased off campus if you hadn't babbled about how we were all going to be up to our necks in pussy."

"We didn't even get to see any ladies thanks to your hyperactivity," Marco said as he gave Robin a shove.

"Man, you assholes like to complain lots," Robin said. "So, Don, what's your big idea?"

"You guys want to go to Santalonia and join the revolution?" I spoke.

"Oh yeah man, three fifteen-year-olds are going to run away to Santalonia, assassinate King Rex and become national heroes when martial law is being enforced and security forces are at their all-time high," Robin laughed. "Get real man."

"Don has a point," Marco said. "The revolution needs as many warriors as it can get. Unless the government topples, I'll never be able to go to university, and I'll never leave the slums."

"We have a responsibility toward our society," I said. "Right now, none of us are doing anything with our lives. Let's try and make a difference for the better. The government has made a lot of changes recently, all of them for the worse. Let's help fix their mistakes."

"Santalonia is pretty far away," Robin said.

"Let's camp in the jungle, it will be kind of like a holiday," I said.

"It's kind of dangerous with weather and wild animals," Robin reminded.

"Are you scared?" Marco teased. "Will you come camping with us if you get to bring mommy or some of your servants?"

"Hey, I'm not a wimp," Robin said. "I'll even bring some camping gear to make things easier for us."

"So, you want to come with us to Santalonia and join the revolution eh?" I grinned.

"Shit yeah," Robin said. "Joining the revolution against that tyrant King Rex and his right-wing government will be the ultimate step of rebellion, and the biggest fuck you to my dad and his selfish corporate greed."

"Right on," I said as Robin and I high fived.

Robin's brief speech was funny, but what was even more amusing was that Robin was joining the rebellion out of ego and alcohol.

"How about you Marco?" I asked.

"I'm totally with you on joining the revolution," he answered. "When someone takes something from you, you've got to take it back. The government has robbed us of health, intelligence, freedom, fun, and security. They have given us fear, paranoia, poverty, restrictions, and hatred. It's time to take back what we deserve and give the government what it hates, disobedience."

Growing up in the slums and coming from a broken home had traumatized Marco for life. His desire to do good for others and correct problems always came from dark internal rage. In his beliefs, whenever someone did something bad, you had to fix it. Only when things were resolved, could you feel happy.

We made a list of items which we would bring and agreed to meet in the park at first light the next morning. It looked like we would spend a few days camping in the jungle before reaching Santalonia. This really excited me because I hadn't been camping in two years. Marco was the most outdoorsy out of all of us and had done a fair amount of hiking, hunting, and foraging. Robin had never been camping outside of his yard, but he would bring a tent.

I had a lot of difficulty falling asleep that night. Part of me thought that I would end up staying awake all night, waiting for the chance to sneak out the next morning. My mom usually got up at 5:00 A.M. to go for a run while my dad had been leaving the house before first light to fetch fruit in the distant forests. Both my parents needed to be gone by the time I left home. My younger sister Julia would want to know where I was going, but lying to a ten-year-old was so easy it made me feel guilty.

I didn't have many supplies to pack in my rucksack: a dagger, slingshot, canteen, a few buns, a bag of trail mix, and a pot and spoon would do me good for the trip. I also had my magic carpet and sword. Robin and Marco would bring a few other items, but for the most part, we would use our magic to survive. Hunting and foraging wild fruit and root vegetables sounded like a lot of fun. Robin also said that he'd bring a load of cash for when we got into the city.

I ended up getting about two hours of sleep that night. Too many thoughts of adventure gave me wild fantasies.

Once my parents were gone, I climbed out from my hammock, and my sister woke up. I'd planned on leaving my parents a note, saying that I'd found a job and would be away for a week. I didn't plan on dying, and if I was going to stay more than a week in Santalonia then I'd send them a letter. Either way, I didn't want my worry wart folks to know that I was running away to join the revolution.

"Why are you up so early?" Julia asked.

Since I was a night owl and was almost always reluctant to get out of bed, Julia's suspicion was understandable.

"I got a new job," I blurted, a thought which came to me on the spot.

"Where?" Julia yawned as she rubbed sleep from her eyes.

"I'll be working on a hemp farm."

"Why is your bag packed?"

"I'll be gone for a week. The farm is about thirty kilometres from here, so I'll be staying overnight in a guest house."

I'd have to keep close track of my lies and not change my story if I didn't want to get busted.

"Why didn't you say anything at dinner last night?" Julia questioned.

"Mom doesn't know but Dad does," I said.

"Why?"

"Mom doesn't want me working away from home. Dad knows, and he says it's okay cuz I'll make a load of money and bring it all home. Mom thinks going away is dangerous, and she wants me to attend class at the school with volunteer teachers, but Dad and I agreed that spending a week away from home is okay."

At least part of that lie was true; there were some free lessons being taught by voluntary teachers. Julia had attended some, but I'd bailed on all of them. Mom didn't want me to find any part-time work though Dad's attitude was that money was money.

"Got to go now," I said, "see you next week."

With that, I was out the door and flew toward the park. I was going to arrive earlier than Marco or Robin, but that would give me time to reflect on things and have breakfast. The lies I'd told Julia clouded my mind, and I kept thinking about how I would resolve these tall tales which would hit my parents by the end of the day. Things were going to be pretty peculiar at dinner tonight when Dad would deny having given me permission to take up a week's work on a hemp farm. I realized that I should have left my parents a note, but Julia had annoyed me, so I'd felt compelled to bolt.

Marco showed up on time, but Robin was an hour late.

"Could you've landed any later," I groaned when Robin finally arrived.

"We were wondering if your mama's overprotective security guards arrested you for trying to run away," Marco said.

"I tell you guys, sometimes being poor makes life way easier," Robin said. "It's hard to sneak away when you have so many damn servants creeping around your house."

"Believe me, life isn't easy when you're forever worried about every coin and wondering where your next meal will come from," Marco said.

"Being rich has its downsides," Robin said. "Most of society resents you; you have a harder time relating to people who aren't loaded; people become so paranoid of losing their wealth that they hire security guards and watchdogs, and you become isolated because you're always getting pampered by money and servants. You street kids are way tougher than I am because you were exposed to the rough side at an early age."

I agreed with much of what Robin had said. Still, I really hated being poor, especially during the revolution. I didn't need to be rich, but being middle class seemed appealing.

"It's time to toughen you up," Marco said. "Let's get the hell out of here and head into the jungle."

With that, we took to the skies and zoomed over plantations on our magic carpets. Since the plantations were owned by large corporations, they stretched for epic distances. Beyond the plantations was a never-ending wilderness of jungle.

There were almost no settlements between O'Jahnteh and Santalonia. Few mountains stood in our way since they mostly existed in the north and east ends of Sionia. We could fly at top speeds without worrying about bumping into anything. Jungle birds didn't tend to fly above the treetops. The thick forests were broken by ponds, streams, rivers, and lakes. We never came across any grassy clearings unless they were around a body of water. Twice a day we stopped for a snack and a swim at a lake.

I wouldn't have thought that running away would feel like such a long-deserved vacation. Part of me wanted to skip out on the revolution and stay in the jungle as a form of escapism from the turmoil that was going on in the city. At the same time, I felt a responsibility to help right all the wrongs. You couldn't evade problems forever no matter how much fun hiding out on vacation could be. It was a bit bothersome to know that so much awful shit was going on while Robin, Marco, and I were having fun. Once the revolution was over, we would definitely need another escape into the jungle. A long vacation seemed like a great reward after battling national issues.

We stopped to set up camp at a clearing next to a river about two hours before dark. Robin and I erected his tent while Marco set up a kitchen and a food hang. After that, Robin and I went to look for firewood. Once we'd brought back a load of kindling, Marco was squeezing the blood out of a python and into the pot.

"Did you get attacked by that serpent?" Robin asked.

"Nah, I chopped his head off and figured that we could eat this guy for dinner," Marco replied.

"For real?" Robin gasped.

"Oh yeah, it's all protein which is what we need," Marco said. "I also picked some mangos, a papaya, and found some potatoes, so we'll have a pretty healthy dinner."

"Have you ever eaten snake before?" I asked Robin. "I know it's peasant food, but it can be quite delicious."

"Nope, but this should be a cool experience," Robin said. "Eating a wild animal is one more way of making this jungle trip savage."

The snake stew was succulent. The wild mangoes and papaya were tastier than any of the fruits from the plantations. River water was fresher than anything from a well. Marco and I couldn't remember the last time we'd had such a good meal. Even Robin (who was catered to by top chefs daily) was impressed with our barbaric jungle meal.

After dinner, Robin had to piss. He got up from his empty bowl of snake stew, walked four metres to the left and started leaking on a log.

"What the hell is wrong with you?" Marco said.

"I didn't know you were a prude who was offended by a dude taking a leak," Robin said. "How about I turn around and piss in your soup? You can get a look at my big cock too."

"Damn it, you're contaminating this kitchen with germs," Marco bellowed. "If you got to piss or shit then you should walk fifty metres into the jungle to do your business."

"How was I supposed to know?" Robin said. "No one told me."

"Ain't you ever heard of not shitting where you eat," I chuckled.

"Whatever," Robin grunted. "I'll check into an inn once we get to Santalonia while you two can snuggle up in the poor house."

"Excellent, you're a stereotypical member of the bourgeoisie who won't share his wealth with others," I joked.

"Fuck a cow," Robin snorted.

"I can't wait for daddy to ground you for stealing funds from corporate tax breaks," Marco added.

"Bite a ball," Robin grumbled.

Robin was the only guy I'd ever met who had indoor plumbing in his house. The rest of us were used to outhouses or squatting in the woods. In addition to having fountains, toilets, and a private bathhouse, Robin's family palace also had elaborate gardens, a swimming hole, a sports field, a horse corral the size of a small farm, and a racetrack for their chariots. I could admire the elaborate architecture and lush gardens around his home, but at the same time, I felt bitterness toward how much his family owned while so many were sleeping in their shoes.

Although Robin's house was massive to say the least, he'd had a very difficult time escaping from it this morning. His mom and some of the servants had wondered why he'd wanted to pack a tent which had only been used once. Robin had told her that he was lending the tent to Marco for a camping trip. Since Robin wasn't allowed to leave his house without permission, he'd had to wait for over an hour for the gardeners and security guards to have their backs turned while he flew off the roof of his house on his magic carpet.

Marco had found Robin's story amusing considering Marco hadn't told his dad anything. I doubted Marco's drunkard of a father would speculate as to whether Marco had been kidnapped or killed. Although Marco hadn't heard from his brother for a while, he took it as good faith that his brother was doing alright since the vigilums hadn't shown up on his door.

Robin and Marco laughed at my story of escape involving my nosy younger sister. My parents weren't exactly overprotective, nor were they drunken and negligent, so I guess I came from the best hand.

Once darkness fell, we put out the campfire and climbed into the tent.

"Man, the ground is hard," Robin said.

"Get used to it princess," I chuckled. "Tomorrow we might be camped atop stone."

"Are you guys sure there isn't a village nearby?" Robin asked. "I'll pay for a room at an inn."

"Baby," Marco gushed. "Why don't you try sleeping outside for ten minutes? After settling down in mud puddles, tree roots, vicious bugs, flapping bats, and snakes on the prowl, you'll be happy to cuddle up inside this tent with two other guys."

"Besides, it looks like it's going to rain tonight," I said.

Robin grunted. Marco and I soon fell asleep. I was pretty sure that Princess Prissy had a difficult time getting shuteye. Between his first camping trip, sleeping on the jungle floor, and the fear of wild animals, Robin probably got little sleep and had fierce nightmares.

It took us another two days to reach Santalonia. We continued to camp by rivers, scavenge produce, and hunt. Robin's whining decreased as he adapted to the outdoors. I was hoping that these changes would lead to future camping trips. Normally Robin's idea of a good time was getting drunk or playing lacrosse, but if he, Marco, and I could go on jungle camping trips, then we would have a lot to look forward to in the future.

One of the greatest aspects of having been in the jungle was that we could forget about all the problems in the city. When in the wilderness, you lived with nature. In the city, you lived with riots, crime, crowds, a useless government, hordes of vigilums, bossy parents, a lack of social benefits, little money, people who had more than you, and people who you didn't want to put up with. Maybe the solution for all of us was to become forest hermits who lived off the land.

Marco and I had never been to Santalonia, but Robin came here at least twice a year. Throughout the journey to the city, Robin had been under mine and Marco's shadow, but now that we'd reached the cosmopolitan capital of Sionia, Robin was the leader.

"You guys are so lucky to have me here," Robin grinned. "If it weren't for me, you'd all get lost, end up in a dirty alley, and then robbed and beaten to pulp."

"I would like to see how you would have handled the jungle without us," Marco said. "You didn't know where to piss, and you got all whiny about having to sleep on the ground."

"Besides, it was my idea to come here," I said. "You told us it was a bad idea so keep your cockiness quiet."

The metropolis of Santalonia was built along the ocean and stretched for endless kilometres. On the south you had ports, rich houses, and beaches. The city centre consisted of rich gated communities, business districts, art communities, city parks and gardens, middle class neighbourhoods, government offices, universities, and a few other cultural relics. The north side of the city contains a mixed bag of residential areas. There were no suburbs or outskirt communities around Santalonia since the city backed onto thick jungle.

Robin checked us into an inn. None of us had gotten much sleep the night before due to intense rain. Robin insisted that he pay for a bed for each of us and buy us a hearty dinner. As much as the evils of money infuriated me, it was beneficial to have a rich friend like Robin.

We took kettle-heated showers, rested on our beds for a few hours, and then dined on catch of the day seafood at the inn café. Since the inn was in a walled community with lots of heavily armed security guards, we didn't see any signs of the revolution. I figured this was what a lot of rich folks liked to do: hide behind walls, indulge in possessions which others didn't have, and pretend that all the atrocities going on outside wouldn't affect them.

The thing was, we were all connected. No matter how much money you had or how many barriers you hid behind, your walls would eventually cave in, and money wouldn't be able to buy you out of anything when the revolution reached its peak. The ironic thing was that a lot of the workers who the bourgeoisie employed and depended on were also members of the revolution.

Robin tried to get into the inn tavern, but the bouncer booted him out. Marco and I laughed pretty hard cuz we'd warned Robin that he wouldn't get in since he didn't have a fake ID and didn't look eighteen years of age. At one point Robin threatened the bouncer with magic and his sword. The bouncer laughed while Marco dragged Robin back to the room. We didn't want anyone getting arrested before we took part in any demonstrations.

In the end, we decided to get a good night's sleep. Tomorrow would be the day that could change our lives forever.

We got up early the next morning. After breakfast, we headed to Dadokoh Square which was the heart of the national rebellion. Protests in Santalonia ranged from laid back pacifist callings for equality to full on riots where stores were attacked and looted, and people were trampled to death, beaten by the vigilums, or locked in prison.

Drums were banged and some people were voicing complaints, but there wasn't any unison chanting going on. People held up signs and banners, but that was nothing compared to the anti-government graffiti which was popping up all over town.

"Man, this is boring," Robin grumbled. "No one is fighting or rioting. Everyone is sitting around like they're at some pacifist love-in, even the vigilums look bored."

Vigilums were usually armed with clubs or short swords and in some cases crossbows. A few of them were walking back and forth across the square. Since the crowd wasn't big and hardly anyone was carrying weapons, the vigilums didn't feel threatened. Violent outbursts usually came unexpectedly, so you'd think the vigilums would be a bit more paranoid. Then again, about a thousand people had been arrested in the last week, so the vigilums were probably thinking that by the end of the season, all dissidents would be locked up, and no protestors would be left among the public.

"Maybe we should make contact with others," I said.

"Since things are peaceful right now, it might be a lot easier to meet up with people and form an alliance," Marco said.

I was glad that Marco agreed with me, but I knew that I would have to do most of the talking. Due to his introversion, it took a lot of willpower for Marco to approach others. Robin and I were extroverts, but I believed that Robin's goofy behaviour would make him look like an ass clown. I figured that I would have to meet up with others, share my political views, and let new faces know about the trip from O'Jahnteh to Santalonia. This was easier said than done. One had to be paranoid of others during a revolution. Some of the seemingly passive protestors could be undercover vigilums.

A crew of painters was cleaning up graffiti which depicted criticism of King Rex. Normally the walls surrounding the square displayed patriotic murals, but now there were splattered drawings of King Rex pissing on historical heroes, having sex with donkeys, and looking like an ugly fool. Phrases such as "King Rex sucks dreck," "King

Rex will never get erect," "Rexist," and, "Death to King Rex," surrounded these paintings.

"Damn those janitors," Robin said. "I ought to steal their paint and write some rude things about King Rex."

"I dare you," I said.

"I will eh," Robin grinned.

When the crew of cleaners took a break, Robin snuck up and stole a can of paint and a brush.

"Hey kid, get back here," one of the janitors called as Robin splashed paint on the ground.

"Get off your lazy ass and get me," Robin laughed.

"What you're doing is illegal," a second janitor howled.

"My graffiti is keeping you cleaners in business," Robin smirked. "You should be thanking me. Tons of government employees have been laid off so janitors like yourselves need derelicts like me to justify your government paid salaries."

I nodded with Robin's point. I found it despicable how health workers, teachers, and garbage haulers had been laid off from government jobs, but folks who covered up slander about the government were still being paid competitive wages.

"The vigilums will arrest you for vandalism," one of the janitors called.

"This is my right as a citizen to exercise freedom of speech," Robin called. "I'm saying what I feel about that imbecile King Rex. Besides, this is a public space, paid for by taxpayers. Since my family's money helped pay for Dadokoh Square, I have a right to decide what it looks like."

I doubted Robin's family's tax dollars had paid for Dadokoh Square. Like many other tycoons, Robin's old man always looked for loopholes and write-offs within the tax system. That and Dadokoh Square was hundreds of years old.

A lone vigilum was alerted of the argument between Robin and the cleaner. A baton was raised in the vigilum's hand, signaling that he would pound first and ask questions later. Robin's eyes caught the weapon. He dropped the paint brush and drew his sword.

The vigilum raised his thin wooden baton. As he did this, Robin's falchion flashed through the baton, breaking the weapon into two splintered hunks of wood. Robin cackled as the mutilated piece of wood rolled across the square and overtop his paint job.

"Man, you're arrogant," Robin laughed. "I guess vigilums who want to work for King Rex need to have an IQ smaller than their shoe size but an ego as high as the clouds. Let me let you in on a little bit of logic big guy, sharp metal swords are more powerful than puny wooden batons."

The disarmed vigilum blew his whistle. One vigilum came from the north, two ran from the east, a fourth dude headed in from the west, and nine others dashed in from the south.

Marco and I nodded at one another. Waves of fear and excitement flooded through me. For years I had dreamed of battling corrupt authority figures.

I unsheathed my katana while Marco pulled his whip out of his satchel. Although Marco was skilled at all weapons, he'd mastered the whip like no one else. I figured that he liked the whip because it invoked so much emotional hatred. Although he never spoke of it, I knew Marco's father had taken the whip to him in the past.

Robin charged toward the sword-wielding vigilum from the north. Blades clashed, parried, jabbed, and flashed as Robin and the vigilum bounced back and forth across the square. It looked like Robin had found his match.

Marco's whip flashed to the east. The whip wrapped around a vigilum's club. With a jolt of the shoulder, Marco tugged the club out of the vigilum's hand. Marco towed the club across the square while the vigilum shook his stinging phalanges.

Once the club had been tossed aside, Marco's whip snapped at a vigilum with a blowgun, cracking the weapon in half. A dart dropped to the ground as the vigilum jumped back in shell shock.

Robin and the swordsman continued their duel as the gang of nine neared Marco and I. Although Marco and I were fairly confident with both our weapons, we both knew that nine foot soldiers would overpower us.

I raised my left hand and gazed at my ring. I envisioned a hurricane of furious winds, destroyed houses, ravaged palm trees, and people sucked away in merciless gusts. The green ball inside my ring jiggled. I glared with ferocity and concentrated on my thoughts of a typhoon.

A massive gust of wind shot from my ring, toward the gang of vigilums. In less than a breath, the wind had knocked each of the vigilums to the ground. Weapons splattered across the square. Bruises and welts were forming while blood was weeping from wounds.

Although I enjoyed sword fighting, magic was always a much more powerful weapon. The problem with magic was that it took time and patience. You couldn't shoot spells from your ring with the wink of an eye. I'd had to concentrate and almost meditate to create the powerful burst of wind. Had the vigilums been closer, I would have been forced into using my sword.

Amid my assault against the guards, Marco and I had forgotten about the vigilum from the west until Marco turned in that direction. I yelped when I saw a raised battle-axe, fearing that my victory against the vigilums would be the shortest lived in history.

Blood exploded from the vigilum's face. Amid shock, I realized that a spiked flail had been buried in the vigilum's head. The vigilum's body collapsed to the floor, knocking over Robin's stolen can of paint. Blood mixed with the spilled paint, creating a pink puddle across the nationalistic mosaic.

The flail tugged backward, and more blood erupted from the wound. I looked to the left and realized that this flail belonged to a guy who was two or three paces taller than me, and I wasn't a shrimp. When Marco and I had our backs turned, this giant must have spotted the axe man and then pulverized his face with the flail. Marco and I owed this tall dude our lives.

Marco and I had seen plenty of dead bodies in our lives, but this was the first time we'd ever seen someone killed. I wasn't sure if I would call this murder since mine and Marco's lives had been saved. I knew that Marco would prefer to not talk about the death, but I needed a second opinion. I hadn't killed the vigilum, but I was still somewhat involved. If the vigilum hadn't been killed with the flail, then I would have probably died. I wondered if this giant was a mercenary who'd killed dozens of people or if he was a commoner like us. Perhaps this was his first kill. I wondered how he felt. Maybe he believed that he'd done the right thing, and knew that if he hadn't defended Marco and me, we would have died. Based on that idea, he was a hero. Maybe he even enjoyed having killed the vigilum? Or perhaps he felt sheer remorse for having been forced to take a life? Maybe he'd only wanted to hurt the guy and hadn't wanted to kill him?

I told myself to stop overanalyzing everything and start talking. Robin had disarmed his opponent. No blood had been spilled, but the vigilum was on the ground and his sword was out of arm's reach.

"I'm Ace," said the tall man with the flail.

"Don," I introduced as I shook his hand.

Robin grabbed the vigilum's dropped sword and then headed toward us.

"Let's talk later," Ace said. "Come on, I can lead you to the refugee point."

Ace pointed to the right and started hoofing it. Robin, Marco, and I each laid out our magic carpets. I called Ace.

"Hop on," I said. "You can be the navigator. My magic carpet is easily strong enough to hold both of us."

Ace climbed aboard and then pointed a few directions out while I telepathically commanded the magic carpet to chart a course. Marco and Robin followed. We flew high above the city. The architecture of Santalonia was much more exquisite than that of O'Jahnteh. Since Santalonia was the capital city of Sionia, it received much more investment. Public forests, gardens, parks, statues, pagodas, historical monuments, buildings with spires, pyramid roofs, and other fancy features were very common. Although I could admire such artistic architecture, seeing all these fancy buildings reminded me that I lived in a dump.

Ace instructed us to land our magic carpets in an alley. After that he led us into an old warehouse.

"Welcome to headquarters," Ace said. "Oh yeah, I forget to introduce myself."

Ace shook hands with Robin and Marco.

"Anyway, I take it you guys are also a part of the revolution," Ace said.

"Damn straight," Robin said.

"What gang are you a part of?" Ace asked.

"I'll explain our story," I cut in.

Marco wasn't likely to speak up and I knew that Robin would exaggerate things to look macho. Although we'd kicked a load of ass in the square, we were still very new to things and joining up with Ace's gang could do us a world of wonders.

"Sure, why don't I get you guys a snack," Ace offered.

"Thanks," Marco replied.

"Do you have any beer?" Robin asked.

"Sorry," Ace said. "We don't allow alcohol in headquarters. With all the chaos going on, getting drunk is too risky."

Ace fetched us a bowl of fruit and put on a kettle to brew tea. Once the tea was served, I told our story. I stated how we'd been facing lots of issues in O'Jahnteh and thus ran away to join the revolution. We all took turns talking about our ideologies regarding society, politics, and the revolution. Although Robin talked lots, he evaded discussing his family's business to avoid judgements.

"I'm an anarchist," Ace said. "I've been participating in the revolution with a number of other rebels since the beginning of the uprising."

"Where is everyone else?" Marco asked.

"A lot of them are in jail," Ace said. "Other people are at jobs, taking care of their families, or doing other business. However, there is going to be a meeting in about an hour. Even though I've just met you guys, I'd really like you to be there. Our group could really benefit from some brave tough blokes like yourselves. Besides, we could use some genie magic."

"We'd be happy to attend," I said.

"Hells yeah," Robin grinned. "Time to whoop some ass."

About an hour later, two other guys showed up. One of the fellows was a stranger, but the other dude looked vaguely familiar. I was sure I'd seen him before, but I wasn't sure where. It would be odd if I'd seen him before since I hadn't previously been to Santalonia. Funnily enough, the mysteriously familiar dude looked a lot like King Rex.

"Don, Robin, Marco," Ace said, "I'd like you to meet Cal and Kyle."

"Prince Kyle," Robin gasped.

"Please, just Kyle."

"No way," Marco said.

"Holy shit," I said.

"Wait, we're a bunch of rebels, and you've just brought us the king's son," Robin hollered. "I knew this was a trap. Don, Marco, grab your weapons and let's kill these traitors."

Robin grabbed his sword and rose to his feet. Ace placed his hand on Robin's shoulders and insisted that Robin sit down. Marco studied everyone closely, waiting for an explanation. I decided to look at everything as pragmatically as possible.

"Woah, woah, hold on there," Kyle said, "Let me explain a few things. I fucking hate my dad."

Marco nodded. It seemed that the two strangers had something in common which would bond them.

"Who doesn't hate him," Robin snorted.

"No, I mean I am seriously pissed off about everything my old man has done," Kyle said. "I am fucking ashamed to be his son."

"Is that why you're here?" I asked.

"Precisely," Kyle said. "You three new guys showed up at a very good time."

"Why, what's going on?" Robin asked.

"We're going on a raid," Ace said. "I'd like you fellas to come since you randomly showed up and took down a load of vigilums. These guys are genies by the way."

"Excellent," Kyle grinned.

"What's going to happen?" I asked.

"There is a secret passage in between Rex's bedroom and some public gardens," Kyle said. "The tunnel is fairly long, but I say we go in there, grab Rex, and then bring him back here as a hostage. We won't release him until he publicly abdicates."

My eyes raised. This was going to be a day to remember.

I also found it funny how Kyle referred to King Rex by his first name. Did he hate his father so much that he wanted to break off all family ties with him? I'd be pissed at my dad if he had done what King Rex was doing, but I didn't know if I could go to the extremes which Kyle was going toward.

"When do we get down to business?" Marco asked.

"I was hoping more people would show up," Ace answered.

"It looks like everyone else has been arrested," Cal said.

"Shit really?" Ace moaned.

"Afraid so," Cal said. "Some of the other hideouts and have been raided."

"Now is the time to act," Kyle stated.

"Six of us could be the perfect number," Cal said, "small enough to stay quiet and not draw any attention to ourselves, but big enough to have one another's backs."

"Let's give'r," Ace said.

Ace thrust his fist forward. Each of us bashed his punch with our dukes. The fellowship had been united. Six of us were going on a hijacking mission that would forever change the course of Sionian history. I still had a lot of difficulty believing everything which was happening. A few days ago, I'd been pissing and groaning like everyone else, and now it looked like my actions could really change things for the better. Life was truly unpredictable; there was no other way to describe it.

We flew on our magic carpets to a public park. After dismounting the magic carpets, we walked for about three minutes into thick jungle bush. All of us followed Kyle since only he was aware of the secret passage.

Kyle halted in his tracks and cleared away foliage that masked a small stone shaft. Next, Kyle tinkered with the lock on the shaft and opened the door. A ladder connected the shaft to the passage. Kyle lit a lantern and instructed us to follow him.

The catacombs were long and made from adobe. Stone tiles acted as the tunnel floor. The ceiling was high enough for all of us, apart from Ace who was forced into crouching.

"We have a ten-minute walk ahead of us," Kyle said. "There are a few twists, bumps, and up and down sections but nothing too rigorous. There aren't any traps down here, and almost no one knows about this place."

Since we were in a small and unfamiliar dark place, danger could easily kill any of us. Although we were well armed, we all needed to be as safe as possible if we wanted to kidnap King Rex. I felt eagerness and uncertainty, the kind of scares which you love but drive you crazy at the same time.

None of us could wait to get to King Rex's chamber. Kyle kept assuring us that we were getting closer and closer to his dad's bedroom. It was hard to tell how far we'd come through the catacombs since there were no markers. Kyle explained that we weren't in a labyrinth so wouldn't have to worry about getting lost.

After the most suspenseful walk of my life, we reached a door which Kyle pushed open. I held my breath. We were breaking into the king's chamber, ready to take him hostage. This was the pulp of fantasy, and my friends and I were playing the heroes. Nothing could be so exciting or scary at the same time.

Kyle, Cal, Robin, and I pulled our swords. Ace let his flail dangle while Marco armed himself with his whip.

We burst into King Rex's sleeping quarters. His bedroom was the largest room I'd ever seen. Tapestries and paintings decorated the walls. Bookshelves filled with antiques, literature, and other collector's items stood out from every corner. A fountain and a small garden rested in the middle of his room. There were so many precious stones in this room that it looked like a treasure chest had exploded. King Rex's bed was big enough to sleep an entire village.

Everything in his room was of the most exquisite quality. I knew that the king had a lot of jobs to do, but if this bedroom was only part of Rex's pay, then he seemed like the most spoiled man in history. All these luxuries totally justified taking actions against the king's policies which were impoverishing the nation.

King Rex stood up from his desk. He turned toward the six of us and let out a smile.

"Kyle, Kyle, what are you doing?" he smiled. "Are you and your new friends trying to live out another delusional fantasy?"

"This is the end Rex," Kyle barked.

"How many times have I told you to call me father?" King Rex grinned.

"Wipe that smile off your face right now," Kyle growled as his sword flashed forward. "I am not your son. I reject all ties to you and royalty."

Rex let out a sigh and shook his head.

"I told you there would be consequences for your actions," Kyle said. "Your regime is over. The monarchy is dead."

"Would you stop being such an immature petulant brat," King Rex said as he backed up toward a wall which had a sword mounted to it. "You'll never be the king if you don't learn your role and start acting like a man."

"Shut the hell up," Kyle called. "You're coming with us."

"Kyle, you poor little boy," King Rex said once he was within arm's reach of the sword. "I am the supreme dictator of Sionia. I don't take orders from anyone, especially my son."

"You might be the supreme dictator but you're the shittiest leader ever," Robin said.

"I will see that you are arrested," King Rex growled as he grasped the hilt of the mounted sword, "the same goes for the rest of your loony friends Kyle. Shouldn't you kids be off doing your homework?"

"We would if you hadn't closed down all the schools," Ace said.

"I am simply acting in the best interest of the economy and the country," Rex said as he pulled the sword from its scabbard. "Nothing is free in life. You work for a little, you don't get a lot."

"Cut the shit," Ace said. "Your policies have fucked over countless people. You're destroying the middle class, making the poor poorer, and the rich richer."

"And you're wasting tax money on security to safeguard your cowardly ass," Cal said.

"Safeguard his ass," Robin laughed. "He's outnumbered six to one. Come on boys, let's show him who the boss is."

Robin thrust his sword above his head while Cal raised his blade. Marco snapped his whip and Ace swung his flail. I raised my genie ring when King Rex swung his sword.

"You know Kyle, if your friends try to kill me in your presence, then I'm sure the curse of youth will be unleashed," King Rex said.

"What's the curse of youth?" Cal asked.

"According to the Alontae, if a member of royal blood murders the king, then a curse will sweep through Sionia," Marco said, "all youth won't age past seventeen."

"The goddesses and gods believe that a country of kids will destroy the nation," I added. "They invented this curse to scare the royals out of fighting with one another."

"You see Prince Kyle, your friends have more sense than a simple-minded fop like you," King Rex said as he slashed his sword forward.

Kyle reached for his belt and pulled out a throwing knife, one which had been concealed by his baggy shirt. Kyle flung back and tossed the weapon forward. The blade spun like a tomahawk until it entered Rex's neck. A thick stream of blood poured from the king's throat. His yellow tunic turned orange. The sword dropped from his hand. King Rex collapsed to his knees and fell to the side. His crown rolled off his head as his skull smacked against the marble floor. King Rex's skin paled to snow as his eyes closed for eternity.

"Kyle, what the hell?" Ace howled. "You killed your old man."

"He ain't my old man," Kyle said. "He was Sionia's greatest criminal. Now he's nothing but one more dead dipshit who got killed for his pompous and selfish attitude."

Robin gave Kyle a pat on the back while Cal glared at the corpse in disgust. Marco looked away while I wondered if Kyle had planned on murdering King Rex or if this had been a spur of the moment kill. The idea of taking King Rex hostage had seemed more like Ace's idea. King Rex had talked down to us and acted incredibly narcissistic, so maybe Kyle believed that his dad was asking for homicide. A lot of people already thought King Rex was asking to get assassinated due to his despicable governing.

On a distant wall was a tapestry of the six gods and six goddesses. Silotious was the goddesses of gods and goddesses. The mermaid Zadeezey was the goddess of the water. The dragon Rahn was the god of fire. An ogre named Phalaetus served as the goddess of agriculture. A ghostly woman called Shilotey was the goddess of weather. The wizard-genie hybrid I'magee was the god of magic. Qiami the cyclops was the goddess of war. An old man named Hermateio was the god of arts. A strange animal hybrid called Nadix acted as the god of the jungle. A beautiful woman called Majatee was the goddess of the mountains. Lazox (who was always changing his animal-humanoid appearance) was the god of animals. Lastly, Zadohkoo was a vampiric god of death.

The tapestry shimmered. Like everything else in King Rex's bedroom, this tapestry was of top form. Many of the picturesque treasures in this room were only allowed to be owned by the king. In ancient times, Silotious had chosen a king to govern Sionia. The royal family would govern over the country though the gods and goddesses held ultimate authority over everything. The monarch was the goddess and gods' tool who took care of politics, something which all the deities hated to be involved with.

The tapestry continued to shine until a light stepped out from it and took human form. Shapes and colours formed. All the candles, torches, and lanterns in the room darkened to blackness and then reignited in big bursts of fire. All hearts stopped while our eyeballs dilated to their maximum.

Silotious was standing in front of us in physical form. The queen goddess was the most beautiful woman I'd ever seen with her wavy brownish blonde hair, eyes which turned from green to blue to violet, smooth skin, longs legs, desirable figure, and angelic face. It was no wonder that she was the queen goddess.

"Prince Kyle," she said.

"Silotious," Kyle said without bowing or showing any signs of worship. "My name is Kyle; I am not the prince. No one deserves such titles."

"As a member of royal blood, it is your duty to take on the role of king," Silotious said.

"I don't want it," Kyle said. "Fuck monarchy. I'm going to abolish the throne and the crown. Every local government in Sionia is run through a democracy. It's about time the federal government became democratic."

"That is your decision, and I will not interfere with how you choose to govern your country," Silotious spoke. "We goddesses and gods do not like to get involved with the political affairs of mortals."

"I am not governing," Kyle said. "The days of kings are forever gone."

"Very well," spoke Silotious. "However, there is a more pressing issue at hand."

"What?" Kyle barked.

"You killed your father," Silotious said.

"Tell me something that I don't already know," Kyle mocked.

"You have inflicted a curse upon the land," Silotious said. "The king could not be killed by any member of the royal family without unlocking the curse of youth.

"As of now, no youth can physically grow past the age of seventeen. You have destroyed all possibilities of anyone reaching adulthood. Once each of you turn seventeen, you will live as seventeen-year-olds for the remainder of your lives."

"So we've got the fountain of youth," Kyle smiled, "that seems pretty good. Our bodies will stay young and strong, and we won't get all of those old fart diseases."

"What'll happen to contemporary adults?" Ace asked.

"They are unaffected by this curse, and they will continue to age," Silotious answered.

Silotious vanished.

I felt the longest and most uncomfortable silence of my life since neither myself nor my companions knew what to say, which questions should be asked, or how we should react to the madness which had happened in the last two minutes. Shock really was one of the most difficult emotions since there was no easy route of escape from feelings of uncertainty. I wondered about the other wild adventures which the future held for me.

BOOK II:

HURRICANE NATION

As promised, Kyle stepped down from the throne and declared that Sionia was now a democratic republic. He called for an election and bequeathed King Rex's former advisors as the preliminary government. Following this, he became a recluse and many rumours of his whereabouts popped up.

Many political parties formed. After a few months of white-knuckled campaigning, a liberal party won the election by a narrow majority. The average Sionian had wanted federal democracy for years. Many were pleased that King Rex had been killed and that the newly elected viceroy re-introduced social services.

The curse of youth couldn't be ignored. Adults were outraged that they would grow old and die elderly deaths while kids would retain healthy youthful bodies for the rest of their lives. Many arguments stated that youngsters wouldn't mature if they always held onto their seventeen-year-old bodies. Some ranted that the young wouldn't live healthily if they always held onto post-puberty bodies. Another popular belief was that the youth wouldn't know how to treat their parents if they were raised by seventeen-year-olds. Some worried that young and less experienced people would have too much power since there would be less distinctions between ages. Others feared that a nation of adolescents would overpopulate the country since Sionia was going to have nothing but kids in a few generations.

Anyone who'd made it to age eighteen on the day King Rex died was going to grow old and wither away while anyone under the age of eighteen could grow very old while still retaining a youthful body. Old people wished that they could age backward and return to their seventeen-year-old selves, but that never happened. Lots of complaining followed, but that's how adults were; they always had to groan and point out the negative aspects of the young.

Ace headed up to O'Jahnteh to visit Robin, Marco, and I a year after King Rex's murder. I was pretty happy to see Ace, but at the same time, it was a bit weird. Since Ace had been in his twenties during the revolution, he hadn't been hit by the curse of youth. While all of us folks under the age of eighteen were moving toward a freezing point, Ace had reached a physical age which Marco, Robin, and I would never attain. I felt kind of sorry for Ace, as I did for many people. They were going to die of old age while the future generations would live in near-eternal youth. No wonder there was so much depression going around.

Ace and I met up in a teahouse which had been built over a marsh. The owners of the teahouse burnt specials herbs and blends of incense to keep the bugs at bay. Drinking tea, feeling the breeze of nature, smelling delicious incense, listening to gentle flute and xylophone music, and being out in the jungle was the perfect escape from the turmoil of urban life.

"I've come up here on a guerilla mission," Ace said. "There is a dragon hatchery in Frosher Volcano."

"You know, I heard that some politicians are buying dragons and that these monsters went out of control and killed a number of civilians," I said.

"You heard true."

"I don't know how those politicians think they're going to win public approval considering owning dragons is illegal and everyone is scared of them. Lazox created the dragon sanctuary in the north to save the people from these monsters, yet the innocent are now getting killed by these political slave beasts. The whole situation is really wacky man."

"I've come up here to stop the madness."

"How'd you know that Frosher Volcano is being used as a hatchery?"

"A spy I know tracked down the sales of some dragons. He even came up here to sneak a peek. A few days after returning to Santalonia, he was killed by an escaped convict who worked with the smugglers."

"Wow, how dangerous is this hatchery?"

"There is a bit of magma and the odd bit of toxic fumes. My man saw five fully grown dragons guarding the place. There were also a few gangsters down there as well. The gangsters control the dragons with a magic orb. If that orb is destroyed, then the dragons will be able to roam free. Since the dragons are not native to the jungles, they will most likely seize their eggs and migrate north."

"Breaking into this volcano to free dragons sounds like a crazily insane adventure."

"I know Don, that's why I'm asking you to help me."

"What about all those revolutionaries you knew in Santalonia?"

"They're all too wrapped up in all the political issues going on. They don't realize that the illegal smuggling of dragons is a crime against the country. Crooks make lots of blood money from selling weapons to killers; it's fuckin' dirty."

"The Joandosya politicians who are buying dragons are no better than the crooks who are harvesting them."

"They're worse man. They're making illegal purchases and keeping the crooks in business. Most gangs can't afford dragons cuz they're so expensive."

"Politicians are government-approved criminals."

Ace laughed as Marco and Robin showed up at the teahouse. Ace retold the story. Robin and Marco were excited and scared by the tale. I could totally understand their feelings, and it was easy to understand why lots of Ace's friends didn't want to get involved in such a dangerous mission. A volcano with magma, smoke, and toxic gas was frightening enough. Gangsters and dragons made it absolutely horrifying. If we pulled a raid on the place, then our attack against King Rex would look like a cakewalk.

"Each of you guys have gifts," Ace began. "You're all courageous, smart, strong, and loaded with magical abilities which most people don't have. You're also independent and willing to act against evil while others hide. If more people did what you guys had done back in Santalonia, then politicians and gangs wouldn't be getting away with actions against humanity."

"I'm in," I declared. "We all have a responsibility to clean up the mess that our country is in. The government is either too useless to solve the problems or too misguided in their priorities. In that case, it's up to us to protect the interests of the people."

"Count me in as well," Marco spoke. "Too much wrong has been done, and too little is being done to fix it."

"Hells yeah, I'm going along for the ride," Robin beamed. "Let's have some fun teaching these bitch criminals a lesson. Power to the vigilantes man."

Each of us toasted, declaring our allegiance to the cause.

Since King Rex's death a year earlier, none of us had been too heavily involved in any causes. Robin and Marco were focused on their academics, so it was understandable why they had veered away from charities. I didn't have too much of an excuse for not getting involved in missions. I'd drifted from one labour job to the next. For months I'd been asking myself what I could do to make my country a better place. A lot of charities wanted people with skills which I didn't have. Other charities were sponsored by corporations, and much of the fundraised money was stolen by the accountants. At times I felt useless for not being involved in more causes. Sure, I'd helped in the revolution, but in the end, it was all about what Kyle had done. I couldn't have done what he had.

Now was my chance to stop bumming about. I was nervous about attacking the volcano but brave enough to overcome my fear. My training in the art of magic would be put to very good use.

Ace, Marco, Robin, and I rose early the next morning and headed to Frosher Volcano. We were all a bit tense on the ride. Ace assured us that we were doing the right thing by acting as a small guerrilla band. The guards at Frosher Volcano weren't expecting an attack so wouldn't have many weapons. Marco hypothesized that none of the guards were trained soldiers, but rather scum from skid row. Ace pointed out that his friend had gotten into the volcano undetected so there was no reason why the four of us couldn't, especially when we had magic carpets.

Frosher Volcano stood out among the thick jungle. The volcano wasn't tall, but geologists hypothesized that it went very deep. There were no trees within a few kilometres of the crater because ash and lava had killed all the vegetation. Trickles of smoke puffed from the top of the crater, but things didn't look overly dangerous.

We halted our magic carpets above the volcano. From what we could see, there was a pond of lava at the bottom of the crater. About three dragons were inside but we couldn't tell for sure. The inside of the volcano contained a few levels as if it were a quarry.

"What'd ya say?" Ace asked.

"Let's do this," I said.

Marco nodded.

"Hells yeah," Robin grinned as he unsheathed his sword.

"Remember, we want to do this as stealthily as possible," Ace said. "Lower your magic carpets slowly into the crater and try to hide in the shadows, but don't get too close to the smoke cuz it could be poisonous and blinding. Let's land, look for the orb, destroy it, and then get the hell out of the crater. If the dragons fly away, mission accomplished."

We all nodded. I couldn't wait to get inside. I was a bit nervous, but procrastination would only make suspense more painful. Brawling gangsters, inferno lava, poisonous smog, stinging smoke, and hellish dragons lay below. There was no way we were going to avoid all the dangers, but we had to keep as low a profile as possible. Stealth was crucial. The destruction of the orb and our survival were the only things which mattered.

Our magic carpets descended very slowly into the crater. Ace was a passenger to Marco's magic carpet while

Robin and I flew solo. Smoke drifted everywhere which made steering our magic carpets difficult.

The three dragons rested near the lava pool, unaffected by the heat. Such resistance to the terrors of the land guaranteed that each of those hellish monsters could easily kill us.

I'd never seen such large creatures before. Their thin bat-like wings spread several paces. Each dragon had a tail of equal length. The tips of their tails were as sharp as a scorpion's stinger. The dragons' large bodies were as leathery as a crocodile. Four short legs held fearsome claws. A dragon's head looked like a combination between a lizard and an eagle. It was hard to tell which colours the dragons were since the only colours which seemed to exist in the crater were red, orange, yellow, gray, brown, and black.

Ace whispered something to Marco. Marco waved to Robin and I and then veered his magic carpet over to what appeared to be a cave. Ace and Marco landed their magic carpet. Robin and I continued to creep behind them. As far as we could tell, no one had spotted our intrusion.

Several fireballs shot in our direction. Ace dropped to the volcanic rock ground. Marco dashed out of the way. Robin and his magic carpet flew to the right. The flames grazed my magic carpet. I feared that I'd been burnt and would crash to the ground within seconds.

After a few long terrifying moments, another fireball shot. Sparkles blasted everywhere after the burning ball crashed into a crater wall.

One dragon raised its head, ready to release another fireball. I raised my hand and aimed my ring at the dragon. Amid the darkness of the volcanic crater, my green ring glowed as bright as ever. I gazed into the jewel and imagined water. As I concentrated at my hardest, the ball inside the jewel shook so hard that I thought that my ring would shatter.

A fireball formed in the dragon's mouth. Flames spewed within seconds. Just when the blast of fire was about to hit me, a geyser of water torpedoed from my ring. The water was as chilling as a glacier. My ravenous geyser collided against the fireball, cooling and suffocating the flames to smoke.

A new fireball shot from the monster. The flame blast collided against a staircase which led from one level of the volcano to the next. Boardwalks lay at the top and bottom of each staircase. Flames crawled along the boardwalk which Ace and Marco were standing atop.

Ace screamed and ran toward the stony ground. Marco raised his ring finger at hanging rocks from above. An invisible propulsion of force shot from his ring and blasted the hanging rocks. Stones fell and landed on the burning boardwalk, leaving the flames to burn behind the rock wall.

I noticed another fireball forming. I raised my ring and visualized intense winds. Right when the blast of fire burst from the dragon's mouth, a gust of wind shot from my ring. The blast of air clashed with the fireball, splashing the flaming sphere into many small fragments which evaporated into nothingness.

Robin flew his magic carpet close to me.

"Those were two wicked shots," he yelled overtop the growling dragons, "but how about shooting those fireballs back at the dragons?"

"That'll kill them," I responded.

"I know how you feel about animals being killed in battle, but it's us or them," Robin said. "What good is saving these dragons' lives if they kill us before we can liberate the eggs?"

I'd always hated the idea of animals participating in battle be they dogs, horses, elephants, dragons, or any other species that had been innocently thrown into the conflicts of humans. If someone assaulted you, kill them. If someone's animal attacked you, slaughter the animal's owner. As hard as it was to accept, an exception had to be made with the dragons.

Robin and I held our ringed hands forward. We each envisioned a force shield. Force shields required much magic energy, and Robin and I telepathically agreed that we should work together to create one large shield.

The magic from mine and Robin's rings created a large violet force shield. The shield appeared as thin as a bedsheet but proved its strength when three fireballs rebounded off it. Each of the fireballs came closer than I would have liked, and each time I'd feared getting scalded if not torched.

Down below, four gangsters approached Marco and Ace.

Ace charged and let out his flail. The spiked ball of his weapon flew forward, digging holes in the lead gangster's face. Blood shot from fresh wounds as the gangster collapsed. Ace picked up his fallen foe, raised the gangster over his head, and tossed him. The chucked gangster collided with his three companions. Each of the gangsters toppled over the ledge and rolled head over heels down the rocky slope. There was no way that any of them would survive getting bashed against so many lava stones.

After viewing Ace's bout, my head spun around to check my back. My eyes caught sight of an approaching dragon. I darted backward and almost fell from my magic carpet. A man was riding this dragon as if he were commanding a horse. A long flame projected from the dragon's mouth. I shifted my magic carpet to the right, narrowly avoiding a barbecuing.

As I evaded my attacker, I noticed an extraordinarily putrid odor, which I assumed was toxic gas. I raised my ring and imagined a breeze blowing toward the poisoned mist. Wind flew from my ring and blew the poisoned gas into the dragon rider's face. The man coughed and was soon choking in silence. His skin turned so pale that flames were glowing off his ghostly complexion. The rider shook in several spasms before falling off the dragon.

My fallen adversary landed on the floor of the volcano. A large puddle of blood formed around his obliterated body. I wasn't sure if he'd died from the poisonous gas or the fall. Either way, I would remember this death for the rest of my life.

I had killed my first man.

I felt like remorse. I wondered if this made me a sociopath. Surely, I wasn't evil. I displayed an immense amount of empathy for others, and I didn't fight people unless danger was lurking. Psychopaths showed no guilt for the pain which they inflicted on others. This man had chosen to sell dragons for the sake of murder. This guy's actions had consequences, and his death was part of the package. War and weapons were a dirty business, and one had to accept that they could get killed. In most cases, your killer had no personal connection to you. If I hadn't killed this guy, then sooner or later, someone else would have. I'd slaughtered him to save my life. I was the one doing the right thing, not him.

Robin landed his magic carpet next to Marco. This was a rather perilous spot since lava was leaking from the walls. Since Robin was a daredevil, he usually ignored dangers in favour of thrills.

Three gangsters approached Robin and Marco. Each of the rivals was armed with a sword and wearing a mask. Robin attacked one of them with his sword. The two of them dueled, bouncing forward and backward across the narrow ledge. I feared that Robin would fall or accidentally step into leaking magma.

Marco snapped his whip forward. One of the gangsters jumped backward, stumbled over a rock, and landed atop leaking lava. The fiery liquid boiled his skin to the blood. More lava pumped from a seeping hole. Molten liquids splashed across the fallen gangster's head and torso, boiling him to the death.

Since Marco had never shown such a flabbergasted facial expression, he probably hadn't planned on killing the guy. I worried that his first action of death was going to cause more harm to his already damaged psyche.

Robin and his opponent continue to duel. The gangster was an excellent swordsman and managed to block one of Robin's attacks and thrust Robin's blade into a hold. Robin squirmed with his sword but was unable to pull it free.

Saliva shot from Robin's mouth, and his rival backed up, releasing his hold on Robin's blade. Once Robin's sword was free, he swung the blade toward his enemy's neck. The gangster jumped backward and fell over the face of the cliff. Death awaited him at the bottom.

Today felt like my gang's baptism of fire. Each of us had killed our first man within the last minute, all while inside a burning volcanic crater.

The third gangster stepped forward and removed his mask. Robin and I were surprised with what we saw while Marco's eyes dilated.

"Hello brother," Devo spoke.

I wasn't sure if Marco was going to drop his whip and talk to his brother or attack him mercilessly. Devo had been missing for months, and the rumours about him working with assassins and illegal weaponry had finally been confirmed. Marco had always stated that his brother made the worst choices when good options stood in front of him. Devo had likely killed others, but how was he going to react toward his brother's slaughter of an ally?

A frenzied dragon flew toward the landing which Devo, Ace, Marco, and Robin were standing on. A blast of fire darted from the monster's mouth. Ace and Robin were out of range while Marco leapt onto his magic carpet and hovered to the sky.

Devo's skin crinkled to cracking blackness. Bones burst into dust. No one could believe how hot a fireball could be. It seemed like the dragons had been blessed by the fire god Rahn.

I wanted to talk to Marco and counsel him. I knew that he and his brother had an endless amount of resentment toward one another, but the dude had just watched his brother's destruction from a dragon. If we hadn't broken into the dragon raising lair, then Devo would probably be alive.

I really wished I could comfort Marco, but now was not the time for sympathy. If having a frenzied dragon on our tail wasn't enough, we still had to find the orb.

Ace dashed off the cliff and landed atop the dragon. He wrestled his way atop the saddle and pulled back on the dragon reins as though he were riding a wild stallion. The dragon nose-dived, ascended rapidly, shifted to the right, bounced to the left, and chased it's tail. Ace looked like a rodeo clown as he held on for his life. I feared that death would come to him if he didn't get the beast under control.

Robin raised his ring and pointed it at the dragon. I wasn't exactly sure what Robin was doing. There was no way that he could use his magic to take possession of the dragon since the deities had banished genies from having the ability to control animals.

I flew my magic carpet close to Ace but was cut off when a stranger on a magic carpet emerged from the darkness. Since only genies could command magic carpets, it looked like I was in for a tough fight. The rider of the magic carpet was very tall and muscular. His bushy black hair, scarred face, and sharp features made him look particularly vicious. He had a sick sadistic look on his face as if he was encouraging me to take my best shot at him. A cutlass dangled from his arm, and I could tell that he couldn't wait to wield it.

The genie flew forward on his magic carpet as I raised my katana. He thrust his sword forward and the two of us started dueling. I deflected several blows and then ordered my magic carpet to fly backward. The rival genie followed me, keeping his magic carpet at exact alignment with mine. Our blades clashed back and forth. Every time I tried to evade him, his magic carpet sped next to mine as though I had magnetized him. My opponent parried all my sword thrusts and was quick to strike forward. I managed to keep my defense system up, but I needed to get better with my offence skills if I was going to defeat this villain.

Marco and Robin searched the landing for the orb. Robin flashed some strange lights from his ring. I wasn't sure what he was doing.

"Help me," a voice called from below.

Robin and Marco peered into a cave. Someone was locked in a cage. Without a word, Marco shot a blast of force from his ring. The force ruptured the lock on the cage, freeing the prisoner.

"Thank you for eternity," the prisoner spoke as he stepped from the cage.

The prisoner was the most peculiar creature I had ever seen. He, she, or it appeared to be half-human and half-dragon. This humanoid lizard was very tall, even taller than Ace. It walked on two hind legs. The creature had arms which were lizard-like, and hands with opposable thumbs and bendable claws for fingers. This mysterious being had long wings on it's back and a head which looked like it belonged on an iguana. Although lighting in the volcano was limited, I could tell that the creature had dark green leathery skin. The voice of the creature spoke with a faint O'Jahnteh accent. I wondered if the prisoner was a human-dragon hybrid.

"My name is Wes," the prisoner spoke, "but I will talk with you later."

"We're here to destroy an orb which is keeping the dragons prisoner," Robin said.

"Beautiful," Wes said. "I know where it is, and I will destroy it at once."

Marco and Robin gazed at Wes as he leapt off the cliff and took flight with his dragon wings. Wes headed toward a dark corner of the crater. I really hoped that Wes knew what he was talking about when he'd said that he knew where the orb was hidden.

I wanted to pay more attention to this Wes character, but my rival genie was continuing to flash sword blows at me. Since Wes's arrival, the enemy genie had come close to taking my skin off, so I really needed to up my concentration.

As the genie gangster and I continued to duel, Ace sought to control his frantic dragon. Dark smoke floated in his direction. The blackness swallowed my friend. Coughing erupted as the dragon screeched. The ruckus grew more hideous when the dragon crashed into a wall of the volcano, throwing Ace aside.

Ace flailed in the air as the dragon rebounded off the crater wall. Time slowed down for several moments as Ace dropped to the hellish pits below. The pool of lava left Ace with less than a destroyed body.

I hated to admit it, but if death was a part of battle, then that could mean the death of my friends. Parts of me wanted to believe that I was hallucinating and that Ace could still be alive, but my instincts kicked in and told me that if I didn't focus on my survival, then I'd join Ace in the grave. Veteran soldiers stated that mourning always needed to take place after the battle which was why funerals were invented. I ordered myself into focusing on my attacker, an enemy who could easily take my life.

The orb flew in my direction from Wes's hands, collided against my duelist, knocked him from his magic carpet, and forced him into a darkened corner of the volcano. I wasn't sure if my competitor was falling to his death or lost in the shadows. His magic carpet fluttered and then fell, something which was never a good sign.

The orb split open against the hardened magma rock. The three dragons squawked like maddened parrots.

Wes approached me.

"Come now," he spoke, "our work here is done."

Robin and Marco mounted their magic carpets and flew toward Wes and I. We three genies followed Wes out of the volcanic crater as he led us toward the jungle.

The three dragons burst from the volcanic crater, flew around several times, and then returned to the hellish underworld.

"What are those dragons doing?" I asked.

"The orb acted as a force shield over the volcanic crater," Wes explained. "Only dragons could not pass through it, which is why you fellows got through it without any problem. Those dragons flew up to the sky to ensure that the shield had been broken. Now they are returning for their eggs. From what I saw, all the eggs are safe."

"Ain't it great that none of those eggs haven't become abortions," Robin snickered.

"Shut the hell up," Marco growled. "You're making jokes right after Ace got killed? What the fuck is wrong with you man? Aren't you shaken up over having lost a friend?"

I waited for Marco to mention Devo, but no further words came from his mouth.

"I think it's best we get out of here," Wes said.

We led Wes to the nearest river, landed on the beach, had a quick dip in the cool water, and then snacked on bread, dried meat, fruit, and tea. Robin complained about how he wanted booze. I agreed that all of us could use a load of drinks.

Wes introduced himself to us and began his story. He had very little memory and feared that he suffered from amnesia. He wasn't sure if he was a human, dragon, mutant, or an unclassified freak of nature. None of us wanted to sound rude, but we found Wes's existence quite baffling.

"I'll take you home with me," Robin said. "After being locked up in that hellish dungeon, you could really use a good holiday, and I'd be very happy to help you out."

"Much appreciated, thank you Robin," Wes said as he bowed to Robin.

"We'll have to report Ace's death," Marco said. "The funeral will probably be held in Santalonia."

"Let's all go," Robin said. "He was such a cool dude, and it fucking sucks that he's dead."

"I'd like to attend too," Wes said. "Although I never knew the man, anyone who died in the pit and assisted in emancipating myself and the dragons deserves my condolences."

"I don't know what to say," I said. "It's wrong that Ace died when he was the one who found about this crime and did everything in his power to prevent it."

"It sounds like he was a very brave and clever leader," Wes said.

"He changed all our lives," I said. "Hell, he helped change the history of Sionia by being a key player in the revolution against King Rex. He was a hero, and he can't be forgotten about."

"We'll remember him for the rest of our lives," Marco said. "We may live to be very old due to the Post-17 curse, but that will include many years of honouring Ace and his heroics."

I waited for Marco to say something about Devo, but he remained taciturn. I wondered if Marco held so much animosity toward his brother that he felt nothing toward his death. Then again, Marco often kept his pain inside and would channel his demons through actions instead of words. The strong silent types were always difficult to read.

After another twenty minutes of rest, Wes and Robin started to set up camp while Marco and I went to fetch fruit, collect water, and cook.

"Dude," I said. "How do you feel about your brother dying?"

My words sounded puny, and I wished that I hadn't been so blunt. There was no easy way to deal with death, which was one of many reasons why death was the shittiest thing ever.

"Devo was forever doing stupid shit despite tons of warnings," Marco said as he gazed into the distance. "He did all this to himself; he insulted the only thing anyone truly has, life."

I couldn't believe how cold Marco was being. I knew that I was sometimes black and white, but I was surprised by Marco's lack of sympathy. I'd never had a brother, but I would be distraught if Julia died.

"I can't remember the last time I thought of Devo as family," Marco whispered, "but maybe now with him dead and my mom in the grave, I'll have a real family to look forward to in the afterlife."

"I bet the next time you see Devo's ghost, it'll be under good circumstances," I said as I patted Marco on the shoulder.

It was possible for ghosts to visit the living in Sionia. One couldn't command the spirits of the dead to visit them whenever they wanted, but it was hopeful and heartwarming to know that even when you were dead, there could still be contact with the living. I wished for Ace to contact us soon.

Wes, Robin, Marco, and I attended Ace's funeral in Santalonia. I was happy that I'd had Ace as a friend, an ally, and an inspiration. He'd died as a good soldier for an important cause. His plan had worked. Dragons disappeared from the black market and gangs stopped using them for combat. I liked to think that the dragons which we'd emancipated were now flying free and a danger to none.

We returned to O'Jahnteh. As promised, Robin's family housed Wes as a boarder. Amid all the flaws of Robin's dad, I really admired him for taking Wes in. Wes was a guy who truly had nothing: no money, possessions, memories, or family.

Although Wes had no memories of his identity, the guy was an encyclopedia. He knew so much about engineering, seamanship, architecture, physics, metallurgy, battle tactics, mathematics; you name it, the dude knew it. It wasn't long before Wes had a job at the local university. Marco started hanging out with him a lot, and he and Wes would go on hikes and do research on various plants. Seeing all of this made me want to go back to school and start taking my studies seriously.

Although the dragons were off the market, crime continued to roar. If it wasn't the mob or street gangs or petty thieves, then political groups were terrorizing one another. Spending more money on vigilums and the military failed to quell crime. I figured this was further proof of how useless the bloody government was.

One night, Marco and I were having dinner. Although he was doing well with his studies, Marco had been more distant than usual. He was still grieving over the death of Devo and was having difficulty expressing this. Thankfully, Marco's dad wasn't aware of Marco's involvement in the raid. I believed that Marco felt partially responsible for his brother's death though didn't want to admit it. Admitting his feelings might have rid him of some internal pain, but Marco had to deal with his grief in his own way. He was going to Zadohkoo's temple of death more often. Perhaps communicating with the god of death was making Devo's death seem more tolerable. I hoped that Marco would get in touch with Devo's and his mom's ghosts at the temple.

I was still waiting for Ace's ghost to visit.

"I think I know what I want to do with my life," I said.

"What's that?" Marco asked.

"I want to be a vigilante."

"Don, you're nosy and you like looking for fights. Vigilantism will get you killed."

"I care about others' safety."

"So do I, and I also care about your safety. I've lost a lot of people I care about; I don't want to lose another friend."

"Then come with me. Both of us have seen a lot of loss, and you have felt so much pain. Instead of dwelling in silent grief, focus that rage on problems. Ace inspired me to do more and to take action. Doing nothing will make us feel small and worsen our trauma. This is our chance to turn things around, to turn ourselves around, and to take pride in what we're doing to make Sionia better. What do you say man?"

"I still want to be a botanist."

"You can do that too. I don't want you to quit work, go hungry, and be too weak to fight foes."

"What about you Don?"

"I'll still make room for fun and learning. Work is worth nothing when you don't get to enjoy the benefits during free time."

"I'll try this vigilante gig temporarily, no promises."

"Good stuff Marco, you won't regret this adventure, I promise."

BOOK III:

ENSLAVED

Marco and I followed through with our goal of becoming vigilantes. We credited Ace as our muse. None of mine and Marco's missions were nearly as bodacious as the dragon volcano. I wasn't even sure if missions was the right term for what Marco and I were doing. Basically, Marco and I would wander around rough areas late at night and wait for something bad to happen. We battled house burglars, street thieves, and a few brutes who went around bullying locals. On your average night, all we did was cruise around and talk. If neither of us had to defend anyone, we considered it a good night. On the downside, if we didn't run into trouble, neither of us could help but wonder if danger was off our radar.

"I feel like I'm really making a difference," Marco said one night.

"That's awesome man," I said. "Good deeds deserve reward even if it's only internal satisfaction."

"No man, I mean working as a vigilante has helped me get over a lot of my personal shit, and I've got a lot of grief to deal with."

"You mean with your mom's death and Devo's destruction."

"Yeah man. Devo was a follower who hung with the wrong crowd and was so easily manipulated. I feel like I'm avenging Devo's death by going after loudmouth thugs who prey on wannabes who lack identity."

For a long time, Marco hadn't wanted to talk about Devo, but after much persistent nosiness, he gave into my questions. I was glad that even the most reticent friend could still open up.

Robin started coming on vigilante missions with Marco and I. At the risk of being exclusive, Marco and I had initially chosen not to bring Robin along. He was our good friend who we still hung out with a lot, but we also worried that he would be a liability. Robin was good with a sword, fast on the magic carpet, and competent with magic, but he viewed crime fighting as a game. I didn't think he understood how poverty and street crime affected guys like Marco and I, guys who'd grown up in the slums. Since Robin looked at crime fighting as a sport, he also ignored a lot of danger. Some days, I wondered if Robin thought that he was immortal or if he was simply clueless toward hazards.

Robin's big mouth was another reason why I hadn't wanted him around at first. His jokes (which were often funny, I'd give him that) and his constant babbling killed the stealth which Marco and I needed when we chased after thugs.

Robin's big mouth didn't only impact us when we stalked crime. I'd heard him babble to people around his house about how we were crime fighters. I didn't want his dad taking a stance against what we did. Vigilante actions, street justice, and citizen arrests got common do-gooders in court. I was sure Robin's old man wouldn't hesitate to warn the vigilums of vigilantes, considering his dad had donated a lot of money to the war on crime.

Although the vigilums were looking to arrest the vigilantes, Marco and I refused to go to crime fighting academy. There was no way that either of us would ever become vigilums. Vigilums served the corrupt government, upheld needless laws, and followed orders like slaves. If all of that wasn't bad enough, vigilums regularly got away with breaking multiple laws. I could never degrade my services, principles, or calling for such hypocrisy and moral bankruptcy.

Marco eventually gained full-time employment as a botanist. Due to field work, he started spending less time in O'Jahnteh. On nights like that, Robin insisted that he tag along. Robin had a good point that patrolling the streets solo was dangerous, but at times, wandering the streets alone and looking for crime allowed my mind to study the criminal world.

Wes kept in touch with us. Every time I visited the guy, he was working on new scientific research with the university. The guy was a genius; he truly was, but the sad thing about him was that he still hadn't found out where he'd come from. He ended up visiting multiple healers, witchdoctors, medicine men, and even a psychologist, but none of them could figure out the source of his amnesia. If all of that wasn't bad enough, Wes remained an unclassified species. No one had ever seen a humanoid dragon before. Some biologists wanted to study him. Wes allowed this research only if the scientists promised that they would help him find out where he'd come from. The zoologists and doctors did their research but found no answers. Some people regarded Wes as a freak and stared at him all the time. This was incredibly unfair, and I really felt sorry for the guy, so I started spending more of my free time with him.

"Don, can I give you some advice?" Wes asked one night.

"Go ahead dude."

"It's about your vigilante efforts."

"Hey, I'm safe."

"I know you are. You don't have any scars or bruises or anything like that."

"So, what's the deal?"

"I think your methods are a bit crude."

"Really? You've never been out on a mission."

Wes disliked any kind of combat. A dragon would have been a great asset to my team of vigilantes, but I couldn't force a firebreather with wings to come with me.

"You wander around town, waiting for bad things to happen," Wes said.

"Yeah so."

"You and Marco have said that sometimes you worry that you don't get to troubled spots in time or that things happen out of your jurisdiction."

"What should we do then?"

Wes handed me a few books on tracking, spying, and undercover infiltration. He also gave me a few wanted posters.

"I suggest studying these books," Wes said. "I borrowed all of them from the library, so be sure to return them to me in two weeks."

"For sure, thanks," I said with sincerity despite not being much of a reader.

"No one can be everywhere at once, but if you follow the advice in these books, then perhaps you can learn to track down criminals, find their lairs, and defeat a whole horde of them."

I was thankful for Wes's books. Robin and Marco also read them. Wes had a pretty good point about how I wasn't pragmatic and that I waited around for obvious danger to happen. Even if Wes didn't want to join in on combat, perhaps he could serve as an intelligence officer.

My sister Julia caught me reading a vigilante book one night. At that point I was in between jobs and sleeping on a hammock at my parents' house. Since I wasn't working the night shift anywhere, my parents wondered why I was always spending most of the night away from home. They also told me to stop leading a nocturnal lifestyle if I wanted to get a day job. I didn't want them to know about my vigilantism.

"I want to come along on a mission with you and Marco," Julia said.

"Forget it," I said.

"Ah come on, I can still kick your ass any day."

Julia had always been tough at kickboxing, wrestling, lacrosse, and running. Recently she'd championed fencing, archery, and stick fighting. For years she'd been able to beat me in a fist fight or a wrestling match, but I could still easily whoop her when it came to magic.

"What Marco and I do is really treacherous," I said.

"Having a third person around will make things way less dangerous for the both of you," Julia said.

"If you die, then I'll be the only heir to the family."

"Don't be a hypocrite, Don. If you die, then I'll be the only offspring of our parents. Marco is already on his own. I'd be doing him and his future kin a favour by looking out for his ass."

"This isn't a good lifestyle."

"Then why do you keep doing it?"

"I have really strong compulsions to right wrongs. I can't explain. I really don't know what else to do with my life. You should do something better."

"Is this unexplainable reason so great that it justifies you not being able to hold a job?"

The funny thing was, I sometimes wondered why I acted as a vigilante. Ace had inspired me. I wanted to do good for my community. I thought the vigilums were corrupt and useless. I hated poverty and how crime was a result of depravity. I loathed how crime that resulted from poverty made the poor poorer. I resented how the government had failed to eliminate the slums.

But why did I put my neck at risk so often?

My answers to that question changed so often. Sometimes I said that I loved the adrenaline. On other days I would argue that putting myself in danger made me hone my swordsman and magic skills. On a few occasions I had said that getting close to death made me comfortable with my mortality. Most of the time though, I stated that I had a responsibility toward a greater good which justified potentially going down like a martyr.

Street crime was declining. Marco, Robin, and I liked to think that our vigilante actions had made a difference in the war on crime. The vigilums deserved some credit for peace times, but my friends and I loathed any praise which they received.

The real reason for street crime declining was the gradual demise of urban poverty. More social programs were springing up. Jobs were being created. People were moving away from the slums and into better communities. Wages were on the rise. The middle class had expanded. The Sionian government was shifting further away from its previous right-wing state. Even though such changes had done much to improve society, there was still work to be done since slums and street crime still existed.

Although my whole family was happy to see the decline in poverty, this happiness was very short lived. Just after my parents bought a new house in a subdivision, they were killed in a flash flood. The tragedy struck Julia and I really hard. Since Julia was younger than me, I told her that she could live in our inherited house while Marco and I would become roommates.

Since Marco was away on research projects for at least half the year, I felt like I was living on my own much of the time. When Marco was home, he was a good friend to me. If I spoke of my parents' deaths, he listened. Marco even opened up a bit more and spoke about his traumatic past. I learned to empathize with his pain while he helped me recover from my loss.

I also spent a lot of time hanging out with Julia. Unlike Marco, I had a sister to fall back on. Being with Julia made me regret that Marco hadn't had a close family member to grieve with when his mom and Devo had died.

The strangest thing which I went through was not aging. In the past, people found change peculiar, but for the new generation of Sionians, not changing was strange and completely normal. Since Marco, Robin, and I had been teenagers when King Rex was killed, we were among the first generation to be hit by the curse of youth. It was kind of creepy to realize that you could look in the mirror when you were seventeen and know that you would see no difference in your body when you were eighty.

A large group of scientists, genies, and wizards attempted to reverse the curse of youth, but no cures were found. Silotious stated that there was no way the curse would ever be lifted and that folks had to accept it. As a result of the curse of youth, adult birthdays became less common. Post 17 became the term for people like my friends and I who had stopped aging.

A socialist party called Wadonshea came to power when I was twenty. A fellow named Bartholomew became the viceroy of Sionia. Social benefits programs had become very popular in Sionia, while the liberal party lost a lot of popularity due to corporate scandals which the government had tried to cover up.

The Wadonshea proclaimed themselves as a socialist party with some communist leanings. Prior to their election victory, communism had only existed on paper. Some folks welcomed the idea of communism while others encouraged an amalgamation of business and social benefits. I was reasonably happy with what I saw.

The Wadonshea Party gave Marco and his colleagues a research grant. He moved to the south-east, where we would stay for up to a year.

Robin's dad threw him out the house when he'd found out that Robin had voted for the Wadonshea. Amid homelessness, Robin moved to the coast and got a job as a bartender.

The Wadonshea government quickly made all forms of vigilantism illegal. I ignored this. At that time, I was acting as a lone warrior.

One afternoon when I was on a leisurely walk with my magic carpet secured to my rucksack, I came across six red vests, capes, caps, and black trousers. It wasn't common to see so many vigilums together unless a disturbance was going on. Some of these vigilums were genies on magic carpets while others were humans who rode cavalry. Each was armed with a short sword and a baton.

"Don of O'Jahnteh," one of the vigilums called.

I wanted to know what was going on but dared not share my name. You could never trust vigilums in any circumstances, but if six of them on magic carpets and horseback stopped you when you were out on an afternoon stroll, then something had to be wrong.

One of the vigilums pulled a blowgun from his satchel. Before I could raise my hands or say anything, the vigilum blew two heavy lungs of air into the weapon. A spray of multi-coloured herbs exploded from the blowgun nozzle.

Psychedelic colours flashed into my eyes. All the noises in the background blurred into a bass-filled drone. Everything started spinning. I thought that I would barf from dizziness. I toppled over, and the last thing I felt was a coarse net being dropped on me.

Sometime later I awoke on a straw mat. I stumbled around, closed my eyes, reopened them a few times, called for others, and scanned my unfamiliar setting. I had no clue where I was. Part of me felt like I was dreaming a nightmare. Another theory was that I'd hit my head and was being taken care of at a stranger's house. I also wondered if I'd gotten drunk somewhere and was now awakening where I'd passed out.

I was wearing rough trousers and a tan long-sleeved shirt which felt like a potato sack. People in the hospital didn't wear such uncomfortable garbs. The thought of perverts undressing me creeped me out. I really wanted to know where my clothes were.

I looked down at my hands and found that my ring was missing. If waking up in a weird setting and being stripped of my attire wasn't bad enough, some freak had hijacked the one thing which made me a genie. That thief was asking to get his ass kicked, but my sword was also missing. I couldn't find my magic carpet either.

"What the fuck is going on here?" I bellowed.

No one answered. I jumped to my feet, scanned my area again, and realized that I was in a small hut. The door didn't have a lock, so I figured that I ought to head out to investigate.

My mind and heart were shocked with what my eyes saw. The hut I'd been resting in had been built next to a very large crater. Miners were inside the crater chipping away at boulders or digging with shovels. Oxen were towing crates of rocks while labourers were pushing wheelbarrows. There were about ten miners at work while fifteen guards armed with whips and clubs patrolled the area. A multi-layered barbwire fence acted as a boundary between the crater and the jungle.

I kept hoping that I would wake up from this nightmare, but the cliché of "it was all just a dream" did me no good no matter how many times I hit my head.

"The new guy is awake," a voice called.

I jumped toward the voice. Someone owed me an explanation. I was expecting to be addressed by one of the guards, but instead two fellas were looking at me. I assumed they were prisoners because they weren't wearing guard uniforms or armed with clubs. One of these guys was an ogre while the other was a cyclops.

"What the hell is going on?" I gasped.

"Relax man," the ogre said. "Take a few deep breaths so you don't give yourself a heart attack."

"Relax?" I exclaimed.

"Hey man, don't get all hotheaded," the ogre said. "The heat today is near intolerable as it is."

"Hey Bashar, give the man a break," the cyclops said as he came forward with a canteen. "Here, have a drink of water."

I took the canteen and gulped down a stomach-full of water, nearly giving myself a bellyache. The liquid was warm, but I was dehydrated, so the drink helped ground me. I didn't thank the cyclops until after I'd chugged most of his water.

"I'm Trent by the way," the cyclops said, "and that loud ogre over there is Bashar."

"Don," I introduced as I shook their hands.

Ogres and cyclops were way taller than humans. Ogres were as fat as sumo wrestlers, but the average ogre was stronger than a bodybuilding human. Cyclops were pure lean muscle. A cyclops eye was five times as large as a human eye, and it stood above the nose. Cyclops also had two stout horns which curved upward from their temples.

"You must be rather distraught," Trent said.

"Hells yeah the guy is distraught," Bashar said. "In fact, distraught has got to be the understatement of the year. Just look at this dude, he's completely shocked shitless which is totally understandable. Hell, he probably doesn't even know why he's here in the first place."

"Guys," I spoke as my eyes slowly gazed off at multiple corners of the crater. "What is this place?"

"Welcome to the gulag," Bashar bellowed. "The worst fucking place in history."

"What's a gulag?" I asked.

"A prison camp," Trent answered.

Well, this was freaking perfect. My worst theories had been confirmed. I was in prison, and for what, I really didn't know. Man, I hadn't even been awake in this place for five minutes and already I'd been told that I'd been shipped to a gulag, a word which hadn't been in my vocabulary until two seconds ago. What I really wanted was a lawyer. Every one of those vigilums who had drugged me with those herbs really deserved to end up here.

"What the hell?" was all I could say.

"A gulag is a prison camp," Trent said. "Unlike traditional prison where you are locked in dungeons and attend rehabilitation seminars or work in shops, a gulag is a slave labour camp."

"But slavery is illegal," I said. "The vigilums poisoned me with knockout dust and I woke up here. We've got to fight back and arrest the vigilums for police corruption."

"I hate to tell you the awful truth," Bashar said, "but this place is perfectly legal. Any amoral action is legal as long as it's carried out by the government, no matter how cruel it is. That asshole Viceroy Bartholomew and his cowardly Wadonshea Party set this place up. This is the first gulag, and they plan on building more. It looks like they'll close all city dungeons, and these gulags will replace the current jail system."

"So, I've been dropped off in a dungeon camp," I said.

"It gets worse man," Bashar said. "You are essentially a slave here. If you don't haul ass mining and chipping stone, then the guards won't feed you. The food here is pretty piss poor too."

"But how can any of this be legal," I cried. "The vigilums poisoned me when I was on a walk. They didn't present me with a warrant or read me my rights or anything. I wasn't even given a trial or the option of consulting a lawyer, yet I've been sentenced to hard labour?"

"The Wadonshea Party have created a wave of new laws which haven't yet been released to the public," Trent said. "Anyone who has been accused of committing a crime automatically loses all rights. Vigilums are now allowed to put accused criminals to sleep. The vigilum chiefs are also allowed to arbitrarily determine whether you deserve a trial or not. If the chief decides not to grant you a lawyer or a trial, then you'll be hauled off here with no chance of appeal. We are also barred from any and all communication with the outside world."

"None of this can be right," I said.

"You're right man, none of this is right," Bashar said. "It's beyond unethical and completely fucked up."

"What the hell are we supposed to do?" I asked.

"That's what we've been trying to figure out," Trent said. "Bashar and I have each been here for two weeks. We aren't even sure where here is. Five guys were here before we showed up, and a few more have come in within the last few days."

"Where are you guys from anyway?" I asked, hoping to try and get a bearing of where this gulag might be. "I'm from O'Jahnteh."

"We're both from the Stodaneatoo area," Trent answered.

I let out a deep gasp. Stodaneatoo was about a two-day journey from O'Jahnteh.

"I have a feeling that we're going to see a lot more inmates showing up real soon," Trent said. "If this is the first gulag and the government plans on building more, then they're most likely treating this place as an experiment, and they are going to want to fill it up with as many people as possible while the new camps are built."

One thing I still couldn't figure out was why I'd been arrested.

"Say, what'd you guys do to get thrown in here?" I asked.

"I'm a journalist," Bashar said. "I wrote an editorial criticizing that twat Viceroy Bartholomew. Basically, I called him a dictator and said that the Wadonshea Party was a gang of no-brain extremists who are going to destroy Sionia."

Bashar sounded just like Robin's dad. Normally I would have laughed at what Bashar had just said, but there was nothing funny about getting arrested for expressing your views. Word had been going around that the Wadonshea Party were limiting free speech and cracking down on the press. I guessed that Bashar was among the first wave of big mouths who were being criminalized for criticizing the government.

"I was arrested for hunting without a license," Trent said. "You see, I live out in the jungle, a few kilometres away from any towns or villages. I like living close to nature and ignoring all the rules of the city. Someone must have ratted me out for hunting without a license because the vigilums tracked me down, gassed me with some weird potion, and then I woke up here."

Hunting without a license had usually only been punishable with a warning. It seemed like every gulag prisoner had broken a minor rule in which the penalties had not been made public. I wondered if every future gulag prisoner was going to be someone who'd committed a trivial bad action. I also worried that murderers, thieves, and rapists would also show up here. I didn't plan on staying here for long, but it seemed way better to be in a prison camp with a disgraced journalist than with hardened killers, especially if I was without my sword and ring.

"What about you?" Bashar asked. "Did you pick public flowers without a permit?"

"Hey Bashar, Don is still pretty shook up," Trent said. "Maybe you shouldn't joke around with him like that."

I found Bashar obnoxious and crass. I really hoped that he would shut up soon. Being stuck in here with a loudmouth would make the experience more hellish. On the other hand, Trent appeared soft-spoken and caring. He seemed like the kind of guy who I should win as a friend.

"I'm a vigilante," I said. "I don't kill; I don't steal; I don't hurt. I protect people from scum. I do what the vigilums fail to do. I fight injustice, cruelty, and malice."

"That explains why you're in here," Bashar said. "I hate to tell you man, but vigilante acts are also illegal. You humiliate the vigilums with your volunteerism. I'm sure you're good at what you do and all, which is why the fucked-up government has criminalized you. The Wadonshea Party wants the government to do everything and the people to do nothing except get bossed around by the government. It's as simple as that. Fuck this socialism shit man."

I hated to admit it, but Bashar was probably right. I had been arrested for my vigilante actions. I'd under-estimated how serious these laws were and figured that the vigilums wouldn't catch me since I was better at catching crooks than they were. I wondered if Marco or Robin would end up here. I'd hate for my best friends to get arrested, but having them around could make this place a lot easier. If they showed up, perhaps we could escape together.

"I know you're a vigilante and all man, but don't bother trying to start a riot," Trent said.

Bashar spun around. Multiple bruises and several fresh scabs decorated the green ogre skin on his back.

"Talking back, getting rebellious, slacking off, trying to escape, or attacking the guards is punishable by a thrashing," Bashar said. "The guards will smack you a few times and then send you back to work. They won't beat you severely at one time cuz they don't want you to be too injured to work. If the guards decide to punish you though, they will whip you three times a day for about a week. Tonight, should be my last lashing though hopefully they've forgotten about it."

"I really hope they don't hit you anymore," I said.

"Thank man, you know you're alright Don," Bashar smiled. "The thing is, I believe that you're a vigilante and all, but you're not that big. Don't you ever get slammed around or are you as quick and sly as a fox?"

"I'm a master swordsman," I said, something which I normally smiled about, but I couldn't force a grin right now. "I'm also an accomplished genie."

"Genie, that's so cool," Bashar said. "Hate to break it to you man, in here you're just an average human."

The idea of being without my ring was too hard to fathom. I couldn't remember the last time I'd taken it off. Since I defined myself as a genie and ignored my human aspects, I always tried to live as close to magic as possible.

A loud whistle blew.

"The guards want us to get back to work now," Trent said.

"Remember, don't think about civil disobedience or you won't get fed tonight," Bashar said.

"What's on the menu anyway?" I asked.

"Rice and gruel," Bashar said, "the worst shit ever. How can they expect us to work hard if they've malnourished us?"

"If you want to stay alive in here, you'll have to revolutionize your diet," Trent said. "Eat all the insects you find. Cockroaches and worms have the most protein. If you see any plants or fungi and are unsure if they're edible, ask me, and I'll tell you if they are toxic. I have a really good understanding of poisonous flora and fauna since I've lived off hunting and gathering for years."

All of this was too inhumane for comprehension. It was no wonder the public was unaware of this gulag. If my story reached the public, there'd be a major social outrage. It was no surprise that Bashar had been sent here for writing a scathing article about Viceroy Bartholomew.

I didn't plan on staying here long, I couldn't. I didn't know how I could work as an obedient miner when I was forced into slavery and threatened with withheld meals if I didn't haul ass. Sure, there were guards all around, and yes they were armed with clubs and whips and probably some other weapons, but us miners had shovels and pickaxes. All we needed was a few more pissed off prisoners to show up and we could pull off a real riot. We were all criminals; disobedience was in our blood. It wouldn't take much to inspire other prisoners to host an uprising given what we were going through. Hell, if we destroyed this gulag then we'd probably scare the government out of building any more.

The first night in the gulag was the longest of my life. Not only could I not sleep from having taken a long nap after having been drugged, but so many dire thoughts spun around my head. I couldn't die here, that thought was too evil. The guards refused to speak with us about anything. Every piece of information I had about this place was through hearsay. The less we knew about this place, the more terrifying it became. The more paranoid we were, the less likely we were to revolt. I would have given anything for the smallest chance of escape.

Since prospects of a rebellion were slim to nothing at the gulag, I got into a routine: chipping stone, digging holes, pushing carts, and sweating like a pig. Smashing rocks and following through with the typical itinerary kept my mind from dwelling over the unfairness of everything.

If one good thing came out of my lousy situation, my muscles grew quite strong. I'd never been the buffest guy in the lands, but after a season in the quarry, I could easily champion any human in arm wrestling. Since we worked long hours and never had a day off, there really wasn't anything else to do but get stronger.

Although I was getting tougher, there was no way I would be stronger than any of the ogres or cyclops. Ogres (particularly Bashar) may have been butterballs, but when they wanted to pump some power, they threw a mad amount of strength into their punches. Bashar could easily lift rocks which I could barely wiggle. He was also into wrestling, and if he sat on me, I was sure I'd be flattened to a puddle.

If Bashar's strength was intimidating, then Trent was a hulking champion. Every muscle of his body was as taut as leather while his bones were iron solid. Trent could crush rocks with his fists and feet while everyone else was nicking at them with pickaxes. It was no wonder that Trent had been able to live in the wilderness with nothing but his brawn.

All of us craved protein, but the food we were fed was completely inefficient, so I took to eating every bug, toad, bird, reptile, or rat I could squash. Initially I had been squeamish about eating filthy creatures, but I got over my fussiness after three days of gruel. Trent taught me how to hunt creatures with efficiency. At night we made small fires to roast poultry, amphibians, rodents, and reptiles. Catching a snake became a mighty treat. Although we'd all taken to eating fierce creatures, caution needed to be taken. One prisoner died after swallowing a scorpion while another choked on his vomit after having eaten a venomous spider.

Trent ended up being the dude who helped keep us alive since he'd lived in the jungle as a forest hermit. Although he'd had friends from the city who would visit him, Trent had refused to go into town. The man prided himself as a naturalist and sough to fully live off the land as a hunter and forager. Trent disliked technology and felt that one's body should be united with their mind and emotions, and that the best way to create a unity through the three was to rid themselves of the ills of the city. Due to his technophobia, Trent insisted on only living with the most basic tools. As an anarchist, Trent hated all governments, and this gulag pushed his anti-establishment beliefs into an extreme direction. Although I'd never affiliated myself with any political party, I liked listening to Trent's anarcho-primitivism speeches.

Trent's knowledge of wilderness survival helped us identify which plants and fungi were edible and which insects and reptiles were toxic. He also taught us how to make a fire out of flint and steel. Since the quarry was extremely hot and with little shade, Trent built small tents out of old tarps and sticks which we could lie down beneath for ten minutes at a time to get shade. One valuable tip each of us learnt from Trent was to suck on a pebble when it got hot out, so that we would salivate and partially quench our thirst. We also created a project of setting up buckets everywhere to collect rainwater whenever the jungle let out a much-needed downpour. Although rain made the quarry sloppy and the work difficult and dangerous, rainfalls were the most exciting things within our day.

New guys came into the prison. Most of them were small time-crooks who'd committed rather innocent acts such as brewing moonshine, spitting on the street, public urinating, or complaining about the government. Based on these new guys' stories, it seemed like the outside world had fallen under martial law. Vigilums and other forms of security guards were everywhere. Anyone who denounced the government was automatically sentenced to a gulag unless they were executed. Common citizens were encouraged to rat out anyone who they felt was in contempt with the government. People were disappearing without explanation though all of us prisoners knew where they were ending up.

Whipping and clubbing happened nearly every day. No one was ever executed or beaten to the point where they couldn't walk because production demands were high. The new guys were almost always victims of the floggings.

Every time Bashar thought I was stepping out of line or complaining too much, he warned me of the beatings. Although Bashar could be abrasive, I came to like him. The guy was funny; he had stories to tell, and most of all he looked out for everyone. He also complained a lot about how there were no women in camp. It was funny how people could whine more about a lack of ladies than beatings, imprisonment, or slavery.

None of the prisoners were allowed to work on the loading docks without major guard presence. A large gate lay between the mining area/prisoners' quarters. If one wanted to push a load of stone onto the loading dock, their arms were cuffed, and their feet were secured to ball and chains. Several guards would accompany them. Government employed traders would load the shipments of stones onto wagons and then take off down the jungle roads.

Every time the gates opened onto the loading docks, each of us dreamed of escape. It would have been so glorious if a prison riot overpowered the guards, but the ratio of guards to prisoners steadily increased. If guards with clubs, sleeping herbs, and whips weren't repressing enough, the multi-layered barb wired fence acted as a spider web of malice.

When I wasn't slaving away, I got homesick. I'd never been the nostalgic type, but in the gulag, I learned the true meaning of longing. Prisoners would go through phases where they would open up to one another, share emotions, and talk about all the stuff they missed. It wasn't uncommon for guys to break down and cry.

Prisoners would also go through phases where they'd hide their feelings. It wasn't uncommon for a sobbing inmate to go sullen and not speak of anything regarding the outside world. This was a way to toughen up, hide sensitivity, and not let lugubrious emotions get the best of us. New prisoners had to be welcomed and shown the ropes, but we had to wait on sharing anything personal or showing any soft spots, in case they decided to exploit weaknesses.

Without my ring I started to feel detached from my genie existence. I felt more and more like an average human. I hated to admit it, but a lot of genies saw themselves as a superior race to average homo sapiens due to their magical powers. With all the hulking ogres and cyclops in the gulag, I felt like I was at the bottom of the food chain. I would have given anything to get my ring back. All I needed was a little bit of magic and I'd be able to liberate all of us prisoners from this pile of shit prison.

There was no worse emotion than feeling powerless. Everything I'd taken for granted back in civilization had been robbed from us. Our lives had been stolen. There were no words for my contempt for the government. Every prisoner in the gulag could spend the rest of their very long lives ranting and raging about the injustice of the slave camp.

Although my hatred for the government was at an all-time high, I sometimes felt dismay toward my own actions. During quiet moments, my mind couldn't help but wander back to the night when King Rex had been assassinated. It went without saying that I would reminisce that memory every day of my life, but Robin, Marco, and I usually had positive feelings about it. Nowadays, I loathed what Kyle had done. I wondered what would have happened had Kyle not killed his dad. Would Sionia have remained a monarchy? Would King Rex still be in power? Would the Wadonshea have never come into office? Would I not be trapped in this fucking gulag? All these questions had no answers and were stupid to ask, but my brain couldn't shut them up no matter how many times I told my intrusive thoughts to shut the hell up.

After too many seasons of smashing stones, we were hit by a famine. The rain season had been rather weak that year. Normally monsoons poured in, but that year the jungle got little more than showers. The rice harvest suffered. Since society lacked rice, prisoners received squat. Production slowed down. Prisoners keeled over in pain. Inmates died from weakness, malnourishment, and heat exhaustion. All the plants inside the quarry dried to dust. Fights erupted over who got to eat insects. Other animals stopped visiting the camp. Bellies ached in agonizing emptiness.

Bashar, Trent, and I managed to hang on. As diabolical as it sounded, cannibalism led to our survival. Instead of burying the bodies of the dead, we cooked them whole. Nothing went uneaten: organs, innards, tongue, eyeballs, brains, and bone marrow became treats. There was no shame in eating genitals. Starvation took a lot of meat off the corpses, but this was still the heartiest food any of us had eaten in the gulag. It seemed kind of cruel that the dead wouldn't have a burial, but every time we scarfed a human corpse, we spoke words of kindness to our fallen prisoners.

When protein wasn't available, we walked slowly, smashed less rocks, pushed smaller loads of stone, spoke little, slept lots, and groaned all day about constant emptiness in our guts. The guards would yell at us to pick up the pace, but we always ignored their whining. Screaming and beatings seemed inconsequential next to starvation.

It was hard to believe that miracles could exist. I'd almost forgotten that word. The only positive energy I felt was through conversation with other inmates. Amid slavery, starvation, isolation, cannibalism, sexual depravity, and disgraced innocence, good things could still be found.

One afternoon I collapsed from hunger. Storm clouds were hanging overhead, and I wondered if this was the end of the world. It certainly felt like the end of my life.

Trent rushed to my side, splashed water on my head, and passed me a canteen. Bashar spotted a cockroach, crushed it beneath his boot, and then offered me the juicy bug carcass as an energy booster. I was very lucky to have such caring friends.

As I recovered from fatigue, I noticed two of the guards going through a bag of loot. Items were passed back and forth, and I realized that the guards were trading.

A powerful phantom surge hit me. Energy jolted through my body. I feared that I was convulsing and would have a deathly seizure due to exhaustion. No one wanted to die, but the last place I wanted to croak in was this gulag. I couldn't let the prison camp triumph over me. I was better than that. I had to be the winner. The gulag may have tortured me and fucked me over for many seasons, but I had to get revenge. It was my destiny to destroy the prison camp and demolish the Wadonshea Government.

My eyes caught a ring. It had a gold band and green jewel. If the guards thought they could trade off my ring, they were majorly mistaken. Stealing my life wasn't enough for them? They had to steal my ring too? Only I could command its magical powers. To anyone else, the ring was nothing but a trophy item.

I concentrated deeply on my ring. Although genie powers could only be yielded when one was wearing their ring, I felt a very powerful bond toward my ring. It had been ages since I'd used magic, so much stored magical energy was pumping through my veins. As a genie, magic lived in my blood. There had to be more to my powers than wearing a ring. If I really was the bionic genie prodigy who my teachers had claimed I was, then perhaps the magic in my blood could connect with the spiritual power of my talisman.

My ring fluttered on the table. My eyes gazed at this treasure. So much of my spirit wanted to run forward and thrust my ring on even if that meant getting a severe clubbing from the guards.

My ring flew off the table and sped toward me. I held my hand forward and the ring slid down my fourth finger. All the magic in my body wanted to explode and radiate fantastic energy. After seasons of spiritual depravity, I was finally complete. I was no longer an average human. I was a genie again.

I pointed the ring at the thick clouds. As I gazed from the clouds to the green jewel in my ring, I imagined a storm. Within a second the cloud ruptured and released a gargantuan amount of rain. As I concentrated harder on the ring, the precipitation blasted like a waterfall blessed by Zadeezey, the goddess of water.

I concentrated on the clouds and told them to only rain on this area. Distant clouds began to cluster over the quarry. It seemed that all the clouds had united as an army and unleashed a merciless attack. Streams and waterfalls leaked into the crater. The bottom of the quarry became a pool. Prisoners sought shelter from the cold downpour.

The return of my ring had been my greatest gift ever, but I still wanted my sword and magic carpet back. The guards had brought the loot from out of a small building, which was always locked and off limits to prisoners, and I wondered if all confiscated possessions were in there.

Most people were too distracted by the rain to notice me when I snuck toward the storage building. I aimed my ring at the locked entrance. A blast of force shot from my ring shattering the iron door.

The shed was littered with personal items which prisoners had been carrying at the time of their arrest. Clothes, wallets, canteens, and rucksacks were among the common items. My sword rested in a bucket with umbrellas and walking sticks. My shaky fingers grasped its hilt. I pulled my katana from its sheath and admired its characteristics. As weak as I was, I really wanted to slash some of the guards with my beautiful blade.

My magic carpet lay on the floor like a regular rug. Upon glancing at it, my magic carpet ascended and hovered in mid-air. I collapsed onto my floating magic carpet and soaked in delight.

My happy lazy time ended. I had a responsibility. Relaxation could come later.

The magic carpet and I flew out of the shed. The two guards who'd been trading loot came forward. One was armed with a whip while the other was eager to club me. Trent and I were the only prisoners who'd never been struck by the guards, and I wasn't going to let them have that opportunity.

"Justice," I roared.

A massive force blast shot from my ring. The guards blew backward and landed in the multi-layered barb wired fence. One of the guards had been flying so fast that his body passed through the wire and was sliced to sloppy flaps of meat. The other guard crashed against the metal and screamed in agony at the sharp barbs which dug into his flesh.

The screaming and the sliced up gory corpse were rewarding sights of vengeance, but I realized that I couldn't take out each guard one by one. I had to find a way to kill all of them without getting any of the prisoners hurt.

The rain continued to pour relentlessly. Everyone in the quarry was swimming. The sides of the mine were too slippery to climb up. In no time the rain would drown everyone in the crater.

Six guards were in the quarry, struggling to stay afloat. Two guards had just been slashed in the fence. That left twelve other guards. All of them had to die.

My magic carpet and I flew over to the edge of the quarry. Each of the guards chased after me with raised clubs and whips. I hovered just above their heads on my magic carpet.

"I'm one of only two prisoners who you've never beaten," I called, "and I'm the man who's going to kill all of you."

A purple force shield sprung from my ring. Guards smacked the violet rays of the force shield with their clubs, but their blows rebounded and bonked these assailants on the head. I cackled at the guards and thought about how these blows were payback for the slave whippings.

As I concentrated my energy on the force shield, I thought about the phantom force thrust. I then used my magic energy to combine the two spells. A force blast shot from my ring and smacked the force shield. Due to the blast, my force shield bounced forward five paces. As the force shield enlarged from the force blast, the guards were hit by the energy and knocked into the flooded quarry.

The force shield disappeared. Rain continued to fall with wrath. Although there was a good chance that all the guards were going to drown, my work was not yet done. I wasn't going to let my fellow prisoners die. All were going to leave the gulag alive while all the guards were going to die.

Two inmates were treading water and struggling to stay afloat beneath the storm. Although I was responsible for their ill state, I wasn't going to let them sink. My magic carpet and I flew above them. The magic carpet lowered so that it was hovering a finger above the water. I offered my hand to each of the swimming inmates and then helped them aboard my magic carpet. Once they were atop the magic carpet, we darted toward solid ground.

All the other prisoners had clustered together and were watching what I was doing. My awe-struck crowd cheered in unison. The cheering felt rewarding, but I could accept gratitude later. An ogre was floating in the water, and I had to rescue him before he drowned or got hurt by one of the guards.

I returned to the flooded quarry. Guards were bobbing up and down in the water. Some of them were sinking while others were treading water or attempting to climb out of the quarry along the steep damp rocky walls.

I helped the ogre aboard my magic carpet. It was a bit difficult to assist such a cumbersome fellow aboard my hovering magic carpet, but the guy deserved to have his life saved. He thanked me as I sped him back to land.

"Don my friend," the ogre said as I dropped him to the ground. "There is a drowning cyclops who does not know how to swim; try and save him if it's not too late."

Although I feared that the cyclops might already be dead, I had to do what I could to save his life. I had promised to emancipate all prisoners of slavery. No one was going to be left behind.

I took a deep breath. Right when my lungs filled with cool air, my magic carpet and I dove into the water. I forced my eyes open. The filthy water stung my eyes. The silt and mud from the quarry made the water very murky. I feared that the water was so cloudy that I wouldn't be able to find the missing cyclops.

The magic carpet and I drifted at the bottom of the quarry. I noticed a drowned guard but couldn't see a cyclops anywhere. I wondered if this cyclops had escaped the flood or if he was floating on the surface. My lungs started to ache, and I desperately wanted air. It looked like I was going to have to rise to the surface, take in more air, and do another dive.

Right when I was about to ascend, I spotted the cyclops. The guy was thrashing around like leaves in a hurricane. I wasn't sure I could carry him to the surface on account of his violent movement. I didn't know how much time the guy had before he'd no longer be able to hold his breath.

I wasn't going to let him die. I aimed my ring in his direction and imagined a giant gust of wind. A ferocious stream of bubbles shot out of my ring. The cyclops floated toward the surface as the bubbles blasted beneath him. The cyclops continued to thrash about, but at least he was heading to the water surface. My magic carpet and I ascended at his side.

When I reached the surface of the water, I filled my lungs with air. The cyclops was having trouble staying afloat so I hauled him onto my magic carpet. Once his upper body was atop my magic carpet, we flew to shore. The rescued cyclops collapsed at the feet of our fellow prisoners. He coughed up several mouthfuls of the dirty water and was then helped to his feet.

I gazed back at the flooded quarry. The beating rain and the flooded crater wouldn't guarantee that all the guards would die. Some of them were good swimmers and could survive the downpour, but I wasn't going to let any of them live.

I raised my ring to the cloud and imagined thunder. Several shots of lightning blasted from the clouds. The water glowed with white light. Electricity zapped the guards, frying the life out of them.

I gazed at the gate which led to the loading dock. One final force blast from my ring gave us a path of escape. Roars of happiness rose from the prisoners when the door of doom blasted open. Everyone wanted to hug me. I had never felt like such a hero.

We marched out of the quarry once we'd looted the warehouse. Everyone made sure to spit on the obliterated gate. None of us looked back. The gulag was ancient history. The jungle would reclaim the land that belonged to nature, that had been stolen from the wilderness by a government who robbed men of their lives. Merchants and other government officials were going to get a real shock when they found guard corpses and no prisoners.

I raised my ring to the clouds one last time. The rain ceased. The land quickly warmed. We all deserved pleasant weather.

We camped in the jungle that night and feasted upon wild boar and a variety of foraged fruit. Each of us confessed that this was the tastiest meal any of us had ever eaten. No one could stop thanking me. All the gratitude was overwhelming.

Part of me was still a bit afraid. I better not have been dreaming. All of this seemed too good to be true. It was completely crazy that a simple mistake by two avaricious thieving guards had led to a one-man uprising that killed all the guards, freed every prisoner, and left the prison in ruins.

Before falling asleep that night, I read the Alontae. One section stated that a genie's ring was naturally attracted to its wielder. If a genie went for a long enough period without wearing their ring, then the ring developed a magnetic bond towards the host so that the talisman could rejoin its owner. Since this trick had revived my identity and helped save many lives today, I vowed to memorize all genie literature.

I was a genie again. No vigilums, prisons, guards, or government could stop me. Although today had been the biggest victory of my life, the war wasn't over. I was going to go to Santalonia. I was going to get revenge against the Wadonshea Government.

BOOK IV:

DEATH DAY

After two days of trekking the jungle road, our party reached O'Jahnteh. Never had home felt so welcoming. I'd never figured myself to be the homesick type but when you were abducted and locked away for over a year, unsure if you'd ever have another place to call home again, you really did long for a place to call home.

A lot of the other guys had drifted off along side roads. Bashar, Trent, and I had agreed to stick together until we got answers on the state of the government. It was unlikely that word of the destruction at the gulag had reached town. None of us were even sure if the public knew of the gulags. For all any of us knew, we could be wanted fugitives.

The three of us headed over to my family house. At first glance I didn't recognize my old abode. It didn't look like anyone was living there, and demolition workers were bashing away at the walls with sledgehammers. All the plants had been torn from the ground.

"Hey there," I called to the foreman.

"What can I help you with?" the foreman asked as he looked up from a set of blueprints.

"I'd like to talk with the owner of this house,"

"Then you'll have to go to the townhall,"

"What do you mean?"

"You look like you've just been in the jungle for a very long time," the foreman chuckled as I nodded. "The O'Jahnteh Municipality just bought every house on this street.

All of them are to be torn down. This entire block is going to be converted into a massive warehouse."

I gazed down the street and noticed that other buildings were under demolition.

"My sister and I used to live here," I said.

"Was your sister Julia of O'Jahnteh?" the foreman asked.

"That's her," I nodded.

"She relocated to Stodaneatoo two seasons ago," the foreman said.

I'd figured that returning to O'Jahnteh would be the warm welcome I'd been dreaming of since my first night in the gulag, but now I felt like I'd solved one problem only to be presented with many more.

"Hey boss, you said that the government just bought up all these houses, right?" Bashar asked the foreman.

"The government ceased property, it didn't buy anything," the foreman said. "The homeowners were given a settlement and ordered to relocate."

"How is that legal?" Trent asked.

"You fellas must have been in the jungle for a really long time cuz a lot has changed within the last year," the foreman said. "The Wadonshea have become a full-on communist government. They own all businesses, homes, and property. The government can do whatever it wants to any building or piece of land, including eviction of residents."

We thanked the foreman and went on our way. I feared the government had become totalitarian, and I anticipated many more unwelcoming surprises.

With Julia gone, I figured Wes would be the best guy to return to. I feared that Robin and Marco may have been arrested for vigilantism. For all I knew they could be in another gulag. Robin's dad would have thrown a major fit over communism, and I wondered if he'd retreated into seclusion with his family and money.

I headed to the university and asked the receptionist for Wes. I was nervous that he may no longer be working there, but to my delight I was told where I could find him.

"Don, I don't believe it," Wes called right after answering the door. "Where have you been?"

Wes put on a pot of tea and offered us a fruit platter while I introduced Bashar and Trent. After having been in the gulag for so long, all food tasted incredible.

"How did you manage to get such good fruit and tea with the famine?" Trent asked.

"What famine?" Wes asked.

"We were told that there was a famine resulting from a drought," Bashar said. "The three of us faced a major food shortage and could barely even get a bowl of rice a day."

"I really don't know what you guys are talking about," Wes said. "We didn't get as much rain this year, but there certainly wasn't a drought. Crops slowed down a little bit, but Phalaetus used her goddess powers to make sure that the harvest delivered enough food for all. Nobody went hungry."

"What the shit?" Bashar said. "I bet you anything the reason why we weren't given enough food was because the prison system was cutting back on costs and figured they should give us as little grub as possible. The guards at the gulag knew we were efficient at feeding ourselves with fungi and bugs and any game we could get, so they were probably pretty confident that cutbacks on food wouldn't kill us."

Wes's dark eyes widened. All of us wanted a lot of questions answered. It was time to tell our stories and figure out whose experience within the last year had been the most perplexing.

We learned from Wes that rumours about gulags had leaked into the public though no one knew exactly what went on in them. Wes was shocked, saddened, and horrified when Trent, Bashar, and I told him what we'd been through. What made the gulag stories even more terrible was that words couldn't accurately describe how horrible the prison had been.

Sionia had become a police state during our time in prison. Vigilum forces were larger than ever. Officers now patrolled every street in town and would arrest suspects without warning or questioning. Many new laws had been introduced. The guys who'd been sent to the gulag for picking flowers or pissing on walls had been telling the truth. Public executions were now common. Offenders were sent to jail without explanation. Families wondered where their loved ones had disappeared to. Newspapers were forbidden from reporting on the gulags. Neither my sister nor friends had any idea about what had happened to me.

The media had become completely state-run. Slander of the government would get one sent to a gulag. Newspapers only printed government rhetoric. Nationalistic propaganda decorated towns through statues, flags, songs, literature, murals, banners, and other art forms.

The Wadonshea Government had ceased control of all industries and private property. Initially the public had been pleased by public education, healthcare, transportation, entertainment, and food stamps. However, many had since forgotten about the perks of social services because there was so much angst toward the governmental cease of industry and property. No one could complain about these new policies, or they would be arrested. Everyone had to be careful about what they said to their neighbours, friends, and even family. Vigilums would pay out small cash rewards to folks who ratted on potential subversives.

It was widely believed that there was a lot of financial corruption in the government. Although kleptocrats were nothing new, there was much evidence that government officials were getting much more money than your average worker despite promises of financial equality. Government bureaucrats also lived in the largest homes, and they were the only folks who were being pampered by servants. Anyone who complained about this was silenced.

Wes had to watch his mouth very closely. Although Wes had never been active in politics, intellects were under a lot of suspicion. The government was paranoid that intellectuals would voice the most discontent against the government and use their knowledge to perpetuate rebellion among the public. The political science and sociology departments in the university had been shut down, and it was believed that nearly every professor from those faculties had been jailed.

"The government wants obedient people who are capable enough to do their jobs, patriotic enough to die for their country, and submissive enough to not question anything," Wes concluded.

Marco had risked being arrested at one point. He'd escaped the vigilums and was now living in a cave out in the jungle, far from any villages or ranger stations. Once a week Wes went out to visit him and make sure that the vigilums hadn't found his hideout. Since Marco was knowledgeable of nature, he'd managed to stay healthy while still studying plant biology. I couldn't wait to meet up with him. Trent found Marco's story very interesting and figured that the two of them would have a lot in common.

Robin had been arrested and his dad had bribed the vigilums into releasing him. Since the jail break, Robin's old man had placed him under house arrest. It had been months since Robin had left his housing premises. The family business had been ceased by the government, but Robin's dad had managed to stash away lots of money. His dad was acting as the manager of the chariot-building factory. The other board members had disappeared or been executed so Robin's dad was too scared to speak out against the communist government.

Basher, Trent, and I stayed at Wes's house that night. The next day we went to Robin's place. Wes had gotten up early that morning and fetched Marco from the woods. After introductions had been made and stories told, Robin suggested that we celebrate being back together and party hard.

We all drank a load of rum and wine. It turned out that Bashar was an even bigger partier than Robin, and the two of them had drinking contests. Trent had never been much of a drinker, but I could tell that he loved the taste of exotic wines. Marco had been unable to get booze out in the woods so gratefully welcomed a few drinks. Wes was more focused on snacks than drinks. I knew I had to be very careful with the booze considering I hadn't had any in ages. However, I was so taken in by the fruity rum cocktails and glasses of wine that it was difficult to ignore common sense and I ended up passing out before everyone else. The last thing I remember was Robin saying, "there's too much blood in my alcohol system, but I'll drink that too."

Hangovers hit Trent, Robin, Marco, and I the next morning. Wes went off to work without a headache. He missed out on a large breakfast of eggs, sausages, bread, and fruit from Robin's hobby farm.

"My ex-girlfriend started a pretty wicked fruit garden out behind my bedroom," Robin said. "No one was supposed to eat any of that fruit apart from the two of us."

"Where's this babe now?" I asked.

"The chick ran off when I didn't give her money one day," Robin said. "Man, girls are an expensive hobby, even under communism."

"I'm sure your dad blamed your miserliness on the rise of communism," Marco cracked while the rest of us laughed.

"At least you had a woman," Bashar said. "Trent, Don, and I were trapped in a sausage factory for over a year. Man, even grandmothers look like foxy ladies after having been locked up with cock for over a year."

"Finding girlfriends should be our top priority," I said.

"I thought your top priority was to find your sister Don," Trent said.

"You want to go on a date with your sister Don, don't ya?" Robin said. "Dude, I always knew your sister was pretty hot, but I never figured you for incest. Man, that prison must have really fucked up your brains and balls."

"You're just jealous cuz Julia shot you down countless times," Marco chuckled.

"How about you Marco, do you have any girl stories to share unlike Bashar, Trent, and I?" I asked.

"Don, you've been asking all of us so many damn questions," Robin said. "Are you trying to write a gossip column?"

"I guess some things stay the same," Marco smirked, "Don's nosiness is one of them."

After our large breakfast and a bit of lazing around, Bashar announced that he wanted to write some letters to his friends to let them know that he was still alive. Robin told him that there was a post office and a printing shop which could be reached on foot within an hour. Bashar told us he would head there and return once he'd mailed his letters.

Trent, Robin, Marco, and I spent the rest of the day lazing around and telling stories. It was comforting to know that I still felt close to Marco and Robin despite having not seen them for over a year. Before meeting up with Robin and Marco, I'd been a bit worried that we would have all grown too far apart and not be able to relate to one another anymore but feeling close with one another after different life experiences was a testament of our friendship. I was also happy that Bashar and Trent were bonding with my old friends.

Wes managed to get off work early that day, so he popped by Robin's place. Bashar still hadn't shown up. We went looking for him amid speculation that he'd been apprehended by the vigilums.

Robin led the way to the printing shop. After a few minutes of searching, we found Bashar at the back of the printing office with over two hundred leaflets.

"Are you writing a book or something?" Robin asked.

"Take a look," Bashar grinned.

The leaflet contained a one-page story about the gulag. Bashar hadn't mentioned anyone by name or talked about the escape. The essay discussed the treatment of prisoners, security precautions, crimes which inmates had been incarcerated for, the lack of food and prisoner rights, and how the gulags were the most likely place where missing people had ended up since Viceroy Bartholomew and the Wadonshea Party had come into power.

"You're going to get your tongue chopped off for writing this," Marco said.

"No one will know that I wrote this stuff," Bashar said. "I'm going to leave stacks of these flyers in public areas for average citizens to read on their own. There is a reason why I left out our names and the escape incident. For all we know, the government may be unaware of the destruction of the gulag."

"Are you guys aware that a lot of political and historical textbooks, and government document are being rewritten by the Wadonshea?" Wes asked. "They're filled with rhetoric favouring the communists who hope that less educated folks and the younger generation will fall prey to state-run propaganda."

"All of this is dangerous, but we have to find some way of getting our story out there," Trent said.

"With state-run media, any zine or DIY publication is now illegal," Marco said.

"The government wants us to be afraid of them," I said. "If we don't get our story out, then we've let them know that we're afraid of them, and they'll think they've won. Well fuck that; they're not going to win. It's up to us to let them know that we are not afraid of them no matter how big they are or how many vigilums work for them. These leaflets will inspire more people to stand up and take action against tyranny. No chickening out."

Wes gazed at some candle-lit windows. I was a bit annoyed that his attention was veering away from my call to arms, but the perplexed look on his face showed much concern.

"Hey guys it's pretty dark out now," Wes said. "We left the house about fifteen minutes before curfew. It's definitely past curfew now so we should get out of here."

"Curfew?" Bashar bellowed.

"They brought it in a few months back," Robin said.

"Man, I thought curfews were only for kids with overprotective parents," I grumbled. "I never thought I'd hear that word again now that we're in the Post-17 generation."

"I'd hoped that the country would be so much better when we got out of the gulag," Trent groaned.

"Things are getting worse by the day," Marco said.

We stepped from the printing shop patio and onto the road. Five vigilums were wandering the streets. Patrolling vacant streets after curfew had to be dull, but I couldn't feel sympathy for the vigilums. They'd chosen a job of boredom. I wasn't sure if violating curfew was more taboo than anti-government literature.

"What do you have in the bag?" one of the five vigilums asked us.

"None of your business," Bashar snorted.

"With that attitude we're going to have to look in the bag," the interrogating vigilum said.

"And where is your printing permit?" another vigilum asked.

"What printing permit?" Bashar blushed.

"No one is allowed in there without a printing permit," the vigilum said.

"It's after curfew too," a third vigilum said. "All of you are in a lot of trouble."

Two of the vigilums came forward to snatch Bashar's bag. I had a feeling that Bashar was going to smash the vigilums to the ground. Each of us rested our palms on our weapons, waiting for a justifiable reason to unleash some insanity.

A fireball blasted forward. Robin and Trent jumped back while Bashar dropped his bag. Screaming erupted from the vigilums as the fireball turned to sparks against a stone wall. I'd figured that Marco had shot the fireball from his ring, but both his hands were on his whip.

A gust of smoke rose from Wes's mouth. I couldn't believe that my most passive friend had finally performed an act of violence. I wondered if the suppression of the government and the horror stories from the gulag had inspired Wes to take up arms against arresters.

"You've been given a warning," Wes said. "Please leave now to avoid getting hurt."

The first vigilum jumped to his feet and hobbled away while the second vigilum rolled across the ground as the flames on his clothes died down. The third vigilum blew his horn while the other two came forward, each with a raised xiphos.

Bashar's palm clenched around a vigilum's wrist, forcing the vigilum into dropping his sword. The ogre thrusted his weight forward and body-slammed the vigilum to the ground. The vigilum groaned and begged for air but Bashar silenced him with a bonk on the head.

Marco's whip snapped at the second swordsman, leaving him with a rope coiled around his neck. With a tug, the vigilum jerked forward, choked, dropped his sword, crashed to his knees, and went silent as his skin turned purple and his eyeballs nearly popped out of his skull. Without wheezing sounds, we knew that the vigilum would suffocate to death. Marco eased up on his whip and let the vigilum go away injured but alive.

A squad of vigilums which greatly outnumbered my friends and I rushed to the scene of the crime in response to the horn blowing.

"Hey horn blower," Robin called. "I bet you got really good at blowing on the horn from all those blowjobs you gave Bartholomew to get this job."

The horn blower drew his sword while Robin's blade swung in defense. I couldn't focus on the blades clashing since my friends and I were outnumbered and going to have to act fast if we didn't want to end up as casualties.

An archer pulled an arrow from his quiver and loaded it into his longbow. I dashed forward and drew my sword. With a quick flash, I slashed the string of the bow. Before the bowman could react, my katana crashed into the quiver, slit the leather, and crunched the arrows to splinters.

Trent's fists swung around in circles, scaring two vigilums from taking a shot at him with their clubs. Right when a third vigilum attempted to thud Trent's wrist, Trent clobbered him in the nose. Trent then tossed his victim's club at another vigilum. The targeted vigilum ran off after the thrown club knocked his weapon from his hand.

Bashar picked a vigilum from off the ground by his throat and tossed the guy against the wall of the printing shop, knocking the wind out of him.

Robin's opponent had yet to fall. Just when the vigilum was ready to chop Robin's head off, Robin dropped to the ground. Robin's free hand pulled a dagger from his belt. The dagger darted upward, burying itself in the vigilum's crotch. The vigilum screamed the most unsettling cry I'd ever heard as he flailed backward. The dagger dug deeper into the vigilum's groin when he fell backward. The excruciating wound would surely kill him.

"Enjoy giving blowjobs as a eunuch, ya dickless dink," Robin chuckled.

From out of the shadows, a crossbow bolt shot through Wes's thin bat-like wings. As Wes cried and shook with shock, Robin dashed to Wes, placed his hand on Wes's wound, and hummed. Robin's ring glowed blue while circles of blue light beamed from his ring and spread across the weeping dragon wing. The wound began to close due to genie healing magic.

The crossbowman loaded a second bolt into his weapon. I flashed my ring forward and focused on the crossbow. Through fierce concentration and genie telekinesis, I pulled the loaded crossbow from the vigilum's grasp. The crossbow floated away from its owner and then pulled a 180. Once spun around, the bolt blasted through the vigilum's shoulder. Like his comrades, this cowardly vigilum fled the scene of the crime.

Bashar had a vigilum pinned to the ground who he was smacking repeatedly across the head. A fellow vigilum came to his rescue, but Trent's jump kick landed the vigilum next to his fallen comrade.

A bowman jumped from the bushes. Marco raised his ring and fired a transparent ray. His force blast knocked the vigilum against a wall, rendering him unconscious.

Two more swordsmen dashed from the shadows. Each had their weapons pointed forward. My sword flashed upward. A vigilum's skin parted, blood drooled, and mutilated intestines spilt from his wound while his deceased body dropped to the ground.

Robin went after the last standing vigilum. Wes was healed, but probably not ready to fight. I'd never healed a dragon so wasn't sure how long it would take for Wes to recover.

The vigilum raised his sword above his head, leaving his chest and face open for attack. Robin leapt forward with his sword in front of him as if it were a lance. The vigilum sprinted into Robin's sword like a war horse who'd galloped into a pike. Spilt blood mixed with the milky mud puddles.

"What should we do now?" Trent asked as he looked around to see if anymore enemies were standing.

"Kill them all," Robin grinned as he smiled at the corpses.

"We don't kill unless we have to," Wes said.

"Since when do you make the rules boss?" Robin said. "I saved your ass. You're the one who started this brawl in the first place."

Wes and Robin bickered back and forth. I took no notice of their spat because there was a vigilum manual floating in a puddle. I leafed through the soggy textbook, trying to see if I could learn any valuable information from the text.

"Look at Don, still as nosy as an elephant," Robin laughed.

"Robin shut the hell up," I said as I passed the book around my circle of friends.

"What's written in the notebook?" Trent asked.

"Apparently Viceroy Bartholomew will be passing by O'Jahnteh in two days," I said. "One of these guards is supposed to rendezvous with Bartholomew's convoy and act as his guard. According to this text, Bartholomew is supposed to spend some time at a spa out in the jungle not too far from here."

"Bloody hell," Bashar said. "He sent us to a derelict gulag while he soaks in a hot spring at some retreat."

"I thought that everyone was supposed to be equal under communism," Marco snorted. "I don't know anyone who can afford to go to any of those jungle retreats."

"So, we've just killed one of his escorts," Wes said.

"That's what it looks like," I said.

"I have an idea," Wes winked.

Wes's plan was for us to ambush Viceroy Bartholomew and his guards while enroute to the spa. The documents stated that Bartholomew would be travelling in a carriage that would look completely average so that no one with a rebellious streak would suspect that the viceroy was riding in there.

Twenty guards were set to escort Bartholomew. Many of the guards would be genies since genies were often selected as elite vigilums and bodyguards. Twenty bodyguards against six rogues seemed like unfavorable odds, but Wes figured that we could surprise the escort.

Wes's idea was for Robin, Marco, and I to dress up in the vigilum uniforms which we'd stolen from the dead bodies of the battle. Next, Wes, Bashar, and Trent would get tied up, and Marco, Robin, and I would pretend to escort them down the road as prisoners. Upon seeing the escort, we were to let Wes, Trent, and Bashar go wild and they would attack the guards while we genies would use our powers to back our allies up. It seemed dangerous, but so was life. Viceroy Bartholomew was a threat to everyone in Sionia, and the only way to end the oppression was to draw blood.

"That's an alright plan," Bashar said, "but I still want to hand out all these stories I wrote."

"I don't think that would be a very good idea," Wes said.

"Are you trying to suppress my writing talents?" Bashar asked. "I was ready to be a hotshot journalist until the media became state-run and filled with propaganda and bullshit rhetoric."

"You could get murdered while handing that stuff out," Trent said.

"We need you for the fight," Marco said.

"Can't have you getting killed before we have Bartholomew's head on a stake," Robin said.

"Once Bartholomew is dead you can hand out those leaflets," I said. "Our story will have more power once the viceroy is dead."

Amid much impatience, Bashar agreed to comply with us. A few times he tried to change our minds, but we always shut him down. I could tell that Bashar really couldn't wait for Bartholomew to die. Hell, we all wanted him dead. Bartholomew was one of the few people who justified homicide.

The two days leading up to Bartholomew's death were long. My comrades and I continuously went over our plans, but there was only so much we could prepare for since we were unsure of the weapons and abilities of these twenty bodyguards. In some ways we wanted to recruit a few mercenaries for our fight, but there was no one who any of us could trust; if only Ace were still alive.

My friends and I awoke early and headed out to the jungle on death day. We chose a very remote spot along the forested road for the ambush. Every second we spent waiting around was held with taut suspense.

Bashar, Trent, and Wes each had their wrists bound by very thin twine. We hoped with all our hearts that everything would go according to plan and that none of us would lose any blood.

Eventually we heard horses coming down the jungle road. None of us could be sure as to whether this was Bartholomew's escort or not. There weren't going to be any markers indicating the Sionian dictator. It would be a travesty if we accidentally attacked an innocent party.

"Alright this is it," Wes said as Trent and Bashar rose to their feet.

"Sweet vengeance," Bashar grinned.

"Don't kill all of them eh," Robin said. "I sure could use some action after all of this boring waiting around."

Robin, Marco, and I stepped forward. I held Wes on a leash while Marco led Trent and Robin guided Bashar. The wagon stopped in its tracks. Several of the bodyguards came forward.

"What be the meaning of this?" the carriage driver asked.

"We have found these three monsters out in the jungle," I lied. "Each is wanted by the O'Jahnteh authorities."

The vigilums eyed Wes closely. Wes must have gotten sick of being stared at all the time and I hated to call him a monster for being a unique species, but sometime weaknesses could be advantages.

"All of them are very dangerous," Marco said. "Do you think you could spare some of your men to help us escort these criminals back to O'Jahnteh?"

I prayed for the squadron leader to say yes. If five vigilums followed us into the woods, we could slaughter them and then return to the wagon. The fight would go so much smoother if we took the guards down in small groups instead of a royal rumble.

"We are protecting Viceroy Bartholomew and are under strict instructions to not leave the convoy," one of the vigilums said.

"But these criminals are extremely dangerous and might overpower us," Marco said.

"You're damn right that we're extremely dangerous," Bashar roared as he charged forward.

I cursed Bashar for his impulsivity and impatience. Wes and Trent broke free. They probably figured that it was now or never and that we'd lost the opportunity to mislead some of the guards. Bashar had started the fight, and the rest of us needed to finish it. Danger was growing by the second.

A genie guard raised his ring and unleashed a blast of energy. Eight sword and club wielding guards came forward once the genie had blasted Bashar to the ground.

Wes unleashed a long and frantic flame from his mouth. A flaming guard dashed into the jungle, igniting branches and singeing vegetation. Since there were no creeks or ponds to dive into, the guard was going to burn to death unless he dropped to the ground.

A flame formed in a genie guard's ring and collided with Wes's fire. Wes breathed harder while the guard concentrated fiercely on his ring of fire.

Trent helped Bashar to his feet as six guards approached them, each with a raised club. The ogre-cyclops team punched and kicked away at the group. Bashar and Trent took thumps from the clubs, but their blows and blunts were tougher than the enemy clubs.

Robin raised his sword and cut his way into Bashar and Trent's fight, slashing one vigilum to the ground. Bashar stepped on top of the vigilum's chest, forcing blood to bubble out of wounds. Robin cackled at his wounded foe and then dueled with a vigilum who was armed with a club and sword.

The genie who'd fired the force blast raised his ringed finger a second time. Marco's whip snapped at the genie's hand, leaving him with reddened digits and a missing ring finger.

"You'll pay for that fucker," Marco's victim cried as he attempted to fire a force blast at Marco.

Despite the weeping blood from his destroyed digits, it took the injured genie a few moments to realize that he'd been disarmed from his magic ring. The genie growled and swore under his breath as he rummaged through the foliage.

Nine guards armed themselves with crossbows. All pointed their weapons at Wes, Bashar, Robin, and Trent. Six archers stood to the left of the carriage while the remaining trio were stationed to the right.

Marco shot a large force shield from his ring, dividing the battlefield. The carriage and the six crossbowmen were on one side of the force shield, while the rest of us were trapped on the other side.

I jumped onto my magic carpet, flew above the battle site, and commanded my magic carpet to hover above the three crossbowmen who were to the right of the carriage. Upon seeing me, the crossbowmen made me their target. A series of blue, yellow, green, and red rays flashed from my ring. Once the vigilum were hit by these stun rays, the guards jittered in seizures before collapsing to the jungle ground.

Robin and his opponent veered away from Bashar and Trent's fight with the clubbed guards. Through blows, parries, forward and backward steps, Robin and his opponent travelled to the left side of the road, away from the protection of Marco's shield.

As Robin's opponent turned toward the six crossbowmen, Robin's sword slid into the rival's temple. Skull cracked as blood seeped. The duelist's body jolted before falling to the ground. Robin pulled his bloodied weapon away and then spun around to celebrate the victory of his melee.

The six crossbowmen fired. Three of the bolts blasted into Robin's chest, piercing his lungs. A fourth bolt dug into his belly. The fifth bolt sank into Robin's heart. The last bolt travelled through Robin's throat and out his neck. Red liquid oozed from the wounds. Robin jittered and then fell backward. His body bumped against the ground, forcing the wounds to bubble more blood.

Marco and I screamed like slaughtered cats. Wes and the fire genie ceased their flames. Bashar and Trent stopped throwing fists while the guards dropped their clubs.

I flew toward Robin's fallen body and placed my ringed hand on his gory chest and began the genie healing ritual. Black circles of light erupted from my ring and travelled down Robin's critically injured body. Blackened healing rays meant that the victim had died. I fired several more rays from my ring, but each blue ring blackened to charcoal. It seemed completely fucked and evil that my friend had to die to stop an inimical tyrant from destroying the country.

The battle had to end now. My friends and I had lost too much. There was no way we could allow ourselves to lose another soldier. There were no words for how devastating Robin's death was, but we had to honour his death by killing every single guard.

The archers got ready to reload as Marco commanded genie telekinesis. The quivers lifted off the archers. The leather casings dropped to the jungle floor while the bolts hovered in the air above the archers' heads.

Marco lowered his ring hand, releasing his telekinesis spell. Bolts sank into the crossbowmen. Arrowheads pierced faces, eyes, legs, arms, chests, feet, backs, and hands. Some of the crossbowmen died from getting bolts to the throat while other guards were pinned to the ground from multiple missiles.

Bashar gripped a clubman's neck and crushed his vertebrae. Once the bones snapped, Bashar tossed the crippled body to the side, ensuring the death of the guard if he wasn't already gone.

Trent bent over and charged forward as if he were a bull. His horns acted as pikes and pierced a vigilums' chest and internal organs.

I dashed forward and swung my katana. The head of a guard rolled to the ground as fresh blood dropped from my weapon. I hoped that Viceroy Bartholomew would be the next man to die by my sword. Bartholomew was truly a chicken-hawk coward if he had to get his posse to kill my friend while he hid behind a carriage while enroute to a spa.

Wes released another fireball. The flame ball travelled into the genie's mouth, turning the guard's insides into an inferno while flames grew and cremated the guard's outsides.

The carriage driver raised his sword and jumped from the carriage with his blade pointed at Marco. Bashar swung at the driver and knocked him flat on his back. By now all the guards were either dead, immobilized, or had disappeared into the jungle.

"Let's burn this chariot down," Wes said.

"Hell no," Marco barked. "We're going to break into this carriage and tear Bartholomew to death piece by piece."

"I deserve vengeance along with every other Sionian," Bashar said as he punched the door of the carriage.

"This is for Robin," Marco said. "Bartholomew, we're going to kill you very slowly so we can watch you die."

"This is for everyone at the gulag," Trent said.

"And it's an act of justice for the betterment of our country," I said. "Bartholomew, your death will be an honour to the Sionian people."

"Tranquility through vengeance," Wes said.

I felt more savagery from Marco than anyone else. He'd been better friends with Robin than the rest of us. With the rest of his family dead or unaccounted for, perhaps Marco considered Robin his next of kin. Robin's death was probably going to send Marco's inner rage to a terrifying level.

Bashar and Trent clobbered at the door of the carriage while Marco chopped the vehicle with a hatchet which he'd retrieved from a dead archer.

Wes and I bent down next to Robin's corpse. Wes meditated, a common practice done to emphasize good luck for reaching the afterlife.

I tried to telepathically tell Robin how sorry I was that he was gone. I even thought that I should have died in his place. In some ways I was mad at Bashar for having been so impulsive. The guy had screwed up our plans of potentially diverting guards away from the fight. Then again, that hypothesized action had been unplanned, and you couldn't fault Bashar for not following through with a spur of the moment tactic which he'd been unaware of.

Part of me felt like I deserved blame for Robin's death since I'd attacked the trio of archers instead of the group of six. I felt like a chickenshit for having gone after the easier targets. If I'd attacked the larger group, Robin would probably still be alive. No one could survive six bolts, but three shots were survivable if you weren't hit in lethal points and were healed quickly. Robin had died before hitting the ground because I'd failed to see the big picture. I was an idiot and a coward.

As my thoughts shifted, I stopped criticizing myself and vented my anger at Robin. He should have stayed within the force shield instead of waltzing into the target of the archers.

All of this was too chaotic. Nothing about battle ever made any sense regardless of how much you knew about logistics, tactics, technology, magic, and strategy. Life was cruel chaos which death triumphed over.

Trent pulled the battered door off the carriage. Wes and I jumped to our feet and dashed toward the opening.

I nearly choked from the foul stench of vomit and carriage corpses. Bashar grabbed each of the stiffs by the neck, hauled them out of the carriage, and dropped them on the jungle grounds next to the dead guards.

We all recognized Bartholomew despite his putrid body odor, tangerine flesh, and bulging eyeballs. Bile encrusted clothes, blue saliva, seeping sweat, and the stench of puss and jock itch made me want to puke. Bartholomew's bodyguard was in the exact same state.

"They've been poisoned," Wes said.

Marco jumped into the puke-filled carriage, thrashed around, and then returned with a sheet of parchment.

"To whoever finds the body of Bartholomew," Marco read. "Viceroy Bartholomew has been poisoned to death. Do not eat or drink anything found within the carriage. All the foods and beverages had been tainted with toxins. By the time you read this, I hope Bartholomew has died from poisoning, be it agonizing and disgusting. This son of a bitch is poisoning Sionia, so it is appropriate that he dies from toxics.

"Mother shit," Marco growled as he ripped the note to shreds.

"I can't believe this," I cried as tears welled in my eyes. "This battle was nothing but a loss. Our actions were in vain. Robin died for nothing. An anonymous asshole beat us to killing Bartholomew."

Marco kicked Bartholomew's body. More puke splattered from Bartholomew's mouth. Each of us spat on the corpse.

After a bit of debate, we left the battle scene. Someone else would find Bartholomew's corpse since no jungle cat would want to eat a poisoned body. We couldn't be tied to the viceroy's or the guards' deaths. None of us survivors were in the vigilante business out of ego, and any type of bragging would get us executed.

Robin's body rested on the back of my magic carpet as we slowly made our way back to O'Jahnteh. Now that Robin was dead, his magic carpet was obsolete. I wasn't sure what we were going to tell his family.

The next day it was announced that Viceroy Bartholomew and his closest bodyguard had been poisoned by a mysterious assassin, while an unknown gang had slaughtered Bartholomew's convoy.

Demonstrations immediately erupted across Sionian. Some of the protests turned into riots. Disgruntled party members and several army generals turned against Bartholomew's loyalists. The Wadonshea government feared impeachment and announced their resignation within the next month. Political parties (which had been dismantled under Bartholomew's tyranny) reformed. Elections were called. Promises were made to abolish the gulags while many prisoners were pardoned for their petty crimes.

My friends and I decided to not get involved in the political crisis. Between King Rex's assassination and Viceroy Bartholomew's death, Marco and I felt like we'd done more than enough to rid Sionia of dictators for one lifetime. It wasn't that we weren't concerned about the direction of our country; my friends and I truly did care about the welfare of others, but we felt that if we didn't take a step back from the turbulent times, then we'd die among the chaos.

Bashar and Trent returned to Stodaneatoo after Robin's funeral. I wanted my friends nearby, but those guys needed to get home after a long prison term. As I bid them farewell, I wondered if life was made of long periods of monotony and then a sudden series of unforeseeable catastrophic events.

Wes returned to the university. He started work on a large engineering project which involved reservoirs and aqueducts. I admired how Wes was using his intelligence and new ideas as a way of healing his pain.

"What are you going to do?" I asked Marco two days after Robin's funeral.

"I need to get the hell out of O'Jahnteh, that's for sure," Marco answered.

"I think I will do the same."

"That's probably a good idea for both of us. Robin's dead and neither of us have any family left here."

"I think I'm going to go looking for Julia. Apparently, she is in Stodaneatoo. If she is, I'm sure I could crash with Trent or Bashar while I look for her."

"Looking for your long-lost sister is truly the best thing you could do after losing Robin. You're a good man."

"Thanks dude, but where will you head?"

"I think I'll go to the west coast."

"Oh yeah?"

"Yeah man, I've never been there before. I'll find some village where politics isn't tearing life apart."

"Good call eh."

"I've always wanted to learn about marine botany but have never had the opportunity. I need to make opportunities for my life."

"Hells yeah dude."

"You know, all lives end prematurely, even Post-17 deaths like Robin."

Marco's words made me realize that Robin was the first guy who I knew who'd died as a Post-17. Some of the guards and vigilums who'd been killed in the last week had been Post-17s, but they were strangers.

"We Post-17s think that we're going to live forever, but we're just as mortal as the previous generations," I said.

"Which is why we have to live just as voraciously," Marco said.

After Marco and I said goodbye, I grabbed my bag, sword, and magic carpet and headed back to the jungle. Julia was somewhere out there.

BOOK V:

DRIFTING IN THE FUTURE

It took me over a week to fly to Stodaneatoo by magic carpet. I could have gotten there way faster but I needed some leisure time. Flying around without boundaries affirmed that I was free from the gulag, free from government oppression. Soaking up the beauty of nature helped distract me from Robin's death. I hadn't planned on taking so long to fly through the jungle, but when I soared above the tree canopies, I kept spotting mountains and rivers which begged me to take a look. Nothing could offer me anything more beautiful than what nature asked me to love.

Every night I camped out next to a lake or river and built myself a rudimentary shelter out of whatever materials were available, be they palm leaves, branches, rocks, moss, or boulders. I'd packed a fishing pole with me and caught fish nearly every morning. Although I'd brought some food with me, I foraged much wild fruit. Water from the river tasted much better than that of a well.

Eventually I touched down in Stodaneatoo. After living like a barbarian, I figured that I should treat myself to a room at an inn. After showering and changing out of my sweat-encrusted clothes, I headed down to the pub.

"Hey Don, how the hell are you doing?" a voice called when I entered the tavern.

Bashar was at a table with a stone mug of ale. I wondered if I was ever going to get away from this guy. He ordered me a beer and recommended that I try the red pork curry. Since your average ogre weighed at least three-times as much as a genie did, ogres could easily out drink and out eat all of us. The portions of food at the pub were massive and

Bashar took much delight in satisfying his gluttony with my unfinished rice and curry.

"I'll go back to work sooner or later," Bashar said after I asked him about journalism. "The country is going through a wave of change, which could make for really good stories, but government information is still highly restricted. I also want to have fun after having been locked up in the gulag for so damn long."

"I'll drink to that," I said as my stone mug clinked Bashar's.

"He's been in here every night," the barmaid said.

"You always said you would party lots when you got out of the gulag," I said, "glad to see that you're living up to your promise."

"What about you Don?" Bashar wondered. "Are you still looking for your sister?"

"I'll go to the hall of records tomorrow and then show up at her address. Until then, I'm sleeping here at the inn."

"Don't be a stranger, you're more than welcome to stay at my house."

"Cool man. What's Trent up to?"

"He's taken off to some primitive village up in the hills. He's been digging some ditches up there cuz it rains like crazy, and the water needs an accurate path to flow, or it will destroy the roads. I'd like him to come down and party with us, but he hates the city and, I think he wants to adjust back to the off-the-grid lifestyle."

"I'm sure he wants some space after having had no privacy in the gulag."

"I guess so. I would like to see his face down here though."

"You should head to the hills and enjoy nature."

"That would be wicked as long as I packed a few kegs of beer with me."

"Let me tell you about what I just did."

I told Bashar about my trip to the jungle over a few more beers. Eventually I needed to be carried up to bed. I was pretty sure Bashar went back to the bar to have a few more rounds once I passed out in bed.

I got up the next day with a bit of a hangover. A bowl of spicy chicken soup, a scoop of rice, two bananas, and three glasses of tea eventually eased the thumping in my brain. Once the headache was gone, I headed to the hall of records to look up my sister's address. After some searching, I came across Julia's name. I wrote down her address, found some maps, and headed to her place by magic carpet.

Like many other areas of Stodaneatoo, Julia's home was built from a combination of bamboo and jungle wood. She had a small lawn out front with a few plants in pots. Her abode looked relaxing, and the home next door was even more impressive. Ivy dangled up the stone walls of her neighbour's house. A pond with frogs rested in the middle of the grassy front yard. Flowers and fruits trees acted as barriers with the road and the neighbouring properties. After having lived off next to nothing in the gulag, all homes looked exquisite.

Julia was playing a solo game of basketball. A net had been bolted into the side of her house and the bamboo walls looked like they'd taken a beating from the rubber ball. Julia played while I stood in the distance, staring at her like a voyeur. I cleared my throat a few times but still felt paralyzed. Eventually I forced myself to call her name.

The basketball dropped to the ground and bounced toward the lawn. Julia's eyes widened while the rest of her remained as still as a statue. Each of us held our breath.

"I'm alive," I said, unable to think of anything more appropriate.

Julia dashed forward. A second later I felt like I'd been slammed by a rolling boulder. I tripped over a pot holding a tomato plant, broke the pottery, and landed on the grass. Julia had always been athletic and had a good amount of buff, but now I was sure she could take on Bashar. Living among giant ogres and cyclops in Stodaneatoo must have really upped her strength.

"Brother, where in the hell have you been for the last ten million eons?" Julia exclaimed. "I thought you'd died or fucked off for the rest of your life."

"It's a damn long story," I said as I made my way to my feet after having had the wind knocked out of me. "How

about we sit down here in the garden? I'm sure you have a lot
to tell as well."

Julia fetched a pitcher of passion fruit juice and
offered me a bowl of nuts while I lay sprawled out on her
lawn. It had been a long time since I'd felt grass. It was
funny how you forgot about the little things in life, and then
when they reappeared, you took so much pleasure in them.

"I'll cook dinner for you tonight too," Julia said when
she noticed me pigging out on the snack. "No meat though,
I've become an herbivore."

"I'm sure a lot of other changes have happened with
the both of us," I said. "Do tell what you've been up to."

I told Julia about my arrest, the time in the gulag, and
the recent events involving Viceroy Bartholomew's death.
Though Julia had a lot of anger toward the government, she
was also angry with me for having been aware that vigilantism
was illegal. The stories of the gulag were hard for her to
swallow but my story of liberation made her proud. The news
of Robin's death saddened her. She'd always pegged Robin
as a clown who would never get in her pants, but his charm
and humour could make her chuckle. Julia could understand
how distraught I felt over the failed mission against Viceroy
Bartholomew. Like many other folks, Julia was happy that
Bartholomew was dead. The last thing I mentioned was my
camping trip from my journey to Stodaneatoo, which Julia
found pretty cool.

Right after my disappearance, Julia had won a
woman's kickboxing contest. A spectating coach was so
impressed with Julia's fighting style that she offered to train
her as a gladiator, which Julia immediately accepted.
Considering my sister already knew a lot about weaponry and
hand to hand combat, it wasn't long till she was competing for
cash.

Once Julia was told that she'd be losing the house in
O'Jahnteh, she ventured to Stodaneatoo. She got a job
working as a blacksmith's assistant and also made money
through underground kickboxing tournaments. There was a
gladiator competition two days from now, and Julia hoped that
I could come out and cheer her on. I was very curious to see

how fierce my sister had become after years of wrestling and playfighting.

Sometime later, Julia's next-door neighbour Sheri came by, and introductions were made.

"You've got a very good garden," I said.

"Thanks, you two should come over," Sheri said.

"I was just going to make dinner," Julia said.

"I can cook for all of you," Sheri said.

"Just as long as there is not chopped flesh on my plate," Julia warned.

"Relax lady," Sheri said, "you can hack away at bodies all you want, but I get the meat."

"I'm sure you can make her a good salad from all the produce growing in your garden," I said.

"I'll make one for both of you," Sheri said.

I got up from my seat, ready to hop over to Sheri's property.

"Don is that a katana?" Sheri asked as she pointed to my stack of clutter which was lying on the ground atop my magic carpet.

"Hells yeah," I responded.

"Darling, that's a wicked weapon," Sheri grinned.

"Maybe I can let you wield it around a bit," I said.

"Unfair," Julia grunted. "Don never let me touch any of his things."

"Cuz you'd break them," I said.

"Oh, sibling rivalry," Sheri laughed. "Don, I have quite a collection of swords myself. Do you want to check them out?"

"Gladly," I said.

Sheri led me into the stone and wooden house she lived in. A longsword and a gladius were mounted above the fireplace. On a different wall: a saber, a khopesh, a scimitar, and a rapier were on display next to a bookcase. A third wall featured a wakizashi, an aikuchi, and a tanto.

"This is a very impressive collection," I said. "Even the hilts on these swords are pretty artistic."

"I hope your sister will make me a broadsword one of these days."

"If Julia makes you a bastard sword, then that's more than she's ever done for me."

"I also really want a katana."

"Let me guess, you brought me over here because you want to stab me and steal mine?"

"I keep all of these babies sharpened for a reason," Sheri laughed as she picked up a falchion (which I hadn't noticed earlier) and then swung it around.

"You want to duel," I joked as I unsheathed my katana.

"Julia tells me that you're an excellent fencer and also a genius at magic."

"Really? That's the kindest thing she's ever said about me. I wonder why she told this to her girlfriend instead of complimenting me."

"Sugar, I think she's trying to set us up."

I had to admit that Sheri was pretty hot, and not just in looks. Sure, Sheri was a sexy tall chick with wicked hair, smooth multi-shaded black flesh, big tits, a voluptuous booty, mysterious eyes, and a wild grin, but there was more to her than that. She was a welcoming person who had a good sense of humour and knew how to make a stranger feel appreciated. Her sword collection was more impressive than any I'd ever seen. Her garden was also very admirable.

I'd been hoping to meet some girls as soon as I'd gotten out of the gulag, but after two weeks I was still on the longest dry spell ever. Listening to Bashar boast about all the babes he'd banged at the tavern hadn't helped. I wondered if Trent had shacked up with a mountain chick. If Sheri ended up being my first girlfriend since leaving the gulag, I'd be hella ecstatic.

"I'm not a genie, so no using any magic if we decide to duel," Sheri said as she waved around the falchion.

"If you win the duel, you can have my magic carpet."

"For real? Julia has never taken me on a magic carpet ride."

"Now that's being a rude friend."

"I would kill to be able to fly over the jungle on a magic carpet."

"I'll take you for a ride tomorrow."

"For real sugar?"

"Hell yeah, it's the least I can do; you're cooking dinner for me."

"Speaking of which, I better get to that," Sheri said as she walked out of the room with the falchion.

"You're carrying that sword with you."

"Maybe I'll use to chop some vegetables and meat. I'll make sure to get some animal blood on your sister's salad."

Julia came over soon after and lounged in Sheri's yard.

"Is Sheri single?" I asked Julia once Sheri was out of ear reach.

"You ask her, I don't want to date her."

"I'll look nosy."

"Since when do you care about being nosy?"

During dinner, I promised to take Sheri for a magic carpet ride the next day. Sheri exploded with excitement and thanked me immediately. I wondered if Sheri had a crush on me. She certainly was a really cool lady. It wasn't every chick who grew a wicked garden, had a chill sense of humour, and collected an eclectic mix of swords. I wondered if we would end up as a couple. The thought of dating my sister's best friend made me laugh.

Sheri and I set off on the magic carpet after breakfast the next morning. We flew over bamboo buildings, stone temples, public gardens, and rice fields before we got out of the city. We then headed toward the jungle mountains.

Sheri kept waving her arms and screaming for joy at the top of her lungs. This was the closest she had ever come to flying. Apart from Wes, genies were the only humanoid species who could control flight. A lot of humans wished that they could be a bird for a day so that they could fly, and now Sheri was getting that opportunity.

As we flew over the trees, our speed shifted from thunder fast to slow as a snail. I pulled a few quick maneuvers on the magic carpet, and we dove into the jungle canopy and then back up to the sky. On one occasion a flock of colourful jungle birds fluttered around the magic carpet. Although the day had mostly been bright, we ran into an assortment of clouds. Passing through the clouds delighted Sheri to a new level.

We decided to have a picnic by a river. Sheri was so pumped with adrenaline that she almost didn't eat her lunch. I'd always found magic carpet rides exhilarating, but Sheri's enthusiasm reminded me to not take my genie powers for granted.

"What other things are you into besides swords and gardening?" I asked Sheri.

"I dig hiking and cooking too. I would like to go to sea and learn about sailing as well."

"Right on."

"What about you, sugar? What are you into?"

"Since escaping from the gulag, I've been learning how to have hobbies again, but I do like fencing, the outdoors, studying magic, that kind of stuff. I've never had a job I was really committed to or anything."

"Julia said that you were quite into being a vigilante."

"Yeah, and it got me sent to the gulag."

"At least you can laugh about it after having had such a terrible experience."

"My friends Bashar and Trent got me through that. I don't think I'd be alive if it weren't for them."

"It's too bad you couldn't make a living as a vigilante."

"I don't do that kind of work for money, and I won't accept any bounty hunter money or anything like that. I fight corruption and crime for the betterment of the community. I consider my work and my principles way more important than money."

"That's really admirable sweetheart. It's not everyone who has that kind of selfless drive to help out others."

"What do you do for a living Sheri?"

"I recently completed vigilum academy and I should be working next week."

I nearly choked on the mango I was eating. The vigilums were tools of the corrupt government who followed the most inhumane orders out of submission. They protected others for the sole sake of money. These pigs broke all the rules. Vigilums were always on power trips and trying to make the public feel small. The vigilums were a legal set of terrorists. I couldn't believe that a girl who I was infatuated with wanted to join these low-lives.

It took a lot of willpower for me to not speak my mind and offend Sheri, but I really did want to scream my disappointment. Luckily, an idea popped into my head before I could ruin the day with my dogmatic opinions.

"I thought women weren't allowed to join the vigilums," I said.

Women's rights groups had been fighting to have equal opportunities in the work force for years. Last I'd checked, women were now allowed to join the military. When I was seven, women had legally entered politics for the first time. In the past women had earned lower wages than men but that had changed after King Rex's death.

"Women have only been able to join the vigilums for a little over a year," Sheri said. "The change must have happened when you were in the gulag."

I had a feeling that Bartholomew had let women join the vigilums because he wanted a much larger security force. I told myself not to say that. As much as I hated the vigilums, women deserved every opportunity which men had. If only there had been a better reason for women being allowed to join the vigilums other than Bartholomew needing a massive security force to enforce his bullshit laws.

"I'm part of a radical feminist group," Sheri said. "For years we have fought for women's rights. Whenever injustice is made against women, the group comes forward and fights for equality and justice."

"That sounds like a form of being a vigilante."

"Oh yeah. You know Don, I know you hate the vigilums. You don't have to hide that from me. I'd probably hate them if they'd thrown me into a gulag."

"You have no idea how much I despise the vigilums. Words cannot explain my fucking hatred for them."

"With Bartholomew gone I think things will get a lot better. Many of his stupid laws are being reversed. The vigilum are gaining less power so there will probably be less brutality against citizens and much less corruption in the forces."

"We can only hope that the new government won't be as evil, but there are no guarantees in life."

"I dig your honesty dear."

"I still think that we don't need vigilums."

"Sugar, if there were more brave DIY individuals like yourself, then we wouldn't need any type of security. The problem is that there aren't enough everyday folks who stand up against injustice and put their neck on the line for the sake of principles."

"It always seems like a lot of vigilums only care about money."

"Yeah, that's the way people are. Money motivates. It's a sad reality, and it's lame that we need vigilums to protect us, and it sucks that we need security to scare people away, and it's really fucking depressing that evil exists, but that's life."

Since I agreed with Sheri's comment about evil, I planned to continue my vigilante activities. I hoped that the government would reverse the laws outlawing vigilantism. I didn't want to live my entire life as an anarchist outlaw while I was doing a public service. I hoped to never see Sheri when she was on a vigilum patrol. I wondered what Sheri would say if she found out that I'd killed a few vigilums. I didn't consider these actions the same as murder because they'd been done in self-defense, but to some people, all kills were homicide.

After lunch, Sheri and I climbed on the magic carpet. Sheri howled at the top of her lungs as we passed over mountaintops, lakes, and wetlands. We forgot about the conversation about vigilums as we absorbed the ecstatic feeling of our magic carpet ride.

Sheri accompanied me to Julia's gladiator match. In some ways I wanted to ask Sheri to be my girlfriend but asking her out at the coliseum seemed kind of weird since we were in a crowded location and watching my sister's battles against barbarian babes.

Although gladiators brutalized one another with every weapon imaginable, none of the fighters died regardless of how severe their wounds were. Zadohkoo (the god of death) and Hermateio (the god of arts and entertainment) had reached an alliance stating that anyone who was mortally injured or killed in a gladiator bout would be immediately teleported away from the coliseum and healed. All fights had to be pre-approved by both gods in their temples, or else the injured fighters would die like anyone else.

The gods' decision to postpone death for the sake of entertainment angered numerous Sionians. Much protest had been made, stating that Zadohkoo should use his powers to revive the lives of loved ones. Zadohkoo argued that death was just as natural as life and that deceased Sionians would be alive someplace else. Hermateio warned Sionians that if they continued to complain about this policy, then dead gladiators would not be returned, and combatants would fight to the bloody death without the privilege of resurrection. As much I understood that death was a part of life, it still seemed like a complete cheat that only gladiators could rise from the dead.

Some gladiator matches featured wild animals. Julia refused to fight any beasts be they horses, tigers, bears, leopards, lions, jackals, wolves, or dragons. Although I wasn't vegetarian, I could totally understand why she considered fighting animals to be an act of cruelty.

Julia was set to compete in an open brawl. It wasn't until recently that women had been permitted to compete in gladiator matches, so the numbers were low, but Julia assured me that they were rising.

The coliseum was a very large stone building without a ceiling. The fighting floor was circular and surrounded by many rows of benches and the occasional stage which featured music and announcements. Six trumpeters and a percussionist were playing the opening music to today's fights. People in the audience cheered in anticipation. Vendors sold snacks, fruit juice, and wine. Gamblers made predictions on who would win which fights.

Julia stood at one corner of the fighting floor while her four opponents stood at their respected ends of the fighting ground. Each woman was armed with one weapon. A few miscellaneous items were scattered on the dusty ground. Julia had been given an axe. She'd been forced into surrendering her ring prior to the match since none of her opponents had magical powers.

The percussionist beat one final drum roll. The trumpeters blasted their last call. A large gong banged. The gladiators rushed from each of their positions. The fights had begun.

Julia stood still, waiting for someone to attack her. I'd never seen her take a defensive stance, so I figured that she was calculating her surroundings and trying to get an idea of what her opponents were like. Some of her competitors were buffer than she was. These rivals were armed with either a club, sword, war hammer, or scythe.

Julia found her first opponent to be a swordswoman. Her opponent's cutlass slit toward Julia's face. Julia dodged the slice, raised her axe, and slammed the axe-head against the cutlass blade. The two weapons clashed back and forth as the audience cheered and sparks flew. Other fighters were doing very little. Dust erupted as Julia and her rivals bounced backward and forward over the rough ground. The sounds of the smashing blades resonated throughout the coliseum.

The swordswoman raised her cutlass. Julia darted forward and brought her battle-axe down as if she were chopping kindling. The head of the axe crashed into the swordswoman's shoulder. The cutlass dropped to the ground.

The swordswoman disappeared. The gong rang, indicating that Julia had won the fight. The swordswoman was temporarily invisible and being healed by the gods.

After much cheering, the enthusiasm of the audience died down though Sheri was still calling Julia's name. The other women had stood neutral during Julia's bout with the swordswoman. Perhaps they were planning on teaming up and overpowering Julia as a three against one match.

Julia made her way across the ground, keeping her axe raised. Along the way she stumbled over what appeared to be a rock. Julia crashed to the dusty ground, and lost hold of her axe. The audience echoed in worry as the scythe woman charged forward. Sheri screamed as Julia felt around for her weapon. The cacophony of the audience and the blinding of the dust must have made it extremely difficult for Julia to sense the dangers which lurked above.

Julia picked up a long and thin item from the ground. It looked like she hadn't tripped over a rock but rather a spear.

The woman with the scythe closed in on Julia and raised her arm for the killing swing. The scythe gleamed in the light. The weapon would be covered in blood and dust within seconds.

Julia leapt forward like a frog. The spearhead zapped into the scythe carrier's belly. Gravity dragged the scythe woman down the pike until the spearhead erupted from her back. The spear held all the gore inside the scythe carrier's belly. This woman vanished seconds later. The gong rang for the second time.

Julia wiped the dust out of her eyes with a rag which was tied around her neck. Just when she regained her vision, Julia noticed the hammer woman. Right before a blow from the hammer could splatter her skull, Julia dropped to the ground. The hammer blow barely zipped over Julia's tightly tied black hair. With lightning instincts, Julia's right foot kicked forward. She spun to the left, tripping her opponent. The hammer woman tumbled backward, landing on her back. Julia rose to her feet, flipped the spear downward, and dropped to her knees. The hammer fighter disappeared right as blood started to puddle out her back from the spear shot.

The audience cheered simultaneously with the ring of the gong. I admired how my sister had become a killing machine and that she was doing all of this without her genie powers.

The clubwoman charged forward and swung her weapon. Julia's spear clashed with the club. It couldn't handle the impact and rattled to the floor. With the spear gone, Julia regained her axe.

The club swung a second time. Julia swung her battle-axe into the wooden club. Chunks of timber flew as the axe-head chopped into the wooden weapon. As the clubwoman tugged back on her club, Julia released her grip on the axe handle. The clubwoman stumbled backward. Julia threw a kick in her rival's direction. Upon receiving a footed blow, the clubwoman gained air. Julia pulled her axe free from the club and then chopped the axe forward, slamming the blade into the clubwoman's collarbone. The clubwoman disappeared right as her body crashed to the ground.

The gong rang as the audience roared. Sheri and I hugged as we chanted Julia's name.

"All those chicks were really foxy, but that one babe with the axe and spear really showed them," a man behind me said.

Although it was kind of uncomfortable to hear other guys talk about how hot my sister was, I was extremely proud of Julia, and happy to know that the coliseum spectators recognized her talent. I thought about inviting Julia along on my vigilante missions.

The following gladiator matches featured animals, so Sheri and I left. We met up with Julia at a bar, and I bought her dinner and a few beers. Sheri and I told her many times about how impressed we were with her fighting ability. Julia said things had been too easy and that she needed some real danger. I thought about how vigilantism would be a perfect method for honing her gladiator skills and an excellent way of utilizing her talents for a benefit other than entertainment.

Some days later, a mountain village on the outskirts of Stodaneatoo called Vadonty became the site of an emergency. Several diseased rat carcasses had been dropped into the village wells. The vigilums were summoned for criminal investigation while medical personnel fled to the hills. Those who hadn't been harmed by the diseased drinking holes were encouraged to flee town until the sick had been healed and the wells purified. Calls for help were being made to Qiami, the goddess of water.

"We'll come along with you," I told Sheri.

"Thanks sweetheart, everyone will really appreciate that," Sheri said.

"I'd really love to put my genie healing powers to some good use; Julia will come too."

"Really? I thought Julia had to do some weapons training with the gladiator club."

"Saving dying people is way more important than entertainment."

Sheri climbed aboard my magic carpet, and we flew to the hills. Julia trailed behind and didn't say anything or make eye contact with us. When I'd asked her to come along, she'd merely nodded. I could tell that she was disgruntled about having to skip gladiator practice, but in the end, she knew that saving the lives of others was more important than beating people up.

The Vadonty Townhall was a large stone building which had been converted into a temporary hospital. People lay in hammocks with puke buckets next to them. Coughing, groaning, and spewing noises echoed throughout the acoustic stone setting. The room reeked of bile, sweat, tears, and shit. Witchdoctors wore crude cloth masks while they administrated potions to their patients.

Julia and I fastened rags around our faces and then got to work. The magical blue healing rays which shot from our rings were much faster and often more powerful than the healing potions which the witchdoctors were using. Our genie powers killed all the germs in the patients' bodies though it would take several days before the patients felt healthy.

Julia and I took our first break after three hours of healing the sick. We'd been coughed at, sneezed on, drooled over, and puked on. Our genie powers were running low and needed to be recharged, but Julia and I made sure to blast one another with blue healing rings to make sure that neither of us had picked up any germs. The witchdoctors had drunk special potions before entering sick hall. Their concoctions kept their systems purified of any pathogens for ten hours.

Sheri paid Julia and me a visit when she was on her lunch break. She pulled out two parchment wanted posters of the terrorists who were believed to have planted the dead rats in the wells.

The first poster was of a guy named Hunter who was from somewhere out on the coast. I took note of his physical descriptions in case I saw him: a tall bald black man of medium build with two scars on his face. When I found out that he was a genie, I realized how dangerous he could be. Few genies lived in this area, and I doubted that anyone around here would be able to fight thugs with magic carpets and genie powers. Perhaps Julia and I needed to take action into our hands.

The second crook was also a genie. He was known as Krull of Valushia. Krull was very muscular, had long messy black hair, an evil look on his face, sharp facial features, and the occasional scar. Unlike the drawing of Hunter, the picture of Krull looked very familiar. He hadn't been a prisoner at the gulag, but I knew that I'd seen his face somewhere. Perhaps he'd been a criminal who I'd once scrapped with in O'Jahnteh.

"These two guys broke into a leprosy camp and stole a load of old blankets and bed sheets three days ago," Sheri said. "This morning we found a caravan filled with sick people who'd bought a carpet from these two criminals."

"But leprosy usually takes about six seasons before any symptoms show up," Julia said.

"Some wizards who were working on a diseased warfare project found a way to mutate various diseases so that they would evolve quicker and infect people with much more severity," Sheri said. "We believe that Krull and Hunter may have used germ warfare magic on the stolen leprosy products."

"This is sickeningly evil," I said.

"A nearby village called Gogalyta is holding an open market today," Sheri said. "Vigilums are heading to the village and to shut down the market until we know the whereabouts of Krull and Hunter. We fear that they are trying to smuggle the diseased fabrics into the village so they can wipe out Gogalyta through biological warfare."

"How many vigilums are in Gogalyta right now?" Julia asked.

"None yet," Sheri replied. "A squad of horseback vigilums is riding that way now, but the villagers of Gogalyta don't know about the danger that lurks ahead."

"We have to get over to Gogalyta right away," I said as I rose to my feet and headed toward my magic carpet.

"Don, I can't let you go there," Sheri said.

"Why not?" I retorted.

"Vigilantism is illegal," Sheri said. "I know that you're a really kind dear who's trying to help, but you'll get locked in jail."

"But the villagers of Gogalyta could already be under attack by germ warfare and not even realize it," I said. "Krull and Hunter may have also placed rat carcasses in their wells too. This mountain terrain is very difficult for the vigilums to ride through on horseback, but Julia and I could get there on our magic carpet very quickly."

"Don, what you're doing is criminal, and you'll get arrested," Sheri said.

"Why am I a criminal?" I barked. "I am voluntarily tracking down crooks who the vigilums are too slow to get at. I might be a bandit, but the vigilums are the criminals if they're going to persecute me for fighting for the safety of my fellow country folks."

"We've all got jobs to do," Sheri said. "Why don't you just stay here and heal the sick?"

"Our genie healing power needs to be recharged," Julia said. "The witchdoctors have the situation under control."

"If we don't act now then everyone in Gogalyta could get sick," I said. "Krull and Hunter will move on to another remote territory. Try and arrest me if you want, but I'm going to Gogalyta."

I mounted my magic carpet and flew into the jungle clouds. Sheri was an awesome chick, but I really hated how her politics were getting in the way of our relationship. She played everything by the book, but the rules needed to be forgotten about. Government rules were what had led to vigilums, bureaucratic corruption, gulags, terrible government policies, and leaders like Viceroy Bartholomew. Sheri didn't realize it, but her actions as a vigilum were contributing toward systemic corruption because she was upholding the laws which protected the politicians.

As far as I was concerned, the only real law was to not do evil. Sure, I was a fundamentalist with black and white views, but I didn't give a shit. If you kept things simple, the world became a lot less complicated, and you didn't need arbitrary and contradictory institutes like political parties and ruling governments. Due to all the problems and contradictions of politics, the rules had to be broken to ensure that common folks didn't fall victim to the perils of evil.

I sped very quickly on my magic carpet. I occasionally peeked at my map, but most of the time my eyes were fixated forward to prevent myself from crashing into the mountains.

A whistle caught my attention and I glanced backward. Sheri and Julia were riding a magic carpet behind me. I slowed down to let them catch up. Part of me was surprised that Julia had enough power in her ring to power her magic carpet considering she'd used up a lot of her magical energy back at sick camp.

"We're coming with you," Julia called as her magic carpet pulled up next to mine.

"Let's just say that I've hired both of you as bounty hunters," Sheri said.

"I'm guessing this is a pro-bono assignment," I laughed.

"Ha," Sheri chuckled.

"Since you don't have enough money to pay for our expensive fees consider this a one-time free offer," I joked.

Sheri chuckled hard. It was good to know that a bit of humour could subside inner frustrations at one another.

We arrived in Gogalyta, which homed about 240 people. Since Sheri was the only vigilum present, she commanded the attention of the market crowd. Julia and I went looking for Hunter and Krull.

Not too far outside of Gogalyta, we saw a lone wagon approaching the town on the winding mountain road. The wagon was being pulled by a horse with two drivers who matched the descriptions of Hunter and Krull.

Julia and I swooped downward on our magic carpets and landed atop the gravely road a few paces ahead of the wagon. The drivers dismounted from their carriage after halting. Krull looked more familiar than ever. It really bugged me that I knew I'd seen him in the past but couldn't figure out where.

"What's the meaning of this?" Hunter grunted. "We have important business to do at the market and you assholes are in our way."

"We are sorry to interrupt your journey, but we are wondering if you would be interested in selling us any carpets, blankets, or robes?" Julia asked.

I smiled at Julia and nodded, hoping that Krull and Hunter would fall for her trap.

"What do you say Krull? Can we sell these people some garments?"

"I don't see why not Hunter."

Holy shit, Krull and Hunter had practically turned themselves in without even realizing it. Wes was right, I really needed to do a lot more undercover work and attempt to fool enemies instead of merely charging at them with violence. Messing with villains through trickery was actually pretty fun.

Julia raised her ring and pointed it toward the wagon. She concentrated with ferocity and a fireball formed above her ring. The flaming sphere blasted toward the wagon as Krull and Hunter jumped out of the way. Flames rose as wagon wood crackled. The diseased fabric smoldered. Blackness grew. Heat sanitized the wagon of germs.

"You fucking cornholes," Hunter cried as he slapped his bald skull.

Krull drew his sword. I unsheathed mine.

"Remember me?" I growled as I glared at him.

Krull swung his sword back and forth, trying to tease me into coming forward with mine. A sneaky malicious look grew across his face.

"You're the little prick from the dragon volcano," Krull said as he continued to swing his cutlass back and forth, "always having to play hero and get in the way of my plans."

"I hope death is one of your plans," I shot. "Between dragons, volcanoes, and germ warfare, one of these days you're going to kill yourself."

Krull let out a chuckle and said, "that's the point. Kill as many people as possible. Destroy this failed race before it can fuck itself over more and more."

Krull's cutlass flashed forward though my katana parried it. Within a second our blades were flashing back and forth so quickly that neither of us could keep track of where each block or attack was coming from. As evil as Krull was with his terrorist tactics, I had to confess that I had rarely come across a villain who equaled me in fencing.

Hunter retrieved a broadsword. The wagon horse was frantic over the fire and feared being set ablaze. Hunter released the horse. Amid its frenzied state, the horse sprinted down the mountain road and separated Krull and I at mid-stroke. I stumbled backward and fell to the ground. Krull flailed over the edge of the mountain bank.

I jumped to my feet. A magic carpet flew from the wagon. Small flames had enveloped it. Krull raised his ring and shot a gust of wind at the fire. After several quick blows, the flames on the magic carpet disappeared.

Krull hobbled atop his burnt magic carpet and then cast off toward the distant mountain peaks. I quickly stepped on my magic carpet and took off, pursuing Krull to the hills.

As I chased after Krull, Hunter charged forward with his broadsword. Julia circled around Hunter until she was behind him and then pushed him from the rear. Hunter toppled forward and dropped his weapon.

Julia was without a weapon so bent over to seize Hunter's sword. Right before she could pick it up, Hunter tackled her. Hunter and Julia wrestled atop the rough ground, kicking dust and gravel everywhere. I wished that I could stay behind to fight, but I had to pursue Krull. If only Sheri had stayed with us instead of going to the village. Her efforts in the village were likely in vain since Julia had destroyed the wagon which was filled with the germ-infested garments.

Although Krull's magic carpet had been damaged from the flames, his speed did not decrease. I had difficulty keeping up with him. Initially Krull had been heading toward the mountain peaks, but when he noticed me gaining on him, he redirected his magic carpet towards the jungle valley. I continued to pursue him and almost fell off my magic carpet when I had to pull a fast downward U-turn after he'd pulled some dodgy maneuvers.

I raised my sword once I got close to Krull. Krull caught sight of me, raised his ring, and let out a wave of colourful stun rays. I yelped and dove my magic carpet toward the jungle ground. My magic carpet halted above bushy baobab trees. I felt branches scratching against the fabrics of my magic carpet. I grumbled several times and then flew back to the clouds. I feared that my magical energy was low, but if Julia had managed to shoot a fireball from her ring, then I should be able to take on Krull with my genie powers.

I raced on my magic carpet until I was aligned with Krull. Krull cackled as he raised his ring, ready to unleash another storm of stun rays. As Krull did this, I commanded a force blast from my ring. A seismic wave of energy shot from my jewel, right when many coloured rays flashed from Krull's weapon. A deflected violet stun ray bounced Krull off his magic carpet, leaving him to flail to the ground. His burnt magic carpet hovered in the air for a second or two, but then flopped toward the jungle floor like a fallen kite.

There was no way Krull was going to survive his fall. If crashing to the jungle floor didn't bash the life out of him then the tree branches would disembowel him. I let out a sigh of relief and turned around. I hoped that Julia was okay and that she'd kicked Hunter's ass. It was rewarding to know that I'd defeated an old enemy, and I hoped that his sidekick would meet the same fate.

The flames on the wagon were still roaring. The horse had disappeared. Hunter was missing. Julia sat on the road, looking upset.

"Hey what's wrong?" I asked.

"Hunter escaped."

"What? How?"

"We wrestled across the ground for a while, and I managed to pull a knife from his belt. I stabbed him just above his hip. I tried to slit his throat, but he knocked the blade aside. I went to grab the broadsword so I could chop his head off. Right before I could behead him, his magic carpet flew forward. He rolled onto it and took off. He was injured, screaming, and bleeding, but he still managed to get away. I hopped onto my magic carpet to chase after him, but I didn't have enough genie energy to power my magic carpet."

Julia had always felt insecure about how her powers were inferior to those of most genies. She had trained hard in the past, but for some reason she'd been born with a small reservoir for magic in her blood while I'd been gifted with a bionic level of mana.

"Hey, this battle wasn't a loss," I said. "If you stabbed Hunter above the hip, then you've damaged his guts, and he'll probably bleed to death very painfully. All the local witchdoctors are healing the victims in sick camp, and Hunter sure won't want to show his face there. It's poetic justice if the witchdoctors can't heal him because they're too busy taking care of his victims."

"I wish we could have won this battle."

"We did win. You did more damage than I did because you blew up the wagon filled with all the diseases. You saved a village, and you deserve the credit, not me and definitely not the vigilums."

"Where's Krull?"

"He fell off his magic carpet above the trees. I didn't see his corpse, but I'm sure the fall killed him."

"At least you defeated your opponent."

"Aw come on Julia, we won this fight as brother and sister. Krull died today, but I really wish I had killed him back at the volcano where Ace died. Finally, Ace's death has been avenged."

Julia jumped to her feet and gazed at her magic carpet. It slowly rose from the ground. Her powers had returned minutes too late.

"I don't know if I would have defeated those guys if it weren't for you tagging along and shooting a fireball at the wagon," I said. "You tricked those guys and what you did was very intelligent, a lot smarter than how I normally fight."

I expected words from Julia but her face remained glum.

"Come on, let's head down to Gogalyta and gloat about how we saved the village and kicked a lot of ass," I said. "You can take the village medal."

Julia hopped aboard her magic carpet.

"I'll bet Hunter's magic carpet has some leper germs on it that will seep into the stabbing wound and kill him very quickly," Julia smirked.

"Hells yeah."

I let Julia do all the storytelling at the market hall. She focused mostly on her actions of blowing up the wagon filled with disease. She mentioned that both Hunter and Krull were guilty of placing rats in the wells of Vadonty and that they were now dead. Although there were no corpses to confirm their kills, I really didn't see how either of them could have survived.

After the big meeting, Sheri and I headed out to a balcony which was built into a cliff face. The light was starting to shine through the thick clouds. The mists between the mountains brightened. This made me happy because I'd anticipated rain on account of the dark clouds from above.

"You know Don, I really admire what you did today," Sheri said. "It was your idea to chase down Hunter and Krull. I know I'm a bit bossy and I like to do things by the book, but despite our different methods, you got things done and you did a damn good job."

"Thanks."

I was very happy to know that Sheri appreciated my methods even though they were very different from hers. Hell, Sheri was taking a lot of liberties with me considering that she could arrest me for vigilantism.

"Julia wouldn't have blown up the wagon if it weren't for you and she is bragging like crazy," Sheri said while we both laughed, "but you Don, you are so modest, not taking any credit when you deserve a medal."

"I do vigilante work because people deserve to be protected and to live their lives in peace instead of fear."

"That's sweet darling. You know, if we can remain friends despite our different methods and philosophies about fighting crime, then that's a testament to the strong bond which we have with one another."

Sheri and I kissed. I couldn't remember the last time I'd smooched anyone. I'd never kissed such a wicked babe before.

BOOK VI:

NORTHERN TERROR

I ended up settling in Stodaneatoo. Officially I was living with Julia, but Sheri and I were soon sharing a bed. Julia got sick of finding my stuff lying around her cabin so eventually tossed my belongings into Sheri's yard stating that I was a freeloader who'd officially been evicted. Sheri made cracks about how Julia contradicted her socialist views by littering in her neighbour's yard, contributing to homelessness, and demanding too much room and board money.

I bounced from a street cleaner job, to cooking, to a salesman in the market, back to street cleaner, back to cook, back to street cleaner. Most of the labour jobs were given to ogres and cyclops due to their superior strength. Wes encouraged me to go back to school, but I really didn't feel like investing in long-term education considering I had so few goals. Sheri told me to join the vigilums, and I told her that I'd rather be a beggar. After a playful wrestling match, she told me to watch my mouth, or I really would become a street rat.

Following the provisional government, a liberal party won the federal election. The liberals knew how to bring the right wingers and leftists to some sort of medium point though a lot of resentment and pressure followed. Corporations returned, social service jobs continued, and the need for vigilums dwindled. Eventually Sheri was laid off.

"The government is really going to regret laying me off," Sheri grumbled a few days after having lost her job. "Just you see, the mayor is going to get murdered."

"You think so?" I asked. "Crime hasn't been this low in years."

Due to the decline in crime, my vigilante patrols had become less frequent. Peacetimes had led to more magic carpet trips out to the mountains and distant lakes.

"The reason why crime is at an all-time low is because the large number of vigilums during the Wadonshea reign scared the socks out of the entire country," Sheri said.

"Yeah, and people like me ended up in jail," I said. "Crime was at an all-time high thanks to all the stupid laws which the Wadonshea passed."

Sheri shut up. Our political views often clashed. That was really the only bad part about our relationship. It wasn't that Sheri had been a communist, but she'd liked working as a vigilum, and she recognized that Viceroy Bartholomew had allowed her to gain work by granting women the right to join vigilums and by increasing the hiring numbers. Sometimes Sheri got a bit carried away with babbling about her job, and I couldn't help but raise my opinionated views on the futility and corruption of government funded security.

"We both know that it's better for the government to spend tax money on public services instead of security forces," I said.

"Ah, you're just happy to see me without a job," Sheri snorted.

"We now have a lot more free time to wrestle, go on trips out to the lake, laze around, have sword fights, and hump and pump."

The play fights, the trips to the lakes and mountains, and the sex were all good, but the bottom line was that Sheri and I needed work. I was unemployed and getting pretty bored of living in Stodaneatoo. Even though I'd grown up in O'Jahnteh, I wasn't much of a city guy. I preferred owning a few possessions and spending my time travelling while I waited for adventures to spring up unpredictably.

"I don't blame you for wanting to get out of the city," Trent said to Sheri and I during a picnic with him at a hilltop lake. "Living off the grid really makes me feel like a natural soul."

Trent was living with a tribe of twenty people. They used as little money as possible and very rarely traded with townies. The tribal folks survived through hunting, farming, foraging, and trapping. Nearly everything they owned was homemade. The tribe was completely team-based and there was no room for putting individual interests ahead of the needs of others. The collective recognized individualism as a means of bringing different and valuable ingredients to a successful team.

"You seem to be living the dream out in the mountains," Sheri said.

"Why don't you guys adopt a similar lifestyle, or better yet join our tribe?" Trent suggested.

"I feel more at home in nature than in a house," I said.

"I don't know if I want to live in the mountains though," Sheri said. "No offence Trent."

"None taken," Trent chuckled. "I love the mountains too much to get offended by anyone's differentiating opinions."

"It's not that the mountains are bad," Sheri said. "It's just that I've lived in Stodaneatoo all my life, and I want a different setting. I've never been to the sea and would like to go there."

"Sheri, you've just given me an epiphany," I said.

"Oh yeah, what's that?" she asked.

"Let's head out to the west coast and get a job on a ship," I said.

"Seriously Don?"

"Seriously Sheri. We can go and visit Marco who is working with sea plants out in Raroaka. He said that merchant boats are always hiring crews. There are also some piracy problems out there so warriors like us are ideal candidates."

"Now you're talking," Sheri grinned.

"This will be perfect for both of us," I said. "You've never been to the ocean, and I merely glanced at it from when

I was in Santalonia years ago. This is our chance to do something new with our lives.'"

"You guys should totally go," Trent said.

"I knew that getting laid off from the vigilums was a blessing in disguise," I grinned.

"Oh, go and shite," Sheri snorted before tackling me to the ground.

Sheri and I wrestled around the lake shore as Trent laughed at us. If he jumped in on the fight, then Sheri and I would have both been flattened. Although Trent had always been a giant, he'd turned into a muscular monster after having lived in the mountains.

Sheri wrestled me into the lake. I raised my ring and pointed it at the water.

"Hey, no magic," Sheri scolded right before splashing me.

Sheri put her house up for rent, and we moved out two weeks later. Julia agreed to watch over the tenants provided that Sheri beat me up if I acted stupid. Sheri had invited Julia along with us to find work, but Julia refused due to her life as a gladiator champion. Julia had temporarily quit work as blacksmith's assistant due to the coin she was bringing in from the coliseum. Although Julia had been offered large contracts in Santalonia and O'Jahnteh, she refused to leave Stodaneatoo due to the wild audiences and the first-rate coaches who she worked with.

Although I wanted to fly to Raroaka on my magic carpet, Sheri insisted that we join an elephant caravan due to the weight of her possessions. I cautioned her that neither of us would be allowed to bring much gear aboard a ship, but Sheri was too stubborn to lighten her bags. I argued that if Sheri packed a lighter load, then a magic carpet ride would be much faster than an elephant ride, but some arguments couldn't be won. If only all of us could live off a sword, two sets of clothes, and a canteen.

Upon reaching Raroaka by elephant caravan, we met up with Marco.

"So good of you to finally come and visit me," Marco said as we high-fived.

"It's great to finally meet you Marco," Sheri said. "Julia and Don have both spoken so highly of you."

Marco was currently working with seaweed farmers and trying to discover new ways to increase the yield in produce. He'd found a way of mixing the crops with jungle herbs to increase the nutritional value of seaweed. He was living in a small but stylish cabin on the bluffs with a magnificent view of the ocean.

Upon gazing at the waves, I knew that I'd come to the coast for a reason. I loved how the ocean held more shades of blue than I'd ever seen. I dug the jungle, but everything about the ocean was different and inspiring. Salty scents, the rise of daylight, the fall of dark nights, legions of cryptic aquatic life, fresh seafood, numerous recreational opportunities, walks along the white sandy shore, and the strength of the sea breeze were all priceless ingredients for beauty and happiness.

"Let's go for a magic carpet ride today," Marco said on our second day in Raroaka.

"Seriously?" I asked. "The wind is freaking crazy right now."

The incoming gale had turned the blue waters into a fury of white caps. Waves crashed against the shoreline boulders and cliffs. Palm trees swayed back and forth, looking like they would snap in two. Coconuts crashed to the ground. Kites were lost amid the breezes. Sailboats zoomed beyond eyesight in no time.

"Wear the tightest clothes you have, and don't bring a hat," Marco said as he tossed his trademark black hat aside.

"Hey don't forget me," Sheri said.

"Sheri, you are in for the wildest ride of your life," Marco said.

Marco mounted his magic carpet while Sheri and I climbed aboard mine. Once Marco and I nodded that we were ready, we piloted our magic carpets off his balcony. In no time we were zooming with the winds. Our magic carpets were flying faster than they'd ever gone. We screamed at the top of our lungs. At times we worried that our companions were yelling in fright. The speeds of our magic carpets were so fast that at times we worried that we would be blown away with hurricane ferocity. As veteran magic carpet riders, Marco and I felt like we'd experienced the closest thing to flying.

Marco winked at me, dove toward the ocean, and I followed. Right before Marco was about to crash into the swells, he pulled his magic carpet up and hovered a pace above the water. I followed his perilous maneuver. Sheri screamed at her loudest, worrying that I was pulling a suicide stunt, but she was also ecstatic over the adrenaline. I managed to avoid crashing, and my magic carpet floated over the waves. Salty breaks splashed against our magic carpet. The water was cool, but the wind speed helped air-dry us. Just when I'd thought that living by the ocean couldn't get any better, Marco had shown Sheri and I a whole new delight to life.

I'd never seen Marco so happy. Amid his dark past, he'd found ways to put a lot of anger behind him. He was truly passionate about his marine botany projects. It wasn't everyone who considered their job a hobby. When Marco wasn't working away with seaweed, he was hanging out on the beach. Amid his new hobbies of canoeing and surfing, he'd managed to stay strong with magic. Marco had adopted a pescetarian diet and ate catch of the day seafood daily. I could see why he hadn't ventured inland.

Although Sheri and I wanted to continue our vacation on the water, we had to find work. Marco put us in touch with some of the guys he knew from the dockyard. Initially Sheri and I were offered deckhand positions on fishing boats and whaling ships, but it was an old mariner who really caught our eyes.

"So, you want to be seadogs eh?" a ship captain said to us.

The captain was the oldest person who I'd interacted with in a long time. His eyes were the colour of the sea and his saggy skin smelt of seaweed. His dangled salt water encrusted hair was somewhere between red and gray. Folks who predated the Post-17 generation would remain common for the next few decades, but I hadn't anticipated working for an old fogey.

"We're thirsty for an adventure at sea," Sheri said.

"If you're thirsty then I recommend heading over to the tavern and ordering a grog because salt water will dehydrate you," the captain said before hollering off a laugh. "Ah relax, I was just seeing if you have a sense of humour. I don't want any boring turds aboard my boat."

The sea captain's ship was called the Vindadong. She was a long caravel with two sails. The mast for the larger sail was in the centre of the boat while the smaller sail mast was near the stern, above the captain's quarters. Caravels were said to be exceptionally fast ships, and they could carry much weight. Unlike the warlike galleons which were moored in the bay, caravels did not require rowing.

"I'm Keifer by the way," the sea captain said. "So, Don and Sheri, both of you kids want some adventure?"

It wasn't often that Post-17 folks were referred to as kids. I didn't totally consider myself a kid, but I didn't consider myself an adult either. Either way, Sheri and I were the first wave of many generations which would remain frozen as teenagers. Sooner or later, folks who were Keifer's age were going to fade into history. Due to the increase of Post-17 citizens, the hierarchal and authoritarian aspects of age were dwindling. If Keifer was captain of a ship and a great deal older than his crew, then I wondered if he would use his age to define his authority. I considered turning away from Keifer, but Sheri wore a huge grin.

"Oh yeah," Sheri said. "We really want to see the ocean and all of its beauty."

"Have you ever been to sea before?" Keifer asked.

"We've been hanging at our friend's place here for two weeks, but I've spent my whole life in Stodaneatoo," Sheri answered.

"I once saw the beach in Santalonia years back, but this is my first true experience on the coast," I said.

"Ah the seas will change you landlubbers forever," Keifer laughed.

I loved land, and also considered myself a sky lover due to magic carpet flying. The more time I spent on the ocean, the more I became a water guy. I believed that going to sea would complete me since I could then call myself a water, land, and air being.

"We are both at crossroads in our lives and eager for some change, so what better way to do that than to go to sea?" Sheri said.

"Oh, just you wait," Keifer chuckled. "As a sailor you'll dine on every monster from the ocean. Salt water will encrust your flesh and become a second skin. Whenever you step on land you will feel phantom waves as if you are still bouncing about in the swells. Swimming will be your new shower. Scurvy and seasickness will be the banes of your life."

"We want a challenge," I said.

"What kind of crazy things have you done in your life?" Keifer asked.

There were a lot of options to list, but I didn't want to make note of my participation in the deaths of King Rex or Viceroy Bartholomew. I also didn't want to make a big deal about having killed vigilums in front of Sheri. She knew that I'd had my scraps with the law, but she was very sensitive over that topic.

"I fought for the right to get women to join the vigilums and participate in gladiator combat," Sheri said. "I've kicked plenty of criminal ass, and I am not afraid to keelhaul or behead some son of a bitch pirates."

"I like it," Keifer smiled. "I like it a lot. What about you, boyfriend? Is your chick tougher than you?"

"I've broken out of a gulag, lived as a vigilante, participated in the revolution, hunted serial killers, fought in a volcanic crater filled with dragons, and I'm pretty tough with both the sword and magic," I boasted.

"Get aboard my boat mates," Keifer howled. "We got a whole load of adventures ahead, and I want the both of you to prove how tough you are."

With that, Sheri and I were officially crewmembers of the Vindadong. Sheri was often the only female crewmember. Sailors came and went but Sheri and I stayed onboard amid calamity.

Keifer hadn't been lying when he'd said that life at sea was tough. It was very rare that Sheri and I could sneak away to have a cuddle and a hump without being interrupted. Buckets became toilets. Fresh water couldn't be wasted.

Seafood was delicious albeit monotonous. Fresh fruit and vegetables were rare, and both Sheri and I would have really killed for a barbecued hunk of pork and a salad. Seasickness was the pinnacle of all illnesses. Showering was scarce. Sheri eventually styled her hair into sexy dreadlocks due to all the salt, but the rest of us dudes looked like waterlogged corpses. I had a feeling that Keifer wasn't that old, but years at sea had worn away on his body.

Despite hardships, life at sea was the adventure which Sheri and I needed. Unlike our other adventures, Sheri and I weren't thrown into combat. In our first two years at sea, we never came anywhere near pirates. Peace times were prospering for Sionia and more and more vigilums were being laid off. I was always happy to hear that the government security forces were no longer needed.

Sheri and I bounced all over the east, south, and west coasts of Sionia. Occasionally some of our friends came out to visit us though Marco was the friend who we saw the most. On a few occasions, we tried to convince him to jump aboard the ship, but he was content with his scientific research.

We visited many ports and villages that few had ever heard of. I was pretty sure that some of the coastal communities were only on nautical charts and not maps. I felt very privileged to know that Sheri and I were witnessing such obscure sides of life.

The villages were cool, but they were nothing compared to the beaches. Every beach we passed, be they white sand, black sand, brown sand, mud, or cobble stone made, Sheri and I wanted to jump overboard and go for a swim. I learned to find equal appreciation for beaches that had either big surf breaks or calm shores. Whenever we had free time at a beach, we always found time to swim. When the opportunities were presented, we enjoyed surfing, canoeing, and rowing. Building sandcastles and other sandy sculptures was also a lot of fun. I didn't mind that the tide destroyed these structures. Knowledge that our art had been washed out to sea reminded me that a part of my spirit was drifting to the heart of the ocean.

Since Sheri and I had never sailed before, we had a lot to learn. Initially Keifer had us doing grunt jobs such as cooking, swabbing the decks, and acting as watchmen. The only aspect of sailing we helped at was hauling the sails up the masts. Due to the high turnover rate of crewmembers, Keifer needed to teach us more about sailing and theory. After three months of learning about knots, points of sail, tacking, and gybing, I was finally allowed to command the helm. The first time I took the wheel, I felt like the captain.

Being at sea also gave Sheri and I further appreciation for the land. When on vacation, we travelled to Stodaneatoo. After meeting up with old friends, Sheri and I went camping in the mountains. The jungles had never looked so beautiful, and the mountains had never seemed as towering. Sheri and I had seen plenty of coastal forests and mountains, but the inland jungle had a feeling like no other.

Trent ended up meeting up with us when we were camped out on a lake, and we almost convinced him to come to sea and find his new path as an oceanic nomad, but Trent didn't think that he could ever adjust to living in such a confined place.

After over three years of sailing in tropical regions, we were given our biggest mission yet: a voyage to the northern coast. Snowcapped mountains in north central Sionia acted as a barrier between the northlands and the rest of the country. To the south, there were thick jungles while in the north there were barren lands which resembled tundra. There were few trees but tons of rocks, craters, canyons, and cliffs. The terrain was a lot hillier, featuring extremes between lofty glacier-covered mountains and the steepest canyons one could imagine. Although forests were scarce, bushes and moss sprung up. Farming was difficult, so the population was small. Most northerners lived along the coast in fishing villages. Some inland nomads acted as yak herders and shepherds. Inland northern towns were extremely rare and always built next to a crater lake or a river filled with vicious rapids. Snow and frost were very common in the settlements.

Many merchant ships refused to voyage north, but Keifer never turned down a challenge.

"Life is one big challenge from birth to death," Keifer said. "If life were easy, you wouldn't die. If you want your life to be interesting, challenge yourself. If you want to survive shit that kills most people, go psycho. We're not suicidal, we're survivors. We pull crazy missions, and we're survivalists."

The journey north was easily the coldest I'd ever been. Instead of dressing in shorts and t-shirts like I'd always done, I wore trousers and long-sleeved hooded coats made from wool. I'd never heard of a toque until Keifer gave me one. The Vindadong fireplaces burnt all day. Freezing winds felt like they were peeling the flesh off exposed skin. Frost decorated the boat. Keifer warned that snow and ice would come next, two things which I feared. Splashed water from cold waves sent shivers to every corner of the body. Sheri worried about crashing into icebergs and drowning in chilly waters. I took to only drinking tea. Soup became my favourite meal.

One night when I was on anchor watch and freezing to death during the dark early hours of the morning, I asked Sheri if I could borrow one of her spare blankets.

"Sucks to be you Don. You gave me shit when we left Stodaneatoo about being materialistic and bringing too much crap, and now you're coming to me crying because you're shivering into a blue ball. Suck it up princess."

Girlfriends were the best people in world but also the biggest pains ever.

Five days later the Vindadong docked at Patassy, a port town in a northern bay. Black stone mountains surrounded the community. The houses were crafted from stone and brick. No trees could be seen. Many fishing ships and longboats were moored off the dock. People were dressed in wool. The sky was overcast and featured many shades of gray, silver, and white. The water looked so cool that you would be frozen for eternity if you fell in.

As shippers, it was our duty to deliver rice and canned fruit and vegetables. We were set to pick up gems and other precious stones from the Patassy Trade Association. I looked forward to sailing home with a light load at a fast speed.

"What do you mean there aren't any gems for us to pick up?" I heard Keifer roar while I was unloading the last crate of canned fruit.

Despite being a bit of an old kook, Keifer normally didn't scream. I quickly delivered my load of produce to the warehouse and ran back to the office to eavesdrop on the argument between Keifer and the shipping manager. All sailors continued with their work. Sheri fixed a look on me, telling me too not be so nosy. When dealing with me, that look was common on her face.

"As of now, Patassy is impoverished," said the warehouse manager. "We have called for military intervention, but the government has been ignoring our pleas for six seasons."

That sounded like the government, only use the military for their own interests.

"I'm sorry to hear this," Keifer said as he lowered his voice. "We all know how useless the bloody government is. What kind of problems are you having?"

"A wizard named Maximus who lives in a cave beyond some of the dead volcanic mountains has conjured up a dragon known as Aurelius," the warehouse manager said. "If we do not pay the wizard a certain quota of seasonal taxes then he sends a giant dragon down to Patassy to wreak havoc. The local vigilum forces have been destroyed and the local militia is futile at battling such a beast. This is the most treacherous racketeering ever."

"I'm terribly sorry about all of this," Keifer said. "I wish there was something my crew and I could do to help."

"You've got help right now," I announced as I burst through the door of the office. "I'm your warrior."

It had been a while since I'd been in a fight, but I was ready for action. Although my combat skills weren't being used regularly, I had continued to practice my magic. Life on the boat had taught me a new level of toughness. I was ready to make my comeback as a fighter. Saving a small desolate town from an avaricious wizard and his bitch dragon seemed like a great way of reviving my warrior lifestyle.

"Lad, I don't think you realize what you are getting yourself into," the warehouse manager said.

"Don's crazy," Keifer chuckled. "Let him get into a fight. I can finally see how fierce he is after years of his big-headed gloating."

"The dragon is far too dangerous for one warrior to take on," the warehouse manager said.

"Life is danger," I said. "Anyone who tells you anything different is trying to pussy you down."

"Nosy Don, always looking for trouble and always getting himself in shit," Sheri chuckled. "The longer you wait, the more bored you get, the bigger the trouble."

"I can guarantee that if he tries to take on this dragon alone then he will be in more peril than he's ever been in," the warehouse manager said.

"Relax dear, I'll be fighting at his side," Sheri said. "I'll probably even save his tail."

"Is your whole crew going to take on the dragon Aurelius?" the warehouse manager asked.

"I'd fight with you if I could," Keifer said, "but an old fart like me is well past his prime. Back in the day though, I was an unbeatable stick fighter."

Keifer had told us many stories about battling pirates. He had a few scars to back up some of his more gnarly tales. Some of the sea shanties which were sung at night had been rewritten to include the ghastliest stories from Keifer's legacy as a sea nomad.

Looking at an old burnt-out warrior like Keifer made me realize how lucky I was since my body would never deteriorate with age. All Post-17s were truly spoiled. We were all going to live so much longer than Keifer and all the folks of the past generations.

Since I no longer aged, I'd stopped celebrating birthdays. I would probably have to look up my birth year in a history text while Keifer was completely in tune with his age. Knowing that Keifer was going to die of old age sooner or later made me kind of resentful that Kyle had killed his dad. Ace, Robin, Cal, Marco, and I had been on the assassination mission, and we should have zapped King Rex instead of letting him babble away. It was King Rex's sanctimonious attitude which had led to patricide. Granted, I couldn't blame Kyle for reversing nature. It was Silotious who had allowed the curse to be unleashed upon the country.

Some two hours later, bells all over town rang and everyone scrambled off the streets. Keifer had checked into an inn along the water though the racket likely awoke him. Everyone was screaming frantically as they headed indoors.

"What's going on?" Sheri asked one of the shopkeepers.

"Aurelius the dragon is coming," the shopkeeper yelped.

"I thought that the wizard Maximus had been paid," I said.

"Sometimes Maximus sends Aurelius down here to remind us of who the boss is," the shopkeeper said. "You folks can take shelter in my cellar, or you can go to one of the refuge centres."

"No thanks, we're going to fight," Sheri said.

The shopkeeper couldn't believe what she'd heard but said, "I'll keep my doors open in case you change your mind."

Aurelius the dragon descended upon Patassy. No one was lying about Aurelius being a giant. The beast was at least ten times the size of the largest bull elephant. Most dragons looked like giant lizards with bat wings, but the most fascinating thing about Aurelius was that he was basically a giant version of Wes. Aurelius had all the same humanoid-dragon hybrid qualities which Wes had: long legs, an erect stance, an alligator face, dark green skin, a yellow belly, arms which were shorter than the legs, and leathery wings which sprung from the shoulder and down the back as though they were a cape. I wondered if Aurelius could speak.

I wished Wes were here now. If only Aurelius weren't an evil tool, he could have really helped a close friend's existential quest.

Aurelius hovered in the sky above wooden shacks and stone buildings with hay roofs. He let out a long wave of roaring flames from his mouth. I hoped no one was inside the burning structures. The ringing of chimes sounded, indicating that the fire brigade was on their way.

Aurelius landed on his feet at the city park and marched over the grounds. Most dragons crawled on four limbs while Aurelius stood straight up and walked like a human. As he stomped his way across the park, Aurelius splashed in the pond, squashed native shrub gardens, kicked over planted imported trees, and squashed pagodas and other monuments which were decorated with precious stones. Perhaps Maximus was going to demand the jewels from these destroyed works of art.

Sheri pulled an arrow from her quiver, loaded her bow, and fired at Aurelius. The arrow stuck into the dragon's yellow belly, but the shaft of the arrow didn't bulge through Aurelius's thick reptilian skin. Aurelius swatted the arrow away as if it were a pine needle blowing in the breeze.

"Sheri you're trying to take on a dragon with a flimsy arrow used for deer hunting," I bellowed. "Are you crazy?"

"Hells yeah."

"So am I, let's destroy this son of a bitch."

Aurelius must have heard us because he inhaled deeply, ready to unleash another blast of flames. I thrust my ring forward and commanded a force shield. The violet shield circled around Sheri and I right as flames blasted from Aurelius's mouth. We felt the singeing heat, though our woolen clothes managed to avoid going up in flames.

The fire disappeared and I released the force shield. Sheri and I were a little toasty, but this wasn't a bad thing given the cold climate.

I could tell that Aurelius was going to attempt to flame Sheri and I again. I raised my ring and projected a fireball from it. My fireball was much smaller than Aurelius's inferno blast, but I managed to blast my shot into the dragon's eye.

I'd gravely insulted Aurelius by blinding him with a small fireball after he'd unleashed a mammoth inferno which caused no damage against his foes. The dragon's stinging eyes snapped shut. He roared several times, and his dangly arms swung. His muscular fists bashed several walls, knocked bricks apart, and smashed cobble stones into smithereens. He then kicked over several very tall inukshuks, leaving a mess of splattered rocks. Aurelius's claws dug into wooden totem poles. These sculptures left splinters in his fingers.

Aurelius's hand darted forward, and he clutched me in his grip. Although I squirmed away from getting stabbed by the dragon's razor claws, he had the grasp of a boa constrictor. Amid his blindness, Aurelius raised me above the ground. I squirmed and struggled but couldn't reach my sword or break free of his grasp. Sheri screamed and fired another arrow at Aurelius, though her arrows were useless against the beast.

Aurelius brought me closer to his mouth. Smoke blackened my vision. Wretched coughing erupted from my throat. I feared suffocation. I could feel one of his fangs tearing my woolen clothes open and I hoped that I wouldn't get stabbed by his sharp incisors. Part of me was scared that Aurelius would release one final blast of heat to cook his dinner. I hated the idea that I was going to get eaten by a dragon and then shat out.

I tumbled down the dragon's throat after getting licked by his dank tongue. Darkness enveloped me. I landed in his gooey stomach. I was mixed in with chewed up yak, sheep, goat, muskox, and reindeer carcasses. The place stunk so bad that I puked. The stench of my vomit and the combination of partially digested animal entrails made me want to hurl again, but my guts were achingly empty.

My spew gave me an idea. I raised my ring and fired a force blast, hoping that Aurelius would spit me up. Should I get barfed up, perhaps I could stab Aurelius's throat on the way up and create a long gash as I travelled upward.

My force blast smacked hard against Aurelius's inside. As the dragon stumbled, everything in his stomach swished around. The remains of his meal of herd animals splattered everywhere. I got hit with several bones and splashed with blood and organs.

Aurelius stumbled a bit more and I slipped backward. I shot down something which felt like a slide and was made from bile and guts. Once the slide came to an end, I realized that I'd slid into the dragon's intestines.

I was never going to eat reptile sausage again. Instead, I was going to be the most painful stomach bug of all time. Aurelius was going to wish that I had been a bulimic meal.

I unsheathed by sword and slashed away at Aurelius's intestines. Blood, unprocessed food, and tons of putrid liquids splattered everywhere. I nearly choked on foul ooze. A few times I thought I was going to hurl as my guts churned.

As I hacked away at Aurelius's intestines, he bounced around. After scrapping and slashing my way through dragon guts, I found the dragon's belly flesh. I blasted my sword upward, hoping to use it as a saw to build an escape hatch through Aurelius's belly. Part of me feared that I'd get shat out. It would be surely grotesque to get blown out of a dragon's asshole as a piece of crap, so I figured that my best method of escape was by giving Aurelius a cesarean.

Once I'd completed the first line of my incision, I cut downward to make a square in the dragon's leathery skin. The twist of the blade created further turmoil in the dragon's guts. Aurelius stumbled about. A few pieces of distorted intestines splattered against me. Amid the disgusting work, I continued cutting away at Aurelius's belly until my escape hatch was complete.

I popped through this trapdoor and tasted the cold misty air. Never had I been so thankful to get outdoors. I pulled myself from the guts, and jumped to the rocky ground, oblivious about breaking any bones.

I hit the rocky ground with a thump but managed to scramble to my feet. After catching my breath, I turned around. Aurelius was lying on his back. Through all my hacking, I must have knocked him to the ground. His eyes were closed, and his mouth was gaping open. Puke hung from his lips.

"Don, are you alive?" Sheri asked as she walked toward me.

"I am but I think I turned into some zombie parasite."

Sheri almost hugged me, but the stench of dragon guts and game carcasses fazed her. I needed to spend the next three or four years in a spa to get fully cleansed of disgusting reptilian organs. The clothes I was wearing needed to be destroyed immediately. I didn't care about the cold weather. I wanted to get naked and washed.

After much rigorous cleaning, I still didn't feel hygienic. My clothes had been tossed in the garbage. I was given a fresh set of leather pants, a woolen fleece, and a toque. Sheri told me that Keifer was waiting for me in the tavern. I was pretty hungry, and hoped to grab pub food, but at the same time I was a bit worried that my stomach wouldn't be able to handle a meal after having passed through a dragon's digestive system.

Nonetheless, Keifer bought me dinner and a few mugs of heather ale. Despite having been surrounded by mutton carcasses while in the dragon's digestive track, I managed to eat rack of lamb, potatoes, and root vegetables.

"I wish I could have seen your fight," Keifer said as he picked away at his meal of goat pancakes.

"I thought he was dead until Aurelius bounced around and keeled over," Sheri said.

"If I weren't such an old fart then I would have gotten out of bed to watch some action," Keifer said. "Damn all you Post-17 runts, living every day full of energy without having to worry about your bodies wearing away or breaking down. One of these days I'll be in my grave while you'll still be bouncing around full of beans and hacking away at dragons, slaying pirates, and doing hell knows what with your fountains of youth."

Keifer let out a chuckle and then ordered two stone mugs of brown ale. Our drinks clinked. Sometimes I worried about Keifer. No one knew how much time he had left. Granted, none of us from the Post-17 generation were immortal. We could die at any minute if we were struck by a murderer or had the wrong disease creep into our systems, but Keifer was prone to old age and more diseases due to his seniority. He could still sail, but you wouldn't see him running up a mountain or brawling in a wrestling match. Too many kids of the Post-17 generation were taking their longevity for granted.

"The shitty thing is that Maximus is still alive," Sheri said. "Don, while you were getting cleaned up, I talked with the inn keeper. Aurelius was Maximus's latest and most vicious creature, but he has used other beasts to cheat people out of their money. There is fear that he'll return with some other grotesque monsters really soon."

"He's going to be wicked pissed over Aurelius's death, so perhaps we should strike him before he can create another freak," I said.

"I agree," Sheri said. "Since he'll be sad and in a frenzy over the dragon's death, his upset state will make him sloppy and more vulnerable."

The next day Sheri and I set out to find Maximus's lair. No one else dared journey with us. The innkeeper gave us a map of the outskirts of Patassy. The wilderness stretched for thousands of kilometres. We were told to look for bonfires, ones with garish smoke would indicate wizard herbs.

Sheri and I rode atop my magic carpet. We took the ride slow because the winds were strong and chilly. Frost had fallen across Patassy that morning. As we flew further from the town, the weather cooled. Fluffy snow was splattered across otherwise barren rocks. Sheets of ice sprawled like islands among the sea of rocks.

Neither Sheri nor I had ever seen snow before. Had we not been on a manhunt, we might have stopped to play in the icy crystals. Although I was a bit curious about this cool white fluffy stuff, snow seemed unnatural despite being a part of nature. I loved water as a fluid liquid for playing, drinking, and bathing but had a hard time appreciating H2O as a crispy cold form of matter.

After about an hour of scanning the wastelands, Sheri and I came across a geyser of green smoke. Since kryptonite vapors didn't normally spurt from volcanoes or steam vents, Sheri and I headed toward the gas, hoping that Maximus was there.

We landed the magic carpet atop a snowbank. The rocky terrain was buried in snow. Jagged gray and black boulders towered out of the fluff as if they were statues. Green smoke was coming from jade flames within a fire pit. A tent made from caribou hide rested next to an ice patch.

A cyclops emerged from the tent. He had the same build as Trent but was much taller, which was saying something considering Trent towered over many of the inhabitants of Stodaneatoo. The cyclops had two horns on each side of his temple. The ivory bones looked like they belonged to a bull, and each was as sharp as a spear.

I wondered if this cyclops was Maximus. Wizards could be humans, ogres, or cyclops. While a genie had to be born to genie parents in order to receive the gifts of magic, wizards were created at random by I'magee when he blessed various births. While some soon-to-be parents became very devout to I'magee in hope of having their kids blessed, there was no guarantee that I'magee would turn your baby into a wizard since he loved to be arbitrary and play games. Many statistics stated that there was only a one in five-thousand chance that I'magee would bless your offspring.

"What do you want?" the cyclops grumbled.

"Maximus?" Sheri asked.

"Yeah," the cyclops grunted.

"Aurelius is dead," Sheri said, "killed by a lone warrior."

Maximus scrunched his teeth. The white in his single eye turned crimson. Growling followed from his gritted fangs. His lone eye shook while remaining as red as a raspberry. His hazel iris sunk into his pupil. A flash of red light shot from the blackness in his eye. The red ray crashed against a large black boulder. Blasts of slatted stone splattered everywhere. Three more eye blasts followed. Two of the red rays disappeared while one of them crashed into the snow, erupting in a flurry of powdery white.

I wasn't sure if Maximus was firing the red rays to show his remorse toward the death of Aurelius, or if he wanted to blast Sheri and I with his rage. I placed one hand on the hilt of my sword and then raised my ring, ready to fire up a force shield to protect Sheri and I.

Maximus dug into his goat hide satchel. He tossed a small vial at the ice sheet which I was standing atop. Glass shattered upon impact with the icy grounds.

I tried moving my arms and legs, but paralysis had taken over my system. Attempts to conjure magic from my ring brought me nothing. No sounds came from my mouth since my words were drowned in silence. I feared that I would die.

After a few silent moments of panic, I realized that Maximus had tossed a wizard potion onto the ice. My body remained frozen, trapped to the ice. I'd read about such a spell in an old book of magic, though such an action was limited to wizards and restricted from genies. Although alive, I couldn't be released until the ice melted. Should Sheri not melt me from this ice cube, I would freeze if not starve to death. I'd never been so thankful for the heavy woolen clothes I was wearing.

Sheri unsheathed her broadsword. Maximus tossed several more vials of the same potion which he'd used to trap me in the ice. Since Sheri was standing atop a rock, none of these vials held any effect on her. She took caution to avoid stepping onto ice. If Sheri ended up frozen like I was, then it would be the end of both our lives.

Maximus growled and beat his chest a few times before blasting several red rays from his single eye. Sheri dashed away from all these optical flashes. A few of the red rays smashed into snowbanks, spluttering flurries of snow. One ray blasted a large boulder into two halves, while two other rays sent piles of stone splattering everywhere.

When Sheri had evaded these eye blasts, she'd neared Maximus. She raised her broadsword and chopped it toward Maximus's skull. In defense, Maximus blasted a ray from his eye. Sheri slipped backward and landed atop a mixture of ice and rocks. The eye blast bombarded a mound of snow as Sheri's sword swung downward. The blade flashed through one of Maximus's horns. His skull bone dropped to the ground.

Maximus flailed around several times, kicked rocks, howled obscenities, and blasted red rays aimlessly while Sheri lay low on the ground. As he thundered about, Maximus slipped on ice and toppled onto his tent. As the tent crashed, a bookcase smashed to the ground while potion vials shattered. Maximus howled even louder.

Although my body was frozen solid, my eyes dilated with what I saw next.

A scorpion emerged from the tent. The tent fabric split in two as the bug grew larger. Eight legs rose from the rocky ground while the long black body stretched out. Two large claws sprung out of the scorpion's long and thin body. A sharp venomous tail keeled upward until it was hanging over the abdomen.

The scorpion was the size of a jaguar. Maximus must have had tundra scorpions in some of his jars. A vial of enlarging potion had likely cracked during the fall, and the scorpion probably crawled into this magical liquid.

The scorpion's right claw snapped and closed on Maximus's neck. Maximum gagged as his face jolted forward. As the scorpion strangled Maximus, the tip of it's toxic tail dove forward. Maximus tried to wiggle his way out of strangulation, but the scorpion tightened the grip on his throat. Right when Maximus's magenta eye was about to blast another ray, the tip of the scorpion tail pulverized his pupil. The scorpion sting dug deeper into Maximus's eye until the sharp point was sticking out the back of his skull.

It seemed completely appropriate that a wizard who'd used his magic to terrorize others was eventually killed by a beast who'd he'd manipulated into doing his evil bidding.

Although Maximus was dead, Sheri was not out of harm's way. I would have loved to jump in and save her, but I was still frozen in my icy prison. Until Sheri released me, I would be nothing more than the battle's sole spectator.

The scorpion crawled toward Sheri. She rolled over and scrambled to her feet. Her collision against the ice must have injured her because she was moving with a limp. I wanted to scream at her to hurry up and watch out for the scorpion, but my words were frozen in nothingness.

Sheri hobbled backward onto the snow. A claw came forward. Sheri's sword flashed and the claw popped out of the scorpion's socket as the blade flew through it. Yellow blood oozed from the wound, decorating the snow with a sickening colour.

The intact claw snapped toward Sheri. She backed away from the grasp though her fleece was torn. I couldn't tell if the scorpion had taken any skin off her flank. As Sheri evaded the monstrosity, she slipped on ice and splattered onto her back. I could tell that she was stunned and if she didn't regain her strength in the next second then she'd be the scorpion's second victim.

Although Sheri was lying on the ground, her sword remained locked in her hands. She smashed her sword against the scorpion four times. Four legs were dismembered from the scorpion's long body.

The scorpion's tail turned toward Sheri. Maximus's blood was still dripping from the sting. Right before the scorpion sting could slice into Sheri's chest, Sheri smashed the wide side of her broadsword against the sting. The scorpion tail thumped backward with the sting still intact. Sheri swung her sword and dismembered the sting from the tail. Poison drooled from the wound. Sheri backed away and clumsily rose to her feet as she evaded the dripping toxins.

Sheri flipped her sword over so that the tip was pointing toward the ground. As Sheri dropped to her knees, the tip of the blade dove into the scorpion's skull and came out the bottom. The tail fell and the left legs collapsed.

I wanted to congratulate Sheri, but I had to wait until I was thawed out.

Sheri burnt just about all of Maximus's possessions. At its closest, the fire was about half an arm's length away from me. Water drooled from my frozen statue state though I would have zero movement until all the ice was liquified.

Once my arms were free, I embraced Sheri and plopped some lavish kisses on her. Had Sheri been killed by Maximus or the giant scorpion, I would have never escaped. Never had I felt so thankful to have a warrior for a girlfriend.

When burning Maximus's gear, Sheri managed to save several large bags of precious stones. We found diamonds, emeralds, rubies, morganites, amethysts, tanzanites, and sapphires among the gem collection. Although tempted to keep some of this loot, Sheri and I agreed to return all of it to the rightful owners in Patassy. I hoped that Sheri and I would get some of the treasure as a reward for freeing the town from Maximus.

Two days later we found out that every gem Maximus had stolen from Patassy was accounted for. By the looks of it, Maximus hadn't spent any of the loot which he'd robbed from the town.

"This Maximus character sounds like he wanted to destroy Patassy by crushing the economy," Keifer said. "From what you guys told me, he lived off the land as a hermit in about as primitive a state as you can get. He probably hunted, scavenged, and then made his wizard potions from off the land. Maybe he had such a hatred toward community and capitalism that he decided to destroy society by hoarding all its wealth. By not spending any of these jewels, he mocked how society is so attached to materialism and finance."

I found Keifer's ideas interesting. While most criminals were in crime for the money, there still were freaks who killed and stole for the fun of terrorizing others. I agreed that society was way too attached to money and materialism. If I valued commodities and cash more, then I probably wouldn't have lived as a nomad or worked as a vigilante for free. I hated how plenty of people who earned legitimately high pay cheques also had their hands deep in corruption money. I didn't think that there was a limitation to greed, and I believed that society would be better off if a maximum wealth limit existed.

There was only one thing which was more interesting than Keifer's ideas: no one thanked Sheri and I for defeating Maximus.

"You know, I almost feel taken advantage of," I said.

"Tell me about it," Sheri moaned. "No one has even thanked or complimented us. Is it too hard for people to mumble a one syllable word?"

"No one else was courageous enough to take on Maximus or Aurelius," Keifer said. "They really ought to pin a medal on both of you, and put up some statues of you in the park instead of reconstructing their pagodas."

"Maybe we should have let them all die to teach them a lesson," Sheri chuckled. "We're obviously tougher than Patassy folks since the two of us took on three monsters; maybe we should be the town's new form of terror."

I chuckled at Sheri's comment and said, "I don't ask for much. I've never been paid for my vigilante efforts, and I don't do any of this out of ego, but I'm starting to feel like I deserve more appreciation. I stick my neck on the line for strangers cuz I think fighting danger will make their lives better, and it will reduce the evils in society.

"Don't get me wrong, I realize that there will always be villains. I might not be able to defeat all of them, but man am I doing a hell of a lot more to destroy evil than most folks."

"Maybe you should finally become a vigilum," Sheri said, "that way society will at least write about you."

"Screw that," I said.

"Suit yourself," she said. "Vigilantism may be legal now, but it is still frowned upon. I don't think that even Bashar will write an article praising your vigilantism, no matter how much good you do."

"I am a damn good fighter," I said. "I do a lot of good work for others, and I have put myself in a hell of a lot of danger. It would be very appreciated if people lauded what I do."

"Don my love, one day you will be remembered as the Lord of the Warriors," Sheri spoke.

BOOK VII:

HYENA OF THE HIGHLANDS

Following our battles in Patassy, life on the
Vindadong continued as usual. Sheri and I slowly became
more acclimatized to the chilly waters of the north. Despite
gaining a stronger tolerance for the cold, we still relished the
tropics.

About six seasons after our encounters in Patassy, we
docked at a port town on the east coast called Fordonchi.
Although Fordonchi was technically on the northern side of
Sionia, grass grew everywhere, the light shined, fir and pine
forests were common, and one didn't have to worry about
freezing to death.

Once all our cargo was unloaded in Fordonchi,
Keifer gave his crew a vacation. Normally individual
crewmembers took leave for a season here and there, but this
was the first time every crewmember was given a break.

Majatee (the goddess of the mountains) had recently
used her geological powers to create an archipelago on the
east coast. This action angered Zadeezey (the goddess of
water) who figured that she had full ownership of the sea, and
other deities couldn't interfere with the ocean without her
consent. Zadeezey coerced the weather goddess Shilotey into
creating tidal waves, floods, and typhoons to bombard the
archipelago while Zadeezey increased the eastern ocean
currents and rose the tides higher to flood the islands.
Silotious didn't intervene in these affairs because she figured

that competition would push each goddess to her maximum potential. Not one ship dared sail anywhere near these waters.

Sheri suggested hiking into the Rognanakh Highlands that were outside of Fordonchi. These rolling hills and mountains were famous for trekking but still considered off the beaten path since this was a remote territory. After having spent the last few years aboard a ship, heading inland was highly appealing.

"Captain's orders state that you have to venture back to the land," Keifer joked. "If I don't see you back here in Fordonchi by the end of the season, then it means you're not cut out for being a seadog and you can stay on land."

"Why don't you head up into the mountains with us?" Sheri invited.

"Ha, are you trying to kill me Sheri?"

"No, but it might be good for you if you got off your butt and got some exercise."

"Ah, an old fart like me is too old to be running around in the mountains like a hyperactive jackal. Are you trying to break my bones by getting me up in the mountains? Or do you hope I'll die of a heart attack so you can take my boat?"

"How are you going to spend the break?" I asked.

"I'm going to be a lazybones, no doubt about it," Keifer laughed. "This area is famous for ales, whiskies, and gins, so I'll become a connoisseur. Plus, I'm going to spend a lot of time relaxing in the hot springs while the rest of you are busting your guts up the mountains."

The next day Sheri and I set out for our hike. We'd packed two large rucksacks with food, sleeping bags, a tent, cooking supplies, canteens, a torch, and other miscellaneous items. I decided to personalize my load by bringing my sword and magic carpet.

"Wow," Sheri said when she saw me securing my rolled up magic carpet to my backpack. "You're not bringing your magic carpet."

"Why not?"

"This is a hiking trip. You're supposed to walk, not zoom around on a magic carpet."

"Let's bring it for an emergency."

"I don't think you should."

"If there is a flash flood, we'll need a fast escape. The highlands get some pretty intense storms, and with all the fighting among the supreme beings, I wouldn't be surprised if one of Shilotey's storms blew this way."

Sheri thought about this for a moment and then said, "fair enough. We'll bring the magic carpet, but we'll only use it for emergencies."

"Deal."

"And you have to carry it."

"Yes boss."

"Ha ha."

I often wondered what it would be like to stop being a genie. Magic had profoundly affected my life and honing my genie powers had been my greatest discipline. I wondered if I would have done better in school or focused more on a career had I not been born a genie. Maybe I had suppressed talents which were waiting to be discovered but were always masked by my interests in magic? Perhaps Julia had discovered her athleticism and knack for metal work because she'd never been too strong with magic?

The more I thought about how my genie powers had impacted my life, the more I wanted to do without my ring and magic carpet during mine and Sheri's hiking trip. If I were to lose my ring, my magic carpet would be futile. Sheri and I would be equals on this journey if I didn't have my powers. The idea of living without my powers excited me. I started to pull my ring off. I figured that I'd leave my ring in a locker with the magic carpet, but I would still bring my sword.

I halted in my tracks. I thought back to how my finger had gone over a year without touching my ring. I'd been robbed of my genie identity back in the gulag and had later sworn to never be stripped of my genie powers again. Had I not miraculously repossessed my ring, then Bashar, Trent, and I would still be locked up in the gulag, if not dead. I couldn't allow such a horrible experience to happen again. If I left my ring in a locker, there was no guarantee that the ring would be there when I returned from the trekking expedition.

I was a genie. I was a prodigy of magic, and nothing was going to take that away from me.

The landscape of the Rognanakh Highlands was a paradise like I'd never imagined. For most people, tropical sand beaches were paradise, something which I totally agreed with. Lots of jungles folks believed that thick rain forests, lush mountains, crisp lakes, and roaring rivers also deserved the term paradise, myself included. Although the snowy mountains, glacier, and rock formations across the barren lands around Patassy had a unique style of beauty, I wouldn't call that paradise due to the brutality of the cold climate.

The Rognanakh Highlands were its own kind of paradise. The hilly landscape turned from rolling hills to mountains back to hillside to jagged mountains. Creeks and waterfalls jutted down mountain and hillsides ensuring that Sheri and I always had drinking and bathing water. Trees weren't overly common though there were some forests of pine and spruce. Thick grass covered much of the remaining terrain. Rocky patches sprouted out like islands. Boulders lay at the bottom of many ravines or along flat patches beneath steep slopes, drop offs, or long hill faces. The weather shifted from t-shirts and shorts to long sleeves, fleeces, and toques. The light was always around, and magnificent clouds decorated the azure sky.

After five days of hiking, Sheri and I hadn't come across anyone. There were no trails, roads, or towns nearby. Nomadic shepherds and yak herders lived in these highlands, but Sheri and I had not come across any of them. Despite no human contact, Sheri and I were happy to see hawks, eagles, rams, goats, sheep, wolves, and bears in the distance.

There were so many beautiful hills worth climbing that Sheri and I sometimes had to restrain ourselves. We would climb up one hill or mountain and then find ten others which we wanted to check out. We realized that if we didn't stay on course, we could get lost. Our maps weren't the best and we realized that if we headed east, we would eventually return to the coast, and from there we could find our way back to Fordonchi or another coastal settlement. I didn't want to bust out the magic carpet unless Sheri and I found ourselves in a dire situation.

One afternoon Sheri and I set up camp at the top of a mountain overlooking many grassy rolling hills. We cooked a stew made from wild herbs, potatoes, and mutton. The fading sky glowed all shades of orange, yellow, and red. The distant hills acted as silhouettes against this magnificent glowing backdrop. Sheri and I cuddled and kissed underneath a blanket with our campfire at our backs.

"I love you Sheri," I said.

"I love you too Don, more than I'll ever know how to express."

"This is easily the best trip we've ever been on."

"You've changed me in more ways that I can express."

"You've changed me, Sheri. You came into my life when I was dark, lost, and confused. You pulled me out of that hole and threw me into a much more positive direction. For that I owe you all that I can give."

"Then we've given one another more than we can repay, so let's keep living that way my love."

"This landscape is a present to both of us, a reward for having done so much good for one another."

Sheri and I made love beneath the glowing sky. Being alone with Sheri in the wilderness made me never want to return to my life as a vigilante. Sure, we wouldn't stay in the Rognanakh Highlands forever; there were plenty of other beautiful places to explore or return to, but I really didn't want to return to the life of fighting injustice. I wondered why I had chosen to live with turmoil. I loved helping others and battling villainy, but right now I was experiencing immense beauty that washed away all the negative things I'd seen. I couldn't have been more thankful for what I was sharing with Sheri. I could only wish that all my friends and loved ones, be they alive or dead, could embrace the same feelings.

Two days later Sheri and I were having lunch atop a hill when we spotted a red object in the distance. The object waved in the wind as if it were a flag. The scarlet object moved closer. Since there weren't any animals of such complexion living in the Rognanakh Highlands, Sheri and I assumed someone was dressed in a scarlet outfit.

A basset hound followed the character in red. Sheri called out to the unknown man and waved. As the stranger got closer, I realized that he was wearing baggy red pants, a long loose top, a hood, and a veil across his face, all of which were bright red. I found it rather odd that someone would have their entire skin cloaked considering it wasn't very bright out.

"Hi there," Sheri said. "Are you lost or something?"

"Nope."

"We didn't think there were any towns around here," I said. "We hiked out here from Fordonchi and didn't expect to see anyone."

"I'm from these lands," the stranger said. "My name is Jason, and this is my dog Sid."

Jason removed the veil from his face and threw his hood off. Once he was unmasked, I saw why he was so heavily clothed. His long thin hair was the colour of pale wheat. The colour of his flesh was on par with the snow of the north lands. There was blue in his irises and an unusual red tinge in his eye whites. Perhaps Jason lived up here in the temperate Rognanakh Highlands to avoid the tropical light of southern Sionia, a place which I'd never seen an albino in.

Sheri and I introduced ourselves. Sid jumped up on Sheri a few times, and she took to rubbing her belly.

"I'm initially from O'Jahnteh and Sheri is from Stodaneatoo," I said. "We're sailors, and our ship captain gave our crew a break because of the fierce storms blowing out to the east."

"Lucky you," Jason said. "I am a native to the Rognanakh Highlands. I was part of the Wadassy tribe."

"Aren't you guys a tribe of shepherds?" Sheri asked.

"Indeed," Jason said. "We have very little contact with the outside world."

"So where are all your sheep now?" Sheri asked.

"I have some sheep locked away in an abandoned horse corral I stumbled upon," Jason said. "When I saw your guys' smoke signal, I decided to come out here and see what was going on."

I'd never imagined that mine and Sheri's little campfire would alert a rescue.

"Thanks, that's really kind of you," Sheri said. "We don't need to be rescued though."

"I'm glad to see that you are safe right now, but no one is completely safe out here," Jason said. "The Hyena Man lives up in these hills."

Jason spoke with such chilling conviction that I immediately became curious. While I had my sword sheathed, Jason was armed with a quiver of arrows, a longbow, and a wooden war club.

"Who is this Hyena Man?" Sheri asked as she petted Sid.

"The only true criminal of the Rognanakh Highlands," Jason said. "He is a misanthropist filled with so much hatred for the world that he seeks to rid himself of all contact with humans. He ordered everyone from my tribe to leave the hills or he would slaughter all of us. Since the Wadassy tribe have lived in these mountains for generations, we refused to believe that one bitter man would force us to evict the heartland.

"One night the Hyena Man and his pack of hyenas charged into our camp, slaughtered over half of us, and killed many of our sheep. Two nights later, he attacked us again. His hyenas are trained to attack people at their most lethal points which is why they have overpowered us even when we were prepared for battle.

"The Hyena Man and his pack have attacked my tribe four times now. I am the last survivor of a group of forty-seven."

I knew what it was like to lose your parents and friends, but losing your entire tribe had to be completely devastating. Nomads generally lived as one large extended family, especially when they were far from civilization. I could only attempt to understand the anguish which Jason felt right now. Although Jason had survived, he must have been plagued by survivor's guilt.

"Jason," I said. "Sheri and I will do everything we can to hunt down and kill the Hyena Man. We are in the vengeance business."

"Don lives for righting wrongs," Sheri said. "And I agree, the Hyena Man needs to be punished. These lands belong to everyone. For his crimes, the Hyena Man deserves to be executed, kicked out of the world by justice."

Jason shook each of our hands and then pointed toward a distant hill. He nodded, indicating that he wanted us to follow him.

"Where are we going?" Sheri asked.

"My camp," he said. "I can cook you guys a lamb stew for tonight, and there is a spring that acts as a water source."

We followed Jason along the ridge which led toward his camp. Like all areas of the Rognanakh Highlands, these hills offered immense beauty. Very long ridges towered over steep ravines which featured long patches of stone, seas of green grass, massive boulders, the occasional tree, the odd creek and waterfall, and a sky that was filled with clouds of all descriptions.

"Don, can we trust this guy?" Sheri whispered when Jason ran ahead to catch Sid, who was chasing a rabbit.

"Neither of us are too gullible. I know you have never lost anyone really close to you, which is a good thing, but after having lost two good friends and my parents, I can channel other peoples' tragedies. Jason spoke no bullshit."

"Even if he was lying, I'm sure we could overpower him."

"We can trust Jason. He ain't a liar, and we'll be doing the right thing by killing this Hyena Man serial killer."

"I agree that this psycho Hyena Man deserves to die for his crimes of murdering and trying to steal land, but shit Don, we can't even have a vacation without getting thrown into some conflict which isn't our business."

"Anytime someone is suffering, and we have the power to turn the tragedy around, it is our business. We have a responsibility to ensure the safety and happiness of others."

"Sometimes though, I wonder if you feel a responsibility or a compulsion."

"Sheri, you must have had a strong calling to help others in dire circumstances if you joined the vigilums. You always like to tell me that you didn't join the vigilums for a power trip or the money."

"I guess you're right, but this Jason guy speaks very little, and we don't know a thing about him."

"I don't distrust him yet, and remember, he knows so little about us, but he came out to our camp to warn us of danger. We owe him the favour."

"I wish there was a bit more certainty."

"We are all part of the unknown. Life would be boring without all the surprises and unpredictability."

We met up with Jason and Sid outside of the horse corral. There were a few yurts, some sheep behind a portable fence, a bonfire, a water spring, and random sprawled equipment. There weren't any other animals around apart from Sid and the sheep, though horse riding gear lay scattered.

"We had horses, yaks, chickens, and a few other dogs around here until the Hyena Man showed up," Jason said while Sheri and I scanned the scattered jockey gear.

Before Sheri or I could reply to what Jason had told us, he walked over to the flimsy fence which secured the sheep in a makeshift pen. Jason unlatched the gate and then walked away. A ram trotted from the pen and headed toward one of the many nearby hills. Every sheep in the herd followed him.

"Aren't you worried about them running away?" Sheri asked.

"Nah," Jason said with a shake of the head. "The great thing about sheep is that where one goes, they all go."

As the sheep dawdled to the hills, Jason fetched water from the spring and then brought it to a boil in a kettle filled with herbs he'd plucked from the ground. Next to the kettle, he heated a pot of lamb stew. Once the food was warm, Jason served Sheri and I our meal with bowls, cups, and spoons made from arbutus wood. The tea was very relaxing, and the lamb stew was exceptionally exquisite.

"Don't you want some?" I asked.

"It feels kind of rude eating in front of you when you're not munching on anything," Sheri said.

"Don't worry about it," Jason said.

"You're one hell of a cook," I said.

Jason smiled, nodded, and then headed to a yurt. A minute later, Sheri and I heard a melody coming from Jason's yurt. Once Sheri and I had finished our meals, we got up to investigate the music.

We found Jason sprawled in a hammock, playing a lute. Sheri danced to the gentle tune. The melody was harmonious and very much suited the tranquility of being up in the highlands.

"Oh hey," Jason said when he looked up from his instrument. "I didn't know I had an audience."

"You're really good," Sheri said.

"Thanks," Jason smiled as he plucked a tune.

"It must be kind of lonely being out here in this camp all alone," I said.

"Yes and no," Jason said. "If you can't be your own friend, then you'll never be totally happy with other people."

"So, what do you do to entertain yourself when no one else is around?" Sheri asked.

"Music, look after the sheep, take Sid on really long walks," Jason responded.

"You certainly have no shortage of great trekking," I said.

"Would it be alright if we took Sid out for a hike?" Sheri asked.

"She'd be the happiest dog in the world if you did," Jason said.

Sheri and I found Sid and then headed up a hill which was adjacent to where the sheep were cluttered. We offered Jason the chance to come on a hike, but he said that he'd like some quiet time, and that he always played himself a lullaby on the lute whenever he wanted to rest.

"That's pretty trusting of him to let us take his only companion along with us," Sheri said.

"Yeah, but do you think he was trying to get rid of us?" I questioned.

"Maybe he's a little shy and needs some space after meeting new faces. If his entire tribe was wiped out, we're probably the first people he's seen, and remember, he rescued us when he thought we were in danger. Usually when you lose people, folks in your community come to comfort you. Jason is receiving everything backward."

On our hike, Sid would run ahead of us, stop, and then bark at us to get moving. Once we caught up with her, she would jump up on us, let out a few happy howls, and then dash ahead. Sheri and I got a real workout by trying to keep up with her as we climbed a rather steep slope. No matter how quickly we moved, Sid was always ahead of us, especially when she smelled a rabbit or a landed bird.

After a two-hour hike, Sheri and I turned around and headed back to Jason's camp. On the way down we decided to trek toward the clutter of sheep.

Jason popped up from a ravine and jogged toward the sheep. We hadn't seen him when he'd been down in the ravine, but anyone would be able to see him up on the hilltop due to his bright red attire.

Sid dashed to Jason upon picking up his scent. Sheri and I followed Sid. Jason ran and the sheep followed him back toward camp. I laughed about how we were playing a big game of follow the leader.

Jason dashed up very steep hills with such ease. Sheri and I couldn't have sprinted as fast as he was moving if we were on flat ground. The sheep moved slowly but Jason kept circling around the clutter of animals to take a head count. Jason also ran down the slope, which was rather dangerous considering mountaineers injured themselves while descending so much more often than they did when ascending. Nonetheless, Jason seemed to have perfect, speed, balance, and agility. Perhaps he had become such a strong runner from having grown up in such hilly terrain.

We ate a dinner of wild potatoes, rack of lamb, and milk tea. Jason headed to his tent to rest and pointed to a yurt where Sheri and I could crash. Although Jason was ready to rest before Sheri or I, he told us to enjoy ourselves by the bonfire for as late as we wanted. Sheri and I cuddled next to the flames until we faded away.

Jason took Sheri and I on a walk the next day. We climbed five different hills. Each high point offered a marvelous view. Although climbing five steep hills was a good feat, there were still many more peaks which Sheri and I wished to visit. Although Sheri and I were in very good shape from combat training and life at sea, our bodies weren't nearly as adjusted to the steep terrain as Jason's. Sheri and I broke considerable sweats, drank much more water, and gasped for breath when we went up some exceptionally steep slopes while Jason remained at ease.

I hated to think this but Jason's laconic state, albino skin, and life in an abandoned camp made me wonder if he was a ghost. There were no corpses or burial points around his camp, which made me wonder what had happened to the bodies of the slaughtered shepherds and animals. The camp was too large for Jason to move on his own, especially when he didn't have any horses or yaks to carry his gear.

As we neared camp, a low groaning echoed in the valleys. These bass groans gradually grew toward a higher pitch until they sounded like a vicious throaty laugh.

"Hyenas?" Sheri whispered with suspicious fright.

Jason nodded as his relaxed facial expression clenched. The reds in his albino eyes darkened and I wondered if his entire outfit would turn to angry maroon. He grabbed a loaded quiver and bow from a pole and then fetched his club from his tent.

"Go find my sword," I said to Sheri. "I'll use my magic."

Sheri was without a weapon unless you included her survival knife. We had hoped that we wouldn't need to arm ourselves while on holiday since we'd expected complete seclusion in the highlands.

Four hyenas sprinted from atop the hill, trampling grass and kicking up loose dirt. Each of them could put Jason and Sid to shame in a race. Their fangs were reminiscent of crocodiles. Greedy eyes beamed toward the sheep which were idly trotting through camp. You could almost smell their blood lust. I wondered if this mysterious Hyena Man had trained his pack to be manically vicious.

Jason loaded his bow and let loose a missile. The arrow bolted into the neck of the lead hyena.

The remaining hyenas scattered in different directions as Jason fired a second arrow. This shot missed the nearest hyena by a few paces, but a third arrow went through a hyena's left ribs and came out the other side.

One of the hyenas charged toward me and dropped his jaw. I got the feeling that the hyena intended on pouncing atop me and ripping my neck open with his gnarly canines.

Diabolical cackles heightened my anxiety. I wondered if many members of Jason's tribe had died from such an attack.

I was not going to become a death statistic.

I raised my ring and blasted a stun ray. The fired ray blasted the hyena onto its back. I wasn't sure if I'd killed the beast or temporarily paralyzed it. Now wasn't the time to confirm the kill. There was at least one other hyena in the vicinity.

Jason charged toward a yurt, which had a hyena outside of it. The quiver and bow had been flung aside. Upon noticing Jason's charge, the hyena jumped upward. I raised my ring, ready to blast the hyena with a stun ray or force blast, but I couldn't get a clear target since Jason was within range.

Amid my predicament, Jason flung his club. The stout club bashed the hyena to the ground. An ear-splitting yelp followed. Jason thumped his club against the hyena two more times, ensuring that the brutality had been beaten out of the beast.

"Is that all of them?" I asked.

"Not quite," a female voice called from behind us.

Sheri emerged with my katana. Blood dripped from the blade while she dragged a hyena carcass with her other hand. A massive gash had split the dead hyena's back.

"They often attack in multiples of five," Jason said. "It must be the Hyena Man's lucky number."

We scouted the area for about ten minutes but didn't see any traces of invaders. None of us had been harmed, and all the sheep were safe, so things seemed all good until the next attack.

"You know, this is the first time I've ever killed an animal in self-defense," I said to Sheri. "Unless you count Aurelius, which I don't considering that dragon was conjured as a puppet for Maximus."

"That's what these hyenas are," Sheri said, "death tools for the Hyena Man. He has trained them as his army. You did the right thing by killing them. Don't beat yourself up over innocent casualties. Animals can't reverse what they've been trained to do."

"Julia does not need to hear about this."

"Ha, she plans on being a vegan in two seasons."

"We can cook the hyena meat if you're getting sick of lamb," Jason said. "I have some recipes, and fresh hyena steaks are delicious, as are hyena curry and hyena jerky."

"Sounds awesome," Sheri said.

"The pelts and bones are also very useful," Jason said. "Since I won't need all of them, perhaps you can sell them for a pretty good price back in Fordonchi or wherever you head next."

"Thanks," I said.

"Don, I didn't know you were a genie," Jason said.

"I didn't plan on using any magic out here," I said. "When I saw the hyena, I figured that a life-or-death situation was good enough to justify breaking this temporary rule."

"You did a good thing by using magic," Jason said.

"I'll take you for a magic carpet ride tomorrow maybe," I offered.

"I'd love that," Jason said as all the anger from the attack disappeared from his face.

That night Sheri and I cuddled very closely in our yurt. The hyena meat was as delicious as Jason had said. We listened to meditative music from Jason's lute, and the bonfire had been especially toasty that night, so Sheri and I nearly forgot about our worries from today's attack. Having sex on a warm and cushy wool blanket made the evening extra special.

"Don," Sheri said right as I was about to nod off. "Do we really need to hunt down the Hyena Man?"

"Of course, we do."

"Maybe we should leave these lands? No one else is here. Is it really worth risking our lives to bring one asshole to justice even though no one will likely see him again based on how remote these lands are?"

"How can you think that? Everything this Hyena Man freak has done is unforgivable. Defeating him is a tribute to the victims, Jason, and justice."

"But these lands are so remote and challenging. We don't know where to look and who knows how many more hyenas he has out there. There are only the three of us, and we're not heavily armed."

"If we let the Hyena Man have the land, then he's won because he wants to have all this territory for himself.

Damn it Sheri, we are professional warriors and Jason is one tough barbarian. The Hyena Man will be brought to death in no time. End of discussion."

"But you and Jason haven't even talked about finding this Hyena Man."

"I'm sure Jason doesn't want to hear you doubting whether we should defeat the Hyena Man or not."

"You know Don, not everyone lives their life on the brink of death due to someone else's bad actions."

I stopped for a moment to think about what Sheri had said. Perhaps I was always finding myself in moments of peril because I subconsciously sought combat. I'd always let other peoples' battles impact my journey. As I thought all this over, I wondered if I'd ever led a healthy lifestyle.

So many people who I cared about had become a part of my quest to rid the world of evil. I was so driven to right wrongs that I couldn't abandon my quest of battling violence, corruption, and eternal bullshit. Due to my calling, I could never separate personal time with loved ones from my mission to destroy villainy. I vowed that I would soon take a break from vigilantism, but not until the Hyena Man was destroyed.

"I'm sorry I yelled," I said to Sheri.

She kissed me. We cuddled tightly beneath our woolen blankets on the cold mountain night.

The next day Sheri and I lay on our backs and stared at the clouds while Jason played his lute and Sid napped. I figured that each of us had earned a day of taking it easy after so much hiking.

A rumble erupted over Jason's lute melody. The ruckus grew louder. Sid barked. The pent-up sheep bleated at a volume I hadn't heard before.

"Oh shit," Sheri said.

Two boulders were rolling down the barren hillside. Grass flattened while clunks of dirt were kicked up. The rolling boulders picked up air as they bounced over hill banks. I considered blasting at the boulders with my ring, but neither a stun ray nor a force blast could stop them.

The first boulder crashed into a yurt which stood along the border of camp. The wooden posts crashed to bits as the roof collapsed. The rolling rock tore large rips in the canvass as furniture crunched.

The second boulder smashed into the campfire. Coals splattered everywhere, clouds of dusty ash rose, sparks flew, and burning timber flattened to a crisp. The boiling tea kettle received substantial dents and leaked steaming water that quelled the flames.

"Was that an avalanche?" I asked.

Jason pointed toward the top of the hill. There was a cloud of black and yellow moving toward us.

"Hyenas," he said. "The Hyena Man is very strong, and he must have rolled some boulders down here as a first wave of attack. He's now sending the hyenas down to clean up what's left over."

"It's time to end this bullshit for good," I roared as I went to fetch my sword.

"Don, I don't think the three of us can take on an entire pack of hyenas," Jason said.

"Then what are we supposed to do?" I demanded.

"I have a plan," Jason said.

"What?" I bellowed.

"Hey Don, listen to Jason alright," Sheri said.

"Sorry, go on Jason," I blushed.

"Don there is a sheep carcass in the yurt next to my tent," Jason told. "Grab it, hop on your magic carpet, fly up to the hyenas, and then divert them away from camp with the carcass. Fly low enough for the hyenas to jump at but not steal the body. Head over to one of the woody hills, make sure the hyenas are still taking the bait, and then drop the dead sheep into the trees and return here."

I nodded and then went to fetch my magic carpet and the sheep carcass.

"Sheri, you and I should get the sheep out of the pen and lead them away from here just in case any more boulders come down," Jason continued.

"Got ya," Sheri said as she jumped to her feet and then unlatched the sheep pen.

I found the hanging sheep carcass. Blood dripped onto my clothes when I pulled the mutton body from the hook which it hung from. Flies buzzed around, and a putrid stench assaulted my nostrils. This wasn't my ideal way of fighting, but Jason's idea of diverting a pack of hyenas seemed clever.

I hopped atop my magic carpet with the sheep carcass and headed toward the pack of hyenas who were within paces of attacking the camp. No more boulders were rolling down the hill. It would have been appreciated if some fallen stones flattened these vicious beasts, but for now it was me against the pack.

I halted my magic carpet and hovered several paces above the hyenas. Their cackling, laughing, and yelping stung my ears, and I would have given anything to listen to Jason's harmonious music. Sharp teeth snapped as the hyenas jumped toward me.

I dangled the sheep carcass over the edge of my magic carpet. The hyenas leapt toward the sheep's dangling legs. I rose the magic carpet a pace higher to ensure that the hyenas weren't able to catch the sheep no matter how high they jumped. Next, I pointed the magic carpet toward a forested hill in the north-east and slowly drifted toward the trees. The hyenas did an adequate job at keeping up with my pace so I increased my speed. If I was going to lead the chase, then I wanted to remain a few paces ahead of the game.

As I increased my speed, innards fell from the incision in the sheep's belly. Bits of mutton stomach and liver plopped to the ground. Some of the hyenas fought over these fallen guts while others continued to chase after the carcass and I.

The tail end of the sheep's intestines spilled from it's guts. One of the hyenas bit the fallen intestine as if it were a hook dangling from a fishing line. The hyena held this raw sausage firmly as I continued my course toward the woods. The hyenas pulled the entire strand of intestine from out of the sheep's belly as though it were a coiled rope being pulled to its maximum length. Several hyenas fought over the guts, tearing apart the sheep sausage while others continued to follow me. A long trail of sheep blood spotted the ground between the yurt camp and I.

I tossed the sheep carcass into the branches of a pine tree. The fallen body splattered across several tree limbs. Blood dripped and the sheep's kidneys fell to the ground. All the hyenas had followed the stench into the forest and were now fighting over the fallen organs or licking the trail of sheep blood. It was only a matter of time till the rest of the carcass fell from the trees.

I had to hand it to Jason; his plan of luring the hyenas with the sheep carcass as bait had worked very well.

I sped back to the yurt camp without looking back at the hyenas. The sheep were a good distance from camp. Sheri was leading the sheep away with a walking stick. Although Sid was a basset hound, she must have been trained to work as a sheep dog considering she kept circling around the flock to ensure that none of the sheep were left behind.

I glanced to the north and saw a red image moving upward at a thunderous speed. I flew toward the hill as Jason made his ascent. At the top of the hill, there was a very large boulder, at least five times the size of either of the rocks which had smashed into camp. I didn't think anyone could move a rock that big unless they were a giant cyclops.

Someone else stood next to the boulder, a very tall and exceptionally muscular man. He wore leather boots, hyena hide pants, a pelt vest, a fur hat, and had bones and fangs dangling from his necklace. I figured him to be the Hyena Man. It seemed a bit ironic that a man who commanded packs of hyenas to do his vicious bidding also dressed in the skins of his allies.

Jason ripped away his red hood and veil. Although Jason was an albino, red rage grew across his milky skin as his blood boiled. Jason raised his wooden club, growled, and gritted his teeth.

The Hyena Man snarled, let out a cackle, fetched a large bone from the ground, and then swung his improvised weapon at Jason.

I wished that I had my sword. Part of me was tempted to sneak up behind the Hyena Man and fire at him with magic, but I feared that if one of my blasts missed, I would kill Jason.

Jason bashed his club toward the Hyena Man, but his foe was quick at evading blows. Every time Jason missed a shot, the Hyena Man let out an annoying cackle. When Jason's weapon tore flesh from Hyena Man's chest, the Hyena

Man let out a masochistic laugh. I wondered if the Hyena Man could talk, or if he only spoke the language of the pack.

Jason smacked the Hyena Man's bone club from his hands. Right when Jason was about to bash the Hyena Man for a second time, the Hyena Man jumped on top of Jason, tackling him to the ground. That did it, I was no longer going to be a bystander floating around on a magic carpet.

I leapt from my magic carpet and landed atop the Hyena Man. This sudden blast shoved Jason deeper into the grassy ground, possibly knocking the wind out of him. The Hyena Man let out his masochistic laugh and then spat several times. He threw me backward, pinned me to the ground, and bit my cheek. Blood rose from my flesh wound. I scrambled vigorously, but the Hyena Man was much stronger than me, and I had never been much of a wrestler. I wished that Bashar were with me to toss this psycho away.

The Hyena Man gave me a shove and I rolled down the hill. After much clawing, ripping grass, tearing holes into the ground, thumping myself against stones, and digging dirt into my fingernails, I came to a halt. I cursed myself for having not blasted the Hyena Man with magic when I'd been pinned to the ground.

Jason whopped the Hyena Man in the back with his club. As the Hyena Man screeched and scrambled across the ground, he picked up a broken bone shard. The Hyena Man flung the fragmented bone at Jason. Jason let out a shriek as blood spilt from his pale skin and stained his scarlet pants.

The Hyena Man scooped up a large femur and swung the bone at Jason as if it were a sword. Jason's club clashed against the bone several times. With a strong parry, Jason knocked the femur from the Hyena Man's hands.

The Hyena Man bent over to retrieve the dropped weapon. Jason swung back on his club as though it were a baseball bat. The wooden club bashed into the left side of Hyena Man's head. The right side of the Hyena Man's face smashed into the side of the boulder. An enormous crack followed as Jason's club swung a second time, blasted through the Hyena Man's skull, and crashed against the rock. Calcium fragmented, blood splattered, and brains popped and spluttered. The Hyena Man's jaw jumped from his skull as teeth fell to the ground. The body of the Hyena Man collapsed to the ground. Blood trickled down the grassy hill like a stream.

I had never seen an enemy destroyed with such gruesomeness. Living in the hills had really taught Jason to fight like a barbarian.

I pulled the bone from Jason's thigh. His face briefly flinched, but he didn't let out any groans of pain. I healed him with my ring. Once I was sure that Jason was alright, I suggested hopping aboard my magic carpet and flying to the yurt camp.

"It looks like all the sheep are safe," I said. "I ditched the hyena pack in the forest and without their master they probably won't come back to camp."

"I knew you and Sheri would do well."

"Why didn't you tell us about your plan to take on the Hyena Man? Sheri and I would have been happy to help, and you might not have gotten injured had we been along."

"I trusted you and Sheri to do a good job and both of you did. The Hyena Man was my fight. I was the only one who could seek true justice for the Wadassy tribe by destroying him."

"You certainly destroyed that son of a bitch; that's for sure."

"We're all extremely tough, but I hated the idea of anyone else getting killed by the Hyena Man. This was a war between the Wadassy and the Hyena Man, and we fought it to the very last blood."

"And you won it one hair away from death."

Two days later, Sheri and I decided to head back to Fordonchi. My biting wound was somewhat healed, and Sheri and I knew that if we got more relaxed, we might miss our departure aboard the Vindadong. Although Keifer didn't expect us back for about a week, Sheri and I wanted to take our time and not rush down the mountains.

"Let's hope that the seas have cleared by the time we hit shore," I said to Sheri as we got ready to trek to the ocean.

"You know love, you don't fight injustice because of compulsion or destiny," Sheri said.

I looked at her a bit puzzled.

"You do it out of your heart."

Sheri and I kissed. Sid dashed over to us and tried to get in on the smooch with her dog drool. Sheri and I laughed as we told the pooch to take a hike.

"What should we do about Jason?" I asked.

Sheri winked and then called him over.

"Why don't you come with us to the ocean," Sheri said.

Jason paused to think this over.

"I know the Rognanakh Highlands have been synonymous with your life, but change can be good," Sheri said.

"Hell yeah," I said. "The need for change is what brought Sheri and I from the city to the jungles, to the ocean, to the northlands, and to the highlands."

"Without my tribe, I have no one to share these beautiful lands with," Jason said.

I sensed much melancholy, and I didn't want Jason to stay alone in the hills. As tough as he was, who knew how much time Jason had before an unforeseeable event would take his life. I really wanted him to come with Sheri and I.

Jason headed to the sheep pen and unlatched the gate. The clutter of wool wandered to an unknown destination in the mountains.

"I think the best way to heal my soul is to do something totally different," Jason said. "I'll give the sheep liberation, and I'll give myself freedom from the highlands."

"Sweet," Sheri said as she embraced Jason in a bear hug.

"Dude, you'll love the ocean," I said. "You can dig both the highlands and the sea. Being away from the mountains might make you appreciate them even more."

"I'll come with you and be a pirate aboard your ship," Jason said, "but you have to let me bring Sid."

"Wouldn't want to leave here without her," Sheri said.

Jason packed some gear and then turned his back on the yurt camp without looking back. It was incredibly brave of him to leave behind the only life he had ever known. I couldn't totally comprehend what was going through his head and heart, but I had a hell of a lot of admiration for him. I'd had big changes in my life, but none quite as large as what Jason was going through.

About a week later, we met up with Keifer at the tavern in Fordonchi. He stunk strongly of stale booze, so perhaps he had achieved his goal of being a complete barfly while the rest of us had explored the hills.

"Seas should be clearing up now, maybe we can go sailing," Keifer slurred as he sipped away on mead. "That is if I don't drown myself in all this alcohol."

"Keifer," I said. "I have a new friend. Sheri and I would like to nominate him as a new crewmember. I know you're looking for new people, and this guy is as tough as anyone you'll ever have aboard the Vindadong."

Sid ran forward and jumped on Keifer's lap, spilling some of his mead.

"Welcome aboard friend," Keifer laughed.

BOOK VIII:

BOUNTY HUNTER ISLAND

Jason took to the seas better than the rest of the crew had expected. Having lived outdoors his entire life had made him very strong. He could stomach cold weather better than Sheri and I due to his life in the cool hills. Although life at sea was very different from living as a shepherd in the highlands, Jason was eager to achieve transformation which was why he fully concentrated on making the transition from a shepherd to a sailor.

Although he never spoke of it, Jason missed the mountains. Whenever the Vindadong docked, Jason went hiking. Sid would tag along behind him while the other guys would combine walking with an afternoon of pub crawling.

Some seasons after Jason had joined the Vindadong, Keifer received instructions that we were to sail to Sixalix, a port town on the south coast. Since we were on the east coast, we would sail due south and then head west. Everyone was happy that we wouldn't have to sail through the chilling northern waters again.

Right before we tacked to head west, we stopped at a port at the very south-eastern corner of Sionia called Gradit. Jason and Sid went for a walk on the beach, which ended up being a run since Sid dashed at top speed down the sandy beach, and only Jason was fast enough to chase after her. Sheri accompanied Jason, insisting that she needed practice and that she wasn't the runner she had been during her days with the vigilums.

I'd been working the graveyard shift for the last week so didn't really have the energy to go for a jog down the beach. Instead, I headed to the tavern with Keifer and ordered a rum ginger punch.

"So where are all of you guys headed?" the bartender asked while he mixed a grog and lime for Keifer.

"Got some cargo to drop off in Sixalix," Keifer responded.

"Really?" the bartender exclaimed. "You're sailing due west to Sixalix?"

"Why wouldn't we?" Keifer wondered. "What would be the bloody good in sailing up to the north lands and then looping all the way down the west coast? By that route, we would have sailed around the whole bloody country."

"Things are pretty dangerous out near Sixalix," the bartender said.

"Dude, the northlands are way more perilous," I said. "The temperature out there can easily kill you, the currents are so much stronger, the fish populations have dwindled, it's the foggy time of year so a lot of boats crash into rocks, seclusion makes it harder to get food or seek rescue in emergency, and there are a ton of psycho dragons and madmen wizards living up there."

"A ring of thieves operates out of Bounty Hunter Island," the bartender said, "not too far from Sixalix."

"How can a bunch of thieves be a threat against hardened sailors," Keifer chuckled. "My first mate Don here is a genie and a brilliant warrior with his katana."

"A gang of pirates have been boarding and raiding ships be they fishing boats, cargo ships, even a naval vessel was attacked," the bartender said. "These aren't a bunch of amateur buccaneers but hardened criminals being run by the mob. Some of the thugs are genies and ogres."

"We can't be scared of some hooligans," Keifer said as he knocked back on his sour grog. "Our cargo needs to be delivered. If we chicken out and take the long way around, then we're letting the hoodlums believe that they own the waters."

We couldn't let the crooks believe that they were the powerful ones. Someone had to challenge them and remind them that the ethical always triumphed over the cruel.

We sailed west to Sixalix the next morning. We passed by a stretch of everglades and were completely secluded. Bounty Hunter Island was still a ways off, but I thought we were ready for a fight. Keifer had recently purchased three ballistas, and every crewmember on board was pretty tough.

Two days later we were nearing Bounty Hunter Island. The watch officer who was stationed in the crow's nest hollered news of an approaching boat from the port-bow side. Keifer grabbed his spyglass and spotted a single mast boat headed toward us. There were about six crewmembers on this incoming boat; each was armed with sabers and archery equipment.

An arrow blasted from an archer on the distant boat. We laughed when the arrow flopped to the water, many paces from the Vindadong.

"I guess these are the hoods who we were warned to stay away from," I chuckled.

"Bunch of amateurs," Keifer laughed as he shook his head.

"Do you want to fire one of the ballista missiles at them?" Jason asked.

"Nah, I'll tell you guys what," Keifer said, "Don, punish their insolence by blasting a fireball at their sail."

"Aye aye captain," I joked with a salute.

With my ring, I created a ball of flames which crashed into the mainsail. Fabric blackened, smoked, and crinkled as ash fell to the waves while burning pieces of fabric fluttered in the breeze. The pirates screeched, screamed, and cried as they tossed water atop the flames. The skipper lost control of the tiller, and the boat headed into the wind. The oncoming gusts spread the flames from the sail and onto the mainsheet, cunningham, and outhaul. The genoa caught fire, causing even more panic among the crew.

This was a story which the crew of the Vindadong would be laughing about for ages. If all the other thieving pirates were as feeble as the archer aboard this small pirate boat, then sailing around Bounty Hunter Island was going to be a lot of fun. I looked forward to teaching other amateur crooks a lesson with simple tricks.

About two hours later, we spotted a schooner with its sail lowered. The anchor hadn't been deployed. No one answered our calls.

"Let's investigate," Keifer said. "Something isn't right here."

The Vindadong anchored. Eight of us packed into a dory and rowed to the idle schooner. It felt eerie to barge onto a strange ship. All crew could be taking a nap for all we knew. Then again, it was very dangerous to let a ship drift, especially when you were near land and the waters were shallow. Common practice stated that two crewmembers should always be on the deck.

We paddled our dory toward a rope ladder and climbed aboard. We called several greetings, but our voices merely echoed across the open water.

"Will you look at that," Sheri said. "The deck is covered in blood."

"Maybe the bodies were tossed overboard," one crewmember said.

"Or maybe these guys were attacked by cannibals who hauled the corpses to a feast," another crewmember said.

"Let's check the hold and captain's quarters to see if anyone is inside," Jason said.

Not only was no one inside the cabin, but many of the rich items which you associated with a captain were missing. The wardrobe and desk were empty.

I headed back to the deck with a few crewmembers. Jason, Sheri, and two other crewmembers popped up from the ship's hold.

"No one was down there," Sheri said, "looks like all the cargo has been hijacked too."

"Nobody was in the crew quarters either," Jason said. "The place was a complete mess, but we couldn't find any valuable items."

"The galley is empty as well," a crewmember said. "The pantry is bare and there's no booze left."

"This schooner was attacked and raided of her wealth," Sheri concluded.

"If hostages weren't taken, then dead bodies were probably tossed overboard," Jason hypothesized. "Maybe that's why there've been so many birds diving to the water. We'd all thought that the birds were hunting for fish, but perhaps they were pecking at corpses which weren't completely water-logged. I wonder if we'll find stiffs washed ashore, if they haven't been eaten by sharks."

The pirate ring out of Bounty Hunter Island now seemed a lot stronger than some amateurs out in a dinghy. Perhaps we had walked into a major gang war. I was happy to have my sword at my side.

We dropped the anchor so the schooner wouldn't drift, and then rowed back to our mother ship. After telling Keifer what we had found, we agreed to drop anchor outside of the main harbor on Bounty Hunter Island and then row ashore. Guards would be stationed aboard the Vindadong in case any pirates dared board us. Keifer advised all sailors to not venture too far inland in case a brawl broke out.

"I think we should contact the vigilums," Sheri said.

"But if we contact the vigilums there will be no adventure for us," I smirked.

"Always more interested in getting yourself killed than enjoying the beaches of a new island," Sheri snorted.

"There might not be any vigilums on Bounty Hunter Island," Jason said. "If there were vigilums then they should have cracked down on the pirates, and they should have had patrol boats out since piracy is a major problem in these waters."

"Or the vigilums could be in allegiance with the pirates," Keifer said. "Maybe the pirates are paying off the vigilums to stay out of thieving operations, or the vigilums own the pirates and are profiting off their enterprises."

We all gave Keifer and Jason's ideas some thought before deploying our dory. Keifer stayed aboard the Vindadong while Jason, Sid, Sheri, and I headed to land. I figured that now was the time to do detective work and ask around about gang activity in the area. Since investigation was never my strongest strength, I wished that Wes was with me. Jason was pragmatic so I hoped that he'd be able to uncover some information.

Apart from rocks and cliffs to the north, Bounty Hunter Island was completely sand. There were no cobblestone streets so all walkways between buildings were very dusty. Many of the people lived in stilt houses along the shore. There were dozens of docks and a good number of grog bars. It didn't look like anyone ate anything apart from seafood and tropical fruit. There were hardly any trees, but plenty of people were selling weapons. Perhaps what should have been an island paradise had turned into dystopia on account of the pirates.

Sheri led the way while Jason, Sid, and I followed. I had a feeling that Sheri was looking for a vigilum headquarters. I knew that she wouldn't be satisfied with our theft theories until she found local law enforcement.

As we walked down a sand road which led toward the cliffs on the north end of the island, we came across a boardwalk. Right as the four of us climbed atop the wood, we heard creaking, which bounced to a boom. The wood gave way and a hole opened. We realized that we hadn't been standing atop a boardwalk but rather a trapdoor.

Sid let out a loud yelp. Sheri growled. Jason shook his head, and I grumbled and swore as we fell, unsure of how deep the hole was. After thumping our butts, we realized that we had fallen a few times our height.

"Everybody okay?" Sheri asked.

"I'm not injured but I hope Sid is alright," Jason responded.

"I'm not hurt, but I won't say I'm alright," I answered. "What the hell is the meaning of this?"

The cave we were in was covered in blankets, pillows, tapestries, carpets, tarps, and plush furniture. I wondered if pirates had robbed a ship filled with bedding cargo and stored all their loot in this cave. I was thankful that the soft fabrics had cushioned our fall, but everything felt surreal.

"Who goes there?" a voice called from a distant section of the cave.

I gazed closer and realized that a boy of about twelve was standing next to a lantern. He was wearing a bandana and had a crossbow. If it weren't for the candlelight, then he would have faded into the darkness due to his ebony clothes and black complexion.

"We seem to have accidentally crashed into your place," Jason said. "I'd love to know where the exit is."

"Hey, I don't know who you are," the kid said as he pointed his loaded crossbow at Jason. "Don't make me fire on you."

I commanded telekinesis with my ring. Through the power of magic, I grasped the crossbow and tugged it away from the kid's hands. The kid yelped as his weapon jolted from his fingertips. I spun the crossbow around so that the bolt was pointed at pirate boy. Through further telekinetic control, I floated the crossbow to my hands.

"I'm not looking for a fight," the kid said. "My name is Huck, and I was told to watch over this area. It looks like you guys fell through the trapdoor and I'm sorry about that. There should be a warning sign above it."

"Alright Huck," Sheri said. "We've got some questions to ask you. If we like your answers, we'll leave you alone."

"Sure, go ahead, ask me anything," Huck said. "I mean no harm to any of you."

Jason, Sheri, and I moved toward Huck so that we could see him clearly. I continued to clutch the crossbow. Sid rolled around on some of the carpets and then looked like she was going to take a dog nap.

I wasn't sure whether to look at Huck as a regular kid or a young criminal. Throughout my life I'd seen youngsters who were as brutal as hardened criminals. Sometimes boys got swayed toward crime but then ran from it. Devo had once tried to turn Marco to a life of crime by coercing him into helping rob a fruit stand. I think Marco stole one orange, but his life of crime ended there. If only Devo had managed to outrun his criminal peer influence like his younger brother had.

"Hey that's a cool dog you've got there," Huck said. "By the way, would you guys like some tea?"

"How do we know you're not going to poison it?" Jason asked.

"I'll brew a pot and have a cup from it if that's what it takes to prove to you that I'm not a bad guy," Huck responded. "Honestly, I hate all the crooks around here, and I'd really like someone to come to Bounty Hunter Island and kill them all."

"Huck, I think we're the people you're looking for," Sheri smiled.

"Really? Seriously?" Huck beamed as he placed a kettle over a burning stovetop. "I'll tell you everything about the criminals around here. You see, I've been living on the streets for two years now. I was desperate for money so some crooks are paying me to watch over this underground holding. Every boy starts off as a guard, and after proving loyalty and climbing up the ladder, they then get to go on raids and stuff."

"Where are the vigilums?" Sheri asked.

"After an ongoing feud, all the vigilums were killed and the townhall was burned down over a year ago," Huck answered. "This place is now being run by a gang called Blood and Bull. They've killed off all rival pirates and employ merchants who sell off the stuff they steal from ships."

"We came across a schooner earlier today," Sheri said. "There was no one onboard, but a lot of blood had been spilt and it looked like all the cargo was missing."

"Blood and Bull take no prisoners," Huck said. "They tend to toss all bodies to the fish."

"We also had some kids in a dinghy try to board us," I said. "I shot a fireball at them and destroyed their sail. Are these kids also a part of Blood and Bull?"

"Oh yeah," Huck answered. "The kids who are out in dinghies are a few ranks above me. Blood and Bull is run as a military dictatorship. You climb the ranks, and after you've served as a crewmember on some of the large boats, you're then assigned a robbery in one of the dinghies."

"We came here on a merchant ship," Jason said. "We're anchored out in the bay and are heavily armed. Do you think we're at risk?"

"Anywhere near Bounty Hunter Island, you're in danger," Huck answered. "Blood and Bull like to surprise people, so they'll probably act really calm and wait for you to let your guard down before they attack."

"You know we're vigilantes," I said. "If you could give us some advice, we'd be happy to set you free and defeat Blood and Bull. I know what it's like to be a slave for criminals."

"For real?" Huck grinned. "The lead mobster of Blood and Bull is this guy named Krull. His right-hand man is this asshole called Hunter who likes to boss kids around and is the one who tries to recruit them into crime."

Son of a bitch, was Krull back from the dead? Again? Exploiting kids and turning them toward a life of crime seemed like the perfect thing for Krull considering he'd sold off dragons to criminals and tried to poison entire villages with leprosy and dead rats in drinking holes. How the hell had he surprised our bout? It looked like he'd crashed to his death, and by the sounds of it, Hunter was set to bleed to death after his battle with Julia. Then again, Krull had survived Frosher Volcano.

The tea kettle whistled. Huck poured each of us a cup of green tea. He took the first drink to prove that the brew wasn't poisonous. Sid woke up when Huck tossed her a beef bone.

"This is good tea," Sheri said. "I'm sorry we've been so rude. I'm Sheri, Don is the guy who stole your crossbow, Jason is the dude dressed head to toe in red, and Sid is Jason's dog."

"I'm happy to meet all of you," Huck said as he came forward to shake our hands. "Don, are you a genie?"

"I am," I said.

"No way?" Huck gleamed as he headed over to a satchel and produced a silver band with black inscription and a red jewel. "I'm not allowed to wear this ring. Hunter confiscated it from me, but the other day I stole it back and have been hiding it down here. I'm always checking on it to make sure that it hasn't disappeared."

"Go ahead and put it on," I said. "I've got my ring, your crossbow, and my sword while Sheri is armed with a double-bladed axe. Jason has a club, and Sid is one beast of a dog."

"Wow thanks," Huck said. "Most people on Bounty Hunter Island are afraid of genies. Krull and Hunter are the two toughest genies on the island, and they only let their most loyal genie thugs carry their rings."

"I'd love to give them a run for their magical ability," I said. "I reached the scholarly level of genie magic years ago, but I still continue to hone my skills."

"That's awesome," Huck said. "I really would love to learn more about magic, but all the temples and magic texts on the island have been destroyed."

"Huck, I promise you that my friends and I will do everything we can to end the reign of terror that Blood and Bullshit is inflicting on your island," I said.

Sheri winked at me. I knew that she'd been waiting for me to declare my death quest against evil.

"Count me in," Jason said. "Sid too."

"Wow, you guys are my heroes," Huck said. "I know this is a lot to ask Don, but do you think you can teach me some more magic? It's been ages since I've studied anything to do with genie life."

"I'll do what I can," I said, "but first we must defeat Blood and Bull. The war is on."

The five of us walked back to the Vindadong. Huck walked with Sid while Sheri caught up with me.

"You know, Bounty Hunter Island is an example of why we need larger vigilum forces," Sheri said.

"Sounds like the vigilums were pretty useless at defending this island from a gang of pirates," I said.

"Which is why they need larger numbers of recruits with more training and better weapons."

"If we can liberate this island of Blood and Bull then it'll prove that ordinary folks are stronger than security forces."

"Oh, you and your anarchy get so tiresome. Just look at what anarchy has turned this island into: a haven for mob rule."

"People like you think that if anarchy occurs then the biggest gang will take over. Well, the biggest gang in Sionia is the government. They came into power and declared that we are not living in an anarchist situation through a load of rhetoric and propaganda. Out here on Bounty Hunter Island, a fiercer gang called Blood and Bull took over the Sionian government and declared that we are living under mob rule; that shows how weak the government can be. Both situations of governing on Bounty Hunter Island are poorly developed anarchist situations."

Jason chuckled and then said to Huck, "the two of them could argue about political ideology all day. Neither of them is ever right nor wrong."

"You know a lot of vigilums were bribed to leave the island or offered mob positions with Blood and Bull," Huck said, "talk about bureaucratic corruption eh?"

I smirked at Sheri, and she snorted before going quiet.

At the Vindadong, Keifer cooked a meal of barbequed manatee, breadfruit, and root vegetables. We enjoyed the food, and Huck totally pigged out. He claimed that the boys in the boarding home were fed nothing much apart from rice, beans, and water. All other foods had to be scavenged. Even though the boys who lived under crime were trying to climb the mob ladder, some of the kids had attempted to steal from upper members of the gang.

"Apart from stealing my ring back from Hunter, I've never wanted to steal from any of the upper mobsters," Huck said. "If you get caught stealing, then you'll live as a slave for the rest of your life."

Keifer pulled me aside.

"Can we trust this Huck kid?" he asked.

"I think so," I replied. "If he wanted to sick the mob on us, he would have done it by now."

"It's a bit dodgy to have a little pirate running around our boat."

"I was kind of like him when I was young. Besides, we've taken away his crossbow and he has inside knowledge about Blood and Bull. I bet he can take us to the headquarters, and we can hit the pirates really hard and end this whole fiasco."

"Oh wow, holy shit," Keifer called looking up.

While Keifer and I were chatting, Huck had climbed onto one of the forestays on the Vindadong's tallest mast. He looped his legs over the forestay, let go with his arms, and then rolled back until he was hanging upside down from his legs alone. He dangled his arm and let out a cackle. Huck then placed his arms back on the forestay and rolled his legs downward so that he was dangling from the forestay by his hands. He swung back and forth a few times and then leapt into the air, letting go of all support. Huck pulled off two summersaults and then landed on the deck of the boat.

"Holy shit," many crewmembers called out.

"Are you a monkey or an acrobat?" Sheri winked.

"I told you this Huck kid is a keeper," I said.

"By the mermaids of the sea, I want this boy onboard," Keifer said.

About an hour later I approached Huck, carrying his crossbow in hand.

"Huck, you've really impressed everyone today," I said.

"Thanks, hope I can continue to make all of you happy."

"I'm sure you will. You're also one amazing stuntman. Most of us onboard can't do a cartwheel let alone a chin up."

"Maybe I can teach you guys some gymnastics, and you can all teach me to sail."

"I'm sure that will happen. I'd also love to help you hone your genie powers."

"For real?"

"Yeah, for real. I'm also wondering if you could get me close to Krull."

"Krull is a truly vicious criminal. I think he lives for the sole sake of destruction."

"Huck, I've dealt with him before, and out of all the crooks I've ever fought, Krull is the most twisted; well either him or Viceroy Bartholomew."

"If you want revenge against Krull I can lead you to his office; he's there most nights."

I instructed Huck to get on my magic carpet. I gave him back his crossbow and told him that he'd earned it. Huck's aura beamed with happiness.

Huck and I flew toward a stone hovel that acted as Krull's fort. After landing the magic carpet in the shadows, we crept toward Krull's office. I kept my sword raised while Huck held his crossbow. He only had one bolt, and I wished that I could give him another weapon to defend himself.

We got to Krull's office. Huck explained that this wasn't Krull's home but a place where he kept information about stolen cargo and the outcomes of missions. I'd never thought of Krull as a record keeper or strategist, but I didn't know him well. Part of what made Krull so dangerous was how little I knew of him. He could put up a good fight, and his plans of evil were truly diabolical, so perhaps he was smarter than I'd perceived. That and he'd managed to escape death twice. Perhaps he was a resurrected ghost? Either way, I wanted answers.

Krull's lair was located next to the boarding house where boys at the bottom of the rank resided. I wanted Huck to stay on the Vindadong tonight. I also wanted to help the kids who were playing soccer in the courtyard, but I couldn't bring too many strangers onboard at once.

"Hey all of you little shits," a hoarse voice bellowed from the shadows. "Get your butts inside right now before I boot your asses. There are a lot of dishes needing washing, floors that need scrubbing, and laundry that needs to be cleaned, so quit farting around, and get the fuck inside, and do your chores."

If this was the kind of abusive slavery which Blood and Bull boys put up with, then I sure as hell didn't want Huck spending another night in the boarding house.

I crept out from the shadows and saw the boys rush inside.

"Leave that soccer ball outside," the warden said. "No getting any mud inside, and no playing around. We've got work to do so get to it lazybones."

I realized that the bossy warden was Hunter. I really wished that Julia had killed him. Had it not been for Hunter's quick escape from Julia's blade, Krull and Hunter may have never taken over this island. I wondered how much other turmoil they'd caused during the long period between Stodaneatoo and Bounty Hunter Island.

As the boys scattered inside, Huck headed to the shadows. We'd agreed on the walk that Huck would stay hidden unless I called his name or blasted magic.

The door to Krull's hovel swung open with ease. Krull was scribbling down notes on papyrus paper using ink and quill. There was a mug of grog on his desk and a cutlass next to him. I wanted to blast him with my ring, but at the same time I wanted answers. Was he a demon who kept resurrecting after death, or a genius escape artist?

"We meet again Don," Krull grinned. "Do take a seat."

I didn't bother sitting. My sword was sheathed, but I liked to keep the hilt close to my hand.

"Don't bother drawing your weapon my friend," Krull teased. "You came here to talk. You would have blasted me with your genie powers if you wanted me dead."

Damn, Krull understood my intentions. I hated how the most observant villains were the most cunning and manipulative.

"Is it our destinies to keep bumping into one another?" Krull asked, though I wondered if he already had an answer. "I'm surprised to see you again, but you must be shocked since I survived our last encounter.

"I'll take your silence as a yes. As you know Don, I am a genie. When I fell off my magic carpet, I used my ring to create a force shield which cushioned my fall and saved me from being smacked to death."

I hated to admit it, but I was learning tricks from my enemy.

"What about Hunter?" I asked.

"Hunter escaped your sister but was very injured. I must say Don, strong warriors run in your family, you should be proud of that. Had Hunter and I not rendezvoused, he would have died because I wouldn't have been able to heal him."

Great, Julia and I had managed to nearly kill two of the sickest fucks to ever walk Sionian soil but by misguided luck, one of them had lived and then healed his brutish buddy. If only the gods and goddesses would intervene more often against agents of evil.

"I take it you and your buccaneers have come here to destroy Blood and Bull," Krull said.

"You'll be dead before you know it," I growled.

"I seem to be pretty good at escaping death at your hand Don," Krull chuckled, "or maybe you can't kill me.

"Perhaps that's it Don, you love the idea of being the good guy, a vigilante, a rogue hero who fights all evil. You have a big ego and pride yourself as having a heart of gold which is why you won't work with the government. Everything has to be your way, and your obsessive quest against evil won't end until you die. Since you save others, you believe that your interloper behaviours are proper.

"I'm just like you in a way Don, except I love being a maniac, a sadistic brute, an agent of malice. I have no boundaries when it comes to evil, and I'm always looking for new ways to commit acts of sadism. I live for pain and always want to outdo myself in a creative way. It's a beautiful art. Robbing people on the streets or stabbing drunks in the bar is boring. I love to pull off deranged artistic acts that will go down in history. Killing is a pleasure, and turning others to evil is truly delicious. All these boys on the island will turn to savages just as Hunter did. He was once a sweet little chap who had many insecurities, but when I taught him that bullying others would make him forget about his problems, he became my number one henchman."

As much as I hated to admit it, Krull had spelt everything out perfectly. I was obsessed with doing good, and I was completely tenacious toward doing things my way. My idealism prevented me from joining the vigilums, and I had to get myself involved with every conflict that I thought I could solve.

Perhaps Krull was my complete opposite: an angel of atrocity who lived to cause problems for no apparent reasons. Maybe he was so deprived of integrity that the only way he could feel happiness was by destroying all the good in the world? Or perhaps he was just like Hunter, a self-loathing twit who needed to harm others to feel strong? Since a guy like Hunter would never find inner acceptance, he'd become addicted to bullying others, and his cravings to harm people and feel powerful had worsened through habit.

"You're not going to kill me tonight Don," Krull said. "You could stab me, blast me with your magic, or even beat me to death, I know you're tough enough to do all that, but you won't kill me.

"If you killed me, Hunter and at least two dozen other boys would rush to my rescue. They would assume you were from a rival gang, and they would do everything they could to avenge me and defend the honour of Blood and Bull.

"You're the good guy Don; you'd never hurt kids who've been brainwashed into lives of crime; you want to save them. If all you wanted was to destroy Blood and Bull, then you wouldn't have snuck in here for a diplomatic meeting but rather sought to exterminate my gang with extreme prejudice."

I loathed how Krull had figured out that I wouldn't kill him tonight, even though it needed to be done. I couldn't hurt the kids. They were still innocent as far as I was concerned. Despite having only known Huck for a few hours, I saw so much good in him. I truly believed that he deserved way more than the criminal life. Huck reminded me so much of Marco. I wanted to see him go down a similar path to Marco's and not end up like Devo.

"Do have a good night, Don," Krull said before taking a drink of grog.

I headed outside, got Huck, and then walked to my magic carpet.

"What was all that?" Huck asked.

"I got some answers, but I can't kill him, not yet at least. It's way too dangerous."

"Are you serious Don? I thought you were a fearless vigilante."

"If Hunter or anyone else catches me fighting Krull, then the whole gang will go after me. I'm not going to fight any of those young boys who've been corrupted into joining the mob."

"Thanks Don, that means a lot to me. I could be one of those boys who attacks you and then gets killed."

"There has to be a better way."

Huck and I headed back to the Vindadong and then climbed into bed. Huck slept well in his hammock. Sheri was cuddled tightly against me, but I didn't get much sleep. Everything from Krull's speech and the idea of innocent kids being turned into hired killers was too unsettling. I really hoped that the nightwatchmen kept a strong guard on the ship that night.

The next morning, Huck and I flew on my magic carpet to the dockyard. Huck needed to get some gear from his lair. He suggested that I stay put on the dock, and I took his word. Things would look a lot less suspicious if he went about his business alone.

Jason had paddled to shore in a canoe that morning. The canoe was docked at a separate wharf from the one which I'd landed my magic carpet on. I wished that I could take the canoe and use it to paddle all the boys away from crime.

As I lazed about on the dock, I noticed a trireme sailing from the opposite end of the island. At breakfast, Huck had spoken of another pier where many of the Blood and Bull pirates kept their raiding vessels. The trireme was smaller than the Vindadong but had a larger crew. Since the winds weren't strong, the trireme was being powered by rowers.

The trireme steered toward the Vindadong. Keifer walked to the bow of the Vindadong and held up a megaphone. The captain of the trireme was doing the same.

"Ahoy," Keifer said into his megaphone.

"Surrender now," the captain of the trireme said. "You have trespassed into Blood and Bull waters. Surrender or die."

"Like hell we will," Keifer roared with enough volume that he didn't need his megaphone. "This morning you shall die."

The Vindadong's three ballistas turned toward the trireme. Crewmembers came forward with burning torches. Each missile of the ballistas had been coated with tar. The ballista missiles ignited in flames as the Vindadong crew aimed the giant crossbow at the trireme. The trireme captain barked orders while the skipper pulled rigorously on the tiller as rowers squawked in terror.

Three missiles projected from the ballistas. The first missile bored a large hole in the hull. Although the missile flopped toward the water, flames grew across the bow. Water seeped into the hole, leading to the first stage of sinking.

The second ballista arrow blasted through the sail, which was picking up very little wind. The sail blackened and folded up into crinkled ash. The mast caught fire and flames spread to the mainsheet and forestays.

The third ballista bolt crashed into the port side of the trireme. Two rowers turned to corpses upon impact. Melted tar dripped across the trireme, spreading the fire to new areas of the boat. Crewmembers jumped overboard while the captain barked orders to put out the fire.

I glanced back to the village to see if Huck was coming. I wasn't going to attack the trireme without knowing that Huck was safe. I saw Jason approaching the wharf which was adjacent to the one which I was on. His canoe was tied to a small dock which was attached to the main wharf by a gangplank. Sid was at his side, and Hunter was following them. I unsheathed my katana and stepped toward my magic carpet.

Sid barked right as Hunter flung a fishing gaff at Jason. Right before the sharp hook on the gaff could connect, Jason turned around and jumped back before unsheathing his club. I raised my katana in hope of stabbing Hunter.

"You can't save him," a voice called from behind me. As I turned around, I stepped off my magic carpet. Krull was standing behind me with a raised cutlass. Sparks flew from Krull's rusty sword when my katana slashed against it. As our blades clashed back and forth, Krull wore a malicious look on his face as if he had a sneaky plan for me.

Jason walloped his club against Hunter's gaff, breaking the wood shaft in two. Hunter roared as the second half of the shaft flopped to the ground.

Krull came forward, forcing me to take a step backward. As I evaded the thrust of his cutlass, I slipped on a strand of kelp. I flopped on my butt, banged the side of my head against a rail, and dropped my sword.

A red stun ray blasted from Hunter's magic ring, knocking Jason to the ground.

Krull stomped his boots onto my shoulders. If my aching head and dizziness weren't bad enough, pain erupted in my bones. Krull lowered the tip of his cutlass and pointed it at my ring.

"Try any magic and I'll chop your finger off," Krull snickered.

Krull aimed his ring at me while Hunter stood over Jason with his ring raised. Did Krull have the same plans as Hunter? Were Jason and I going to die?

Sid sprinted in front of Jason. She snapped her jaw open and tore into Hunter's wrist. Hunter yelped like a little puppy as Sid's canines ravaged his flesh.

Krull bounced to the side. His weight shifted which inflicted much more pain into my shoulders, but he soon stumbled off me. His cutlass dropped from his arm. Amid pain in my shoulders, I reached for my weapon. Once I wrapped my fingers around the hilt of my sword, I climbed to my feet. I felt pain in my tailbone and my head was quite woozy, but at least Krull no longer had me pinned to the bird-shit covered dock.

The arrowhead of a crossbow bolt stuck out from Krull's right bicep. Blood dripped from both the entrance and exit wounds of the bolt. Huck stood several paces away with an unloaded crossbow.

"The little local loco had to save the big genie warrior," Krull hissed. "Pathetic, wouldn't you agree Don."

Jason grabbed Hunter's hand and ripped the ring from his finger as Sid nipped Hunter's face and scratched his chest. Jason chucked the ring into the ocean, leaving Hunter without magic.

Krull stumbled onto his magic carpet and hovered away from the dock. He was without a weapon apart from his ring and the crossbow bolt sticking through his arm.

Hunter moaned, pushed Sid aside, and dove into the water. Although the tide wasn't low, I hoped that Hunter would hit his head, crack his skull open, break his neck, and drown.

"Come on Don," Huck said. "Finish him. Kill Krull."

I blasted a stun ray toward Krull and missed him by an embarrassing distance. My vision blurred and stars popped in front of my eyes.

"Took a bump to the head big guy?" Krull laughed. "Well Don, I know you're not thinking clearly, but I bet anything that you'd rather put out a fire and save the innocent than kill me."

What the hell was Krull talking about?

"Oh shit," Huck gasped. "Don, the boarding house is on fire. Krull, you son of a bitch. You set that fire. I know you did, you fucker. Those kids who devoted their lives to your gang are going to die."

"Hells yeah," Krull cackled. "Don, you and Huck have a choice: kill me or save the kids. I know what you'll choose, Don. It's not the choice I would make if I were in your position."

Amid his injury, Krull flew like a speed demon toward the burning trireme. The flames on the ship continue to burn despite futile attempts to put the fire out. Few crewmembers remained onboard.

I glanced toward the town. Smoke rose from the boarding house which was next to Krull's hovel. Flames could be seen through the windows of the smoking building. Damn it, Krull knew me well enough to know that I would rather save the lives of innocent kids than kill my greatest enemy.

"Come with me," I said to Huck as I stumbled onto my magic carpet, ready to take flight to the burning building. "Is Jason alright?"

Jason heard me and gave thumbs up as he walked down the gangplank to his canoe. Out of everyone I knew, Jason seemed to be able to stomach pain better than anyone else. Jason and Sid climbed into the canoe and paddled toward the Vindadong. It looked like the ship was still anchored and the ballistas had been reloaded. None of the missiles were burning.

As Jason and I had been combating Krull and Hunter, six pirates in a dinghy had snuck aboard the Vindadong. Most of the crew had been too focused on the ballista projectiles and the burning trireme to notice the stealthy invaders.

It wasn't often that Keifer took up arms in his old age, but when it came to pirates boarding the Vindadong he was ready to fight to the death. Since Keifer didn't have any weapons on hand, he armed himself with a fishing gaff.

Keifer smoked a pirate in the head with the gaff. The pirate toppled forward and plunged face first into the ocean.

Keifer swung the gaff a second time. The razor hook of the gaff dug into the left side of one pirate's neck. The tip came out the right side of the pirate's throat followed by drips of blood. With a sturdy yank, Keifer pulled back on the gaff. The hook of the gaff ripped the pirate's throat open. The pirate collapsed to the ground, sprayed a splatter of gore, and leaked an enormous puddle of blood from his fatal wound.

Sheri armed herself with an axe and charged after the four other invaders. With a downward chop, Sheri slammed the blade of the axe into the head of one pirate. As the pirate lost his life, he stumbled forward, thrusting his machete. Right as the pirate died, he stabbed one of his mates in the belly with the machete.

Sheri flashed the axe a second time and beheaded the third invader. Right as her enemy's head bonked to the ground, the fourth pirate shrieked in fright, dashed toward the starboard side of the Vindadong, and dove overboard.

Sheri swung the axe a third time giving the machete wounded pirate a mercy kill. Once the terminally wounded pirate had bit the dust, Sheri tossed the fresh Blood and Bull corpses into the ocean. Killing had never come so easy and it was obvious that Krull had been employing rookies who were nothing more than insecure bullies looking to assert themselves through pseudo-tough guy crap.

My magic carpet came to a halt next to the burning boarding house. There were no clouds in the sky so I wouldn't be able to raise rain to quench the fire, but there was a water tower next to the boarding house.

"Huck, I need you to aim my ring finger so that it is targeted at the water tower," I said. "I'm still feeling a bit dizzy."

Huck did as requested. I concentrated with all my effort on the water tower despite my migraine. The colour in my ring shifted and a blast erupted from the emerald. Wooden boards split to splinters. Hardware toppled. Water blasted out of the ruptured tower as if a bathhouse pipe had burst.

The water drenched the fire of the burning boarding home. The structure had been made mostly from brick, so it had been hard for flames to spread. There hadn't been much furniture inside though it was obvious that the wooden roof and other belongings had been destroyed by Krull's arson.

I flew closer to the water tower. Huck remained as still as a statue, and I almost forget that he was copiloting my magic carpet. I shot a gust of wind from my ring, hoping to drain the tower of all remaining liquid. Puddles of moisture sprayed from the reservoir tower. Plops of water assaulted flames that had yet to be quenched.

Huck and I landed my magic carpet. Kids had crowded in the courtyard. Locals had come to aid the kids who were covered in ash and soot.

"Huck, I want you to go inside and make sure that everyone has escaped," I said. "Scream like hell if anyone is in danger."

"You got it," Huck said as he dashed toward the building.

A few others followed Huck on his recovery and rescue mission. I saw three boys who were screaming and crying from burns, so I took to healing them with magic. A local medicine man was taking care of a victim of smoke inhalation while other villagers were feeding the escaped fire victims and doing what they could to calm them down.

Huck returned with two of his fellow boarders. The guys he'd rescued looked pretty shell shocked, but they didn't appear to have any physical injuries. Huck took a headcount and concluded that all the boys from the boarding house had survived the fire. As much as I scorned Krull for attacking kids to lure me away from killing him, I was grateful that none of the boys had been killed or seriously injured.

Jason, Sheri, and other crewmembers from the Vindadong came ashore. Keifer stayed stationed with other crewmembers and kept the ballistas loaded. The trireme had sunk and some crewmembers had made it to shore. Nothing had been seen of either Hunter or Krull though I was fully convinced that both of those assholes had escaped death. I hypothesized that sooner or later I was going to run into them while they were pulling off another crime against civilization.

We spent the afternoon nursing the kids from the boarding home and assuring them that things would be alright. Jason, Sheri, and a few others patrolled the streets to make sure that there weren't any vengeance-filled pirates lurking about. Right before dinner time, a village meeting was called in the market square.

"Greetings Bounty Hunter Island citizens," Sheri said. "It appears that Blood and Bull have been defeated."

A wave of cheering erupted. Sheri waited till all the celebrating voices subsided before continuing her speech.

"Krull and Hunter have likely fled the island. Many pirates were killed this morning and the large trireme has sunk. Today is a glorious victory for all of us. My crew and I will soon sail to Santalonia and request government intervention. We hope that the navy will arrive with government officials to help you set up a preliminary town council. Vigilums should also be sent here. It looks like any surviving gangsters won't want to start any fights now that the good outnumbers the evil. None of you have to live in fear anymore."

More applause followed. I knew Sheri was happy about announcing the future arrival of vigilums and politicians. I chose not to argue with her. Although I thought it would be more appropriate for the locals to take over island affairs, perhaps the villagers wanted government intervention. The sailors on the Vindadong couldn't act as the island's bodyguards forever.

"As for all of you boys who have survived the fire," Jason said as he took the stage, "we are leaving you with two options: you can stay here on Bounty Hunter Island and wait for aid workers, or you can sail with us to Santalonia. The crew I am part of has recovered a moored schooner which Blood and Bull attacked, though left in good condition. Some of my fellow sailors will sail this ship to Santalonia and you are all welcome to come along for the voyage. Once in

Santalonia, you can check into orphanages or other social services and schools."

As people praised Jason's delivery, I thought about the orphan boys who'd been lured into piracy. How many of their families had been killed? Had the surviving town folks been too frightened to stand up to Blood and Bull? It seemed like the villagers had acted as support staff for the pirate operations after all societal structure had fallen. Krull had been trying to breed a generation of criminals. Such a thought was truly petulant. Although I often thought of myself as a kid due to having the fountain of youth, I saw myself as darkened and experienced in comparison to the young boys who'd been lured into piracy. Hell, Huck was the first guy I'd hung out with in ages who hadn't reached the Post-17 age.

I really hoped that Bounty Hunter Island would find peace and that the likes of Krull and Hunter wouldn't be showing up again. I could justify vigilum activity if it meant that Krull was gone for good. Since Krull had fled the fight and set fire to his subordinates' home, I theorized that he wasn't interested in building a fortune for himself, but instead he wanted to turn paradise into dystopia as a way of feeding his desire for destruction. I feared the kind of carnage he would get up to next.

That night Sheri cuddled with me very tightly in bed.

"Don, you have done a lot to liberate all these people, and you're taking it so modestly."

"You kicked a lot of ass today too. Today was the first time the Vindadong was boarded, but it sure wasn't ransacked."

"I know you complain that people don't give you much credit, but everyone who really cares about you thinks very highly of you, and these town people are never going to forget you. They are truly grateful for what you did today. You've given them a very hopeful future."

"Thanks Sheri, but we all deserve credit. I may have put out the fire, but today was very much a team effort."

"You are in my positive aura, my love," Sheri said with kisses. "Never forget it."

Two days later we set sail. The cargo which Keifer was scheduled to deliver eventually made it to port, but the

Vindadong took a detour to Santalonia. As planned, the schooner followed behind. About half of the orphan boys who'd been recruited into crime sailed with us to Santalonia while the other half stayed on Bounty Hunter Island and were taken care of by the locals. Once we'd docked in Santalonia, social services intervened on the boys' behalf.

"Huck, we have a proposal to make," I said to him the day after social services met up with the boys. "How would you like to join the Vindadong?"

Huck's jaw dropped, his eyes widened, and he beamed like a beacon.

"For real?" he exclaimed.

"I'd love to have a cabin boy onboard," Keifer said, "and who better than a pirate kid with a crossbow, a knack for acrobatics, and a flair of adventure."

"I can also train you to be a magically affluent genie," I said. "You can be my apprentice."

"I don't know what to say," Huck gushed, "this is the kindest thing anyone has ever done for me."

"Say yes," Jason said. "It's what all of us want to hear."

"Yes, yes, yes," Huck said as he jumped for joy.

"Welcome aboard," Sheri said as she hugged Huck.

BOOK IX:

THE PIT FIGHTERS

Keifer claimed that Huck took to the sails better than any crewmember he'd ever encountered. Despite having resided on Bounty Hunter Island, Huck had little knowledge of sailing prior to being taken aboard the Vindadong. Nonetheless, Huck quickly advanced his sailing skills, and in rapid time he was promoted from cabin boy to watch officer.

Although Huck was a born seadog, he was a bit of a slow learner when it came to magic. I tutored him nearly every night on the use of his genie ring.

Huck came to learn that genies had magical energy in their blood, and that genie rings had a spiritual link to this energy. Spells required concentration and visualization, hence many genies having vivid imaginations and a determined focus. It took much practice to synthesize mind and magic so that a spell could be cast. Patience was essential to studies since the mental exercises were tedious. Magic levels in the blood increased through learning and practice. Training allowed genies to move to spells which required a higher level of mana within one's blood.

We also spent much time reading magical texts written by I'magee. Since Huck's literacy was poor, our book sessions involved improving his reading skills. I couldn't blame Huck for being a weak reader or slow at learning magic. His parents had died under mysterious circumstances when he was eight or nine. The school on Bounty Hunter Island had been shut down, and the pirate gangs who'd ruled

Bounty Hunter Island forbad use of magic in fear of a genie uprising.

Despite slow progress in the art of magic, Huck kept an optimistic attitude. He was the kind of guy who was generally very upbeat. Even when he was pissed off, you could tell that he was a genuinely positive fellow.

I knew it was wrong to compare my friends since everyone was a unique individual, but I couldn't help but feel like Huck was almost the opposite of Marco. Both Huck and Marco had grown up amid gang wars, fear, and depravity but had gained polarizing views on life. Marco was generally moody, quick-tempered, and found light in very few things. His desire to right wrongs was the result of a vengeance streak against all the turmoil he'd seen in his life.

Unlike Marco, Huck didn't dwell in morose. He was happy to be around others, and he liked to chat. His desire for adventure came from curiosity and he was always asking others lots of questions about their experiences. Huck claimed that such stories inspired him to live an exciting life.

Even if Huck was a bit slow with the ring, he'd become a competent magic carpet rider. The two of us went for magic carpet rides almost daily. Huck continued to impress everyone with his acrobatic ability, a talent which no one else on the ship came even close to.

After a few seasons of sailing, Keifer gave our entire crew a vacation. We sailed the Vindadong up a deep inlet on the east coast of Sionia and then headed west to Stodaneatoo. Sheri missed home and I figured that heading back to the city would give me the opportunity to see old friends. Huck had never been inland, so was very excited about seeing a new side of the country. Jason promised to take Huck on a trekking trip into the mountains. Keifer decided to tag along, saying that he wanted to do some hiking to prove that his feet hadn't turned to flippers after having spent years at sea.

After two days of travel, we reached Sheri's old house in Stodaneatoo. Weeds had replaced the flowers in her garden while stray cats and dogs roamed the property. The little fishpond had manifested with frogs. Despite the house looking dilapidated, we were thankful that no one had burglarized the home.

We all slept in late the next morning. The plan was to rest and recuperate before going to the market to fetch food. Sheri and I hoped to host a barbeque, and we wanted Julia, Trent, Bashar, and some of Sheri's old friends to come by. In the last letters I'd exchanged with Julia, I'd asked her to write to Marco and Wes and invite them to stop by for some catch-up time.

Sheri decided to do all the shopping on her own because she knew how impatient I got in the market. Jason and Huck went for a walk to explore the city. Sid joined Huck and Jason after she'd chased all the cats and monkeys out of Sheri's jungle-like yard. Keifer settled in a hammock with some alcoholic jungle juice and eventually drifted to sleep. Although he was a tough dude, I was very unsure if Keifer could climb a mountain since he'd refused the offer to go hiking in the Rognanakh Highlands.

Julia stopped by Sheri's place right when Sheri started to barbeque wild boar. It seemed totally appropriate that my sister would be reunited with her best friend right as her vegan principles were being violated.

"I was hoping that you would have imported a load of aquatic plants so that I could have a seaweed salad," Julia said.

"I'll eat your sister's pork," Keifer said right as he poured himself another mug of jungle juice. "Say lady, how'd you like some jungle juice? I promise there is no bat blood or water buffalo milk in it."

"I'll take you up on that old man," Julia said as she helped herself to a bamboo mug of jungle brew.

By the time Jason and Huck had returned from exploring the city, Marco and Wes had arrived.

"It's great to finally meet another genie," Huck said.

"We've got to practice some magic," Marco said.

"Hey, what about me?" Julia said.

"How about we go to a gladiator match," Jason said. "Julia, I've always wanted to go to one and I'll cheer you on. We can fly there on your magic carpet so you can show your true genie spirit."

"It'd be awesome if you brought your dog Jason," Julia said. "I love pooches, and my last one died not too long ago, so it would be good to have another pup to walk."

Wes decided to take over the cooking so that Sheri could join others in conversation.

"I'm really glad that you invited me out here," Wes said. "I can't remember the last time I took a vacation."

"Cuz work is your hobby," I cracked.

"True enough. I guess I need to find a hobby away from the university. I really admire how you and Sheri have managed to live the adventure life. Your other friends seem pretty happy with the sailing lifestyle based on the stories they're telling."

"Wes, you've got a cool life too. All that research you do at the university is important, and it must feel rewarding to know that the knowledge you pass onto others really helps them out."

"Thanks Don, that makes me feel appreciated."

"Maybe you should come out with us on the sailboat. With your big brain, I'm sure you could teach us a few things about marine engineering. Hell, maybe the rest of us can teach you a thing or two as well."

"That'd be great. Marco has also been trying to get me out to the ocean. Biology isn't my field, but I believe that any knowledge is valuable, and Marco seems to be next to Zadeezey in terms of knowledge of the ocean."

Wes didn't make any mention of Aurelius or my theories of Maximus having enlarged and enslaved a dragon who may have been Wes's kin. I figured that Wes hadn't found any evidence to support this theory of mine. Since Wes's existence was a touchy subject, I chose not to bring up the dragon. I really wished he had been around for the fight.

Bashar came by as we sat down for dinner. He stomped through the mangled garden and was carrying a war hammer. I found it peculiar that he was carrying such a heavy weapon to a party. The rest of us warriors had left our arms inside.

"Everyone," Bashar bellowed. "Tomorrow morning we're all going to head north to kick a load of ass."

"Thought about saying hi to anyone?" Julia said. "You haven't even met Huck, Jason, Sid, or Keifer. Did you leave your manners at home?"

Bashar's green pigments faded to red.

"Oh hi new guys, my name is Bashar and I'm an old friend of Don's. I'm sure he's told you about how we lived in the gulag for way the fuck too long, and I hope he's told you lots of really cool things about me. If he hasn't, then he isn't a very good friend.

"Any who, the reason why I'm late and announcing a mission is because our friend Trent has been kidnapped. Two days ago, some guys came by his tent, hit him with some knockout potions, and then locked him in a wagon and headed up to Xatica."

"Wow, wow, wow," I said as I rose to my feet, knowing that I would have to get a bit dramatic if I wanted to shut Bashar up. "You're saying Trent's been kidnapped?"

"Bull's eye Don," Bashar said. "A gang called Paleeshii has been kidnapping cyclops and ogres in this area. Some of the other jungle boys who Trent hangs out with have also been captured. The kidnappers demanded a ransom of more money than Trent's tribe has. I talked to the vigilums, but they don't have any leads beyond hearsay. Some of the jungle folks are saying that the Paleeshii gang is based in Xatica, and the captives are being taken to a pit fighting prison. If the kidnapped don't entertain their captors through gladiator combat, then their food is withheld. I'm not sure if the prisoners are also working as slaves in a gulag, but either way, we've got to do something about this; it's a fucking travesty against the beauty of life."

"Xatica is a lawless territory," Wes said. "That land has been taken over by mobsters seeking asylum, and there is no law apart from the sword. The government is either too afraid to intervene, or they're hoping that the gangsters will destroy one another in a turf battle."

"Sounds a lot like Bounty Hunter Island," Huck said.

"Precisely," Wes said.

"I wrote a story about Trent's kidnapping and the Paleeshii gang as well as the activities which are going on in Xatica," Bashar told. "I'm hoping to create awareness, but until the vigilums or military do something, it's up to us to rescue Trent and all the others.

"You guys are the toughest warriors I know. Huck, Jason, Keifer, I'm sure you're all incredibly strong warriors if you've taken down pirates and barbarians in the highlands. I am asking all of you to come on this mission to free Trent and the others. This will be our way of letting the Paleeshii pukes know that they cannot escape justice even if the government is giving them their own territory and turning a blind eye on the innocents who are being harmed. What do you all say? Are you in for an adventure and a quest for justice?"

Bashar raised a mug of jungle juice. Keifer's mug flung up, something which surprised everyone due to Keifer's age. Upon seeing Keifer's toast, I raised my drink. Huck, Sheri, Julia, and Jason followed. Wes picked up a cup and raised it. Marco was the last guy to raise a glass.

"Let's destroy this bullshit," Marco said.

We toasted to Marco's words and drank.

The next day we headed to Xatica. Bashar had rented four elephants to help us trek through the jungle. Wes, Julia, Marco, Huck, and I decided to alternate between flying and riding atop the elephants. It had been years since I'd been on an elephant, and I definitely preferred elephants over horses but nothing beat riding a magic carpet. Out of all of us who could fly, I think Wes enjoyed riding the elephants the most because unlike us genies, he exhausted his physical energy while flying.

"We'll take a break every two hours," Bashar said. "We'll spend half an hour relaxing, eating, drinking, and possibly swimming if there is a lake, river, or creek nearby. This will also give me time to write down some notes."

"What do you need to write?" Huck wondered.

"I'm a journalist," Bashar responded. "Like Don, I'm real nosy but my inquisitiveness is a lot more justifiable since I share all my knowledge with everyone as if I'm the teacher of the nation. I'm going to write a major story on our journey to rescue Trent from the Paleeshii; this will be the biggest crime story in decades, and let me tell you man, I've written a lot of stories about crimes from all over Sionia."

"Don told me that you wrote a number of stories about the gulag and how you all pulled off that fluke of an escape," Huck said.

"Hells yeah," Bashar said. "We sure rocked a lot of ass that day."

I decided to let Bashar be boastful and garrulous rather than remind him that I was the sole hero behind the escape. Moments later my thoughts told me that I was being arrogant considering Bashar and Trent had helped me survive the gulag. Had it not been for them, I might not have lived long enough to have retrieved my ring. My anti-authoritarian streak would have probably gotten me killed had Trent and Bashar not given me regular warnings about the risks of being beaten by guards for insubordination.

It was taking us a lot longer to gets to Xatica than expected, but the elephants' sluggish pace made us really appreciate the jungle. Huck had never seen forests with so much density. Wes was almost always too busy with work to get away on vacation, so he greatly appreciated the journey into the wilderness. The rest of us (save Bashar and Julia) had become complete seadogs, so we badly needed a change of scenery despite the ocean being just as beautiful in its own way.

So many trees needed climbing. The fruits we scavenged from the trees were more succulent than anything I'd ever eaten. Monkeys, hippos, gorillas, rhinos, gibbons, panthers, tigers, jaguars, and orangutans lurked just beyond the old jungle road which the elephants were trotting down. We played games to see who could spot the most animals. The mosquitoes didn't bother us because Wes had brewed up an anti-vampire bug concoction.

"Hey what kind of birds are those?" Huck blurted out every time he saw a winged creature which had a different set of coloured feathers. "How about those trees, what kind are they, and what are their distinct traits?"

Marco could answer most of Huck's questions. While Marco had spent many years on the ocean, he still remembered his jungle botany.

"Maybe you should transfer back to the jungle," Huck said. "You know so much about inland and coastal plants so maybe you should do a comparison study between the two."

"That is a pretty good idea Huck," Marco said. "I'd also like to get up north where I've never been before."

"This jungle is so amazing though," Huck said. "Man, I can't believe that I've never wanted to come here before."

"I prefer the ocean," Marco said. "Still, you're showing true appreciation of the world if you love the ocean and the jungle."

We stopped for a picnic. Sheri designated herself as the crew cook and boiled a pot of black bean soup. The rest of us fetched fruit.

"I know all that fruit is delicious, but don't ruin your appetite on it," Sheri said.

"Succulent jungle fruit made becoming a vegetarian so easy," Julia said.

Sid smelled a monitor lizard and dashed into the jungle as Jason was filling his canteen at a creek.

"How about we have a race to see who can capture the pooch first?" Julia suggested.

"No one is faster than Jason," Keifer said, "except maybe that dog of his."

"I'm up for a challenge," Jason said. "Let's push one another to be our most."

"I dig your competitive spirit," Julia grinned.

"I don't see pushing one another as a means of triumphing over someone else, but rather two people cooperating to be the most that they can be," Jason said.

Julia and Jason nodded and then dashed into the jungle after Sid. Despite the thick foliage, it wasn't too hard to track Sid due to her barking. The monitor lizard which Sid had chosen as prey was a speed demon, so it looked like the race could go on for a long time.

"You guys need to invite me on more trips," Wes said after lunch. "I really can't remember the last time I've been on an outing."

"Maybe you should take a sabbatical from the university and become an adventurer," Sheri said.

"He'd miss his work too much," I joked.

"Marco, I need to be like you," Wes said. "You work hard and love your marine biology, but still know how to throw adrenaline into your life."

"Cuz I don't live in O'Jahnteh," Marco said. "The city will make you so lethargic that you won't be able to go out on an adventure no matter how bored you get."

"I dare you to say that about Stodaneatoo," Bashar smirked as he showed off his new war hammer. "No one dares talk about my homeland that way."

"Stodaneatoo is awesome cuz it's built between the mountains," Sheri said. "Wes, you need to give yourself a break from your research even if you are a science genius."

"Maybe this odyssey will teach me something about science, and I can start writing papers on adventure science," Wes smiled.

"Going on a journey will be the best way to do that research," Huck said.

It seemed a bit peculiar that we were speaking so highly of adventure when the purpose of this mission was to rescue Trent. It was cool that we were having fun, but so many ugly factors had led us to this excursion. We didn't know what we were up against with the Paleeshii. For all we knew, we were probably going to be outnumbered in a fight to the death. Maybe we needed to enjoy the times leading up to the fight as much as possible so that we wouldn't let worry and fear bog us down? It seemed like a good idea to be happy with what we had. This was the biggest reunion of friends I'd ever had. I couldn't wait for Trent to join the party.

After Sid had been dragged back to camp and Jason and Julia had eaten, we got back on the elephants and headed north. Sid, Jason, and Julia rode one elephant and chatted away. I couldn't remember the last time Jason had babbled so much. He sounded like Bashar but with more modesty. Wes and I were on another elephant while Sheri and Marco followed on a different one. Bashar and Keifer swapped stories on the lead elephants while Huck flew above us on his magic carpet.

"You guys got to give the magic carpet ride a shot," Huck said. "Flying above the trees is the most amazing thing I've ever seen."

"Glad you've joined that club," Marco said.

"Why don't you take me out on your magic carpet?" Jason said to Julia.

"I'm not the strongest flier in the world," Julia blushed, "or the greatest genie."

"You're a damn good runner, and from what I've heard, you're a champion gladiator, so I bet you could beat your brother's butt any day," Jason chuckled.

"He'll never admit to the countless battles he's lost to me," Julia laughed, "not once has he even won a wrestling match against me."

After a few hours of elephants trekking, we set up camp at the top of a ravine. There was a creek down below to bathe and wash dishes in. Marco and Bashar poached three large jungle fowls for dinner. Sheri insisted that she be the camp cook.

"You got it mom," we all joked.

"You can be the cook as long as you fix me a veggie meal," Julia said. "And I get first dibs on the fruit."

Jason and Julia went off on another hike. Sid came along and was most likely going to chase after a baboon or a jungle hare. The rest of us swam in the creek. Huck had never been for a dip in fresh water prior to this trip.

"Even though I'm happy that I'm not constantly inhaling salt, fresh water feels so weird," Huck said. "It's still really refreshing though."

Wes had fun shooting fireballs into the creek water. We created a game where we'd toss fallen sticks at Wes and he'd set the wood on fire. The burning pieces of timber would crash into the creek water and then we'd see how long the flames would smoke for. We all got really excited over this game, and Keifer said that we ought to play a similar game on the ocean, which would entice setting enemy pirate ships on fire. Huck and I very much welcomed that idea. Bashar said that he'd go on his first ocean voyage if we played that game.

"I don't think I've been on a hike since I was Huck's age," Keifer said.

"So that was about a hundred years before the rest of us were born," Bashar cracked.

"You watch your lip," Keifer chided. "I might be an old fart, but I'm as vulpine as a viper."

Little had Bashar realized that Keifer had dropped a chicken head into his mug of tea. Several moments later Bashar screamed, spat out a soggy skull, spilled hot liquid on the crotch of his loincloth, and shouted a monologue of vulgarity. The rest of us exploded in laughter.

"I guess I'm chicanery and you're a chickenshit," Keifer chuckled. "Normally it was the chicken who ran around frantically after it was beheaded, but now a massive ogre is throwing a conniption fit over a birdbrain."

"Someone is going to get a walloping," Bashar grumbled as he went looking for his misplaced war hammer, which he ended up not being able to find until the next morning.

The next day Julia and Jason went for a morning run before the rest of us were up. By the time my eyes were open, they'd finished a long jog and were practicing archery. Jason had always shown competence as a bowman, but Julia gave him a few pointers.

"This is easily the best bow I've ever used," Jason said.

"I won it in a contest," Julia said.

"No way."

"You're doing pretty good with it yourself. You should really come to Stodaneatoo's next archery tournament and win your own bow."

"Deal. If I win though, you have to use my lucky club in your next gladiator tournament."

"You're on."

Sheri called me over for a cup of tea and noodle soup, which was heating over the fire. Since another long day in the jungle lay ahead of us, a hearty breakfast was essential.

"Julia and Jason seem pretty close eh?" Sheri said.

"Jason is closer with her than Robin ever was," Marco grinned. "You know, I think I heard them sneak off last night into the bushes."

"Shut up," I grunted.

"I'm serious man," Marco chuckled, "and when is anyone serious about sex?"

I'd never seen Jason talk to girls much. He'd always been so reticent and introverted, and I wondered if he had difficulty getting close to people on account of being an orphan. It was very rare for him to speak of his past, and he'd never mentioned any girlfriends. For all I knew, Jason could have had a lover who'd been killed by the Hyena Man, and he chose not to speak of her death as a way of suppressing pain. Considering Jason never spoke of his parents, a murdered spouse seemed highly plausible.

I glanced toward Jason and my sister. Julia was using her genie powers to levitate the arrows from the quiver. With her telekinesis, Julia slowly shot the arrows into the bull's eye on the archery target. Jason clapped in applause. I was tempted to jump in on the praise but held back since I didn't want to seem like I was spying on them. If Julia thought I was being nosy, she'd make a big stink about it.

At the same time, Julia rarely had the confidence to perform magic in front of others. I wondered if she felt alright performing in front of Jason because he was without a drop of magic in his blood. Either that, or she thought that she could impress him. I wondered if Jason was boosting her confidence.

"You sure they're only teammates?" Marco asked.

"Whatever," I said. "Jason is a good friend and I approve of him as a boyfriend for Julia."

"I'll second that," Sheri said. "Two of my best friends getting together, what more could I reasonably ask for?"

"Something good ought to come of this mission," Marco said, "considering all the evil shit that's going on."

"What do you mean?" Sheri asked.

"Trent's been kidnapped, again," Marco said. "Who knows how many others have been taken hostage. A lot of people have probably been killed, and as always, the government isn't doing a fucking thing about the real problems which are going on."

"Evil is going on, but instead of dwelling in pessimism, I think we should look at this journey as a party that is looking for one more person," Sheri said. "We find Trent, we win, we really party."

"I won't feel good about any of this shit until we've won," Marco said. "I've been living a good life, but evil needs to be punished. The good things in life necessitate the need to destroy evil and protect innocent folks who deserve no malice."

I figured that I'd always worry about Marco. He'd been happy the last few years, but realistically he would never get over the demons that haunted him. Since Marco knew he'd never overcome his anger, he sought to distract himself, and he'd done a good job at evading his past by living on the coast as a biologist. I knew he really cared about Trent and didn't want evil to happen to others, which was why he'd come back for one more mission. Nonetheless, I worried that too many of Marco's repressed demons would rise and lead toward him doing something rash and dangerous.

After breakfast I told everyone to get packed. I could tell that Jason and Julia wanted to continue archery and hiking while Wes and Huck were enjoying a flight over the jungle canopy. Keifer and Bashar had been lounging around while Sheri had enjoyed picking fruit and observing the different flowers. Sheri really appreciated the arcane biological information Marco had passed onto her.

I would have liked to stay around and have some fun, but we had to get to Xatica as quickly as possible without exhausting ourselves. It seemed unfair that a hike in such a beautiful place had to be given a time limit due to outer evil.

"Don, I don't need you bossing me around," Bashar said after I asked him to get off his rear.

"All I did was ask you to pack up your kit," I said.

"Don isn't the bossy one," Keifer said, "you are."

"Quit complaining, go take the elephants for one more drink, and then get the food hang packed," Bashar ordered.

"Point proven," Keifer said. "You can bury the latrine considering you made a big mess in it this morning. Do I need to announce that loud enough for everyone to hear?"

Bashar bitterly buried the shithole. By the time he was done, Wes, Huck, Julia, and Jason had packed the elephants. Marco and Sheri had done the dishes while I'd swept the campsite to make sure we weren't leaving any belongings behind. We then took off north-west, getting closer to both our friend and the terror which lay ahead.

We had a very long day of trekking. The elephants held up though my companions started to moan and groan at four in the afternoon. I encouraged everyone to keep going and that we should use daylight for all it was worth.

"We'll need daylight to set up camp and get dinner cooked," Jason said.

"Good point Jason," Bashar said. "Hey Don, you should listen to others for once. Who made you captain of the expedition? This whole rescue trip was my idea, and not all your ideas are good, so let's be a democracy and listen to others eh?"

In fear of mutiny, I gave into my complaining comrades and agreed to stop for the night. Keifer and Wes fed the elephants. Sheri, Marco, and I set up camp. Huck and Bashar fetched drinking water. Julia and Jason headed off into the bush to gather fruit. They asked if any of us would look after Sid while they were away from camp.

"I'd be happy to," said Wes. "Having a dog around makes me want to get a pup of my own."

Marco snickered once Jason and Julia were out of earshot.

"Ha ha," I said.

"I tell you man, they're going off to hook up and they want Sid gone cuz she'll interrupt their humping and pumping," Marco laughed.

"Go and shite."

"Bashar is right, you are really bossy."

We got up at a reasonable hour the next day. After a three-hour trek through the jungle, we arrived in the vicinity which the Paleeshii were located in. Since we didn't want to bring the elephants into criminal contact, we left them chained up by a waterhole with plenty of foliage to chew on.

"The pit fighting stadium is about a three-minute walk from here," Bashar said as he looked over his map.

"How do you know that Trent and the other prisoners are being held at the place on your map?" Jason asked.

"This is the only known arena in the area," Julia said. "For generations, the most brutal criminals brawled in that pit. It may be the last pit fighting arena in Sionia considering most of them were closed during a crackdown on illegal gladiator combat."

We made our way through the small forest which separated the elephants from where this pit supposedly was. Just as Bashar had told us earlier, the pit was in a clearing. Scattered human skeletons decorated the ground. Dust stung our eyes while daylight beat down on the arid ground. Bashar and I gave one another a look, telling each other that this was reminiscent of the gulag. It was probably very traumatizing for Trent to be a prisoner here. I really felt sorry for my friend. Living in the gulag had been damaging enough but getting sent back to a desolate jail would severely deepen somewhat healed scars.

A large hole in the ground lay a few hundred paces from the tree line. Each of us dashed to it very quickly. We had to know if this was the place where the prisoners were being held. What if Trent was down there right now?

"Holy shit," Huck said.

"God damn Bashar, you were right," Keifer said.

"And now we're going to righteously kick a load of ass," Bashar roared.

The hole was about fifty paces deep by forty paces wide. Torches illuminated the bottom but it was hard to get a good view of what was going on from the top. An audience was watching the fights from bleachers. From what we could see, two groups were brawling. The fights were made up of mostly ogres and cyclops though there was the odd human among them. No weapons were present, so the fighters were bashing with their bodies.

"That's Trent," Bashar said.

A rival cyclops dashed toward Trent. Trent quickly evaded the tackle and bashed his forearm against his rival's back, stunning his opponent. I was happy that Trent was getting the better end of the fight, but it was saddening to know that he'd been forced into fighting for his life. Since Trent was a prisoner, it was safe to assume that all other fighters were otherwise decent folks.

"What the hell are we waiting for?" Bashar said. "Don, Julia, Wes, Huck, Marco, fly in there and save some ass."

Wes spread his wings. Huck, Marco, and I grabbed our magic carpets. Jason had been carrying Julia's magic carpet and was about to hand it to her until he pointed at an object down below.

"What's with that wizard wand down there?" Jason asked.

All of us peered at a long thin metal rod sticking up from the ground. The ruby and turquoise stone at its top glimmered despite the faint light.

"It's just a pole," Bashar said.

"It could be a wizard's tool," Wes speculated.

Huck raised his ring and fired a stun ray at the hole. The hole in the ground turned from transparent to turquoise. Each of us dropped to the ground as the stun ray rebounded off the turquoise light, narrowly missing Huck. Sid yelped and ran around frenzied for about half a minute before calming down.

"They've set up a force shield," Marco said. "We'll have to find whatever entrance the gangsters are using."

"Holy shit," Keifer blurted.

We all turned around, fearful of what surprises lay ahead.

Nine human skeletons were walking toward us. Each was carrying a cutlass. I'd heard stories about wizards resurrecting skeletons and using them as zombie warriors, but I never thought that I'd see the spells put into practice. Though each of the skeletons was armed with a blade, their bony bodies stumbled along the rocky ground.

"Nine of us, nine of them," Huck said. "Is this the best you pussies can do?"

Huck blasted a bolt from his crossbow. The bolt smacked into the lead skeleton's eye socket and knocked the head off the spine. Once the head crashed to the ground, the rest of the skeleton's bones collapsed. Huck let out a victory howl.

The rest of us charged toward the eight remaining skeleton warriors. Jason snuck up behind one skeleton, swung his club, and bashed the skeleton to the ground. After a few swings, the skeleton was nothing but cracked bones and dust in the dirt.

Marco swung his whip at the nearest skeleton. His whip wrapped around the skeleton's sword wielding wrist. With a tug, Marco ripped the skeleton's hand from it's forearm. The skeleton tried to retrieve the dropped weapon with it's one good hand, but Marco slammed the sword into the skeleton's skull, killing what was left of the brainless dead.

Bashar banged his war hammer against another skeleton. While the blow took out the skeleton, Bashar continued to beat down on the bones with his hammer. Since Bashar was new to his war hammer, he was still in the honeymoon phase, and pulverizing enemy bones to dust gave him much delight.

Wes blasted a fireball at a skeleton, blasting the bonehead backward. The skull crashed into a pile of rocks and shattered like a broken bottle.

Sheri and I clinked our swords as a toast before we took on two separate opponents. To both our surprise, the skeleton warriors fought back. The swordsmanship of the skeletons was at a respectable level. I wondered why they hadn't pulled any fencing tricks against my friends. After a few close shaves, I remembered that zombie warriors always had a strong attraction toward the tools which they'd been given by their conjurers. Had these skeleton warriors been given hammers and crossbows, then they would have put up a solid fight against Huck and Bashar.

Sheri managed to dodge an attack right before she slashed her blade into her opponent's spine, crippling the skeleton to a random pile of bones.

I dodged two blows before Sid bit the ankle of my opponent. My friends screamed, fearing Sid would fall victim to the sword wielding skeleton. Before the bony warrior could make any offence against the basset hound, I flashed my sword against it's neck and beheaded the living dead. The skull dropped to the ground while Sid continued to gnaw on the anklebone, which still had meat in it.

Keifer flung his staff in between the right ribs of one of the last remaining opponents. As he pulled his staff downward, the weapon dislodged the ribs. Rattling bones fell to the ground. With a second thrust, Keifer pulled the same move on the left side of the skeleton's rib cage. Since the skeleton couldn't feel pain, it continued to advance toward Keifer though tripped over it's fallen ribs. Upon collapsing to the ground, the skeleton cracked it's remaining bones, rendering it a futile pile of calcium.

The final skeleton warrior collapsed to the ground without any warning signs. No one had flung their weapon at this bonehead. All the arrows in Julia quiver remained in their housing. I was surprised that she had her ring raised.

"Did you just blast that skeleton down?" Jason asked.

"Oh yeah," Julia said.

"That's amazing," Jason said as he high-fived her.

"I'll say," I said. "I thought you never used magic in combat."

"Surprise is a powerful weapon," Julia gloated.

Now I was sure that Jason and Julia were a couple, and that Jason had given Julia the confidence to finally use her magic in battle.

"All this adventure and getting away from my old man routine really makes me feel young," Keifer cackled. "I think I'm almost Post-17."

"Wait till you have a real fight grandpa," Bashar cracked.

Right after Bashar's word echoed in the clearing, a blue gas rose from the cracked bones of the skeletons. Within a second, we were feeling woozy. Sid and Huck collapsed to the ground. Before I realized what was going on, my friends and I fell next to them. Everything went blurry and I couldn't keep my eyes open.

Sometime later I awoke on a filthy rock-hard floor. Wes, Jason, and Marco were awake but Julia, Sheri, Huck, and Keifer were snoozing. Bashar was missing.

"Don," Wes said. "How are you feeling?"

"Groggy," I responded. "What's going on?"

"We've been trapped in the fighting pit," Jason answered. "The same force shield that covers the roof has also divided the pit into a hexagon and each of us are trapped in a different section."

My head still wasn't entirely clear, and I couldn't really understand what Jason was explaining.

"Watch this," Marco said as he picked up a rock.

Marco chucked the rock toward Jason. The flying rock hit an invisible point in the air and rebounded. A wall of turquoise light erupted between Jason and Marco, creating a shield between the centre of the pit and the perimeter of the pit. It looked like the same wizard magic, which had kept us from climbing into the hole, was keeping us divided. The weak skeleton warriors who'd been loaded with knockout gas must have been sent to drug us so we could be captured. I loathed how our rescue mission had been a failure so far. I feared that we'd become the new pit fighting slaves. And where the hell was Bashar? Had he been thrown into a fight with Trent? Where were the other pit fighters?

Sheri, Huck, Julia, and Keifer awoke in that order. Sid slept at Julia's feet. It seemed peculiar that we'd been spared the dog. What was even stranger was that each of us had retained our weapons. Genie rings hadn't been removed either. As always, Trent had fought with nothing but his fists, and maybe his opponents had also come in without weapons. Did our captors want us to participate in weaponry bouts?

"Prisoners," an unseen voice said. "Welcome to Paleeshii Pit. You can fight to your death, or you can fight to your freedom."

Each of us raised our weapons.

"Wait," Sheri said. "We might be forced into fighting civilians who've been kidnapped. It would be wrong for us to hurt them."

Eight doors opened, one for each of the eight sections of the hexagons. From each entrance, a human stepped out; one fighter for each of us. While some warriors were fit and armed with tough weaponry, others were exhausted, frail, and ill equipped.

My opponent was armed with a battle-axe. Though I felt battle equipped with my magic and sword, I remembered Sheri's words. The Paleeshii were manipulating us into killing innocent strangers. There had to be a better way of getting out of this trap than through bloodshed.

I stepped on my magic carpet and rose toward the opening in the ceiling. It looked like I could fly out of the pit, but I knew better. As I rose, I paid attention to the jewel on the wizard wand in the centre of the pit. Perhaps the jewel was a tool of wizard magic which had created the force shield. Wizard and genie magic didn't share any similarities, so I wasn't entirely sure how much merit my theories held. I'd never paid too much attention to wizardry studies while in school and was now cursing myself for having been a lackluster student.

My opponent lowered his axe and sat on the floor. We nodded at one another. I was unsure if he was trying to trick me into coming down so he could bury the axe in my neck, or if he understood that I was trying to avoid a forced conflict.

Keifer lowered his head and slumped to the ground. His ankles twisted outwards, and he limped around. His combat staff became a cane as he hobbled around before crashing to the rock ground.

"You wouldn't hurt a lame old man, would you?" Keifer whimpered.

"Come on, I can take on a way tougher opponent," Keifer's rival said. "Are you guys calling me a pussy or something?"

As Sheri laughed at Keifer and his opponent, Sheri's rival charged forward with his spear. Sheri gulped her chuckles and dashed out of the way of the incoming spearhead. Before her opponent could reposition his course, Sheri jumped on top of him. Dust splattered as the spear clunked to the ground. Sheri sat atop her rival with her sword positioned above his spine.

"No funny business or I'll carve out each of your vertebrates, piece by piece," Sheri growled.

It was funny that the woman who'd told us to be compassionate pacifists was using scare tactics to stay alive.

A crossbowman took aim at Marco. Marco's ring glowed and blasted a gale of wind. The crossbow bolt ejected, but then spun around once the wind charged toward Marco's target. The crossbowman flew off the ground, got speared by the bolt, crashed into the stone wall, and thumped to the ground. Blood dripped from the missile wound in the archer's collarbone. The man's head slumped to the side like a drunk.

"Oh shit," Marco gasped.

Wes dropped his jaw and let out a fireball. The burst of flame clashed with the otherwise transparent force shield. Right as the force shield came to light, the fireball rebounded off the turquoise light and then burst into a storm of sparks across the opposing force shield wall. Wes's malnourished and battered opponent jittered and huddled into a ball.

Jason ran around in circles. While Jason was a born runner, equally comfortable with sprinting and long distances, I'd never seen him move so quickly. When most people ran around in a confined space, they often went around in circles, but Jason kept bouncing between random points between the two opposing force shields. His opponent couldn't get a clear aim with his slingshot due to how fast Jason was moving. There didn't appear to be any rocks littered on the floor of Jason's quarters, so his opponent had only one piece of ammo.

Huck climbed up the wall and hung from a bar which a banner was draped from. His rival was short, and his sword swings didn't come close to slashing Huck.

"Quit being a coward," the swordsman barked at Huck. "Come down and fight me like a man you little shit."

"I'll make you a deal," Huck said. "If you can climb up here, I won't fire my crossbow or use my magic."

"You're a sneaky little cheat," the swordsman said.

Huck pulled a handstand on the pole and stuck his tongue out while his rival grumbled in rage. I couldn't help but laugh. It was comforting to know that humour could still be found in dire and powerless situations.

Marco was standing overtop his rival. The archer looked close to death though Marco was blasting healing rings across the wounded body. I was glad that Marco was doing all he could to preserve innocent life. A lot of people wouldn't have considered the archer innocent for having taken aim. In the past, Marco would have probably killed his rival without second-guessing. I wondered if Marco's time on the ocean had healed his soul and taught him that rage wasn't the way to win a war.

Julia and Sid were sitting on the floor. The dude who'd been assigned to clash with Julia was giving Sid a belly rub.

"I love dogs," the dude said. "I grew up on a farm that raised dogs and now I'm going to the Santalonian Veterinarian College."

"Right on man," Julia said.

"Dogs are truly a man's best friend."

"A woman's too."

"I hope I can have a dog as cool as this one as a graduation gift."

"Sid actually belongs to my boyfriend."

Wow, love was being announced right when we'd been assigned to kill strangers. Huck, Wes, and Keifer chuckled. I couldn't see Jason clearly but really wondered what his reaction was. I was sure Marco would have made a big deal about the love story, but he was too preoccupied with trying to save the archer's life.

Jason's rival tossed his slingshot at the invisible force shield. The wooden weapon turned to ash right as it bounced off the turquoise light. The rival grumbled, kicked the ground, and spat at his smoking weapon.

"Hey everyone," Jason said. "Instead of trying to tear one another's heads off, how about we work together to escape?"

"The force shields are being powered by the jewel on the wizard wand in the centre of the pit," I said.

"Jewels don't have a very high melting point," Wes said.

"Let's melt it," Huck said.

"Genie fire isn't hot enough to melt stones," I said.

"Dragon fire is," Wes said. "The only problem is that the force shields will rebound my flames."

"Genies, use your force magic to knock the jewel into Wes's direction," Jason said.

"Jason you're a genius," Julia said. "Come on guys, let's all do this."

Julia left Sid with the dog lover and then stepped toward her corner of the hexagon. She pointed her ring toward Wes's direction. I floated on my magic carpet to the corner, keeping a notable distance between myself and my rival. Huck did a backflip to the ground and then headed toward his corner. The swordsman tailed behind Huck until he raised his crossbow.

"You attack me, and you'll never be released," Huck said.

"Come on Marco," Julia said.

"Yeah man, I don't want to spend my entire retirement in this shitty excuse of a nursing home which doesn't even have a toilet," Keifer smirked.

"This guy is pretty hurt," Marco said as he looked up from the archer.

"If you haven't saved him yet, then you've done all you can do," Sheri said. "What's important is that you save your own life. You tried to save his, and you can still save a lot of other people."

Marco headed to his corner. He pulled several checks on the archer. The fallen crossbowman was no longer bleeding, but who knew how bad he'd hit his head against the stone wall.

"On the count of three, I want all of you to fire force blasts in my direction," Wes said.

On Wes's guidance, we four genies fired force blasts. The entire pit lit up with turquoise light. The wizard staff jolted slightly toward Wes while each of us genies fell onto our backs from force blasts which rebounded from the force shields.

Wes unleashed a long stream of flames from his ferocious mouth. Everyone cheered him on while I stumbled to my feet. I'd been knocked off my magic carpet and hoped that my opponent wouldn't use my sudden misplacement as an opportunity to slaughter me. I unsheathed my sword but realized that my rival had kept his distance and maintained a lowered weapon. He probably didn't want to fight any more than I did. Huck and Julia were back on their feet, while Marco was playing nurse to the archer. No one needed to get hurt.

The jewel melted to a blackened puddle after half a minute of incineration. The pit briefly flashed turquoise light before the colour disappeared to nothingness.

Sid dashed toward Jason without bumping into any boundaries, confirming that the force shields had been destroyed. While all of us were happy to have destroyed the force shields, we'd only broken out of our cells. We still had to escape prison, find Trent, Bashar, and free the other prisoners.

A cluster of ogres and cyclops stood in the spectators' seats. Even though the light was dim, I was pretty sure I recognized some of these folks from Trent's fight. While there were some humans among the crowd of cyclops and ogres, there were even more corpses.

"Victory," a voice which belonged to Bashar roared into a megaphone.

Trent stood at Bashar's side. Waves of relief flooded many souls.

"Excellent," Trent said. "You guys made the buffoons at the gulag look undefeatable compared to these Paleeshii pussies."

"Where the hell did all of you guys come from?" I asked.

"These two guys helped break us out of prison," a random ogre said.

"Oh man do I have a really boss story to tell you," Bashar said. "So, I woke up inside a separate dungeon than the rest of you, an ogre and cyclops only dungeon cuz it was meant for big brutes. I must have woken up a lot earlier that you guys did because the knockout gas wouldn't have much of an effect on a fat ass like me.

"Anyway, I woke up and my hammer was lying next to me. Even crazier, Trent was there too. I wasn't sure if I'd died or not, but after Trent told me what the deal was, I clued in and realized I had to do everything and anything in my power to get the fuck out of the dungeon.

"Those guards were really stupid to not confiscate my hammer from me. I ended up bashing away at the door of my cell until three prison guards were alerted. Right when the three of them came in, each with a sword and ready to go slice and dice on my ass, Trent picked me up. This totally struck me as out of the blue, but I was happy to oblige. Anyway, Trent tossed me at one of the guards. I just barely missed getting sliced by his sword, but luckily I landed flat on a guard's skull. I crushed the son of a bitch like a little bug.

"Right before the second guard could take my head off with his sword, I swung my hammer and crunched his skull to a salad of spilled brains and cranked bones.

"Trent picked up the third guard and tossed him onto one of the swords, which had the tip of its blade sticking up at a weird angle. Anyway, the guard died which is all that's important.

"Trent and I used the guards' keys to get out of the room we were in. Since pit fighters were always blindfolded when they were taken to the ring, Trent wasn't entirely sure of where we were going. We ended up coming across three wizards.

"I'd never seen Trent fight like such a mad man before. He was so vicious against the wizards. I didn't want to get close to him in fear of accidentally getting slaughtered.

"The first wizard swung his staff at Trent. Right as the emerald at the top of the staff lit up, Trent grabbed the wand and snapped it in half. The wizard was powerless without the staff so tried to run away. Trent grabbed his neck like a crab squeezing prey and crushed the wizard's neck. Right after every disc went snap, Trent tossed the paralyzed body aside, leaving the wizard to die in crippled hopeless agony.

"The second wizard froze in fear. Trent dismembered the guy by tossing his staff to the side and then twisting his arms behind his back until they popped out of their sockets. The wizard collapsed to the ground along with his arm's right as a mad amount of blood started gushing. I'm not sure if the wizard died from blood loss, drowning in his gore, or shock.

"The third wizard actually shot a few rays at Trent. Trent managed to dodge each blast, and every time he jumped away from a bolt from the staff, Trent got one step closer to the wizard. Once in arm's reach, Trent punched the wizard, knocking him to the ground. When the wizard tried to climb to his feet, Trent booted him in the face. I thought Trent was only going to knock out teeth or give the wizard a bloody lip, but Trent ended up kicking the wizard's head off. I'd never seen such a crazy fight before.

"Anyway, we then went about releasing prisoners from cells. We ran around back and forth through many corridors until we were absolutely sure that everyone was out of their cell. A few guards tried to fight back against us, but we quickly overpowered them, and they're all nothing but a bunch of lifeless losers right now.

"We couldn't leave this hell hole without you guys. We came into the arena right when you guys were pulling off your acts of peace. I must say, I really admire what you did. I tell you, I probably would have freaked out and fought with my fists. It really sucks that Trent was forced to fight people who he had no problems with, but back to the story.

"Since you guys were trapped behind the force shield, you couldn't see us. There was one wizard and a bunch of other Paleeshii gangsters watching the fight. The wizard tried to fight us and so did some of the gangster spectators, but we killed them all. We prisoners outnumbered them at least five to one. I totally love how the prisoners overpowered their captors; we truly are the best warriors in Sionia."

"Thank you blabber mouth Bashar, are you going to gab until we've aged beyond Post-17?" Julia smirked.

"Blabber mouth, how about bladder mouth," Keifer chuckled. "He just bored the piss out of us with his monologue."

"He told the truth pretty well, but I agree, let's get the hell out of here," Trent said.

We found an exit passage and left the pit. Along the way, a few guards' huts were raided for food, water, and any other supplies which would be of value for camping. In addition to the rescue party, forty-two prisoners walked free from the hell hole.

Though many prominent members of the Paleeshii had been killed during the prison break, the gang was still alive. A large wave of escaped prisoners would incite a major story in the media. Bashar would be writing about the epic escape for ages. He guaranteed that this tale would be the biggest story for the next few years. I would have loved to have seen Trent's revenge and the prison riot, but I would have to take Bashar's word as a storyteller. Although Bashar loved to yak, he allegedly never bullshitted due to journalistic integrity.

On our way out, Marco and I flew our magic carpets. Most others were marching along the jungle road while the elephants carried group gear and folks who were taking a break from trekking.

"I kind of screwed up pretty bad," Marco said.

"What do you mean?" I asked.

"I really lost control when dealing with my attacker back in the pit."

"Dude, that wasn't your fault."

"I could have killed him with my magic."

"But you didn't; you ran forward and saved him with your healing powers. You did a good thing man. Sure, he's riding on an elephant now, but by tomorrow I'll bet he'll be walking, and he probably doesn't hold anything against you. You had a crossbow pointed at you after all."

"I should have used telekinesis to steal his weapon."

"We all act impulsive when faced with death. As a warrior you know that better than most of those pit fighters."

"But you guys were all peaceful. I wasn't, despite Sheri's warning."

"Forgive yourself man, that guy sure has."

"I don't ever want to become a monster again."

As I thought about what Marco had said, I wondered if it had been a mistake to bring him along. Since I felt the need to save Marco from his rage, perhaps I needed to keep him away from volatile situations from now on.

Trent never spoke of what happened in the pits. When questioned, he said he was happy to be away and wanted to focus his thoughts on nature, the place which he was most happy in.

BOOK X:

SWAMP BLOOD

      While the Paleeshii were far from destroyed, the stories from the escaped prisoners motivated the Sionian government to send the army into Xatica. Bashar liked to claim that his news coverage created a wake-up call to the lawlessness of Xatica. The army invaded and cracked down on the kidnappers, the slave trade, and other criminal factions, but peace wasn't exactly brought in by the government.

      I'd given up years ago on the idea of governments bringing peace to the land. I'd also completely given up on the idea of people ever living together with civility. It was easy to live harmoniously among a small community, but on the whole, people were volatile, selfish, competitive, and paranoid, stupid too. While a person was often smart, other people brought out the idiocy in an individual. It seemed ludicrous that an army would bring peace to the land. The armed forces could kill off a load of gangsters, but that always led to new terror units being formed. I'd always believed that the government caused more crimes than criminals. The only real difference between the crimes of the government and the criminals was that the courthouses tolerated the crimes of the government.

      Jason took a hiatus from the Vindadong since he and Julia were going steady. They moved to the hills, not too far from where Trent was living. Julia got a job as a blacksmith while Jason became a mountaineering guide. Sid loved accompanying Jason on hikes, and the tourists spoiled her with treats.

Huck and I were happy to be back at sea, but Sheri was growing sick of the nomadic lifestyle. After two seasons of groaning, she asked Keifer for a vacation. At that point Keifer was commanding a very confident crew, so he told Sheri to take off as much time as she needed. Though I was quite content with the sailor's life, I wanted to go travelling with Sheri.

"It's not that I don't want you Don, and it's not that I hate the ocean or the sailor life, but I really need some time to reflect on what my life has become and where I want to head in the future," she said. "I love you lots, and we're not going to break up."

I accepted Sheri's decision to take leave without me. She was a heartfelt free spirit who needed to do something different to stay true to herself. Keifer and most of the crewmembers could understand where she was coming from, while Huck had a bit of difficulty figuring out why she wanted to leave the adventure life for the city.

"Taking a vacation will make returning to the ocean so much more fun," Sheri said. "You loved the jungle eh."

"Oh yeah," Huck said.

"I love the jungle and the ocean too, so I want both of them in my life. Two seasons in Stodaneatoo will mean I won't grow bored of the city or the jungle, but when I leave I'll have had a healthy dose of what the ocean can't offer."

"With my girlfriend gone I'll be able to train you with more magic," I told Huck.

"Right on," Huck said.

Five days before we were set to pick Sheri up at an east coast port town called Laleaka, Keifer collapsed. He'd been standing at the bow of the boat enjoying the splashes of waves, something which had always been a daily habit. As he fell into the ocean, some of the sailors thought that he wanted to cool down and have a swim. When we didn't see Keifer moving, we got worried. Two crewmembers dove overboard to recover his body.

Keifer's last feeling was splashing against the waves. I thought it was beautiful that a diehard sailor's final sensation was the ocean. Though we were all saddened by his death, we were glad that he died as a happy man without any suffering.

The non-Post-17s were dwindling. Since the Post-17 generation weren't going to face the medical hardships of old folks, medicine men were focusing their efforts on cures for non-age-related diseases. No one had died of a heart attack in the Laleaka area in five years, and it took the coroner awhile to figure out what had gone wrong with Keifer's body. Watching an old man die made me wonder if Keifer would end up being my last friend who wasn't a Post-17.

Sheri was greatly disheartened when she returned to a dead captain. At first, she was angry about her trip, but Huck reminded her that no one had foreseen Keifer's demise.

"Why let his death ruin your beautiful past," Huck said.

"I loved Keifer, and I wish that the last time I saw him was a bit happier for both of us," Sheri said.

"He understood why you needed leave," I said. "He was happy for you."

"Do you still love the ocean?" Huck asked.

"Very much," Sheri answered. "I love the ocean, the city, and the jungle. I love life."

"You also loved Keifer, so let's go sailing."

Sheri, Huck, and I did as Huck suggested.

A few weeks later, the Vindadong was sold off and the crew dispersed. Sailing the boat didn't feel right without Keifer. Huck started school in Laleaka while I got a job working as a longshore man. Sheri had hoped to join the local vigilums, but all positions were filled, so she got a job as a combat trainer for the local fighting club.

I was happy that Sheri hadn't received the vigilum job. She knew this, even though I didn't express it. Moreover, I was happy as to why she wasn't hired as a vigilum. Crime was at an all-time low. There were no rivalries going on between different territories. Military personnel were without battle, so they committed to disaster relief and farming. Prisons were becoming vacant. No one was paying attention to the war goddess Qiami. Bashar liked to boast about how his articles on the Paleeshii had led toward the crackdown on the mob and the peace times which had followed.

The gap between the rich and the poor had drastically shrunk. The lower class was steadily decreasing. No one complained about tax dollars being spent on public services. Hermateio, the god of arts, had become the most popular deity of the zeitgeist renaissance.

Things had never been better for Sionia. I liked to think that this utopia came from people living together peacefully as opposed to stepping on one another's toes in that strange, selfish, quarrelsome social pyramid known as society.

The baffling thing about peace times was how mundane things got. Maybe I was too used to chaos. I'd spent my entire life living on the edge. Death had never been far out of reach. I'd regularly gone out of my way to put my life in danger, and I liked doing so. I loved crushing evil and triumphing over scumbags.

I wasn't the only one who felt out of place during peace times. Sheri had shaved her head and started to groan about work. She moaned that she didn't think her purpose in life was to explain things to others and that she needed to be challenged more. Many told her that there was much honour in passing on her combat knowledge. Sheri retorted that she'd never liked school and that combat knowledge wasn't going to go far if she or others weren't hired as vigilums. Despite groaning about work, Sheri was popular with her students.

Huck was more lost than Sheri and I. I could understand where his discontent came from. So much of his life had been spent at sea or living in a criminal community. The transition to civilization was difficult, and there were so many things which he didn't understand about society. I regularly heard him groan about how the world didn't make sense.

"Why are people wasting money on all this crap they don't need? Shouldn't they at least try to share with people who have less dough than them?

"Back on Bounty Hunter Island, all the kids were really friendly which is saying something when you consider that they were all raised as criminals. Around here I say "hi" to someone and they look away, or they don't want to have a conversation. How can we have a society if no one wants to establish a friendly community?

"Too many people are sitting around inside. Why don't they go out on an adventure or a vacation and take advantage of all the beauty around here?

"People around here are so fucking arrogant. I'm sick of listening to everyone boast about how cool they are only to have others try to one-up them.

"People were looking at me like I was a weird crook today. Why can't I wander around town and do my own thing? Who is anyone to judge me if I'm not doing any harm? Are these nosy judgmental pricks angry with themselves, bored to death, jealous of me for doing my thing, or are they ingrained with prejudice?"

"Huck honey, you have very valid complaints, and even if we have answers to those questions, a lot of people don't bother to make the solutions happen," was a typical answer from Sheri.

"You should really get together and complain about that stuff with Trent," I once said.

"Sounds like Trent is really smart," Huck said. "He lives the life he wants, only goes to the city when he has to, and gets away from society before it makes him sick."

"Along with people being dicks, people are also self-destructive," I said. "It's why we die. Problems are regularly passed down from one generation to the next."

"That's a bit pessimistic Don," Sheri said. "A lot of things have improved in the last couple of years."

"We might be in the golden age, but we will never get to utopia," I said.

"If people felt better about themselves, thought more about others, and let go of discrimination and ego, life might be a lot happier," Sheri shared. "You have to model what you expect of others."

"Life is boring around here," Huck said. "Boringness is a quiet crime. We don't need goons, but people still have a lot of social weaknesses which they need to improve."

One day when I was coming home from work, I decided to take the long way by walking down the forest path.

"Stop that thief. Don't let him get away."

This sudden cry from a stranger stopped me in my tracks. I turned toward the voice of distress. Three teenagers were chasing after this one dude. All of them were below the Post-17 age. The dude being pursued was carrying a flag. The old sheet didn't look like much but who knew what was beneath it. Petty theft was rare nowadays, but maybe this guy thought that it would be easy to steal during peace times since societal calmness had led toward people lowering their guard.

Though I'd stopped carrying my sword, I would have been naked without my ring. Without question I fired a stun ray at the thief with the flag. The ray bounced the thief backward. As he crashed onto his back, muck kicked up everywhere while the flag flapped upward like a rising kite. There didn't appear to be anything wrapped around the flag.

"What the hell?" one of the pursuers yelled. "What the shit did you just to do him?"

I wasn't sure if the chasers were shocked by my powers or surprised that I'd zapped the thief.

"Oh man, he's in trouble," another one of the pursuers screamed.

The third pursuer bent down next to the fallen flagbearer. She was a genie and used her ring magic to heal the guy who I'd floored.

"What gives?" I asked. "I thought this guy was a thief."

"Stupid. We were playing capture the flag," the genie girl growled.

I'd never regretted any action of mine so much.

"Let me help heal him," I said. "I'm a supreme class genie."

"Fuck off already," the girl growled. "You've done enough damage, and I'm a good healer."

The girl was right about both comments. When the runner with the flag came back to his senses, I offered an apology and compensation.

"You want to do me a favour?" the flag runner said, "go fuck a cow."

I turned my back on the kids without looking back. For the first time in my life, I felt like an abusive adult. No longer did I feel like the hero of Post-17 who would forever be a youthful warrior who helped others live to eternity by slaying all evil. I had attacked kids who were having fun. I wondered why violence was always my first response to problems.

"Why can't I get with the times and enjoy serenity?" I asked Sheri after I'd told her the horror story. "I helped create peace times."

"Sweetheart, you grew up in a time when the norm was to solve all problems with rage," Sheri said. "Your young days weren't too different from Huck's upbringing."

"So are rough young years the reason why Huck and I can't adapt to society?"

"Huck's a very sweet kid, and he expects civilians be more adventuresome and friendly; his expectations are too high."

"Maybe my expectations of people are too low. I've always assumed that danger lurked around the corner. Maybe I'm a distrusting misanthrope."

"If you're a misanthrope then why did you fight for improvement for so many years?"

"It didn't seem right that so many people lived under so many forms of oppression."

"See love, you're a good person, an amazing person. You're nosy, paranoid, and occasionally ignorant but still a noble heart."

"How do I redeem myself after nearly killing an innocent person?"

"Have more faith in the good in others."

For the next few weeks, I felt shitty about having blasted that capture the flag kid. At the same time, I kept telling myself that others were good. Most people who committed crimes did so out of desperation. Now that the economy was on the rise, poverty wasn't leading to crime. I didn't need to worry about the actions of others. I could smile instead of scowl at strangers. If the vigilums were bored due to a lack of crime, then a vigilante should be too.

One afternoon I was wandering around the park after work. I heard screaming and I wasn't sure if someone was hurt or whether people were having fun. I told myself that it was probably some kids horsing around, and that if anyone was hurt, it was through accident rather than violence.

Since I had the power to heal victims of accidents, I decided to follow the screaming. Two guys were wrestling very viciously. Part of my mind told me that the dudes were play-fighting while my cantankerous side growled at me to take action.

After a bit of internal debate, I turned aside. As I was walking away, a flash of light caught the corner of my eye. One of the wrestlers held a dagger above his rival. A fireball torpedoed from my ring right before the blade could slice any flesh. The flame ball smashed into the knife-wielder, knocked him back, singed his clothes, and blackened his face.

"Thank you, I owe you my life," the victim gasped.

The knife-wielder lay in shock as I seized the fallen dagger.

"Hold it right there, this is vigilum business," the approaching vigilum squad called from behind me.

I loathed how the vigilums had showed up two seconds too late, and that I hadn't noticed them until the fight was over. This was the only time I'd pulled off an act of street justice during peace times, and now I was at risk of arrest since vigilantism had once again been outlawed.

"Hey, it's Don, Sheri's boyfriend," one of the vigilums said.

"The famously nosy vigilante," a second vigilum said. "I bet he'll be really happy about getting arrested for interfering with our mission."

"I stumbled upon the crime by chance," I said. "I got here before you did and if I hadn't acted this man would be dead."

"Yeah, ease off of him would you," the guy I'd rescued said.

"Don, people who take the law into their own hands create more street violence," a vigilum said.

"Vigilantes clean up what you people can't," I protested. "I undermine the power of you vigilums."

"Quit the arrogance."

"No, you quit the ignorance."

Before any of the vigilums could raise arms against me, I stepped onto my magic carpet and took off to the ocean while the vigilums remained grounded.

I flew around for twenty minutes before heading back to the cabin I lived in with Sheri and Huck. Huck wasn't home, but I called Sheri into our room.

"You know I've been thinking," I said, "how about we go to Stodaneatoo?"

While wandering about on my magic carpet, I had thought of a tactic to duck out of getting arrested. A warrant would need to be drawn up for my arrest, but if luck stayed on my side, I could get out of the house before the vigilums came knocking.

"Sounds good, when do you want to go?" Sheri asked.

"First thing tomorrow morning."

"Love, this is really random."

"If we leave early in the morning, spent all day travelling north-west, then we'll be able to see Wes's presentation at the University of Stodaneatoo."

On the Naflit River in southern Sionia, Wes had designed the largest dam in history and was getting an award for it. Since water had to be halted, the water goddess Zadeezey had demanded much worship during construction. The land was swampy, but when it dried, many caves had been revealed. Legends claimed that the caves held many secrets.

"Huck is also on a break from school," I said, "and you deserve a vacation before going to boot camp."

Sheri had been accepted into a new vigilum program, which allegedly had groundbreaking teachings. It looked like a job had come up for her. Although I was irritated about Sheri joining an organization which I'd had endless problems with, now wasn't the time to bitch and moan about politics even if Sheri's colleagues wanted my head on a stick.

"We could also see the whole gang too," Sheri said. "Trent, Bashar, Jason, and your sister who you don't see enough of."

"You only see your family more often because you have a much larger one."

"Since Julia is your last of kin, you really need to spend more time with her."

"If I saw Julia more often, then we'd be squabbling like little brats. You hang out with her, while I chill with Marco cuz he's also going to be at the presentation."

"Ha, prioritizing your boy over your sister makes you a real man."

"Whatever Sheri. Are you coming or not?"

"I am, but why did you wait till the last minute to spring this idea?"

"Life here is boring and we really need to see our friends more often. Wes deserves our admiration."

"Life isn't that bad here. It's good we're going to see old friends, but you could be more social here."

The front door opened, and Huck stepped inside.

"Hey Huck, want to go to Stodaneatoo for Wes's award ceremony?" Sheri asked.

"That's a wicked idea," Huck said.

Huck headed out the backdoor to the balcony. Before turning his back on Sheri and I, he gazed at me with much darkness and nodded. I waited until Sheri had gone to the kitchen before I retreated out back.

"What's the deal?" I asked Huck.

"The vigilums were down the street looking for you."

"Where?"

"Don't worry dude, they're gone now. They stopped me and I said you'd packed your bags and fled to the highlands."

"Thank you so much Huck, I owe you."

"Don, I'd be fucked without you, and I think getting mad at you for citizens justice is bullshit. If anything, the mayor should put a medal on you."

"Don't tell Sheri about this, not yet at least."

"I don't want to listen to complaining on a trip to Stodaneatoo. Rescuing that guy was a blessing in disguise."

We got up as the light was rising the next morning. I was really excited about getting away from town to have fun. Working six days a week didn't give me many opportunities to go off and get wild.

Huck flew on his magic carpet with the majority of our gear while Sheri rode with me on mine. The journey to Stodaneatoo took all day, and by the time we'd arrived in the city, we decided to get a room and crash for the night. We didn't bother eating dinner, but the next day we had a massive breakfast.

"Since Jason and Julia live outside of town, we should find Bashar first," I said at breakfast.

Huck and Sheri agreed. After our large meal, we headed over to his place.

"Bashar ain't home," one of his neighbours said.

"When will he be back?" Huck asked.

"Probably not for at least a week," the neighbour responded. "He's in the hospital with thoolithay."

"Oh shit," Sheri exclaimed.

"He's had it for two weeks but is making a lot of progress and should be fine," the neighbour said. "Don't worry, we have very good medicine men around here. I'll give you the address of hospital where he's staying at."

A few years ago, anyone who got thoolithay would have died from vomiting, fever, or dysentery. Due to recent advancements in medical technology, it was becoming common to survive thoolithay. For many generations, thoolithay had been extremely lethal because magic couldn't heal it, but science had recently found a way around this malady. I liked to think that public healthcare had led to cures for pathologies which had been fatal during the times of privatized healthcare.

"What the shit?" Bashar said when Huck, Sheri, and I walked into the room. "I thought you guys had forgotten about me."

Ogres were chubby by nature, but Bashar looked thinner than most humans. If seeing him two-thirds skinnier wasn't perplexing enough, his skin had shaded from lime green to blueberry. He wasn't sweating, which showed that he was getting healthier. A large vat of iced tea was stationed next to his bed. A steady breeze was blowing through the window that his bed was next to. There were many flowers decorating the room, so it looked like he was getting top notch care.

"Come on, give Big Bashar a hug," he said. "I'm not contagious, and I'm too emaciated to crush you with my famous fat."

"I've been so worried about you all day," Sheri said as she embraced Bashar.

"Nonsense, no one needs to worry about Big Bashar," he said. "I'm recovering. Hanging out in the hospital is actually pretty fun. This place has a good library; this is the cleanest room I've ever been in; I get to eat whatever I want as much as I want; all the nurses here are totally smoking hot, and all this new medicine the doctors are giving me is loaded with alcohol, so I spend most of the day drunk."

"We found out about your condition this morning," I said.

"Damn Trent," Bashar snorted. "He was supposed to write everyone; damn jungle beast doesn't understand the postal system."

"We came here to see Wes's award ceremony," Huck said.

Huck had promised to stay shut about my arrest warrant. Escaping Laleaka undetected had been a miracle. I still had a hard time believing that the vigilums had fallen for Huck's lie. I'd always assumed that most vigilums were pretty dumb, but maybe they were completely gullible as well.

"Have a beer in my name with him, each of you do that," Bashar said. "As soon as I get out of here, I'll definitely have a few drinks with that genius."

I found Bashar's optimism very inspiring. I'd never been seriously sick, but I always figured that if I ever had to go to hospital, I'd be moaning and suicidal. Bashar had found all the perks in the medical environment, and it looked like he was going to ride them out for as long as he could. Perhaps I needed to take more advantage of the benefits of living in Laleaka. It seemed kind of messed up that my friend enjoyed the hospital more than I enjoyed my posh town on the coast.

After our visit with Bashar, we headed up to the hills to visit Jason and Julia. They'd recently moved into a cabin on a mountaintop lake. On the flight up the mountain, Huck kept crowing about how beautiful this place was. Although

I'd flown through this area multiple times, its beauty never ceased to amaze me.

Julia and Jason greeted Sheri, Huck, and I with much love though Sid made the most noise and got the most affection out of anyone. Between seeing old friends, my last remaining kin, a dog that was howling in happiness, and a mountaintop cabin that overlooked a panoramic jungle valley, I felt like I'd walked into paradise. Julia and Jason had done a good job with their garden, and I couldn't wait to go for a swim in the lake.

"You guys are living in paradise," Huck said.

"If you take me on magic carpet ride, I'll show you an even more amazing view," Jason said.

"Deal," Huck said.

"Don, why don't you go along with them," Sheri said, "that way Julia and I can have some lady time."

"Sheri will tell me secrets I already know, and I'll gossip about Jason too," Julia smirked.

I went along with Huck and Jason while Julia and Sheri lounged around the lake with a pot of tea. Jason acted as a tour guide as Huck and I piloted our magic carpets overtop mountains, through low hanging clouds, and above jungle canopies. Toucans and parrots flew passed us. Huck kept complimenting the scenery. I couldn't agree with him more. Returning to the jungle mountains made me want to quit my job and live off the land as a mountain man.

When we returned to the cabin, Jason and Huck jumped into the lake. I decided to get changed before taking a dip. My gear was in the spare bedroom, and I could hear Sheri and Julia chatting on the balcony.

"What are you going to do?" Julia said in the background.

"I'm really not sure," Sheri responded.

"Why don't you move?"

"That would probably make Don happy. He's so bored with the town and there is no reward to his job. He gets little time off work and when he does have free time, he's usually too tired to even want to go out to sea."

Sheri definitely understood my woes, one of the many reasons why I loved her.

"You guys should move out here," Julia said.

"A change of scenery would be good for Don, as would permanent escape from his job."

"I bet Huck would really like it here too."

"He only has one more semester of school left."

"Then come on out here. You've got family, Don has lots of friends, living inland would be a big new step for Huck."

"There's just one complication though."

"What's that?"

"I've been offered a vigilum job."

"Take the job and then ask for a transfer out here."

"If I ask for a transfer, I'll be put back on a wait list. I don't want to spend my entire life waiting. Getting put on one more wait list will throw all my patience to waste."

"Life is how you waste time before death."

"I'd be doing something so much more important and meaningful by working as a vigilum. I hate the idea that the cadets I train will become vigilums while I wait and wait for nothing."

"Does Don understand this?"

"Don will never understand my ambitions to be a vigilum. I love him, but he is so obtuse and dogmatic. He loves being a vigilante, so I don't get why he won't accept money for his crime fighting. It's not like I'm going to work as a bounty hunter."

I hated to eavesdrop, but Sheri's words were totally my business. I was bored of my job, and I really wanted to move away from Laleaka. I wanted Sheri to be happy, but I really didn't want to stay around in Laleaka just so she could be happy with her job. I never wanted her to be a vigilum, but if she did take the path of darkness, I'd rather we were living in a place which we would both be happy in.

"Has Don had more trouble with the law?" Julia asked.

I held my breath, waiting for Sheri to mention that she knew about my arrest warrant but hadn't bothered to confront me.

"He's been behaving himself really well," Sheri chuckled. "There is so little crime that he can't get in trouble, which is why he's so bored."

I let out a sigh of relief, which probably gave away that I was spying on the conversation. Huck had kept shut, and I was out of the Laleaka jurisdiction, so I didn't have anything to worry about. I could now go for a swim and forget about all my worries.

Trent and his fiancée Larissa came by shortly before dinner. Jason barbecued trout from the lake while Julia made a fruit salad and a potato salad, only using ingredients from her garden. It was the best meal any of us had enjoyed in a long time.

"I'm really touched that you've all come out to meet us," Larissa said. "This might as well be an early wedding present."

"We should stay till the wedding," Huck said.

"I'm up for that," I said after taking a sip from my goblet of wine.

"What about work though?" Sheri asked.

"I'm totally up for quitting," I answered.

"Don't let us get you in trouble," Trent said.

"I really want some change," I said, "being in the mountains is good for me."

"I know you guys love the ocean, but in my opinion, you can't do better than the jungle mountains," Trent said.

"I'd say the mountains are equal to living on an awesome beach," Jason said.

"Living in a town has been a disappointment," Huck said. "Folks aren't as friendly as I thought they'd be, and people are more focused on buying ostentatious crap than they are in getting out and going on an adventure."

"You'd love it up here," Larissa said. "When you live with few possessions, you become so much more focused on your mind, your environment, and your relationships."

"Wow that's really beautiful and deep," Huck said. "Every moment I'm getting more and more inspired to move out here."

"You're always welcome buddy," Larissa said. "Sometimes life is a bit harder out here, but I'm way happier up in the mountains than I was in Stodaneatoo."

I could totally see why Trent and Larissa had fallen in love, and I wished that Sheri and I could go back to having a similar life.

My love for the mountains had never been stronger, and Huck was about to be reborn now that he was nearly seventeen. The only problem was trying to convince Sheri to leave Laleaka. It was wrong of me to stay in a town I didn't like, and at a job that took the life out of me. It also didn't seem right for Sheri to turn away from the job which she considered her calling, but it would also be improper if Sheri and I weren't together.

We went to the University of Stodaneatoo the next day to witness Wes's award ceremony. A large banquet had been laid out. Many notable academics and scientists were present. Wes was the only recipient of an engineering award. Other prizes were given for physics, chemistry, mathematics, architecture, forestry, zoology, botany, and agriculture.

Wes's friends were supposed to wait until he'd been handed his trophy, but we couldn't help but clap and whistle when he took the stage and headed toward the master of ceremony. Wes was dressed in a long velvet robe, the first clothing article I'd ever seen him in apart from old cut-off jeans. He bowed with his award after shaking hands with the master of ceremony. More whistling, clapping, and words of congratulations followed.

After several more winners received their awards, the banquet began.

"I'd like to sit with you guys," Wes said to his friends.

"Aren't you supposed to eat with the other award winners?" Marco asked.

"You guys came all this way to my ceremony, which means so much to me," Wes said. "It would be wrong if I didn't spend time with the people who are making me feel proud."

"You're making all of us proud to be friends with you," Sheri said.

The winners of the physics prize and the agricultural award followed Wes's example and ate with those who'd shown up to honour them.

"Marco, you've got to win a big award so we can have another party like this," Huck said.

"Next season I'm starting a project on the diets of river sharks," Marco said. "You guys should come on a whitewater odyssey if you want a real adventure."

Wes looked happy and he was dressed at his best, but he didn't spend any time boasting. He didn't even talk about the Naflit Dam throughout the meal but asked the rest of us about our lives. Wes was sorry that Bashar couldn't attend but also very interested in Larissa and Trent's wedding.

I had little to say. Life in Laleaka was too boring to talk about unless I wanted to complain. The biggest thing that had happened to me was nearly getting arrested and I didn't want anyone else to know about that yet, not even Marco. Jason and Julia had stories to tell about hiking. Sheri was excited about becoming a vigilum, and Huck was keen on finishing school. Wes said he'd like to attend Huck's graduation.

Right when I was about to head out the door of the banquet hall, Wes stopped me and handed me a slim book.

"I found this right when I was leaving the dam," Wes said. "No one came forward to claim it, but it looks like it's filled with genie content, so I bet you'll like it."

"Thanks Wes, I'll take a look through it," I said.

Sheri and I headed back to our room at a nearby inn. The plan was to head down to the tavern for a few drinks afterwards. I decided to kill time by skimming through the notebook which Wes had given me. The hotel room balcony looked out over a garden, so that seemed like a good place to do some quick reading.

After a few moments of fingering through the book, my eyeballs dropped into my stomach. The damming of the Naflit River had unearthed access to Yefhati Cave: a massive cavern with many entrances, labyrinth twists, and dark secrets. Genie mythology spoke of death cults who'd used Yefhati Cave as a spot for invoking the darkest of genie apocalypses. Fables dating to before written history told of massive blood drinking monsters, vicious dragons of unusual intelligence, and genies who could fly without magic carpets and summon mysterious and dangerous powers. The weather goddess Shilotey had created a massive hurricane to flood Yefhati Caves and kill all the genies who were involved in the death cult.

I read a few more pages from the notebook. There were many drawings of the river and the dam, but after a little snooping around I came across pictures and profiles of various genies who I assumed were part of a new terrorism group. None of the names or portraits meant anything to me until I came across one that looked strangely familiar. Sionia had plenty of big white dudes with messy dark hair and facials scars, but the piercing blackness in one set of eyes alarmed me.

Holy shit, I was looking at a picture of Krull, even his name was below the portrait. Since Bounty Hunter Island I'd been unsure if he was alive or not. After flipping pages, I found a picture of Hunter. As I flipped back and forth between Krull and Hunter's pictures, I wondered if it was my path in life to continuously battle Krull.

I had to get to Naflit River and see if Yefhati Cave was accessible. I felt like the entire nation was under attack by an insidious apocalypse.

Sheri knocked on the door of the balcony.

"Sheri, can you get everyone in here real quick, I have an important announcement to make," I said.

"What gives?"

"Just get everyone in here right now."

Sheri left the room and returned with Jason, Sid, Marco, Julia, Huck, and Wes. Larissa and Trent weren't present since they'd gone down the road to sell foraged pineapples to the market.

"You're pulling us away from drinks at the pub," Julia said. "This fuss you're making better be something meaningful."

"Wes, this book you gave to me," I said as I waved about the book, "has information about the doom cults at Yefhati Cave."

"What's the big deal?" Sheri asked.

"Wes, that dam you built, it dried up a lot of land eh?" I asked.

"That's right," he said.

"It has also unearthed a passage to Yefhati Cave," I said, "a place where evil genies practiced acts of annihilation many years ago. From what I gathered from this journal, killer genies have gone back to Yefhati Cave to raise damnation once again."

"What makes you so sure of this?" Jason wondered.

"Every genie knows about Yefhati Caves and the dangerous spells that went on there," Huck said. "The genies conjured blood sucking monsters, legions of killer dragons, and some nasty diseases. If it weren't for the caves being flooded by Shilotey, we'd all be dead."

"Thank you, Huck," I said. "Also, the logbook has profiles of known criminal genies including Krull and Hunter."

"I thought those sons of bitches were dead," Jason said.

"The Yefhati Cave may have some unknown magic which has given rise to their return," Marco said.

"A group of genies financed the dam construction on Naflit River," Wes said, "though I never saw Krull anywhere."

"What should we do?" Huck asked.

"Tomorrow we should fly south to Naflit River to investigate the caves," I said. "If there's nothing there, we're fine."

"That's a pretty long journey to go looking for nothing," Sheri said.

"I have every reason to believe that evil is bubbling down there," I said. "If we don't act now, the most vicious evil in history will slaughter, if not destroy the entire country."

"Don, I know you won't like this idea, but shouldn't we get the army involved?" Julia suggested.

"It'll take them a long time to get assembled," Marco said, "plus that little notebook won't provide enough evidence to warrant a major investigation."

"I'll contact the vigilums down by Naflit Bayou," Sheri said.

"There will be no vigilums," I affirmed.

"Quit with the anarchist outlaw crap," Sheri scoffed.

"I will go to jail if the vigilums come around," I confessed.

Julia laughed. Marco shook his head with a smile. Jason and Wes exchanged suspicious glances. Sheri's teeth gritted. Huck made eye contact with me, and I nodded.

"A warrant has been drawn up for Don's arrest," Huck said.

"So that's why we came all the way out here," Sheri bellowed. "You're on the run, again."

"Hey, don't get mad at him," Huck said. "Don was busted committing an act of civilian justice. If he hadn't acted someone would have died."

"I thought you'd given up on that vigilante crap," Sheri said.

"I haven't been patrolling the streets," I said. "I came across someone who was about to get stabbed so I acted like any half-decent person would. It's not my fault that the vigilums were too slow and in the wrong place at the wrong time."

"Don't worry, the vigilums haven't followed us up here," Huck cut in. "I told them that Don had gone to the hills, so we're safe."

"Great, you've taught Huck to lie to the vigilums," Sheri yelled.

"Sheri, I grew up on Bounty Hunter Island, I know the difference between real lies and doing what it takes to look out for your clansman," Huck said.

"Wow, everyone hold on," Jason called.

Everybody silenced.

"Okay, we've got a problem ahead of us, so let's not create any more conflicts right now," Jason said. "It sounds like genocide is ahead of us. If that's the case, then I'm with you Don. I will do all I can to stop evil from happening."

"Count me in too," Julia said.

"Same with me," Huck said.

"I was at this area most recently, so I think I'd be a great help too," Wes said.

"Don't forget me," Marco said.

Sheri scanned everyone before saying, "Don, can I talk to you in private?"

Our friends left while Sheri and I went out to the balcony.

"Don, I know you are trying to do a good thing, but I think the vigilums should get involved."

"I will not allow myself to be locked in jail for trying to save my country."

"The government wants to take care of the people, and they're doing a good job of it right now, that's why we're living in the golden age."

"I have no reason to trust the government. The justice system wants me dead because I'm an embarrassment. I do what they cannot."

"You're throwing Jason and Julia into this calamity; they are lovers now."

"I would never sacrifice my sister or good friend. They're as good as warriors as we are."

"What about Huck? He might not live to be Post-17 if he comes on an extermination mission against a death cult."

"Huck is every bit as tough as us, he'll be seventeen in a few weeks, and he's in good hands with a guy who helped create Post-17."

"How far are you going to take this gallivanting? Are you sure this isn't all about your ego?"

"This isn't about me, it's about our people. It's about you too Sheri, and all our loved ones. We will win, and no one will die along the way. I am the Lord of the Warriors."

Sheri swallowed. We loved each other deeply but there were some things which we would never agree on. Politics had permanently warped both of our lives, and we were forever on opposite sides of the fence. I hated to yell at Sheri, but I cared too much about this crusade to let her political ideals get in the way.

"If you're going to Naflit, I am too," Sheri said. "You're not going to die without me."

"I told you already, no one is going to die."

"Good, cuz when we return, I am going to become a vigilum and I am not going to accept any protest from you. One little complaint and I sure as hell won't be your ticket out of jail."

"Very well."

We held each other and kissed for a long time. Anyone always needed a good amount of smooching after a session of jarring.

"I love you Don, even if I'm on the side of the law and you're a hell-bent anarchist outlaw."

"I care about others, I fight crime, and I'm on my own side of the law. I make no apologies."

Sheri forced a smile before suggesting that we head down to the pub and meet with the others. We did so, and I bought the first round of beer.

"You know Marco, you don't have to come on the mission if you don't want to," I said when I met him at the dartboard.

"Why wouldn't I want to come?" Marco asked.

"I thought you were busy with that biology project where you'll be studying the diets of river sharks and how invasive species are affecting their habitat."

"I'll be back in more than enough time for that assignment."

I took a long drag on my beer as I thought about what to say next.

"Are you sure? I won't ask Trent to come cuz of his upcoming wedding, and Bashar can't come due to his health. Your project is just as good a reason to opt out."

"It sounds like you don't want me to come."

"I know you're tough enough for the mission. You're equally skilled with magic, fist fighting, weapons, and magic carpet flying."

"You're afraid of me losing my temper."

"You got me."

"Members of a genocide cult seem like the perfect target to let inner rage out on," Jason said.

"Jason has a good point," Marco said. "I won't have to worry about killing any innocent prisoners like that poor guy back at the pit."

"I'd hate to drag you away from your happiness and pull you toward the darkness," I said.

"Don, you fight crime because you hate evil and believe that cruelty and unfairness should not be done to anyone," Marco said. "I am the same way. We're one, but we're different. I don't want malice to come to anyone, and I empathize with victims because I felt enough harm when I was young. I fight my demons by helping others battle their darkness. When we win the battle, I see hope, and I forget about my past plights."

"Why don't we raise a drink to our journey tomorrow," Huck said.

We took Huck's advice and drank to winning another battle.

We set off early the next morning. It took two days to reach Naflit Bayou by air. None of us had a lot to say. While we'd all faced larger than life terrors in our lives, the concept of a death cult was strong enough to shake fear into the most courageous warriors.

"How many genies were in the logbook?" Jason asked one night around the campfire.

"There were six listed in the notebook," I answered, "four men and two women."

"There are seven of us plus Sid so this mission should be a piece of cake," Huck said.

"I didn't see many genies around the river," Wes said. "The ones I worked for paid me and all the construction workers in cash, and from what I could tell, they were running a pretty legitimate operation."

"Dropping the genie book was key though," Julia said. "Had you not found it, none of us would be here now."

"In the future, when people write about how we kicked a load of evil genie ass, you're going to be remembered as the savior spark," Sheri said to Wes.

I was glad that Sheri had warmed up to the mission. There hadn't been any more bickering about politics or vigilums between us. I knew that Sheri was nervous, but we all were. Our fear was understandable considering we knew so little of what lay ahead. All we had to evaluate this mission on was ancient mythology and a drenched littered notebook. It was easy to believe that all the monsters from mythology would be resurrected in Naflit Bayou, but every so often I liked to tell myself that folklore had been exaggerated and we didn't need to worry about disease or death.

When we reached Naflit Bayou, it was as murky as a latrine. The monsoon season was coming into full swing so most of the waterlogged ground was submerged. Some trees sprouted out from murky waterholes, but apart from that, there was little land or vegetation which rose above the water. All the swamp islands looked like they would sink if you put weight on them.

"Follow me toward the dam," Wes said. "We've still got quite a lot of marsh to get through before we reach the dried-out area of Naflit River."

Wes took the lead while the rest of us followed on magic carpets. Flies and mosquitoes buzzed past us. The gray clouds burst, soaking all of us with spitfire rain. Bolts of lightning flashed in the distance, indicating that more dire weather lay ahead of us. I really wished that we could have come to the swamp in the dry season.

After twenty minutes, we came to the Naflit Dam. Wes's crown jewel was certainly an impressive piece of engineering. Hundreds of logs had created a wall in a canyon. As a result of the dam, the Naflit River had been reduced to a large creek. Yefhati Cave had to be around here somewhere.

We landed on the once flooded riverbed. The ground was dank, so we had to move very carefully. While much of the ground consisted of rocks, we were also met with mud patches. Sid had a difficult time on the slippery surface, so Jason told her to stay put while the rest of us snooped around for caverns. Before any of us found any openings into the underground, Sid was barking, jumping, and running around in frenzy.

"What's your pooch smell?" Marco asked.

"Down there," Wes said as he pointed to the opposite side of the dam.

Buzzing grew louder as a cloud of black and gray approached us. The cloud swarmed around in a spiral as it moved north. Those of us who were literate in genie mythology knew what was coming after us.

While your average pesky blood sucking bug could give you an itch at best and malaria at worst, the elephantine mosquitoes were at least twice the size of my head. Getting bitten by one of those gargantuan blood suckers was like getting stabbed by a dirk. To make matters worse, mammoth mosquitoes had the ability to drain your body dry of blood.

"Guess mythology and your theories of a death cult were correct Don," Sheri said.

"Yeah, and if we don't act now, we're going to be bloodless carcasses," Julia said.

"I have an idea," Wes voiced. "Mosquitoes fly very close together. If I set a few of them on fire, then they'll crash into one another and the whole cloud will erupt in an inferno."

"That's a brilliant plan," Huck said.

"You'll have to be careful though," Jason cautioned. "Some of the mosquitoes might break away from the cloud to bite you."

"I'll blast them away from us with wind," Marco said.

"Wes, we'll stand by you as guards," I said.

We made our way across the slimy land. The buzzing grew louder as the cloud of blood suckers got closer. They'd smelt our blood. The horde was going to attack us at any moment.

Wes nodded to Marco. Marco raised his ring and created a blast of wind. Rain blew to the south while mud fluttered off the miry ground. The mosquitoes came to an uneasy halt.

A few of the bugs broke free from the wind and came after Wes. Without hesitation, Wes unleashed a burning blast from his dragon mouth. Five mammoth mosquitoes caught fire. Flames singed their wings to crisp while insect hairs perforated. The burning bodies crashed into the rest of the scrounge. A massive fireball erupted, forcing us to jump away from the flaming sphere. We wanted to run, but the ground was too slippery. Sid barked louder than ever. The burning flock of bugs grew larger as more blood suckers caught fire. The entire gulley lit up in tangerine light.

"Wes, you are a genius," Sheri said.

"With all of these chain reaction techniques maybe you should give up engineering and become a full-fledged warrior like the rest of us," Huck said.

"Hey, don't forget about me," Marco said.

"You've always been a master of combat," I said. "I'm glad you came along."

Although blackened and burning mosquito bodies were dropping to the ground, five renegades from the fire flew toward their attackers. Sheri flung her sword to the left, slicing a mosquito in half. Blood and guts spilled across the moist riverbed, creating an even fouler stink. My blade flashed next, beheading an approaching blood sucker. A mosquito flew low, and Jason bashed his club against it, flattening the vampire bug against a boulder. Julia tossed her spear. The pointed weapon pulverized one mosquito while knocking a second mosquito to the ground. The fallen mosquito had an injured wing and difficulty taking flight. Sid dashed toward the fallen flier and gnawed at the bug's body. The enraged injured mosquito let out the most heinous cries I'd ever heard while Sid tore the battered bug apart.

Now that the area was clear, we continued to make our way down the river, searching for an entrance to Yefhati Cave. Along the way, Huck slipped on a rock and tumbled into a mud puddle. He struggled and couldn't break free from the sticky mud. Sheri and I stopped to give him a hand. Wes noticed more approaching mammoth mosquitoes, so the rest of the gang got ready for an attack.

Jason repeatedly swung his club as if he were a blacksmith trying to obliterate an anvil. Four demolished mosquito carcasses dropped to the ground while bug juice and blood camouflaged Jason's trademark red cloak.

Julia repeatedly flung her spear upward with rapid fire. After half a minute she'd speared three mosquitoes. Each of the bug bodies rested on her spear as though they were skewered shish kebab meat.

"You may have killed one more than me, but I get the stylistic point," Julia smirked at Jason.

"You always have to make a competition out of everything eh," Jason chuckled.

"Hey, I easily killed more than both of you combined," Wes burst in.

"I'll show both of you wild style," Marco boasted.

Marco grabbed an approaching mosquito by its proboscis. The rest of us gasped at such a dodgy move. A warrior often had to take big risks if they wanted to win a battle, but Marco was edging toward suicide.

Marco jerked his captured mosquito by it's blood sucker. He then stabbed a second flying gore fiend with the mosquito straw, which remained in his grasp. The second mosquito died quickly while the captured mosquito drained blood and bodily fluids from the bug it had been forced into stabbing. Marco held a tight grip on the mosquito's proboscis. Rumour had it that if you squeezed a mosquito's straw when it was draining blood, the mosquito would suck in too much liquid and explode. Marco held a tight squeeze on the proboscis until the mosquito exploded like a water balloon. Blood and scraggly bug parts decorated us while Marco raised the blood sucking straw above his head like a trophy.

"How's that for style," Marco gloated.

Sheri and I gave Huck one final tug and he rose to his feet, completely caked in glue-like mud.

"Ah, my buddy Huck has risen to give me a standing ovation," Marco said.

A mosquito buzzed behind Marco and dropped it's needle into Marco's back. Marco's cackling turned into sorrowful wailing as blood escaped his body. His flesh paled as his body flopped over.

Huck blasted a bolt from his crossbow and pinned the blood-draining mosquito to a dead tree. The mosquito fluttered in pain. The more the mosquito fought against the staking bolt, the more it tore apart it's punctured body.

I rushed to Marco's near-lifeless body. Never had I put such energy into the healing powers of my ring. Waves of magic traversed through Marco's bloodless body. I feared that I'd lost a friend. Since I'd promised that no one would die on the mission, I increased the healing energy from my ring and could feel my level of magical energy dwindling.

"Is he gone?" Sheri asked.

"He's breathing," Wes said.

I felt all magic leave my body and ring. Never had I shot out so much force from my ring. Marco was alive, but barely. I'd practically resurrected him from the dead, and it had taken all my magic. It would take several hours till any notable amounts of magic would be recharged to my ring.

Marco opened his eyes. He was pale, couldn't speak, and his breathing remained questionable. Huck took over medicinal duties and blasted healing magic from his ring.

"There's only so much a ring can do," Julia said. "We'll need to let Marco rest."

Jason and I picked Marco up and walked him toward a small cavern where he'd be out of the rain. Several thunder strikes burst above us, indicating that the worst of the storm was nearing our way.

"You guys go looking for evil," Huck said. "I'm staying behind."

"Are you sure that's a good idea?" Sheri asked.

"Someone's got to watch over Marco to make sure he doesn't die," Huck said. "My genie powers are stronger than Julia's, we have a cave for protection, and I've got Marco's weapons plus my crossbow."

"Keep Sid with you too," Jason said. "If things get rough around here, get her to bark like crazy and we'll come back for the two of you."

I hated to leave Huck and Marco behind, but the entire mission couldn't be sabotaged due to one injured soldier. The mammoth mosquitoes had confirmed that the genies were up to evil, and I feared that more peril lay ahead.

"Don are you sure about letting Huck stay behind?" Sheri asked.

"Huck's tough," I said. "He's confident, I have faith in him, and we still haven't even found an entrance into Yefhati Cave."

"I don't want anything bad to happen to Huck," Sheri said. "I almost think of him as my son."

Sheri and I had never talked about having kids. We'd always been too caught up with adventure and vigilante efforts. Maybe the reason why Sheri wanted us to settle down and establish careers was so we could start a family.

I told myself that now was not the time for future familial matters. If we didn't act fast, the family of Sionia would be doomed.

We searched for a cave entrance for around ten minutes. There were many small caverns along the emptied riverbed, but none of them looked like they could lead toward a major underground passage. I hoped that the cave entrance would be notably big and that we hadn't accidentally passed by an inconspicuous opening.

Eventually Wes came upon an entrance with strange emerald light coming from it.

"That's got to be the entrance," Sheri said.

"Definitely," I said. "Legend says that unusual emeralds lights used to combine with potions and strange herbs to create genie made plagues."

Jason pulled a few torches from his backpack and Wes ignited each of them with a blast of dragon fire. Once the torches were alit, we entered the cave. Although the limestone surface was slippery from stalactite drips and mucky stalagmites, the cave was drier than the torrential bayou. Since the emerald light was growing brighter, our torches weren't needed for light, but they kept us warm as we moved forward on our spelunking expedition. Had we not been on a mission to destroy a death cult, I would have spent more time admiring the astounding geology which looked like no mountains I'd ever seen. I'd seen amazing rock formations in the northlands, breathtaking cliffs on the coast, and uncanny karst stones in the jungle, but nothing compared to the cave formations. I decided that as a reward for defeating the cult I would do some caving.

"Wow, check out these," Julia said.

Animals, genies, and humans were painted on the cave walls.

"It's beautiful, but let's stay focused on the mission," I said.

"Quit being bossy," Julia retorted.

"Seriously, you think I'm being bossy while you're wasting combat time to look at cave scratching," I growled.

"Look closer," Sheri advised. "Nosiness doesn't always lead to death and destruction."

To humour Sheri, I gave the cave paintings a second glance. On take two, I noticed dragons which looked vaguely human. The painted dragons weren't large or on all fours like a horse, but instead they stood erect like humans. The dragons had small wings, they breathed fire, and they stood side by side with people. It then hit me that these drawings looked exactly like Wes. Until now, Wes had been a unique creature: a human-dragon hybrid, most likely a mutant or an experiment.

"What if I am a genie?" Wes wondered. "What if I was transformed through magic into a humanoid dragon? What if it is possible to transform others into anthropomorphized dragons?"

"Don, your ring is glowing," Jason said.

Though the stone on my ring was lime green, my jewelry looked like a flame was being held against an emerald. I'd never heard of rings glowing on their own. It seemed peculiar that my ring would transform on account of dragon paintings. What was even more puzzling was that my genie powers were completely drained from my body, and I was still unable to cast any magic from my ring.

Wes nodded, affirming that it was time to move on. We headed toward the source of the light while my ring continued to glow. I could feel much uncertainty among my companions as we neared the light.

From the dragon mural, we walked along a faint path which led toward a cliff. Emerald lights glowed from a pit below the cliff. Mist hung at the bottom of the canyon, clouding over the ground and light source.

Two female genies sat meditating by the edge of the cliff. Neither seemed to notice our approach. We hadn't been stealthily so perhaps they were deep in thought. Maybe their act of meditation with the emeralds light was part of a ritual for giving rise to another plague.

Sheri unsheathed her sword and swung it toward the first genie. The genie's head toppled to the green misty ground. Emerald lights turned the genie's blood maroon. Just after Sheri had beheaded the first genie, she pulled back on her sword and buried the blade it the back of the second genie.

We kicked the two genies' bodies over the edge of the cliff to hide our tracks. After another hundred paces of exploring the lighted pit of Yefhati Cave, Jason spotted two more genies. Each genie raised their ring. Jason's bow and arrow were the only long-distance weapon we possessed. I wished that I had Huck's crossbow. Without sufficient missile weapons and magic, we were nearly defenseless.

A yellow flash started to form in one of the genie's rings. Right before the light was expelled from the ring, Jason's released an arrow from his bow. The arrow flashed into the genie's elbow. Upon getting slammed in the arm, the genie's forearm turned to the left and he accidentally targeted his ring at the second genie. The targeted genie fluttered in the yellow light from his ally's ring. After a few moments of jittering, this genie lost footing and fell into the emerald lit pit.

Wes swooped in front of the genie who Jason had shot. Before Wes could slash his claws or vent a blast of fire, the genie jumped back in fright.

"You're all supposed to be dead," the genie said.

The genie continued to back away from Wes as if Wes were a phantom. Along the way, the genie lost his footing, fell over the edge of the cliff, and joined the three corpses which lay at the bottom of the emerald misty light.

Legends spoke of genies creating dragons down in Yefhati Cave. I wondered if Wes had been created by evil genies without realizing it. Afterall, Wes had no memories of life before Frosher Volcano, yet he'd been armed with a name and a massive amount of knowledge. I theorized that severe amnesia may have destroyed all of Wes's lived experiences without altering his scientific knowledge.

As we ventured deeper into the cave, a strange buzzing grew louder. The buzzing and the emerald light led us toward a mosquito nest, which was the size of an elephant. The nest rested on top of a large iron altar as if it had been conjured in that spot. I felt tension rising in my guts as dozens of mosquitos fluttered around the altar. Direct hits had been a good way of pulverizing individual bloodsuckers, but with a nest, we were completely outnumbered. Marco's injury had proven that one quick peck could nearly kill you. I feared that we were going to have to run and find answers on how to destroy a death squad.

Julia raised her ring. After a few seconds of concentration, a blue lightning bolt bulleted from her finger jewel and banged into the large metal altar. Electricity lit up the entire cavern, masking all emerald light. The mosquito nest blackened to crisp. Flakes of ash crinkled to the damp ground. Smoke rose while the boom of thunder rang our ears. Mosquito carcasses dropped while burning bugs crashed into one another.

"Holy shit," Sheri said.

"Julia," I said, "that was by far the best magic I've seen from you."

"You really ought to stop feeling like an underdog in magic," Wes said. "Don, Marco, and Huck couldn't have thought of something that brilliant."

"We'd all be dead if it weren't for you," Jason said.

"As of now I have the highest death toll and the most stylistic points," Julia cheeked. "You suckers really have a lot of catching up to do."

I let my sister enjoy her cockiness since the demise of the mosquito nest was a huge relief. The deaths of the last four genies had also been a triumph, and I had a feeling that we were nearing the source of the death group. The logbook Wes had found stated that there were six genies involved in death acts at Yefhati Cave. By that logic, Krull and Hunter were the only criminals left. Julia, Wes, Sheri, and Jason had had their glory. Now it was my turn to hunt down and destroy my lifelong nemesis.

The limestone path my friends and I had been walking on turned to cobble stone. We weren't sure where this manmade path was taking us, but we felt like it would lead us to the heart of the crime.

Jason and I were in the lead. Although the ground had been solid, we stepped on a loose stone. Before either of us realized it, we were falling. There was no ground beneath us for several paces. The emerald light glowed brightly.

Jason and I landed with a thud in a deep canyon. My ankles stung as I tumbled forward, scraped my knees, and battered my palms. Jason groaned about how badly he'd lumped his ass upon landing. Sinister chuckling caught our attention, making us forget about our injuries.

Krull stepped from out of the emerald-lit mist. His cackling grew louder and louder. I wondered if Sheri, Wes, and Julia could hear him and if they would jump down the trapdoor to look for us. I really hoped for their rescue. I still had my sword, but my magic energy was weak despite the continual glow of my ring.

My sword leapt out of my hand. Jason's bow, club, and quiver of arrows jumped toward Krull. Krull's ring was glowing, and from that, I deducted that Krull had used telekinesis to steal our weapons. I couldn't remember the last time I'd been in such an oh shit situation.

"Just when I thought things couldn't get any better down here, you showed up," Krull grinned.

"Forget about your death cult Krull," I growled. "We've killed the other four genies and the mosquito nest is fried."

"Ah forget that shit," Krull chuckled. "I get to teach the peoples' champion a thing or two before he dies. I didn't think that any of my kills would be personal, but if anyone deserves a face-to-face slaughter, it's you Don."

"You stupid sick lowlife," Jason said. "You'll die along with the civilians. Genies aren't immune to dragon fire, lethal plagues, or elephantine mosquitoes."

"I'd die a blissful man knowing that thousands of others perished at my hand," Krull said. "Some days I feel like I've had enough of life, and that I might as well die with a bang and take others down with me. It's better to commit suicide than to be killed by someone or something else."

"Evil always dies, good always survives," I spoke.

"Don you poor little man," Krull said. "Good is merely an opinion. Sionia has reached its golden age, I'm sure you and the rest of the country thinks that's a good thing. You look at myself and the other genies down here as disturbed self-loathing misanthropes. Well let me tell you something; we need to remind society that it's not as good as it thinks it is. The country is weaker than it realizes, and so many people are going die regardless of how happy they are. It's appropriate to have an apocalypse at the height of social arrogance. Not everyone will die. The survivors will remember darkness. Maybe they'll learn from the apocalypse and remind others to not get too cocky or confident, to not get too happy. For generations everyone remembered the first apocalypse, but those stories shouldn't have been forgotten. All of you are only as strong as your great weaknesses.

"But Don, I admire you. No matter what, you're resilient. I am too. We're just determined about different things. You seek to purge evil while I strive to take darkness to all. You've slowed me down, but never defeated me. Since we're once again face to face, I'll finally give you the chance to kill me."

My sword came flying at me. I clutched the handle of my katana and held it tightly, anticipating that Krull would use his telekinesis to pull my sword back and drag me along.

Hunter stepped from out of the shadows carrying a bow-staff. I'd forgotten about him during Krull's monologue.

Jason yelped as Hunter struck him multiple times with the bamboo weapon. After getting thumped on the ass, Jason collapsed. Hunter had exploited the wound which Jason had received when he'd come tumbling down to this level of the cave.

I slashed by sword toward Hunter. With a flash of the blade, I chopped Hunter's weapon in half while Jason lay on the ground and groaned.

"You stupid son of a bitch," Krull laughed. "I gave you the chance to kill me, but you chose to save your friend. This is your major flaw Don, you care too much about people. People will ultimately destroy you, which is why you have to start fighting them instead of trying to save them."

Krull disappeared into the shadows while Hunter armed himself with Jason's club. Without a word, the two of us began a duel. The stalagmite ground created many obstacles. I decided to fight from a defensive standpoint to avoid tripping over bumps in the ground. Hunter bashed the club toward me in many directions. Although the club was wider and heavier than my sword, I managed to parry the attacks. Chunks of wood cracked out of the club as my blade collided against it. I hated to destroy Jason's prized weapon, but Hunter had to be taken down. More than anything, I wished that I still had magic within my ring. Saving Marco's life had been crucially important, but I could have easily taken Hunter down with magic. My ring continued to glow, and I wondered if the glow meant that the damn thing was broken on account of being out of magic. I hoped that my hypothesis was incorrect.

An arrow flashed toward Hunter and pierced his skull. Hunter's eyes darkened as he collapsed to the ground. Jason crowed as he raised his bow above his head.

"Brilliant man, I owe you," I said as I fetched Jason's dropped club.

"I was returning the favour," Jason said. "That Hunter bitch sure is a dirty fighter, spanking my already battered butt, what a loser eh."

A few torch flames pierced the darkness. Footsteps grew closer. I hoped that more genies weren't coming even though we'd ticked off all culprits from the logbook.

Jason and I felt immense relief when our friends stepped through the shadows. Sheri and I met with a hug and a kiss before she jumped in on sharing Julia's embrace with Jason.

"Easy," Jason groaned. "I'm happy for your love, but my ass is on fire."

"Jason, I'll heal you lover," Julia said as her magic ring did healing work on Jason's wounds.

"What the hell happened here anyway?" Sheri asked.

"You didn't happen to see Krull did you?" I inquired.

"You found him?" Wes said.

"He gave us a monologue about how this death club is a vendetta against the arrogance of Sionia's golden age," Jason said. "He got away, and we had a bout with Hunter, but the arrow in his head has pinned him in his place."

"We're really happy to have found you," Sheri said. "We thought we'd lost you."

"And we've found something that can destroy this damn forsaken cave," Wes said as he showed us a wooden drum of oil.

"Is that thithaleeth?" Jason asked.

"Indeed," Wes answered. "I am going to spill it all over the dam and then set it afire to drown out the cave and re-flood the dry area of Naflit River."

"Wes you can't do that," I said. "You'll destroy your life's work."

"Don, you're being a kind guy, but if you want to be a really good guy, you'll let me destroy the stupid dam," Wes said. "I was too foolish to question the guys who were paying me to build it. I should have been a lot smarter because a dam shouldn't be built in a remote bayou in swampland wilderness. If the dam goes, this cave will be buried for good, and we won't ever have to worry about any Yefhati death cult magic again."

"He might kill Krull too," Sheri said.

"You have a good point Wes, but I'm sorry," I said, "just a few days ago you'd won a major award for this dam, and it sucks that it has to be destroyed to save others."

"At least it will be destroyed by my hands," Wes said.

I admired Wes's stoicism. If I'd had to destroy my masterpiece I'd be bellyaching forever. In a lot of ways, I wished we could find Krull, kill him, and then not have to worry about any more curses rising from the cave. Considering other genies were dead, there probably wasn't much of a chance of any other evil rising from the ground. Then again, we only had a very limited knowledge of the cave. Wes had made a good point when he mentioned that if we flooded the cave then there'd be no chance of more wickedness rising.

Julia helped Jason to his feet, and we made our way out of the cave. We didn't run into Krull or anyone else along the way. Hunter appeared dead but I had a feeling that he and Krull would find some other sneaky way of escaping. It seemed that the two of them were eternal spirits of evil.

Once we were out in the open, Wes flew to the dam with the drum of oil. Lightning was flashing much more frequently. Rain blasted us as if we were being sprayed by geysers. Sid was barking in the distance, so we hurried toward the animal calls. Worrying about Huck and Marco's state arrested my mind.

Marco was on his feet and looked better, but not in any shape to fight. The sight of Huck took me to another level of worry. Krull stood several paces away from him. He was armed with a bastard sword and was looking to take Huck's head off. Huck was without a weapon, which seemed incredibly foolish. Several massive mosquitoes buzzed over Huck's head. Sid was dashing back and forth frantically and yelped like the end of the world.

Jason loaded his bow with an arrow. Julia, Sheri, and I charged forward with our weapons raised. Huck flashed his ring and created a force shield. Each of us stopped in our tracks. The mosquitoes buzzed toward the force shield as if they were magnetized by the violet light.

"I created those mosquitoes," Krull said. "My beast won't harm me. Don, your protégé is even dumber than you are."

"Watch your mouth," Huck said. "The name is Huck in case you've forgotten. I'm the son of a bitch who blasted a crossbow bolt into your arm, but you're the real chickenshit Krull. You fled Bounty Hunter Island at the first sign of danger. You could have won the battle even after Keifer set fire to your ship, but you had to outrun your embarrassment and your fear of an uprising. Since you set the headquarters on fire, you willfully self-destructed. You're a loser and your own worst enemy."

Huck stepped toward Krull. The mosquitoes flew toward the violet light until they'd completely clouded around the force shield. Krull swung his sword back and forth as more and more blood sucking bugs approached him. Two slashed bugs fell from Krull's blade, but many other mosquitoes crowded around him. Three of the mosquitoes pierced Krull's skin. Blood sprayed from the incision wounds as Krull collapsed to the sewage-like ground. The mosquitos sucked him dry as his body sponged into the muck. Krull's bloodless flesh paled to chalk. The mosquitos continued to buzz around him. I knew there was a chance that Krull might live, but I hoped for his death.

Huck aimed his ring at the bugs and blasted a fireball. Each of the blood suckers caught fire. I couldn't see any other mosquitos, and I prayed that no others were hiding and ready to ambush us.

"Fuckin' eh all the way Huck," Sheri said.

"I showed this piece of shit that I'm not a stupid protégé," Huck laughed.

"Huck, it looks like you and I have both done better with magic today than this big shot," Julia said as she gave me a punch to the bicep.

"Hey, I revived Marco," I shot.

All the victorious laughter ended when the dam erupted in an inferno. Wes had spilt oil across the wooden river wall, and a lightning bolt had set it aflame. Flames spread across the dam despite the hefty amount of falling rain and reservoir water. Burst of waters blasted through burnt section of the dam like blown aqueducts. Wes flew toward the rest of us.

"I can fly my magic carpet out of here," Marco assured. "Huck is a really good healer, and he did a good job at chasing off the leftover mosquitoes. I owe him one, and I owe you a lot too Don."

"You helped Wes kill a lot of mosquitoes," I said. "We've all done well as a team."

Marco sat atop his magic carpet and rose toward the rain clouds. Despite some apprehension that I was too drained of magic to pilot my magic carpet, Sheri and I were able to float away on the genie's trademark vehicle. Julia and Jason ascended on their shared magic carpet. Huck fetched Sid onto his magic carpet and then joined us. Wes met our hovering party.

Fire burned at every corner of the dam. Pieces of burnt timber drifted in the river current while vast amounts of water flooded the already bogged up swamp.

"You don't need to watch this Wes," Sheri said. "Let's get out here."

"We might as well celebrate our victory far away from this stinky swamp," Wes said.

We flew to the next town, which was about three hours away. After a long shower and a large buffet dinner, we collapsed to our beds. Initially we'd planned on heading back to Stodaneatoo the next morning but decided to take another day off to relax around our inn, drink tea, and gluttonize the delicious local curries. We spoke about how we'd kicked a lot of evil genie and mosquito ass but didn't speak of the destruction of the dam. It was probably going to take Wes a long time to get over a major loss right after an enormous success.

My ring had stopped glowing as soon as we'd left Yefhati Cave. My magic returned to full strength which I was thankful for, but I couldn't help being curious about the mysterious glow.

"What if it was tied to the dragon paintings?" I asked Wes once we were back in Stodaneatoo.

"I'm going to do more research on dragons," Wes said. "I've spent enough of my life in science, now it's time to learn about anthropology and mythology."

"But the cave paintings were destroyed. Wes, I'm really sorry you had to do that."

"You genies know a lot about mythology; you'll probably be a good teacher, and we can study together."

I needed to be more like Wes since he saw positive outcomes in dire situations. I didn't want to be like Krull, a pessimist who had to find the worst in everything.

Bashar was feeling a lot better when we reached Stodaneatoo, so he decided to write a story about our adventures in Naflit Bayou. Some detractors stated that his prose was ornate, but I didn't believe that he had embellished the story at all. The magazines that published our story reached record sales, and magic scholars and other journalists wanted to interview all seven of us adventurers. Trent's beautiful wedding to Larissa helped get us out of some tedious interviews. Bashar was happy about cancelled interviews with other reporters since he wanted his article to be the definitive piece on the heroes who'd defeated a newly resurrected evil.

Marco went off to study river sharks while Wes took a sabbatical to research dragons and ancient mythology. Wes declined interviews which were focused on the destruction of his dam since he'd already told the whole truth to Bashar.

"We had an agreement Don, remember what it was?" Sheri asked when we were about to go out for dinner with Jason and Julia.

"Oh man," I groaned.

"We're going back to Laleaka, the most boring place ever," she chuckled, "and I'm going to become a vigilum. I've got a half-year contract."

"It'll be lame and boring. These days random people get stopped and interrogated by the vigilums since the power trippers have nothing to do. Man, I thought I was a nosy twat until I met the Laleaka tyrants."

"Don, you are the rebel who fought with reason, and I love you for that, and I want you to come back to Laleaka with me."

"So I can get arrested by my own girlfriend."

"All charges were dropped."

"Seriously?"

"Seriously."

"You're just saying that to get me back to boring town."

"I went by the vigilum station, and the warrant was tossed. Bashar's article convinced the justice department that if you had been arrested then the entire country would have faced an apocalypse. You're a national hero, and the justice department has forgiven you for your crime. To contradict your anarchist opinions, most vigilums are not cold-blooded power-hungry fundamentalist pricks."

"I guess when we return to lame old Laleaka there will be one more vigilum who I will have to evaluate on that criteria," I chuckled.

"Maybe you should think of a career; you might not feel so mundane. If you're bored all the time, maybe it means you're becoming a dull guy. It's kind of depressing actually."

Sheri was right about one thing. I'd never thought about a career. It seemed boring. I'd always wanted nothing but a life of action.

BOOK XI:

HARMONIOUS CHAOS

Sheri won the argument and we returned to boring old Laleaka. She began work as a vigilum and started bossing me around less, probably cuz she was so busy ordering around would-be crooks or innocent folks who were viewed as potential suspects.

Huck stayed around for a little while and then moved to the mountains outside of Stodaneatoo. He found a girlfriend out there, made new friends in the area, still hung out with the old gang, and said he'd never been happier. I couldn't blame him for not being too interested in visiting Laleaka.

I took up work as a building painter and then got a job selling weapons before becoming a farmhand. Life wasn't great but it could have been worse.

One day when I got home from work, I found a letter from Marco and instantly ripped it open to see what was inside. Marco had temporarily moved out to Danjia and was volunteering as an aid worker. Marco's cousin Damon was among the refugees whose village in Danjia had been destroyed by a wildfire. Since Danjia was made up of grasslands with the odd small lake and river, roaring blazes spread quickly. Despite bush fires being common, there were many herds on the plains, and the best meat in Sionia always came from the Danjia savanna.

My rucksack was packed by the time Sheri got home from work.

"Just like that, you're up and leaving to Danjia?" Sheri said.

"Why not?"

"What about work?"

"I'm going to get laid off sooner or later, just a week ago a few guys were cut. Since all the other surviving dudes have kids, I'll be the next to go."

"Isn't this a bit sudden?"

"I didn't expect to get a letter from Marco this morning saying that he was an aid worker, and that I was invited to come and help out."

"I agree that this could be good for you."

"Don't you have some vacation coming up within the next season?"

"Yeah."

"Look at things this way, you'll get a vacation from me for a season. I'm sure I'm so annoying you need space from me right now. If you do miss me after your harmonious holiday from me, then come on out to Danjia on your paid vacation from the vigilums."

"Sounds good."

The next morning, I flew to Danjia, which was north-west of O'Jahnteh. Stepping out of the jungle and flying above the grasslands was an amazing spectacle. I loved soaring above lions, rhinos, zebras, gazelles, giraffes, and elephants. Flying above the jungle canopy had always been awesome, but foliage always masked the number of animals that lurked among the trees. Travelling to new areas of Sionia always gave me more appreciation for my country. After my time in Danjia, I wanted to travel to an area of Sionia which I had yet to journey to.

I passed by the occasional pack of nomadic hunters/herders but was alone for much of my journey. Many settlements (which were marked as villages on my map) had been destroyed by wildfires. On two occasions when I'd wanted to stop for a rest, I was met with an island of ash. I was very thankful that Shilotey had used her goddess of weather powers to bring rain to destroy the wildfires. While rain may have quelled the bush fires, Danjia was prone to flooding due to being so flat. Some camps had been washed away by the rain. Such destruction made me wonder why folks would live in such a dire area, but at the same time, I felt the appeal of living wildly in the savanna.

Marco's yurt camp was located at the top of a hill, the only high point which could be seen within eyesight. A modest-sized river ran below the hill. Since the day was growing late, many of the camp inhabitants were finishing the day's chores.

"Are you new here?" a random villager asked.

"Yeah, I'm looking for Marco of O'Jahnteh," I said.

"No way, I'm his cousin Damon," the stranger said with a handshake. "You must be Don?"

"Yeah, I got Marco's letter and decided to come on out here."

"He'll be really happy to see you, surprised too; it's very hard to send any mail out of here due to our isolation."

"It's pretty cool to be so far away from civilization. I love all this land you guys can roam around in."

"Jungles and mountains are cool, but the grasslands will always be my home."

Damon showed me around the camp. I offered to help with feeding the animals and any other chores, but the tribal folks told me to relax after a long day of journeying. Lion steaks were being cooked over a communal fire, and local grain bread was served as an appetizer. Both delicacies were quite delicious.

"We haven't been given any aid from the government and very little help has come in from any donors," Damon said. "Out here we don't have much use for money and prefer to trade collateral."

"Danjia beef and other game meats are highly coveted throughout Sionia," I said.

"When we sell meat, we usually barter for staples, tools, or items that these lands don't offer."

Marco came by the communal dinner right after I'd finished my meal and washed my dishes.

"Don, holy hell, so glad you could make it out here," he said.

"I'm glad you invited me," I returned. "You gave me an excuse to leave Laleaka."

"I guess Sheri didn't come with you."

"She's busy with work but will come out here on vacation sometime in the near future."

Marco helped himself to dinner and then sat down next to me while Damon ran off to chase down a runaway dog.

"Don, you can sleep in my yurt tonight," Marco said. "Things are pretty crowded here, and you probably don't want to be cooped up with strangers."

"Sounds good," I said.

"People here are alright though."

"I'd hope so. It would be brutal to lend aid to a bunch of assholes."

"It would, but these people are the real deal man."

"I can't believe that the government is doing nothing to help these nomads after their camps were destroyed by wildfires. If Shilotey can intervene, why can't the government?"

"We both know that the government is particularly useless at helping others. The excuse I heard was that the government wants the nomads to move into cities and assimilate with the rest of society. Giving wanderers a handout after a natural disaster would encourage them to continue living a barbaric lifestyle."

"What the hell is wrong with wanting to primitively live off the land? Man, so many people love the food resources from the grasslands."

"The government dislikes how these bands of nomads don't involve themselves with the rest of society. They remind the government that it doesn't control all."

Damon returned sometime later. He tossed me a campfire blanket and told me it was mine for however long I wanted.

"Thanks," I said. "Since I'm staying here, I'd like to contribute toward some jobs."

"Would you be willing to dig some ditches tomorrow?" Damon asked. "We want all the rain to run down the hill and into the river, so our camp won't flood."

"Sounds good, I'll do that and anything else I can."

I spent nearly a week digging ditches. It was tough dirty work, but I got stronger. We were encouraged to take breaks regularly, and whenever I wanted to rest, someone always jumped in to fill my place. There was enough food to go around for everyone, and no one went with less provisions than anyone else.

"Nomads have never lived with much authority," Damon told me one day. "Since no one was giving us orders, we learned to take voluntary action. Since we believe in self-responsibility, we're always quick to help others so that everything remains stable."

"Do you ever get lazy selfish people who don't want to help?" I asked.

"Sometimes, but such vices are sourly frowned upon. When your ego is small, you become more interested in others and less focused on individual materialism."

"Man, I wish more people would follow such advice. You must be kind of shocked that the government and rich people haven't donated anything to you guys. It doesn't seem fair that tsunami victims along the west coast were given aid but you plains folk weren't."

"It's lame that the government has failed to help us, and it sucks that many rich folks are too ostentatious to give us charity, but we nomads like doing things our way. If we can function without the help of the government, then we're doing a pretty good job on our own."

"You're all fed, recovering, and getting along, so who needs failed government bureaucracy?"

Once the ditches had been dug, I switched to collecting wood, gathering wild fruit and vegetables, and planting crops. I was told that I'd done enough ditch digging, so others would dig wells and pit toilets. The nomads figured it was a good idea to educate yourself with all trades and that one shouldn't be tied into a monotonous role. I was very happy to hear this considering my body was aching all the time from so much ditch digging.

Damon was an expert at herding animals and building new yurts. Marco did a bit of hunting but was better at tending crops. Since many bison and cows had been killed in the fires, livestock numbers were small, but the vast fields of green and yellow grass gave the herds more than enough nutrients to fatten up on.

As more yurts were built, people gained more privacy. Meals and work were communal, but solitude was encouraged during free time. While some people read or played music during their free time, I relished flying my magic carpet over the grasslands. In the past, I'd heard people moan about how boring the prairies were, but from my flights on the plains, I realized that these whiners hadn't experienced the land properly. Zooming across open space and chasing after different animal species sent high levels of adrenaline into my heart. When I wanted to calm down, I gazed at the clouds while warm breezes and tingling long grass soothed me to tranquility.

"Do you miss the ocean?" I asked Marco.

It was mine and Marco's first time working together since my arrival in Danjia. We were constructing a corral with newly scavenged wood from a small forest. Though animals were given free range during the day, we'd decided to pen them up at nighttime to keep them from wandering into lions or other predators.

"A little," he confessed. "How about you?"

"I sure don't miss Laleaka," I chuckled.

"But Laleaka was on the ocean."

"If you wanted to go to the beach or out boating, you had to pay all these fees since the yacht clubs and access points to the beach were owned by rich bitches. I rarely had enough money to cough up the coin."

"Laleaka was designed as a town for the bourgeoisie who wanted to escape from the city."

"All those wealthy folks relied on the service industry, but thought it was okay to pay us dirt wages."

"Which is why it's a good thing you came here. Have you heard anyone talk about money?"

"No, not at all."

"I'd really like to take this lifestyle and put it on the ocean."

"Maybe after our adventure out here we should get a sailboat and be sea nomads. Live off fish, adventure, and strong gales."

"Hells yeah."

"There are a lot of people around here who would probably also like to come sailing," I said as I thought back to the long-gone days of the Vindadong. "I dig the people around here because when I ask them questions, they consider me friendly, but in the city when I make conversation with others, they find me nosy."

"Maybe this is the tribe which you've always been searching for?"

One afternoon when I was on my daily break, Damon came by and saw me practicing fencing.

"Why do you have that weapon here?" he asked.

"I don't go anywhere without it," I said.

"I don't think it's a good idea to be swinging it around."

"I don't plan on fighting with anyone."

"Around here weapons are pretty frowned upon."

"But you have sickles, axes, spears, and stuff like that."

"Axes are for chopping wood. Sickles are for cutting grass. Arrows and spears are for hunting, and blades are for cooking."

"I know that you're all pacifists and get along with one another really well, don't get me wrong I really admire that, but don't you ever get worried that once in a while someone will freak out and you'll need to take up arms."

"Knowledge is power, and we like to invest that knowledge into peaceful living rather than defense."

"That's a cool idea, but it seems a little simple."

"When people don't have the opportunity to fight, they can't bout. We seek to abolish all reasons to squabble. I know you're a lifelong vigilante, and Marco had told me some incredible stories, but I'm sure you know that many crimes come from poverty."

"Too true."

"And poverty is the result of not providing people with enough to live off. The top priority of our nomadic lifestyle is to make sure that no one goes without what they need. Part of that includes making sure that no one has too much. If one person has too much, others will get jealous, and we'll have the crime of greed rather than the crime of poverty."

"Those ideas are beautiful, but they wouldn't work in society."

"Which is one of the reasons why we don't live in civilization, at least not in the mainstream one. We nomads evaluate society by how peacefully you live with one another and nature, not by wealth and technological expansion."

"People around here have gone through so many hardships with the wildfires," Marco said when he came by with a bucket of buffalo milk. "They are thankful to be alive, which is why they don't want any other problems. We should really get Trent out here cuz he'd fall in love with this place."

"I really admire how no one is looting one another or using this humble situation as an opportunity to form a gang and rise to power," I said.

"People are happy, which is why they're not tempted to act like a bunch of assholes," Damon said. "Don, the act of regicide you and Marco and your other friends pulled many years ago, that was a true act of defiance against the system, and nothing has been the same since. Out here on the grasslands, we're pulling our own act of defiance through civil disobedience. This is our way of rebelling against society, and we hope to inspire people to start living a different way."

I sheathed my sword. My katana was my baby, and I loved how my sword had helped me crush evil. I also loved recreational fencing, but after hearing Damon's words, it seemed paranoid and pugnacious to carry a weapon around pacifists.

"You're an anarchist Don," Damon said, "take advantage of the peace and enjoy anarchy."

Sheri came out to visit some time later. She'd given up on her shaved head and grown an afro. Most female vigilums had short hair, and I would have been delighted to death to hear that she'd quit her job, but I also knew to not have unrealistic expectations. Seeing her after a long break made me happy, so I told myself to not think about our opposing views of the government.

"Traveling across the Danjia plains in a caravan was pretty amazing," Sheri said. "Don, I think you and Marco should get rid of your magic carpets and ride horses and elephants."

"I'm all for that," Marco said.

"How about you Don?" Sheri asked. "You look really happy."

"It's cuz you're out here after a really long break," I said between kisses.

"Sweet man, but what have you been doing out here?"

"I've learned how to help others without battle."

BOOK XII:

THE ACCIDENT OF LIFE

I spent a few more seasons among the grasslands. Marco and I continued our aid services with the exodus of refugees. We also did a bit of camping out in the wilderness, which Sheri and Huck joined us for. Huck and his girlfriend had split up right before the camping trip so time in the wild soothed his soul.

About two seasons after our camping trip in the Danjia wild, I got a letter from Wes asking me to come to O'Jahnteh. His note told of new discoveries he'd found which related genie magic to a deceased species of dragon. All this shed much light on the peculiar cave paintings we'd found in Yefhati Cave, so I headed to O'Jahnteh with Sheri. Huck was in the mountains of Stodaneatoo and was bouncing between girlfriends, seasonal jobs, and parties, while Marco was working at a plantation to the north of Danjia.

Returning to O'Jahnteh felt odd. It wasn't until Sheri and I arrived there by magic carpet that I realized that I'd never seen this city with Sheri at my side. I hadn't been to this neck of the woods since Robin's death. There'd never seemed to be much reason to return since whenever I met up with Wes, we always visited somewhere else. From what I saw, things hadn't changed much in O'Jahnteh, which reminded me why I'd walked away from a city which had shown me poverty, death, and hardship.

Jason and Julia had moved to O'Jahnteh a season ago. Julia was training fighters and competing in gladiator events while Jason was working as the sous-chef at a mutton restaurant. Since Wes lived in a small apartment, we decided to crash at my sister's tree house.

"What the hell Don?" Julia said when I randomly landed my magic carpet on the balcony of her tree house. "I never expected you to show up without a letter."

"Hey what about me?" Sheri said as she got up to hug Julia.

"Don't get me wrong, I'm happy to have both of you here, I really am," Julia said, "but I didn't expect to wake up this morning and have the two of you relaxing on my balcony."

"This is only my second time visiting O'Jahnteh," Sheri said.

"I thought you guy were still out in Danjia," Julia said.

"Wes sent a letter asking me to come out here," I said. "He says it's a real big deal."

"Wes ha, I haven't seen that guy in a really long time," Julia said. "He's become such a recluse, and he is trying to track down really ancient arcane scripts."

"Wes was always a nerd though," Sheri said.

"He's not into science anymore though," Julia said. "I guess he really did take mythology and those cave paintings to heart."

"He asked Marco and I to see him in private," I said. "Marco's working on a plantation, and I don't know when he'll show."

"How about you head over to Wes's and let Sheri and I have some girl talk," Julia said. "If we're not here when you get back, there's a tea house down the road where we'll most likely be, and Jason will probably be there too."

I followed my sister's advice, something which I almost never did since Julia's advice almost always consisted of bossing me around.

I headed to Wes's apartment. Before I stepped through the door, my ring was glowing. The jewel hadn't given off any uncalled light since Yefhati Cave.

Three piles of books and a mess of old scrolls were stocked on Wes's coffee table. A few primitive paintings of humanoid dragons hung from the walls.

"Don," Wes exclaimed. "I'm so glad you're here. Come on in friend, thanks for coming. Would you like a snack? There's a pot of tea on the table, help yourself."

"Say Wes," I said when he returned from the pantry with a bunch of grapes and a baguette. "My ring has started glowing again, and it hasn't done this since Yefhati Cave."

"That's really good news, really awesome news. It means you're attracting new magic."

"I'm practically a magic master. Few genies are as skilled in magic as I am unless you include I'magee, but there's no way I'll ever be in the same league as the god of magic."

"According to some archaic literature, many spells have been suppressed and censored from mainstream media. I'll tell you all about them, but I have to tell you another story first."

I was curious about Wes's story, but I was even more interested in learning about various spells which had possibly been hidden from public knowledge. The idea of learning new and secret magic really excited me, especially when I had surpassed most of my magic teachers at a young age. I was tempted to ask Wes to continue with the magic talk but decided to let him do the speaking because I'd never seen him so enthused.

"You see this dragon?" Wes said as he unraveled a scroll which had an illustration of a dragon who could have passed for Wes's brother. "That is Dirotalo: the dragon god."

"There is no dragon god."

"You've never heard of him because most evidence of him has been destroyed. Dirotalo was a big deal back when most Sionian were illiterate. Right after he died, most evidence of his existence was destroyed."

"Hold on Wes, you're telling me that Dirotalo was the thirteenth god?"

"Oh yeah."

"And he's dead?"

"Believe it. I know it's hard to imagine a god dying, but it's possible."

"And the reason why no one remembers him is that few people could read during his reign, and most of the books written about him were burnt or whatever?"

"That's right. I hate to brag, but I own the largest collection of books and paintings on Dirotalo and his legion of tathika dragons. Cost me an arm, a leg, and both my wings to get all these archaic paintings and scrolls. The books were even harder to get, and most of them were marketed as works of fiction to be displayed as historical items at literature museums."

"Hold on Wes, you're moving a bit too fast for me. What's a tathika dragon?"

"You see how these paintings of dragons look like me, kind of like the cave paintings back at Yefhati Cave looked just like me?"

I nodded in response to Wes's rhetorical question as he pointed at the illustrations of humanoid dragons.

"Dirotalo also looks like me," Wes said.

"If I didn't know any better, I'd say this was an illustration of you."

"I am a tathika dragon, the only one in existence, the last survivor of Dirotalo."

For years Wes had struggled with existential questions. It was understandable why Wes felt alone considering he was a unique species who had randomly fallen out of the sky. I realized that sharing this information with me was a very cathartic experience for him. It was no surprise that he'd asked Marco and I to be the first two people who he'd disclose this information to.

"Tell me more," I said.

"Dirotalo was the god of dragons, kind of like how Lazox is the god of animals. For many lifetimes, Dirotalo only ruled over the animalistic dragons. What distinguished Dirotalo from other dragons was that he was very anthropomorphic. He was verbal, had an intelligent mind and developed emotions, stood erect, and lived like a human; there really wasn't anything different between him and humans apart from physical characteristics.

"Dirotalo learned magic from I'magee and the two of them created a legion of disciples: humanoid dragons that became known as tathika dragons. Dirotalo's goal was to create a new race which could live side by side with humans, ogres, and cyclops.

"Things went badly though. A gang of evil genies (many of whom worked out of Yefhati Cave, hence the cave paintings of tathika dragons) used their powers to take control of Dirotalo's disciples. The tathika dragons were very easy to control considering I'magee had used his genie magic to help create them."

"The ability to control animals is a banned action of genie magic," I interrupted. "I'magee outlawed this act because some evil genies stole livestock, created stampedes, and used animals to terrorize small villages."

"True Don, but this was the first major instance when genies controlling animals became dangerous. Evil genies used Dirotalo's disciples to terrorize the country. Entire towns were destroyed by dragon attacks. Even though many of the tathika dragons were intelligent creatures, they were powerless against hypnosis spells because they'd been partially created by genie magic."

Such a thought sent chills through my mind. I was very glad that genies could no longer control animals or dragons. I could only imagine how horrible things would get if Krull or some other criminal took possession of Wes. Battling Aurelius had been difficult enough. I really did wonder if Aurelius had been an enlarged tathika dragon who was controlled by Maximus's wizard magic, but I would never get an answer. I made a mental note to later ask Wes about potential tathika dragons in the northlands since I didn't want to interrupt his passionate teachings.

"I'magee felt partially responsible for the havoc which had been wreaked upon the country," Wes said. "After feeling guilty for the deaths of so many innocents, I'magee decided to atone his actions by creating a plague which would only kill dragons. This plague swept through southern Sionia, killing all tathika and animalistic dragons."

"There must have been some survivors considering we still have animalistic dragons."

"The northern dragons survived because Lazox created immunity for them before the plague could sweep north. Under Silotious's permission, Lazox adopted animalistic dragons, which is why dragons are now classified as animals which live under Lazox.

"Dirotalo was the last of the tathika dragons. I'magee lured Dirotalo to Frosher Volcano and killed him. This created much backlash amongst the goddesses and gods, but Silotious pardoned I'magee as a murderer. I'magee had feared that Dirotalo would try to recreate his disciples, and that tathika dragons were too dangerous to live in a world where they could be easily manipulated by evil genies.

"The idea of a god being murdered was deemed too horrifying a truth for Sionian folks, so all but a few records of Dirotalo and his dragons were destroyed."

My blood ran cold. I couldn't speak since I had taken in way too much information during one sitting. I wanted to complain about how it was unjust to destroy an entire species of dragons based on the actions of a few criminals, especially when the tathika dragons were innocent of any crime. I also wanted to know how my magic was tied in with tathika dragons. I really wanted Wes and I to visit some temples and then have Bashar write a story about this phenomenon.

"You're speechless Don, and I don't blame you," Wes said, "but I'd like us to take a trip to Frosher Volcano."

Wes and I flew by wing and magic carpet to Frosher Volcano. I hadn't been there since that unforgettable day: the discovery of Wes, the deaths of Ace and Devo, the emergence of Krull. The volcano was dead so there was no danger of toxic smoke or lava, but I couldn't help but sense peril ahead. I knew that Wes was withholding information and that he'd be more comfortable with sharing the story once we arrived at the holy site.

Wes and I landed in the crater which was now hardened volcanic rock. My ring glowed brighter than ever. Several bright rays shot from my ring in all directions. The lime-green lights were bright enough to temporarily blind me. I felt like the forces of magic were trying to tell me something, and that they'd also been trying to share secrets with me at Yefhati Cave.

"Wes," I said. "What's going on? I'm not doing this."

"Point your ring at me," Wes said. "Please Don, I promise that neither of us will be hurt."

It was hard for me to aim my ring due to the brightness of the light, but with so many rays getting blasted in all directions, I figured that one of them would hit Wes. I was worried about blasting him, but Wes was confident about this situation, so perhaps getting flashed by my ring was part of his plan. Since I was unfamiliar with these green rays, I wondered if they were merely lights which would cause no harm.

Wes was struck by light and stood still. The sporadic rays stopped flying from my ring. Petroglyphs of tathika dragons appeared on the volcano walls.

"Wes what's going on?"

"Don, I believe you are resurrecting Dirotalo."

"How so?"

"That petroglyph on the wall is of him."

I gazed closer and realized that the largest dragon petroglyph was of Dirotalo.

"Hold on Wes, I can't resurrect anyone, let alone a dead dragon god. Zadohkoo forbade all forms of resurrection."

"Perhaps many magic rules don't apply within Frosher Volcano. After all, this is the site where I'magee killed Dirotalo and banned many forms of magic. Your ring also glowed at Yefhati Cave, and that site also featured forbidden magic."

"Are you trying to tell me something?"

"I believe I was resurrected when you, Ace, Marco, and Robin were fighting Krull and his dragon gang."

"How could that have happened? None of us knew anything about resurrection."

"What about controlling animals? You'll tell me that I'magee and Lazox banished controlling animals with magic, but I want you to try to control me."

I wasn't sure what to believe. There were so few explanations for the mysteries which Wes had presented to me, so I figured why not. An electric-green ray fired from my ring, collided with Wes, and did no damage.

"Wes," I said, "I order you to fly around the volcano three times."

Without any acknowledgment Wes took to flight. I hoped my magic was making him do what he was doing, and that he wasn't playing a game to trick me into believing his theories. Wes had always been honest and integral, and I'd hate for this to be his first episode of dishonesty.

"Do a few back flips in the air," I said.

Wes obliged. He didn't stop until I ordered him to. I commanded him to shoot three fireballs and he did so. Next, I told him to nosedive to the ground and stop within an arm's reach of crashing. He followed my commands precisely. I told him to land, and he did. Within a second, I ordered him to hover above the ground. He flew a pace above the ground as if his mind had no control over the actions of his body.

"Alright I believe you," I said. "I'm not going to jerk you around even though it's really fun to have you as my slave, but this is totally hard to wrap my head around."

"Thanks Don. How about firing a second ray at me to release me from your slave control?"

"Ah man, I wanted you to be my slave so you would do my chores all night," I smirked right before I fired a release ray. "Say, I wonder if I will be able to control you or any other animals outside of the volcano."

"We'll have a lot of experimentation to do. I'm sure I can write some first-rate academics papers on the subject. Don't worry, you'll get plenty of credit."

"But what does all of this have to do with resurrection?"

"My first memory is of Robin trying to control one of the dragons during your battle here. Robin may have failed to control those monsters which the goons were flying, but I think he accidentally brought me to life."

"No way."

"Yes way. It's completely preposterous man; that goof Robin is responsible for my life by sheer accident."

Wes and I erupted in laughter. Everything was making sense, but it was too crazy for logic. I wished that

Marco was here, Robin too. It was hilarious to think that Robin had tried to break magic rules and control wild dragons while Ace had played rodeo clown with one. If only Robin could realize what he'd accidentally created.

"I have an idea Don," Wes said, "point your ring at that rock carving of Dirotalo. I want you to try and control him just as you controlled me."

I was ready to believe anything so took aim with my ring. A green ray blasted the petroglyph. The light enveloped the rock carving. The light grew brighter, solidified, and took shape. A figure grew before our eyes. The apparition became a solid form which looked like a dragon.

Dirotalo stood in front of us. I couldn't believe that I had turned a rock carving into a tathika dragon or that I'd resurrected the dead. Never had I felt so surreal.

"Dirotalo," Wes said as he bowed down.

"Wes," Dirotalo spoke. "You do not need to bow down. You and your friend owe me nothing. I owe both of you everything. You have freed me not only from death, but from being forgotten about. Both of you are very special geniuses."

Wes shook Dirotalo's hand and thanked him. I wasn't sure how to react, though I gazed at Dirotalo and Wes with very open eyes. Dirotalo and Wes looked like twins. Wes was nearly crying.

"Dirotalo," I spoke. "Are you Wes's father?"

"No, but Wes you are still an extremely special individual," Dirotalo said. "You are the first resurrected member of an extinct species. Here in Frosher Volcano, many magic laws do not apply, which is why your friend was able to resurrect both you and I."

"His name is Don," Wes said.

"Pleasure to meet you Don, I will thank you in a minute," Dirotalo said, "back to you Wes. Frosher Volcano is a cemetery for many tathika dragons. When you were resurrected, dozens of different dragon spirits came together through reincarnation, formed one hybrid, and you were born. Since you were new to this world, you had no memories, but all your skills and knowledge came from dead tathika dragons. Wes, you are the sum of many dead dragons, and from what I can see, you inherited the best of traits: intelligence, bravery, and integrity."

Wes went quiet as he thought this over. He'd spent his entire life looking for answers to his orphaned existence, but the truth was almost too overwhelming to handle. The rest of us had two parents while Wes had so many different ones.

"I know this is so much for you to handle right now," Dirotalo said, "but I think your friend Don deserves an award for bringing the both of us to life."

Dirotalo raised his hand. A genie ring glimmered from one of his dragon talons. Was Dirotalo a genie? Could Wes learn magic?

A blue ray fired from Dirotalo's ring and flashed through me. I felt no different. What had Dirotalo given me? I hadn't planned on receiving any presents. I was pretty happy that Wes had received answers, and that was more than enough to call this mission a success.

"Don, I have bestowed you some genie spells which I'magee has outlawed," Dirotalo said. "You won't have all of them yet, as many will have to be reached through study. Don't expect to be able to revive the dead, but you can control all animals now."

"I can't thank you enough," I said. "I am completely beyond words."

"Just don't boss Wes around too much with your animal manipulation," Dirotalo said.

The three of us laughed in unison.

"Do you want to hear another funny story?" Dirotalo asked.

"For sure," I said.

"Do you know how genies were created?" Dirotalo asked.

"Who doesn't?" I shrugged. "I'magee selected a group of humans to be magic workers and gave each of them rings which embedded them with magic in their blood. As I'magee's chosen people, the race of the genies was created."

"That's the story from the Alontae, but it's not a true story," Dirotalo said.

"Really?" I said. "Please correct the bullshit for me."

"In very ancient times, I'magee kidnapped a group of humans and turned them into his slaves," Dirotalo said. "These slaves could perform acts of magic when they were under the command of I'magee, but when he had no use for them, he locked them in bottles filled with gases as if these magical slaves were vapors.

"One day Dirotalo gave a slave woman an iron ring with a jewel. This talisman allowed the woman to break free from I'magee's bondage and gain full control over the magic powers which she possessed while she'd been under I'magee's control. With the arrival of more rings and more escaped slaves, a revolution was born in which the magical slaves overthrew I'magee and became completely independent. Thus, the genie species was born. This tale has been eliminated from the Alontae to avoid humiliating I'magee."

"I'magee is a total fool who really doesn't know how to use his powers responsibly," Wes chuckled while Dirotalo and I roared in hysterics. "It's no wonder so many stories about him have been censored. I really need to find other embarrassing anecdotes about the god of fop."

Right as our chuckling died down, a cloud of smoke appeared at a nearby corner of the volcano. I worried that the volcano was about to blow. Between the new magic, extinct dragons, and answers to Wes's existence, I wouldn't be surprised if Frosher Volcano was ready to erupt again.

"You have disrespected me and will be punished," a strange voice growled.

I'magee appeared as the clouds of smoke dispersed. I recognized the god of magic because he was a blue-skinned human who wore a tan turban with a ruby in its centre. I'magee was flying on his magic carpet and was carrying a wizard staff. Unlike other genies, I'magee wore a genie ring on each finger.

"Dirotalo," I'magee growled. "You are to stay dead."

"Zadohkoo spoke to me right before Don brought me back to life," Dirotalo said. "I have been released from the afterlife and have rejoined life. More tathika dragons will rise. Today is the end of extinction."

I'magee fired a white ray from his wand. Dirotalo disappeared upon impact with the light. Wes screeched in astonishment and got ready to set I'magee on fire.

"Don't worry Wes," I said, "that was only a disappearance ray which wizards use. Dirotalo has vanished but he's not dead, and definitely not in the underworld. He's probably among the gods and goddesses."

"Shut your face Don," I'magee barked. "You've always loved to stir up trouble; you really don't know how to use your magic properly. It's no wonder you have a reputation for being a nosy interloper."

"If resurrecting innocent souls who you've murdered makes me a troublemaker then I'm your proudest dissident," I said.

"And you'll pay for it, you son of a bitch," I'magee sneered.

A ray fired from the ruby on I'magee's turban. I got ready to evade the blast, but the flash hit Wes, locking him in a force shield.

"Your mischievous friend isn't hurt, but I'm not going to let him interfere with our fight," I'magee said. "Neither he nor Dirotalo would be walking around if it weren't for you and your cretins always disobeying rules."

"I fight for the betterment of this country while you and the rest of the gods and goddesses ignore all the problems of Sionia. Fuck you and fuck worship."

I'magee fired ten stun rays at me, each from different rings. Before any of the rays could catch me, I created a force shield from my ring and deflected the rays.

"Is that the best you can do you pussy?" I taunted.

Though I'magee was the auspicious competitor, it was still fun to mock the god of magic. I pointed my ring at the volcanic floor and envisioned a burst of lava. Geysers of magma erupted like waves beating against the beach on a stormy day. I'magee fell to the ground and his magic carpet and turban melted to napalm. His flesh crisped but all wounds were quickly healed due to his self-healing magic. While it would have been great to kill him with the lava, I was happy that new forms of magic had come to me so quickly.

"You're learning quick Don," I'magee said. "You've always been powerful, but you're not tough enough to survive death."

I raised my ring and fired three lightning bolts at I'magee. Blue and white electricity jolted through I'magee's body as he convulsed on the rocky ground. I then conjured a blast of water and targeted it at I'magee. Smoke exploded from his jittering body. His flesh disappeared while his organs and gore dropped from his skeleton. Little flashes of blue and white lightning flew about and fried his damp bones. I smirked in accomplishment.

"Here's an off-the-record piece of magic I've never used on anyone before," a ghostly voice said. "I'm happy that you're the first freak who I'll use it on."

Pain throbbed in every cell of my body. I could hear nothing but snapping sounds which resembled crackling kindling. I wanted to scream and cry and die, but I lost all feeling within a moment. I feared paralysis since I couldn't feel my body. Terror and helplessness clouded over my anger. My eyes closed and my mouth shut, but my ears remained open. All movement and life seemed to have been shattered from my body. Had I died? Was I a blind ghost floating around the site of my death?

"That's called the bone breaker," I'magee said. "I used rapid telekinesis to break every bone in your body. You can't even open your eyes or feel pain, that's how bad this spell is.

"Don't worry Don, you're not dead, just completely useless. This is what you get for misusing the gifts of magic. Paralysis is an interloper's poison."

I'magee let out another cackle. I had never felt more hopeless. Why hadn't I figured out how to self-heal myself? With all the magic Dirotalo had given me, self-healing should have been among the package.

Had battling I'magee been my biggest mistake? I had always been impulsive and loved to fight, but anyone would tell you that fighting a deity was beyond stupid.

"I'll release your little pal," I'magee said. "Dragons are weak against the powers of magic; having one freak among the crowd won't cause any problems."

I was unsure if I'magee was taunting me or not. Was he actually going to release Wes, or would he kill him?

"Don, I'magee is gone," Wes said. "I'm free."

I couldn't respond to Wes. It was funny how paralysis kept your ears strong but destroyed the rest of your body.

"I'll get you out of here man, I promise," Wes vowed.

I was unsure of what happened for a very long time. After what felt like many lifetimes, I heard Sheri's voice. She was telling me not to worry and how much she loved me and that everything would be alright. These were sweet words, but also phrases which usually carried little hope since they were often said to terminally ill patients on death's door. Jason also promised my survival. Since I wasn't hearing Robin, Ace, or Keifer, I assumed that I was still alive and not in the afterlife. Would I survive, or would I fade with my eyes closed?

My eyes remained closed, but I saw blue lights. Was I being shot to the afterlife? Was Zadohkoo taking me to a new stage of existence? All these questions drove me crazy.

The bluish light waves continued to pass through my closed eyes, but the lights gradually turned green. I could hear Sheri, Jason, Julia, and Wes, but couldn't make out their panicked words. These were my friends, my loved ones, and they would hold my hand as I died. I wished that Marco and Huck and Trent and Bashar were here, but I was extraordinarily lucky to have some of my friends at my side.

My eyes fluttered open. Julia was standing over me and her ring was glowing the brightest I'd ever seen from her. She was healing me, but her magic levels were low. I had so many memories from our youth of how she would justify low magic by her athleticism. Whenever I boasted about how good I was at magic, she tackled me to the ground like a rugby player. We'd wrestle and I would get scolded for unfair fighting after using telekinesis or creating force shields.

If I died, where would my memories go?

I thought I saw Zadohkoo, but he quickly disappeared against the bluish green light. I'd never felt so delirious and demented.

Tears flowed down Sheri's face. Wes was holding her tightly. Jason looked like he'd seen a ghost. Sid barked frantically. Julia was lying on the ground, ready to crash. There was no light coming from her ring. I tried to speak, but words couldn't fall from my mouth. Julia's ring disintegrated to invisibility.

"He's alive," Jason said.

Sheri hugged me. For the first time in what felt like an eternity, I could feel something. I savored Sheri's tight embrace, her lush kisses and tears on my flesh. I kissed her, confirming that I was still here and not in the afterlife.

"I love you so much," Sheri said between kisses. "I thought you were dead. Wes, Julia, we can't thank you enough. We really can't."

"I love you too Sheri," I managed to say. "I am alive. I owe all of you my life."

"You owe Julia and Wes your life," Jason said. "Wes brought you here from Frosher Volcano. He even remembered your sword and magic carpet. I've never seen anything fly so fast. Julia healed you once you were inside."

"Julia," I said. "Did you just sacrifice all your magic to save me?"

"I am no longer a genie Don," Julia said as tears streamed down her face, "but I wouldn't have it any other way."

I didn't know how I'd ever thank Julia. I would have never been able to shed my life as a genie to save the life of another. I had used a lot of my magic to revive Marco after he'd been bitten by the massive mosquitoes, but I didn't have the selflessness to be a martyr and lose my magic forever. Julia had put so much healing energy into saving my body that she'd lost all her magic permanently. She would never be able to regain her powers or call herself a genie again. From here until death, she was a human.

"Julia, there is no way I'll ever be able to thank you," I said.

What she had done for me was more powerful than what Dirotalo had gifted me. Today really had been the craziest day ever for both Wes and I.

"Just remember, I can still kick your ass," Julia smirked.

BOOK XIII:

WAR OF THE LOSERS

I was in and out of my waking state for a few days. I was busted sleepwalking a few times only to fall over cold. Sometime after my zombie resurrection, I came to relatively clear senses. When it was determined that I was lucid, Jason cooked me a bowl of mutton stew and handed me a beer, both of which made me feel alive.

"While you were out of it, you missed major national news," Sheri said. "It's not as cool as what you and Wes discovered."

"Let me guess," I said, "no one knows anything about Dirotalo yet."

"He's a personal god for the two of us," Wes said, "and they say guardian angels don't exist."

"Sionia has gone to war," Julia said.

"What else is new?" I snorted. "This entire bloody country has been designated as a sprawl of conflict by Qiami, that's the kind of culture we get from having a goddess of war."

"This ain't funny Don," Sheri said. "Santalonia has gone to war with O'Jahnteh and Stodaneatoo."

The food in my mouth stopped tasting so good. It wasn't that I was overly surprised about politicians from different cities fighting so much as I feared that many innocent civilians had been caught between two belligerent forces.

"It turns out that O'Jahnteh and Stodaneatoo are both built over major mining deposits," Julia said. "The federal government wants to floor these cities, migrate all the inhabitants elsewhere, and build major mining sites. Many politicians from Stodaneatoo and O'Jahnteh have been assassinated. Santalonia is sending many troops from the national army north. A number of local forces have banded together as a rebel alliance to battle the invaders from Santalonia."

I couldn't think of anything to say apart from, "holy shit."

"The O'Jahnteh government is calling for conscription," Sheri said. "If you don't enter military service without a valid reason, then you'll be considered a traitor and sentenced to hard labour."

"In other words, you have to fight imperialism or live as a slave, though I don't see much of a difference between the two options," Jason said.

"Forget about all of that," Julia said. "We're in a land war and we have to do all we can to save our homes."

"I've been able to use some of my vigilum connections and pulled some strings," Sheri said. "It looks like all of us can be on the same platoon. I've also contacted Marco, Huck, and Bashar, but am still trying to get word to Trent. Hopefully, we can all be on the same troop."

This invasion couldn't have come at a worse time, but war never came at a good time. I liked the idea of fighting side by side with my friends, but more importantly I wanted to spend some peaceful time with my buds during my recovery. I still hadn't figured out how powerful I had become since Dirotalo has bestowed me with forbidden powers.

"An invading force is nearing O'Jahnteh," Wes said. "We should get ready for the attack."

A week later I found myself in a jungle camp south of O'Jahnteh. Since the jungles were thick, it looked like all the battles were going to be fought through guerrilla warfare until one side penetrated the wilderness and ended up in the city. Both sides could pray as much as they wanted, but there was no guarantee that either opponent would win no matter how optimistic, strong, or prepared they were.

Sheri came through with her promise and managed to pull enough strings to put together a team of fierce veteran warriors: Julia, Bashar, Huck, Wes, Jason, Marco, Trent, herself, and me.

So many rumours were swirling around the country, and no one knew what to believe.

"I am going to get to the truth behind this war," Bashar said. "I will write the most important piece of war journalism ever, and it's all going to be told from my own first-hand account. No bullshit, no propaganda, no embellishment."

"Won't that be something," Huck cracked. "You're already the cockiest guy I know."

"Piss up a rope," Bashar said.

"I for one would really like to know what this war is all about," Jason said. "It seems odd that precious minerals were randomly discovered beneath the second and third biggest metropolitan areas of Sionia, especially at the same time. These cities are pretty far from one another too. Even if there are tons of precious stones, the federal government should realize how dangerous it is to dig up two major cities which are prosperous in so many other ways."

"I agree with Jason," I said. "Everything has been so crazy recently, and if anyone knows what crazy is, it's us."

"I think it's wrong that we have to fight someone else's war," Trent said. "I happily live in the jungle, far from Stodaneatoo and O'Jahnteh. This war is about greed, and it should be fought between politicians and businessmen. Why do we common folks have to be martyrs for squabbling bureaucrats?"

"Trent, we have a responsibility to our homelands," Sheri said. "It is up to us to defend our territory, to look out for one another, and to punish evil. Society has given to us, and now we have to give back."

"I never really wanted anything to do with society which is why I live in the wilderness with a primitive tribe," Trent said. "I'm only here because of conscription, and I'd rather fight than be forced into slavery for a third time."

"I know you have a caustic view toward politics but look at this war as a way of defending your tribe," Julia said.

"The best way for me to take care of my tribe would be to go back home and be with them," Trent affirmed.

"There is nothing I want more than to be at home with my pregnant wife."

We all stopped in our tracks. Bashar let out a chuckle, indicating that he'd been waiting for a secret to spill. Sheri bear-hugged Trent and Julia jumped in. Huck high-fived Trent while the rest of us guys shook his hand.

"Why does such wonderful news have to come up during such shitty circumstances?" Trent said.

"This is why we are going to fight damn hard to win the war really quickly," Sheri said. "You will be home well before Larissa gives birth."

I agreed with Sheri that we should hit our enemies real hard and end the conflict as quickly as possible. I really wished that we could get the gods and goddesses to scare the Santalonians out of the war, but Qiami had decided to play the role of passive-aggressive sadistic spectator and not intervene in combat despite being the goddess of war. Worshipping a deity of war seemed like a complete juxtaposition to life. My recent near-death experience had made me appreciate life even more, and I wasn't ready to throw myself into another life-or-death situation despite invaders being at the door.

During our first three days in the war camp, we patrolled the jungle, played lacrosse with others during down time, and climbed trees. We'd been ordered to hold a defensive stance which suited each of us.

On our fourth night at the base, we were awoken by a large barrage. The ruckus shook me from my sleep, and I dashed out of my tent without my sword. Sheri chased after me without rubbing any sleep from her eyes, though was carrying a cutlass and a lantern. Our only lights came from a few torches and our campfire, which had been reduced to embers.

Our aphotic setting became alit by a rapid blaze as flames grew across a tent, which soon collapsed.

"Is everyone alright?" Huck asked.

Julia, Jason, Wes, Trent, Bashar, and Marco emerged from their tents. While I was happy that everyone was well, it seemed odd that our spare tent had burst into fire.

"That tent must have been hit by a fireball," Jason said.

"There is probably a catapult nearby," Wes said.

"Or a genie is lurking in the shadows," Marco said.

Sid barked. Through the trees we could see a faint light. Since there were abandoned roads near our camp, it was possible that artillery was being transported down them. The dim light in the trees started to travel upward and strange noises passed through the foliage.

"Oh shit," Wes said.

Flames rose above the trees. Wes took flight and let out a massive blast of fire from his dragon mouth. Burning bombs fell to the ground as the incoming fireball burst open due to Wes's attack. Though Wes was a beast born from a volcano, he'd gotten way too close to the incoming fireball. The rest of us dashed into the trees to avoid the falling inferno.

We were unsure of how many catapults lay veiled within the trees. For all his heroics, there was no way Wes could defend us forever from incoming fireballs.

Sid dashed toward the thin light between the trees. Jason and Trent chased after the dog. We hoped that Sid would lead our team to the invaders.

Wes swooped to the ground and said, "I'm going to fly above the trees and see if I can spot any more invaders. I will do all in my power to destroy any bombardment."

"We already owe you our lives man," Huck said.

Everyone gathered their weapons before following Trent, Jason, and Sid. By the time we'd caught up with our allies, Jason and Trent were in the middle of a fight with four Santalonian soldiers. Two oxen stood next to a catapult and a bonfire. Jason had clubbed two adversaries to the ground. His club swung once again and he knocked a third enemy into the bonfire, which acted as fuel for the catapult fireballs. The fourth soldier tried to run from the fight but bumped into Trent and was then stomped into the ground with a few kicks from colossal cyclops legs.

"Kick ass job guys," Julia said.

"Thanks," Jason said, "but these clowns weren't alone. I heard one of them say that there were others out there, which is why the guy who Trent booted was trying to run away."

Jason pulled Sid toward one of his slain victims. Sid got a good whiff of the soldier's blood-stained clothes.

"Go on now pooch," Jason told Sid, "find our other enemies."

Sid dashed into the jungle and the rest of us followed. I really admired how Jason had trained his dog so well. Basset hounds had the second-best scent of any dogs, and Jason had taught Sid to use her nose for something apart from sniffing out food and rolling in dead fish.

Since Jason was the fastest runner in the group, he was able to keep up with Sid. He also seemed to have very strong night vision since he was dodging trees and bouncing over logs and rocks with grace. He didn't have a light while the rest of us were carrying torches and lanterns. Huck, Marco, and I had left out magic carpets behind because the darkness made dodging trees very challenging. Bashar was having a hard time keeping up with the rest of us, so Trent stopped to wait for him despite Trent being the second fastest runner of our troop.

A phantom ruckus vibrated through the forest. Wood cracked. A boom echoed from the forest floor. Sid barked in frenzy. There was no light coming from any corner of the jungle.

Our troop came across a large boulder which lay atop a pulverized timbered tree trunk. Shattered wood and sprayed branches lay everywhere.

Julia let out the fiercest wail I'd ever heard.

Jason lay beneath the fallen tree trunk, pinned to the ground. Dark blood tainted his skin and blackened his trademark red cloak. I crouched next to what I feared was a corpse. Healing rings shot from my ring across his body, but they quickly turned black, indicating that there was no life left in Jason's body. I hoped by some miracle that my magic would send his soul back into his corpse.

Nothing made any sense in war, and nothing was predictable. One moment your buddy was taking charge of the situation and doing better than anyone, and the next he was an empty body.

Julia stepped closer to Jason's corpse, and I backed away. It seemed wrong that I had brought Marco back from near death with magic, and Julia had lost all her genie powers when she'd brought me back from the dead, but a human like Jason couldn't be healed with magic.

Wes landed after spotting our lanterns and torches.

"I've found the other catapult---," he said before he realized that we were having a silent funeral.

"Go on and kill those sons of bitches," Julia barked. "We'll have the funeral later. We need to kill those assholes before we have a group memorial."

Wes took the lead, and Huck and Marco followed. Sheri hugged Julia.

"Leave me be," Julia said. "Don and I will join you soon."

Sheri placed a kiss on Julia's head and joined the others. I wasn't sure why Julia had asked me to stay, unless she believed that I could revive the dead with my new magic powers. I'd heard that people often made irrational choices during heated conflict, and I wondered if everyone would start behaving more enigmatically due to the insidiousness of war.

"Where's Bashar?" Marco asked as Wes led them away.

We all looked around, but the ogre wasn't about.

"He must have gotten lost," Trent said. "I'll go find him."

Trent took off with a lantern. Our group was broken five ways. How the hell had the war gotten off to such an ugly start? How much evil lay ahead of us?

It was hard to imagine Jason having been killed so quickly: the fast runner, the club fighter, the archer, the dog lover, the chef, a great friend, the fellow who easily bounced from the mountains to the ocean to the jungle, the dude who was practically my brother-in-law, a quiet smart guy who analyzed everything and always saw details which the rest of us rushed over. With his life gone, only our memories could carry on his magnificent character.

Julia's crying caught the attention of five approaching troops. She broke her embrace with Jason's corpse and dashed toward them with her sword raised. Her blade caught two of the troops by surprise, slashing each of them to the ground. A third soldier began a duel with her.

Both opponents bounced between the trees as their blades slashed back and forth through the darkness.

Sid jumped off a log, tackled a fourth troop, and bit into the troop's neck with spitfire jaw action. They said animals had a sixth sense when it came to relationships with owners, and Sid was settling her vendetta.

I used my telekinesis to levitate a broken branch above the ground. I fired the improvised spear toward the fifth troop. The splintered wood shot into his neck, killing him on impact.

My fallen victim caught the attention of Julia's duelist. When the man's eyes flashed to the right, Julia's used this momentary distraction as an opportunity to dismember her foe from shoulder to waist. Although it was very dark out, I saw crimson juice piercing the blackness.

"Let's check on our friends," Julia said. "We'll come back for Jason's body later."

Julia and I followed the path which Wes had created. I wanted to talk and counsel Julia about Jason's death but didn't know what to say. Too much was going on, and we hadn't had enough time to process such terrible emotions.

We came across our friends a few minutes later. I nearly tripped over a Sionian corpse which had a crossbow bolt sticking from the chest, courtesy of Huck. Sheri was dueling a swordsman. Bashar snuck behind her adversary and buried his hammer in the guy's skull. Marco's whip snapped toward a spearman. The whip wrapped around the spear and with a taut tug Marco ripped the weapon from the spearman's hand. Upon seizing the spear, Marco chucked the missile back at its owner, spearing him in the gut.

A catapult and two oxen lay next to a few lanterns and a large pile of rocks. These slain troops must have been the guys who'd fired the kill shot at Jason.

"Where's Trent?" I asked.

Everyone looked at one another without an answer.

"Oh shit," Sheri said. "He went looking for you Bashar. Thanks for hammering my foe in the head."

"I didn't spot any other fires when I was flying above the trees, so there probably aren't any more nocturnal attackers out there," Wes said. "Let's find Trent before he gets totally lost."

"Should we destroy the catapults?" Huck asked.

"Let's retrieve them in daylight," Marco said. "We'll take the oxen too."

Though we all feared that Trent may have gotten lost, we found him on account of Sid's tracking skills. Trent thanked us for being worried about his state, but he didn't seem scared since he was a jungle man who'd spent so much time in dark forests without a light. He offered to retrieve Jason's body and take it back to camp.

None of us spoke until we reached home base. It had been silently decided that we would burn Jason's body in the tent which was flaming from the fireball. Julia pressed her lips on a small spec of Jason's flesh which hadn't been touched by blood or tears, bidding him much love and farewell. Bashar tossed the dead body into the fire. Moments later Huck chucked Jason's war club into the flames. It was considered good luck among many northerners to take one precious item with you into the afterlife.

"Thank you, Huck," Julia said. "I would have forgotten that tradition, and I know Jason will be thankful for that."

As Jason's body burned, the rest of us telepathically communicated how hurt we felt and how sorry we were that he had to go while the rest of us got to live. I'd certainly felt survivor's guilt when Robin and Ace had died, but now I feared that more unpredictable deaths lay ahead, and that it would soon be my turn to join the trend.

"If you guys don't mind, I'd like some alone time," Julia said, "just Sid and I."

We all agreed. Julia hugged each of us. Though it wouldn't be light out for a long time, none of us were going to get any sleep. Marco, Huck, and Wes decided to patrol the skies. Trent headed back to his bunk while Bashar squatted next to a lantern and made notes in his journal. Sheri took me by the hand and led me to bed. We ended up screwing pretty vivaciously that night but no matter how great the orgasms were, we couldn't fuck the pain away. Some said that love always overpowered hatred, but I wasn't sure if that idea applied during war.

As the weeks rolled on, many lies and rumours swept the nation. Some called this conflict the Great Sionian War while detractors claimed that the word great should not be used to compliment something as horrible as war. Others called this conflict the Sionian Civil War but was there a such thing as a civil war since war was anything but civilized. Bashar referred to the war as the Battle for the Land in all the articles he wrote for the newspaper. His entries were popular due to his descriptive writings of battles, his embellished yet eloquent prose, and his rhetoric that we were triumphing over evil.

"All my writings are going to be published in one thick volume as soon as the war is over," Bashar said. "It'll be the definitive take on the war."

Much to the surprise of Santalonia, O'Jahnteh was so far winning the war. Many of the southern troops had little experience in jungle combat and had expected large full-scale battles.

"It's pretty arrogant of Santalonia to think they can beat us on our own turf," Trent said one evening after a long patrol in the jungle. "We are from the jungle while Santalonians are from coastal plains, so they really don't know how to survive in the rainforest."

"They'll probably have a strong advantage against us when we head down south," Wes said. "Most troops from Stodaneatoo and O'Jahnteh don't have much training when it comes to naval or open-field combat. Besides, we'll be exhausted from traveling while their forces will be close to home."

"Don't say that Wes," Huck said, "be positive man."

"How the hell am I supposed to be positive?" Trent scoffed. "My wife is due to give birth, I've been conscripted into war, stolen from my homeland, and forced to kill."

"Would you ever consider fighting with weapons, just for once?" Wes asked. "I know you're the strongest, but the war might go by faster if you fought with a lance or a sword."

"To hell with weapons," Trent said. "There is no way something as evil as war will make me forget my principles."

"I'm worried that your admirable idealism will get you killed," Wes voiced.

"Nature has always protected me because I know how to live with it," Trent said. "We're winning jungle combat because we know how to live with the jungle. All societies should be close with nature. Politics, corruption, feuding businesses, and war are all the result of the over-expansion of society. If we went back to our natural roots as hunter-gatherers with primitive tools and some farming, then we wouldn't be caught up in this bloody war."

Knowledge of the jungle wasn't the only reason why Stodaneatoo and O'Jahnteh were winning at jungle combat. Many towns and villages had sided with us, citing that they hated how much of the nation's wealth was hogged by the capital.

Though Jason had died, no new members joined our troop. Julia rarely talked about Jason's death though she remained close with Sid.

"Winning this war is how I'll honour what Jason died for," Julia once said at dinner.

"It's also how we'll honour our homeland and our metropolitan governments," Sheri added.

"Fuck that," I said. "The governments are what got us into the war in the first place."

"What would you rather do Don?" Sheri asked. "Pack up and watch O'Jahnteh and Stodaneatoo crumble to the ground so that a quarry can be built while countless people are displaced."

"Are you sure that's even the real story?" I asked.

"Why are you always so paranoid of the government?" Sheri questioned. "You're so quick to fight evil if you're doing it on your own terms, but as soon as politics step in, you automatically brand the government the enemy even if you're fighting for the same thing. Stop jumping to such spiteful conclusions man."

"I hate fighting soldiers," I said. "Fighting criminals is guilt-free because those individuals chose to do terrible things. With the military, average folks are being forced into fighting. The soldiers we battle are probably decent people who've been fed too many lies and are dying for the wrong reasons. Send out the chicken-hawk politicians to fight; I'll happily behead them."

"War is brutal and bloody and we're all in real deep shit," Julia said. "The only way to end the terror is to win the war. The faster we win and the quicker we kill others, the sooner the slaughter with end. None of us are deserting and that's final."

Since the Battle of the Land was the first major conflict with female soldiers, certain citizens were uncomfortable with having women in war. Some military officials suggested that women step down and let the men do the fighting.

"Fuck that," Julia said. "I'm a gladiator, a combat coach, a woman, and a warrior. I have kicked plenty of man ass in my time."

"It's ludicrous to want women to step down from war," Sheri said. "We need as big an army we can get, so let's bring in as many ladies as possible."

"There aren't as many female soldiers in Santalonia," Wes said. "Getting attacked by women could really throw off the Santalonian forces, and surprise is a key to victory."

"There is no way the war is going to erase what myself and so many other women fought hard for," Julia declared.

"Our rights as soldiers are going to be protected just as long as we vote for the right candidates in the upcoming election," Sheri said. "We'll get better weapons, higher quality supplies, more advice from generals, and there will be more women in battle. This is why we the soldiers need to align with the politicians."

I decided to let Sheri believe that the government would help us win the war. As cynical as many soldiers were, we all needed hope. If the government gave Sheri hope, who was I to criticize her? I kept my comments quiet, and I held hope in magic. I wasn't entirely content that magic would save us, but I found it much more reassuring than politics.

After countless days of pushing south, we came upon the northern banks of Eftalous Lake, the largest lake in Sionia. Zadeezey got sick of the lack of naval battles, so she called for some action on the lake. Many foresaw more naval battles coming as the war grew closer to Santalonia. A lot of troops feared ocean combat since O'Jahnteh and Stodaneatoo were landlocked. Huck, Sheri, and I had informed our superiors that we were more than willing to participate in naval combat. As a result of our volunteerism, our troop was drafted toward the Battle of the Rowers.

For many weeks, ships had been fighting back and forth across Eftalous Lake as if it were a chessboard. Shilotey opposed the war, so she used her goddess powers to ban wind from the lake, so all the boats were rowed. Exhausted muscles and the futility of sails had made it difficult for either side to gain victory. When my crew was presented with a small trireme (armed with an onager), our chances of victory looked far from favourable.

"How the hell are eight of us supposed to row this beast and fight our rivals?" Bashar said. "I wonder what the public is going to think when I write a story about this."

"Not so fast Bashar," I said, "having a small number can be advantageous."

"Don, quantity over quality can be important in war," Bashar retorted.

"Our enemies will think a small boat is weak and easy to overpower," I said, "but they will overlook one detail of us underdogs; we have three genies on board. We can use magic to make wind for the sails while our enemies will be stuck with paddles and sore arms."

Our trireme pushed off from the dock. Sid barked several times as we drifted from land. While Sid always stayed close with us in combat, we knew not to bring her out on the boat since she would get too distracted by the lake birds.

Once we'd rowed several paces from the dock, I used my magic to create wind for the sails. Ever since Dirotalo had bequeathed me with heightened magic, it seemed that I had an endless amount of power in my ring. Though I kept my sword at my side, I never used it in combat any more since so much magic was at my finger. Julia didn't say anything, but I could tell that she was jealous of my new abilities. Whenever I tried to talk to her about her sacrifice or how grateful I was for her selflessness, she changed the topic as if she didn't want to be reminded that she was no longer a genie. As always, she sought to prove herself as an athlete. Jason had helped her become a better runner, and right now she was better with weapons than anyone in our troop.

There were four enemy triremes ahead of us. It didn't look like we had any allies nearby. Four to one was frightening, especially when each boat had at least three times the crew of our boat. My friends and I had always done an excellent job at triumphing over near impossible odds, and I liked to attribute our success to our unity as a team. I really hoped that our friendships would once again help us surpass our adversaries.

An enemy trireme rowed toward us. Our boat ran with the wind and headed to the rival at a speed which surprised them. The Santalonians soon struck their oars and climbed up to the deck of their boat, armed with arrows and javelins. Once our port side was parallel to their starboard, I killed the wind from my ring and created a large force shield which surrounded the port side of our boat.

"Alright crew," I said. "I've created an advanced force shield. Weapons can pass through it on our side, but nothing can pass through it on their side."

Julia and Sheri armed themselves with bows and loaded quivers while Huck packed a bolt into his crossbow. Marco had never been a great archer, but I assured him that his magic blasts could pass through my force shield without doing any damage to our protection. Wes's fire blasts didn't have the range to hit our rivals. While I always wished that Jason was still alive, our lethal situation really made me wish we had his archery skills.

Many arrows, spears, and javelins blasted from the deck of our naval rival only to be deflected by my force shield. Sheri, Julia, and Huck blasted bolts and arrows from their weapons without any fear of the missiles ricocheting off the force shield. Speared sailors fell into the water or were bombarded to the deck of their boat from incoming arrows and bolts. Marco fired several rays from his ring, blasting enemies away.

"Hold up" Wes called. "You guys are all doing a great job, but we only have a limited number of arrows. Instead of trying to kill each troop individually, why don't we destroy the boat?"

"Wes you're a genius," Sheri said.

Wes headed to the bow where our onager lay. Trent followed and placed a stone (which only he was strong enough to pick up) into the bowl-shaped bucket on the onager. Wes blasted the stone with flames until it was a glowing coal. Right when we thought that the boat's catapult would catch fire, Wes launched the onager.

The burning stone flashed through my force shield as if it were invisible. While many of the crew had been shot dead, those who were still alive screeched at the incoming terror.

Wood blasted from the ship as the stone smashed it. The trireme keeled so far to the right that the boat capsized. Some crewmembers fell into the lake while others scrambled upward on their half-sunk boat.

"They're useless now," Trent said. "Let's move onto the next boat."

Trent pulled the tiller to the left. I shot magic wind at the sail, and we sailed toward our enemies in the distance.

I felt strange optimism. It wasn't often that one felt positive during war. Although feeling hopeful was a good thing, I ordered myself to not get overconfident.

"Would you look at this," Bashar laughed as a dinghy with three swordsmen rowed toward us. "Let me teach these arrogant buccaneers a lesson."

Bashar jumped over the side of our boat and pulled a cannonball. Horror struck the guys in the dory. The obese ogre crashed into the rowboat, shattered the wood, flailed the oars, trampled the crew, and sank through the bottom of the vessel. Water splashed, waves grew, and bits of the once remaining boat bounced in the wake. Bashar let out a cackle as he emerged from the water.

"You guys were brave but stupid," Bashar laughed at the swimming buccaneers. "I won't kill you if you fuck off forever."

"You were pretty stupid too Bashar," Sheri said. "You could have landed on one of those swords."

"If you're going to be a cocky idiot, don't expect us to heal you," Marco said.

"Stop being wimps," Bashar laughed. "Bravery wins."

Bashar climbed aboard our boat using a rope ladder. We continued to sail toward more rival boats. Wes decided to take flight and check the area to see if we had more than three enemy ships within our vicinity.

Moments after soaring into the sky, several arrows flew from one of our enemies. Two of the arrows darted through Wes's leathery bat wings. Our dragon friend let out a lizard cry, flopped backward, and crashed into the lake, sinking as blood wept from his wounds.

"Oh shit," I said as I dove into the water without giving any thought to the incoming arrows.

I was not going to let Wes die. Jason was going to be my only lost friend from this war. During my life as a vigilante, I'd lost a lot of important people, and all the deaths were to end with Jason's.

I dove deep into the cool lake water, pulling myself to the abyss. Wes was sinking very deep, but I was gaining on him. I worried that I might run out of oxygen. If I re-emerged to lake-surface to get a breath of air, then I would surely lose Wes.

Right when my lungs were wheezing for air, I remembered one of my new genie powers. The lake water stung my eyes, but I glanced down at my ring and called for an air bubble. A large bubble of air shot from my jewelry. I placed one hand inside the bubble and with my other arm I paddled toward Wes. After a few strokes I grabbed Wes's arm. Using all my strength I pulled Wes into the bubble.

The two of us passed into the cavity of oxygen as if its walls were transparent. Once inside, I took in several deep breaths of air. Wes was breathing faintly and continued to bleed. I took to healing his wounds with magic. The bleeding holes in Wes's wings closed. After a minute he started breathing at a normal rate.

"What happened?" Wes wondered. "Don what's going on?"

"We're inside an oxygen bubble. You were shot, I dove down here to rescue you, and I used my magic to create this bubble."

"Don, I owe you my life."

"Dude I wouldn't even have this magic ability if you hadn't brought me to Frosher Volcano; this is one of the powers Dirotalo gave me."

The bubble floated to the lake surface, and Wes and I climbed aboard our trireme. To our surprise, the ship which had attacked Wes was sinking.

"What happened?" I asked.

"Your girlfriend is a real hero," Huck said.

"That's heroine," Julia scolded.

"When you were down rescuing Wes, Marco created a force shield to protect all of us," Huck said. "The only problem was that we had to fire our weapons over the force shield. Sheri got Trent to load another rock into the onager. It was a difficult shot, but she managed to fire the rock over Marco's force shield. The rock crashed into the centre on our enemies' trireme and made a shipwreck worthy hole. Most of the crew abandoned the boat once it was sinking. It was the most unreal shot ever, and Sheri might as well dub herself the queen of catapults."

"That's really sweet of you Huck," Sheri said as she pinched his cheek, "but don't forget Marco, his force shield saved us from a load of spears."

"There are also alligators around here," Trent said. "Some of the crew got chomped up when they were fleeing the sinking ship."

"Bashar, Wes, and I are really lucky that we haven't been bitten by these beasts," I said. "Let's make it a rule that none of us go swimming again."

The third trireme neared our boat. Our vessel was rocking back and forth motionlessly since I wasn't powering the sails with wind, and no one was rowing.

"I have an idea," Julia stated, "hand me the torch."

Though it wasn't nighttime, there was a burning torch at the bow of our boat near the onager. Marco passed Julia the torch and she used it to light one of her arrows. Right before her bow could go up in flames, Julia fired the arrow. Sheri then ignited her arrows and fired at the nearby boat. Huck smiled at what they were doing but feared that igniting his bolts would burn his crossbow.

A small fire grew on the enemy trireme. Some sailors attempted to douse the flames with buckets of water, but the fire continued to burn.

"Our arrows were dipped in thithaleeth oil," Julia said, "that boat is going to burn to crisp, and there is nothing the soldiers can do about it."

We complimented Julia and then took to sailing toward other rivals. The waters became shallow, and I wondered if he'd bump into any of the hippos who were resting among the swampy shore.

"Holy shit, an alligator," Bashar exclaimed.

A gator had crawled onto our boat using the rope ladder. This didn't seem possible, but war wasn't the time to contemplate what was or wasn't real. The gator snapped it's jaws at Wes, who still hadn't fully recovered from shock and wounds.

"Don't shoot any fire," Julia warned. "You'll burn the boat down."

Trent leapt forward and tackled the alligator. The two of them wrestled across the deck as the gator's claws scratched Trent's taut skin. Sheri surrounded the alligator and was waiting for an opportunity to spear it, but worried that she might stake Trent. I had tried to use magic to control animals in the past, but it was a skill I had yet to learn. Julia wanted to intervene and understood that Trent's life (and possibly the lives of everyone on board) was in danger, but her veganism paralyzed her.

The alligator's jaw snapped open, revealing dozens of vicious vampire teeth. Trent jumped back. The gator darted forward and snapped it's jaw. A hunk of meat was ripped from Trent's thigh. The cyclops groaned, spat, and jumped forward. Blood leaked from Trent's wound at an alarming rate. Trent's hands balled into fists, and he swung his dukes at the gator. I wanted to jump in and heal Trent, but he was focused on clubbing the gator in the skull. Before haze could leave the alligator's eye, Trent drove his horns into the belly of the gator, piercing it's lungs and heart. While the first headbutt probably killed the beast, Trent rammed his horns into the gator several more times to confirm the kill.

"Holy shit," Trent said.

I crouched next to Trent and healed his wounds. Blood attracted carnivores, and we feared that Trent's ripped flesh and spilled hemoglobin would lure more gators.

"Trent, that was the most badass fight I've ever seen against an animal," Bashar said.

"Don't be proud of that," Julia scolded.

"Relax," Bashar laughed. "The man didn't have a choice, and we can all have a healthy dinner tonight, reptiles are pure protein."

"I admire that gator for being a fighter, and we're definitely going to eat it," Trent said. "I could really use some extra muscle right now."

"You guys take a look at that," Wes called, stealing our attention.

The catapults on the fourth boat had fired three shots. The first shot had poor accuracy and was going to land far from us. The second shot didn't have much range so would flop into the water. The third shot was burning red and ready to bash our trireme and set it afire.

"I got it," Huck called.

Huck raised his ring and blasted wind. The sudden breeze caught the burning missile. Small bits of embers blew off the incoming projectile. Right when it looked like the flaming ball was about to crash into our boat, Huck heightened the power of his gale. The wind blew the fireball backward. The shot flopped into the water. Cool liquid smothered the fire to ash.

"Holy shit Huck, you saved us," I said. "You keep getting better and better at magic."

"Now is the time to get them," Sheri said, "let's slaughter them before they reload."

"Leave that to me," Marco said as he stepped atop his magic carpet.

Marco took flight and headed toward the last standing enemy ship.

"Is he trying to commit suicide?" Wes exclaimed. "There are tons of troops with arrows who could easily shoot him down."

"Marco was always a loner who could take care of himself," I said. "Only once did I ever have to save his life, and let's hope that he'll never need his neck saved again."

Several bows fired at Marco, but he managed to dodge each arrowhead using his keen magic carpet agility. The onagers were being loaded, and I wondered if the siege weapon operators would consider realigning their catapults to blast the genie on his magic carpet. While we watched what was going on, Huck used telekinesis to maneuver a rock onto our onager since Trent wasn't ready to lift such a heavy object.

Marco flew to the stern of the trireme. He targeted the sail on the boat and fired a force blast from his ring. I couldn't figure out why the sail was rigged considering there was no wind anywhere.

Several more force blasts flew from Marco's ring. The force blasts caught the sail and pushed the trireme forward as if winds were blowing at it. The trireme glided forward until it crashed into several submerged stones. Wood smashed and holes grew in the bow of the boat. The mast cracked and toppled downward.

Marco flew back to our boat right before a gang of archers could fire at him.

"That ship is now beached against a rock," Marco told. "It's filling with water, and if they try to row away from the rocks, they'll make the hole bigger, and the boat will sink. I say we paddle away and leave them marooned."

"Paddle," I snorted. "Magic has done us favours. Let's sail away and laugh at those rowers. I don't want anyone to have sore muscles after we kicked so much ass."

Marco, Huck, and I put our rings together and created a strong gale which caught the sails on our trireme. We sailed back to our dock at a broad reach while Bashar commanded the tiller. Everyone onboard smiled. For many, this was their first battle at sea. We'd overcome some incredible odds and near-death incidents, but each of us was walking away stronger than before. Perhaps the Santalonians would lose the lake faster than they'd predicted.

"Do any of you guys want to go to the tavern?" Marco asked once the boat was docked, and we were heading up the gangplank.

"I'm all for it," I said.

"No thanks dude, I've got a lady to hit up," Huck grinned.

Huck had recently hooked up with some chick who was on a different platoon, and he'd been sneaking away at every opportunity to get laid.

"Since none of us have seen this babe, she probably isn't real," Bashar cracked. "Are you sure you're not sneaking off to jerk off?"

"Suck a ball," Huck said.

"Not today," Wes said. "I've got some reading to do."

Julia and Sheri had a warrior women's meeting to attend while Trent wanted some quiet time in the jungle. Bashar said he'd joined us shortly, but he wanted to get some writing done while his memories of the lake battle were still fresh in his head.

The tavern was in a cove at the most northern tip of the lake. The allies' navy surrounded the waters south of the cove, shielding this from an attack. This watering hole had once acted as a haven for tourists but was now a retreat for northern soldiers. Patrons packed the pub to participate in chess, billiards, darts, arm wrestling, and cards. It was comforting to see that even with war going on, people were still escaping to the pub for fun. The kickboxing ring was empty which made me happy because the thought of watching recreational combat seemed out of line given our circumstances.

I ordered a lager while Marco settled with a pint of pale ale. The bartender offered us a complimentary bowl of trail mix. There was a sword and a large dragon skeleton mounted on a distant wall. Though the bones were from an animalistic dragon, I couldn't help but wonder about Dirotalo. He was a character who would be a great asset to our troop.

"To Jason," Marco said as he held out his glass.

"To Jason," I said as our glasses clinked.

After draining suds from our pints, Marco said, "the dude has been dead for quite some time, and this is the first drink we've had in his name."

"That's horrible. This fucked up war is really distracting us from the good things we should remember."

"The war sure is evil, but I think it might be doing me some good."

"Marco, how the hell can you say that?"

"Hear me out. I've always struggled with anger and trauma from my past. Fighting crooks used to help me unleash some rage, but it was never enough. I'm thinking that this war can be my ultimate purge to cleanse myself of all my pent-up anger. Nothing I face in the future will ever be as awful as this war, so perhaps I will get over all my unresolved issues when I walk away from the last battle alive."

"That's an interesting idea man, but what if you end up even more traumatized by the evils of life because of this war?"

"I really don't think I'll ever go back to combat once the war is over. We're winning, and we've had luck on our side."

"You know, this war is really making me question my own life as a warrior."

"How so?"

"As a vigilante, I always called the shots. I chose my battles. I acted as the judge and jury, and I never had to follow rules or politics. Things are different now that we're working for the government. I'm not even sure we're fighting on the right side."

"No one is ever totally right in war."

"Exactly, that's one thing that really frustrates me. I never felt remorse when I fought freaks like Krull, but now I'm fighting average, most likely ethical people who've been conscripted into war. It's totally fucked man."

"I agree with you on that Don, don't think I don't. I think any sane person would agree with you on that. I hope my warrior side will die with this war, and my tranquility side will grow after the war."

"I'll drink to that."

Marco ordered a snack of bannock and insisted on paying for another round of brew. Just as our drinks were coming, two wizards entered the bar. Both were dressed in traditional robes, carried staffs, and bee-lined to Marco and I. As the wizard duo approached us, they raised their staffs. Marco raised his beer glass to the wizards while I raised my ring.

The orbs in the wizards' staffs glowed red, an indication of assault. I created a force shield to surround Marco and I. Rays darted from the wizards' staffs and bounced from my force shield. I had a terrible feeling that my shield wouldn't hold against wizard magic. Several more rays flashed as my force shield trembled. Such a sight made my powers feel weak against wizard magic.

Marco blasted several stun rays at the wizards. Each ray swerved toward the orbs in each wizard staff despite having been fired at different targets. The orbs in the staffs must have had magnetic force which redirected the paths of magic.

I released my shield and fired several bolts of lightning from my ring. Each series of storm bolts fired as triples blasts. Since gaining new genie powers, I'd been able to shoot up to five bolts of lightning at a time. Despite my heightened powers, all my magic blasts headed into the wizards' staffs.

Flames erupted at the tips of the wizards' staffs as if they'd turned into torches.

"Water magic," Marco said right before the flames blasted.

With sheer concentration, Marco and I used our magic to call upon all nearby liquid be it beer, water, whiskey, rum, moonshine, or jungle juice. Liquid splashed from kegs, glasses, and dish washing buckets as though we'd used telekinesis to create geysers.

The first fireball was hit by dishwater and beer and died on impact. The second fireball was splashed by moonshine, rum, jungle juice, and a few other forms of liquor. Alcohol complimented the flames and the fireball burst like a firecracker. I dropped to the floor while Marco jumped over a table, knocking it over. Smoke wavered across the bar while the explosion rang in my ears.

Right as Marco and I climbed to our feet, we noticed that about a dozen whiskey and pint glasses were levitating. I feared that the wizards were going to telekinetically throw the glassware at us.

I shot a force blast from my ring. Shattering sounds rung in my ears. Bits of glass dust scattered over Marco's clothes and bandana but he didn't appear to have been cut.

Before Marco or I could exchange thoughts or react against the attack, I felt an unusual pull against my ring as Marco grasped his ring.

"They're trying to magnetize our rings," Marco said.

"Run to the dartboard," I yelled.

I squeezed my ring as the magnetic pull continued. I could feel the flesh around my finger being ripped to the bone. Marco dashed to the dartboard, and I met him there a second or two later.

"Put your ring next to a dart."

Marco did as I commanded. The darts popped out of the corkboard and flew toward the wizards. While most of the darts missed our attackers, one wizard got poked in the cheekbone while the second adversary was pierced in the arm.

The wizards' magnetic energy had knocked the dragon skeleton and the sword to the floor.

I found it perplexing how no one seemed to notice what was going on. Regardless of our bout, none of the patrons had been hurt or were paying any attention to our fight. The bartender continued to serve drinks while the tavern attendees drank, played games, and chatted away, oblivious to the fighting and broken glass. Had Marco, the wizards, and I turned invisible? Were the patrons protected by a strange force shield? The sheer absurdity of this situation really made me wonder what else was going on.

I collected the fallen sword despite having not used a blade in a long time.

"Why don't we have a real bar fight?" Marco called as he unleashed his whip, "skin against skin, weapon against weapon."

Each wizard shot a ray from their wand. I dropped the sword right as a wizard ray hit my weapon. The sword turned red, indicating that it was too hot to touch even with its strong hilt. When Marco's whip was hit, the leather weapon turned to reptilian skin. The tip of his whip thickened and grew a head with beady eyes and fangs.

"Holy shit," Marco gasped.

Marco let the black coil slip from his fingers. As the mutated weapon slithered across the floor and hissed, we realized that the wizards had morphed the whip into a cobra. The snake slithered on the barroom floor, completely confused but ready to deal with the calamity through violence. As the reptile wiggled through the dragon bones, ideas popped through my imagination.

I pointed my ring at the dragon bones, envisioned necromancy, and commanded the deceased beast to come to life. I'd never concentrated so hard on a spell. As I put as much magic energy into the skeleton as possible, I thought about Dirotalo, how he'd been accidentally resurrected, and how Wes had come alive as a sheer fluke.

The dragon bones jittered. For the first time in a long time, I felt magic leaving my body. Right when I felt like I'd been drained of all magic energy, I felt an explosion in my ring. I jumped back, landed on my back, and briefly closed my eyes.

When I looked up, a dragon was in front of me. The dragon was small for it's kind but still the biggest creature in the bar. Marco gasped, and the two laconic wizards showed emotion for the first time. I was happy that fear was the first and only feeling they displayed. The snake slithered away from the dragon and hid underneath a fallen bar stool. None of the bar crowd could see the dragon, but now wasn't the time to question our realm of reality.

The dragon dropped it's jaw, unleashed fire, and scalded one of the wizards. As the wizard attempted to stop, drop, and roll, the dragon bit the wizard's torso and chomped down on the burning body while puffs of flames burst between the dragon's fangs. Wizard blood, the blackened staff, and the charred robe dropped to the floor.

The dragon spread its wings, flew upward, and blasted a hole in the restaurant roof. Debris fell from the new skylight while the dragon carried the first dead wizard to his grave.

The snake slid out from it's hiding place once the dragon was out of sight. Marco aimed his ring at the cobra and called upon the whirlwind spell. Using his genie wind powers, Marco created a small tornado. The serpent got caught in the windy cyclone and spun up and down in the wind cone. Marco directed the twister toward the last standing wizard. The wind blew the snake into the wizard and the tornado continued to spin. My eyes widened as I watched the snake travel up and down the wizard. Venomous serpent bites decorated the wizard's skin as the snake travelled up and down.

Marco killed his wind spell, and the snake wrapped around the wizard's neck several times. As the wizard asphyxiated, his neck snapped from the tightness of the choking cobra. The snake bit the wizard several times, delivering painful venomous blows as the wizard wheezed his last breath.

When the wizard collapsed, the snake morphed back into a whip. Marco was reluctant to collect his trademark weapon, but the whip didn't slither or bite him.

The wizard corpse turned invisible. Marco and I looked at one another in shock. Nothing made much sense right now.

Smoky clouds grew in front of us, and a figure formed in the mist. This apparition turned from ash to red to green to blue. I'magee appeared in the colourful fog.

"You are a very tricky warrior Don," I'magee said. "Your friend is an amazing sidekick."

"His name is Marco, and he is every bit my equal," I retorted.

I'magee was the last creature who I wanted to see. I would have rather bumped into Krull and Hunter. Ever since I'magee had nearly killed me at Frosher Volcano, he'd been my eternal enemy. Being a genie and hating the god of magic was almost like patricide, but I would never thank I'magee for my magic no matter what.

"You killed two of my assassins," I'magee glared.

"Our magic is stronger than yours," Marco shot. "We offered them hand-to-hand combat and they chickened out."

"You're allied with the Santalonians," I accused.

"Indeed, Don I am," I'magee grinned. "The genies of O'Jahnteh are my people, and you're on the losing side. You're a brilliant warrior and a much better genie than you deserve to be, but much horror lies ahead of you."

"You're not going to get away with this," I said.

"Are you threatening me mortal man?" I'magee laughed. "I fully commend you for killing the two assassins who were sent to murder you, but your magic is not enough to win the war. Evil will forever haunt you even if O'Jahnteh triumphs over Santalonia."

I'magee let out a cackle before teleporting away. Once he'd vanished, I concluded that he must have used force shields or some other spell to protect the other bar patrons. If only the other gods could protect more of us from the war.

"What the hell was he talking about?" Marco asked.

"I don't know," I answered. "He talks a lot of shit, but his comment on what is ahead of us is kind of scary."

"I don't like how he mentioned how evil will always haunt us."

"Every war veteran is shell shocked, but I have a feeling that I'magee was referring to something much more insidious."

Once Eftalous Lake was secured a week later, the war came to a slow pace. There was still plenty of killing going on, but the Santalonians took a defensive stance. They held their southern territories strong, and many platoons perished when trying to penetrate their blockade. Guerrilla warfare no longer seemed to be working. Wes joined a council of strategists to figure out a new method of invading our enemies.

Both sides became very devoted to Qiami. Sacrifices, prayers, and worship tried to persuade the war deity into helping each of the opposing sides. I think Qiami loved all the attention as well as the fierce competition between the two sides for her love.

Qiami wasn't the only deity who started to get a lot of attention. On a daily basis, I saw many soldiers bowing down to worship Nadix. Troops hoped that the jungle god would make things easier during attacks since the thick forests were no longer acting as an advantage. Trent and everyone from his tribe had always been quite devout to Nadix and Majatee, so Trent built an altar to these supreme spirits. Since there were some mountains in the area, Trent thought we should give both gods plenty of attention. Other soldiers warmed to this idea and hoped that Majatee would create an avalanche which would crush enemy camps.

Many soldiers (particularly genies) were surprised to learn that Huck, Marco, and I didn't worship I'magee. All were alarmed when they learned that I'magee had sent assassins after me.

"I hate I'magee just as much as I hate the government," I said. "I'd really love it if we could forget about the government and devolve back to more peaceful times before politicians were fucking everything up."

"You got it Don," Trent said.

"You and your never-ending pejorative views toward politics," Sheri said. "We're doing the south a favour by destroying the federal government. Since the beginning of time Santalonia has neglected so many other communities."

"I think when Santalonia falls, the entire country should adopt a socialist government so that no one is left low," Julia said. "This war is our calling to punish Santalonia for not treating us as equals. So many problems in this country have come from bad Santalonian decisions."

"You know it girl," Sheri said. "Santalonian bureaucrats have pocketed our money. This is the war to end all of that, and we have a chance to be heroes until the end of history."

I didn't feel like arguing with Sheri. To keep morale up, some people needed to believe they were doing a good thing and that their government was right. It was no secret that Trent fought to avoid jail time. Everyone knew I was dubious about the stories we were being told, but nonetheless I kept fighting. Sometimes I felt like fighting was the only way to get anywhere in life considering I wasn't too good at much else.

One afternoon Julia, Huck, Sid, and I were wandering through a very thick area of the jungle. Things had been quiet for the last few days, and we felt that some tranquility in the jungle would ease our souls. Enjoying the beauty of the forest seemed like a way of worshipping nature. I definitely preferred hiking over bowing down to an altar to honour Nadix.

"What do you know," Julia said after we'd been hiking for around twenty minutes. "Some Santalonian assholes are interrupting our nature stroll."

"Maybe we don't have to fight them," Huck said. "For all we know they could be a bunch of guys like us who want some peace and quiet."

"It's too risky," Julia said. "They could be planning an attack, or they might spot our camp and then report our location to the rest of their platoon."

"So, everyone is guilty by association?" Huck complained.

"Huck this is war, there is no innocence," Julia said before charging forward with her battle-axe raised.

Though we could only spot a spearman and a swordsman, there were probably more foes lurking in the bushes. Neither of these troopers noticed Julia until Sid barked.

The swordsman raised his weapon, but Julia decapitated him with a chop from her axe. Right as blood splashed and the soldier's head became a piece of compost, the spearman lowered his weapon and charged toward Julia like a jouster. Julia dodged the spearhead right before it could pike her. She positioned the head of her axe so that it was in front of her opponent. The spearman tried to brake but skidded on the slippery jungle floor and crashed face-first into the axe-head.

Sid dashed south and Julia chased after her. Huck and I were without our magic carpets, and we had difficulty keeping up with Julia. Dodging bushes, logs, trees, and rock made the game of follow the leader exceptionally difficult. While Huck wasn't a fast runner, he could dodge obstacles through a combination of jumps, handsprings, somersaults, and flips. Since I wasn't gymnastically inclined, I had to rely on maneuvering my body away from obstacles.

"Don, are you hurt?" Huck asked after I'd bailed for the second time.

"No twisted ankles or blood or anything."

"I can heal you with my magic."

"Save it for later man. I think you might need it."

"No, you won't," a strange voice said.

Two Santalonian bowmen were standing a stone's throw away from Huck and I. The jungle was doing a good job at hiding our enemies and I really wondered if maybe I should have prayed to Nadix at the altar. These phantom warriors made me wonder if Julia had gotten into a skirmish.

The first archer fired his bow at Huck. Before the arrow could pierce Huck, he sidestepped to the right like a dancer. Right after pulling off his showman move, the second bowstring rung, and another arrow darted toward Huck. Huck leapt with lightning dexterity into the air, grasped a low hanging tree branch, pulled a chin up, and lifted his legs above the path of the arrow. The Santalonians exclaimed as Huck pulled himself into a standing position on the tree branch and then pulled a forward flip. Huck dropped onto one of the archers and crushed the man's neck to the point of fatality.

The second bowman jumped back in shock and armed himself with an arrow. Huck fired a lightning bolt from his ring before the archer could stake him with the arrow. The boom and echo of the lightning bolt followed right as Huck's enemy dropped to the ground.

"Holy shit Huck," I said after my bones had calmed from the thunder, "that was some pretty impressive acrobatic work."

"Thanks man. Are you okay to walk, or should we wait around until Julia finds us?"

"Let's find her and Sid."

Huck and I took our time exploring the jungle. We didn't want to call Julia or Sid in fear of attracting attention. Since Sid was conspicuous, we figured her barking would lead us toward her, if not Julia as well. As Huck and I veered further from the faint hiking path, we came across a gully.

Three Santalonian spearmen were down in the ravine. I got ready to fire death magic from my ring, but before I could unleash any blasts, Huck jumped on a vine and swung toward the gully.

Huck swung on the vine with grace and ended his elegance by kicking one of the spearmen to the ground. Before the spearman could reach for his dropped spear, Huck pulled a knife from his belt and stabbed his fallen enemy in the heart.

Fear struck me when the two remaining spearmen closed in on Huck from opposing sides. The foe on the left attempted to stake Huck, but Huck pulled a cartwheel away from the jab. The spear flew forward and stabbed the Santalonian on the right. The man on the right dropped to the knees and fell backward from the spear. His killer shrieked in remorse, but his guilt was short lived since Huck blasted him in the face with a crossbow bolt.

"Holy crap Huck," I said. "I've never seen you kick so much ass before. When this war is over you really ought to become a gladiator cuz you fight with style man."

"I'm doing a good thing for my fellow countrymen," Huck said. "Having fun and putting style into things takes the horror away from the war. I think we should all let war know it's not as horrible or powerful as it thinks it is."

"A lot of people would disagree with you on that. Many veterans feel war deserves no comedy and should always be looked at as the worst thing in existence."

"Ah fuck Qiami. I'm sick of her being so grim and obsessed with mutilation."

I couldn't help but chuckle at Huck's insult toward the war goddess. Once my laughter subsided, I hoped that Qiami wouldn't retaliate against Huck's blasphemy.

Huck and I wandered through the jungle for about twenty minutes without hearing any signs of Julia, Sid, or Santalonian forces. More bushes and dangling vines crowded our paths. Leaves and other foliage grew much larger. Eventually Huck and I could no longer see one another due to the thick vegetation.

I came across a large mud puddle. I wasn't sure how deep it was and didn't feel like getting soaked or having my boots stuck in the sludge, so I decided to swing across the swamp on a vine. I knew I wasn't a gymnast and that Huck made acrobatics look easy, but I was confident that I could make it across the gunk on a natural rope swing.

I took a vine in my hands, walked backward, stood up on a log, and pulled on the vine until it was stretched to its maximum bounce. I kicked off the ground and swung over the puddle, barely missing the mud. On the spur of the moment, I decided to jump off the vine and pull a spin. I leapt from the vine, pulled a 360, landed on the balls on my feet, tipped backward, and bonked my head on a log.

Everything went black.

Sometime later I awoke in a hammock. I wasn't sure if I was dead. War always took unexpected tolls on life. Maybe I was on my way to the afterlife. It was said that when you died, you had a meeting with Zadohkoo before passing into the afterlife. My head felt turgid, and I really hoped that I wouldn't have to wander through the afterlife with the pain and injury that had killed me in my previous one.

"Don?" Sheri said as she entered the dimly lit tent. "You're awake, thank goodness."

Sheri dashed forward and bombarded me with a bear hug and tons of kisses. I was really happy to see her, but her yelling infuriated my headache.

"I was so worried about you sweetheart, so glad you're better," she said before showering me with a few more kisses.

"What happen?"

"Sid found you by a mud puddle, it looked like you tried to swing across it on a vine and hit your head."

"This is why I prefer magic carpets."

"Julia followed Sid's barking and brought you back here. She would have healed you if she were still a genie, and for the first time she actually grumbled about not having any powers."

"I have an incredible sister. She's saved my life twice, with and without magic."

"Julia kind of likes not being a genie. A few days ago, she was talking about how being a human without powers had allowed her to shed her skin, find a new identity, and completely focus on her athletics, which is how she's always defined herself."

"You can say that again. Still, I can't help but feel a little guilty that she had to reinvent her existence upon saving me."

"But you've saved so many other people too."

"But I don't know what I would do if I wasn't a genie. I surely wouldn't be much of a warrior without my powers."

"You're a good swordsman."

"And you're an even better one now that you're using my katana."

"And I'm never giving it back."

We both laughed and Marco came into the room with a kettle of tea.

"I brewed a medicinal recipe that will heal your pain," he said. "You have no injuries cuz Huck healed you. He's swimming down at the lake right now, but he feels pretty guilty about you getting hurt. He says that it wouldn't have happened had he stuck with you closer."

"Thanks Marco," I said after taking a sip of tea. "Huck shouldn't feel guilty either. He took down five troops single-handedly, really impressed me. If he still feels guilty when he gets back here, tell him that healing my wounds was his penance."

"I'm going down to the lake," Marco said. "I'll pass on your words."

Sheri and I hugged again after Marco had left.

"I'm kind of scared Sheri," I said.

"Sweetheart, that's the first time I've ever heard those words from you."

"Jason's dead."

"People always die in war. No troop goes without a fallen soldier."

"What if I'm next?"

"Don't think that way."

"I pulled off a stupid cocky move cuz I was jealous of Huck's acrobatics, and it nearly killed me. My accident should have happened to an overconfident smartass on the playground, not a career vigilante."

"You lived my love, others wouldn't have, be thankful for that," Sheri said as she wrapped her arms around me tighter.

We kissed some more. Our clothes came off. I buried my face in Sheri's tits while she jerked me. I returned the favour to her crotch by rubbing her clit while I fingered her. We switched toward the sixty-nine position and then went from foreplay to fucking. Marco's pot of medicinal tea was helpful at easing my headache, but sex with Sheri was the real healer. She was the magic which I needed to bring me back from the land of fear and death.

As the weeks went on, the effects of the war started to travel across the rest of Sionia. Initially soldiers had been rather aloof to other matters in the country because if we weren't fighting, we were being barked at by superiors or listening to tales about combat missions from other platoons. Since Bashar was writing propaganda articles when he wasn't on jungle patrol, more newspapers flooded our camps, detailing what was going on in the rest of the country.

"This is so typical of our sick and twisted society," Julia said, "sell tragedy to make money."

Julia was referring to how weapons manufacturers were making a killing off arms and siege weapons sales. Robin's cousins had also made good coin from selling military chariots.

"At least some people are getting money," Huck said. "Amid all this terrible shit, something good has to happen."

"Those greedy capitalist twits are going to pocket the money themselves," Julia said. "They like how people are dying, and they're building weapons and artillery cheaply, so it will get destroyed, and the government will then buy more. It's fucking evil."

"No shit," Marco said. "And Huck, don't ever look for good things in war again. You might be an optimist, but the only thing which you should be hopeful about is staying alive."

"Maybe optimism will help us end the war," Huck said.

"I like your thinking Huck, but the continuation of war is out of our hands," Sheri said.

"I hope you aren't telling Huck that we should continue our duties as soldiers and leave it up to the politicians to make decisions," I said.

"Hell no," Sheri said. "War is bizarre, arbitrary, oppressive, and cruel. We are scapegoats for problems that politicians don't know how to solve."

"Sheri, that is maybe the first contentious thing I've ever heard you say about the government," I said.

"I know you're all surprised," Sheri said. "This war has really changed my perspective on the government cuz no act of the government has ever had such a profound impact on me."

"You've got to feel sympathy for the civilians too," Trent said.

"Oh, fuck yeah I do," Sheri said. "So many towns have major food shortages because most food is being sent to the soldiers. Sure, we need all the nutrition and energy we can get, but it's not right to starve the public to feed the army."

"The folks living in small villages and towns are losing out the most," Trent said. "In my last letter from Larissa, she mentioned that some villagers came out to her camp to barter for food. Some of my friends gave these starving folks free food because they felt so bad for the famished villagers. The camp has since grown and townies have been learning hunting, gathering, and farming."

"It's always the proletariat who suffers the most," Julia said. "All the more reason why the profiting weapons manufacturers are amoral and why we need a socialist government."

"There's also a lack of medical access in many places," Marco said, "too many healers have faced conscription."

O'Jahnteh wasn't facing a lack of medical access since so many genies lived there, but other towns had lost many healers. Even though many medical professionals had been stationed at military bases, genies such as Marco, Huck and I were regularly asked to heal wounded soldiers from other brigades.

Julia also helped out in the medical tents. When I saw her distributing medicine, changing sheets, or cleaning vomit, I knew that she missed having her genie powers. Had she still had her magic ring, she would have been healing as many soldiers as possible, but now she was finding a different way to do just as much good.

"Academia is suffering too," Wes said. "University enrollment has dropped drastically, and many of my colleagues are no longer focusing on beneficial research. So many intellects have been ordered to do research on military. Cronies of mine who were pacifists can no longer focus on designing bridges, buildings, vehicles, or urban housing plans because the government wants them to concentrate on designing military camps, artillery, and naval ships. Even health researchers are being forced to work as dietitians for the military instead of improving agriculture or learning more about healthy eating."

"That is so criminal," Trent said, "especially when famine is plaguing the populace."

"Why do people always look to combat as the first way of solving problems?" Wes questioned. "We like to think that we're smart, but we are so dumb when it comes to diplomacy."

That night when I climbed into my bunk with Sheri, I said, "Wes's words really got me thinking."

"How so?"

"People are so volatile. I'm no different."

"Don, my love, you are totally different than the politicians. You didn't start this war."

"True, but I almost always solve problems with violence."

"But you don't start the problems, you finish them."

"When I was with Marco and Damon in Danjia, I really liked that. There were problems, but we solved them through heart and hard work. Wes usually solves problems with his intellect. Why can't heart and intellect end the war?"

"Winning the war will require hard work and heart and intellect. Our virtues will be temporarily blackened due to the evil nature of atrocity."

"I'm starting to wonder if I could have done something to prevent this war."

"Love, you may have been involved with lots of conflicts in the past, but you've never done anything on a major enough scale to ignite a national war."

"Sionia will be warped until the end of time due to the revolution I helped out in."

"You can't blame yourself for the war, and nothing from King Rex's death triggered this war either. Political squabbling and greedy fights have been going on since the beginning of time. Stop beating yourself up and get some rest sweetheart."

I shut up, but it was hard for me to fall asleep, even with Sheri resting against my chest.

The next day Sheri and I were out by Snake Mountain, a very steep peak which had an old road that zigzagged back and forth across the mountain. It wasn't too often that we got romantic privacy, but whenever the opportunity came up, the two of us had to get away to get love into our lives.

Right as Sheri and I were getting lost in nature, we heard voices ahead.

"Just can't get any privacy," Sheri said.

"I wonder who's ahead of us," I said.

Since war was a time of paranoia, we always had to investigate everyone to find out if they were an ally or an enemy.

Three Santalonian troops emerged from a forest of very tall ferns. Two of the soldiers were armed with clubs while the third carried a battle-axe. Without any acknowledgment, the Santalonian warriors charged toward Sheri and I.

Sheri unsheathed her katana; the sword which had once been my trademark weapon was now hers. She flashed the blade at the first clubman, and a skull dropped to the jungle floor. Gore sprayed the second clubman as he bounced back in alarm. Sheri pulled back on the katana and jutted it into the second clubman's chest, destroying all vital organs in his upper torso.

The third warrior swung his axe at Sheri as she bounced back, missing the axe blade by two arm lengths. The axe warrior swung his weapon a second a time as Sheri sliced her blade in his direction, chopping his wooden weapon into two. The axe-head dropped to the ground, leaving the Santalonian with a wooden staff. The warrior tried to attack Sheri with the stick, but she quickly ended his life with a blow to the head.

"I really fucking hate killing," Sheri said as she turned away from the fresh corpses.

"Any real warrior does. We don't kill unless it's to save our lives. We are warriors, not murderers."

"I can forgive myself somewhat if I deal out painless deaths."

"You don't need to apologize or seek penance or beat yourself up. We are not the bad ones in this war."

I wanted to say more, but I heard approaching troops coming up the mountain road.

"Stay tight I'll take care of those goons down the road," I said as I dashed down the mountain path.

The four Santalonian troops on the lower side of the mountain road were armed with swords and spears. Before any of them could touch me, I created a force shield. When the Santalonian soldiers realized that I was a hard target to attack, they snuck off the trail. I wasn't sure if they were evading or if they thought they would sneak behind me and stab me in the back. Either way, I couldn't let them live. I hated to act as executioner, but when it came down to it, no soldier was really a killer.

I fired a series of lightning bolts, each one shocking the soldiers to death. I was glad that lightning had taken its toll on their lives and that I hadn't had to shoot fireballs. It was better to die from cardiac arrest than to burn to death.

I turned around to face Sheri. Her boots were stuck in the mud, and she was pulling hard against her feet, but the muck offered no release. She bent over to untie her bootlaces so that she could leap to dry land in her socks.

A Santalonian horseman stood at a flat spot on the mountain road above Sheri and I. Beneath him, a battering ram was bumping its way down the side of Snake Mountain at an ever-increasing speed. Sheri lay directly in this siege weapon's rampaging path. I raised my ring and got ready to pull Sheri out of the way using telekinesis.

The front of the battering ram crashed into Sheri. She smacked backward, fell off the mountain road, and flailed toward the trees. Sheri thudded against the trunk of a very large tree. The zooming battering ram smashed into her, pinning her against the tree. Her head thumped forward, smacked against the front of the ram then rocketed back and slapped the tree trunk. She slumped to the side. Gore erupted from her pulverized chest while her last breath bubbled blood.

I fired healing rays from my ring before I could cry. The rings of life magic darkened, telling me that I could do nothing to heal the love of my life. If I couldn't heal Sheri with magic, then I had to bring her back to life. I fired conjuring magic and revival rays from my ring, but the colourful magic quickly turned invisible. I put more energy and concentration into my magic acts, and more love into Sheri's spirit, but nothing came about.

What the hell was happening? Why was it that I could turn a dragon skeleton into a living monster, but couldn't bring Sheri back to life?

"She's gone Don," I thought I heard Zadohkoo say.

I refused to believe that Sheri was dead. Pulverized ribs, a battered jaw, a hurricane of blood, splattered guts, blunt force trauma to the head, and a lifeless corpse weren't enough to stop me. I had killed enough people in my life to know which individual didn't deserve to die on the battlefield.

I turned away from Sheri and looked up to where the battering ram had been pushed down the mountain. The little scumhole who'd killed her was going to pay.

I fetched Sheri's katana: the sword which had once been mine, had become hers, and was being returned to me through Sheri's death. I charged up the hill to where the horse was eating leaves from a bush.

Sheri's killer was lying on the ground. Sweat flooded his flesh, piss and shit stained his pants, and vomit was splattered across his clothes. Blood blasted from his coughs.

I had never seen someone so ill before. Was this lowlife dying in agony and disgust as punishment for having killed my beloved?

A snake slithered across the mountain road and disappeared into the leaves. Fang marks and blood seeped from a wound on the murderer's cheek. The snake may have given him a death blow, but the serpent's venom wasn't going to kill him.

"Time to die," I growled.

The katana flashed, slit the troop's throat, but didn't quite chop his head off. Blood, vomit, and mucous splattered. The chop of the blade had destroyed his neck bone, but untouched flesh still held his head to the rest of his body. He had a very creepy facial expression which reminded me of a demonic clown I'd once seen in a nightmare. I turned away. There was no way I could look at Sheri's killer any longer.

Killing Sheri's murderer wasn't needed, but it's what I'd wanted to do. Certain crimes should only be punished by people, not by nature. Maybe I was a murderer now. Maybe I had become a killer, a freak who needed to assassinate to make sense of this sorry fucked up world. Too many thoughts were spinning in my head, and I couldn't comprehend any of them. I didn't want to die, but I didn't want to be alive. Life was so baffling and cruel, and I wanted nothing to do with it. There were no solutions to the problems of life; not even death could solve such ills of the worlds. Such a thought made life so much more fucked up.

I couldn't bring myself to go back to Sheri's corpse. I cried off and on. When I couldn't cry, I felt kind of fucked up.

Bashar retrieved her body.

"You've got to finish writing those papers," one officer said.

"Fuck the papers," Bashar said.

Trent dug a deep hole, and we buried Sheri's body with flowers before putting any dirt atop her grave. Since we'd been going to so many funerals (often of people who we didn't know) all eulogies and words of condolence had become clichéd. Silent funerals had become the norm.

Julia had ached with pain since Jason's death, and Sheri's death emphasized all the more that any one of us could be next. My friends did a better job at giving Julia condolences. For some, group therapy was key when it came to getting over sorrow, but being with other depressed people reminded me that everyone in the country was suffering.

I waited and waited to see Sheri's ghost, but nothing came about. Sometimes my friends sought to comfort me while other times I was so standoffish I felt like I was killing them while slowly committing suicide.

The war continued as if nothing had happened.

"We are going to win this son of a bitch war and I am going to be the Lord of the Warriors," I randomly said during a rather taciturn meal a few evenings after the funeral.

If Sheri's death wasn't going to take us to victory, it was going to take us to the grave.

While soldiers continued to be slaughtered, civilians now suffered since a Santalonian general had derived a terrorist method of raiding farms. Crops were stolen, farmers were slaughtered, hay was torched, and cattle were rustled. Phalaetus felt sorry for the civilians so used her agricultural goddess powers to accelerate the harvests of all crops. Her actions caused much controversy among the deities, and she was scolded for choosing sides. Phalaetus argued that she hadn't interfered with politics but was trying to prevent a famine and that she was on the side of the civilians, not the soldiers. Either way, Shilotey decided to get vengeance and used her goddess powers to create a storm which had very detrimental effects toward farmlands and crop yields.

Since we couldn't rely on the goddesses and gods to fight our battles, many platoons were ordered to patrol farmlands to prevent raids. Initially I enjoyed flying around farms on my magic carpet, but all of that changed when my sergeant introduced two new but old faces to my troop.

"I would like you to welcome Krull of Valushia, and Hunter of Bounty Hunter Island to your squad," the sergeant said.

"No way," Huck said.

"This is insanity," Wes howled.

Marco gripped his whip.

"What the hell is wrong with you?" Bashar demanded. "Those guys are criminals and serial killers and should be locked in jail. How loco have you gotten?"

Trent balled his hands to fists.

"Are you trying to get us killed by our fellow comrades?" Julia growled.

Sid barked.

I was too flabbergasted to speak. Krull let out his trademark sadistic chuckle while Hunter smirked. Several soldiers who were on different troops could sense an explosion boiling.

"You guys have lost too many fighters and your troop needs some replacing," the sergeant said.

"But why the hell them?" I asked. "Can't you send them to a different platoon?"

"Or to jail," Julia said. "There have been death warrants on both of them for years."

"We need all the troopers we can get, so many criminals are being pardoned for crimes until the war is over," the sergeant said. "Many jails have been emptied of inmates and if convicts serve well in the forces, then their sentences will be dropped."

"Are you trying to kill everyone on our troop with our lifelong enemies?" Trent asked.

"Enough of this crotchety backtalk," the sergeant barked. "I order all of you to accept Hunter and Krull on your troop. In one hour, you will head to the south-west to patrol Dadeaka."

"Aren't you guys going to shake my hand and welcome me to the crew," Hunter snickered.

"I'll bet they're all upset about evil bureaucracy and their autocratic sergeant," Krull smirked. "Fighting side by side with your greatest enemies is sure going to be fun."

Our nonsensical team headed out to Dadeaka, a treeless plateau which consisted of mud huts, pastures for water buffalo, and rice fields. Julia and Sid rode with me on my magic carpet, Bashar took flight with Huck, Marco piloted his magic carpet with Trent, and Wes kept up to us by wing. We tried to outrun Krull and Hunter, but the two of them followed on their magic carpets. They teased us by flying close, stopping, and then pulling funny moves which consisted of pretending to crash into us. I had never been more tempted to kill anyone. There were no words to express the insanity of working side by side with lifelong enemies who were the most notorious criminals in Santalonian history. Part of me wondered why Krull and Hunter hadn't died in the swamp, but the two of them had a natural talent for escaping danger. Perhaps Krull wasn't a person but a spirit of evil who kept reappearing at the worst times.

The villagers of Dadeaka welcomed us. The fields weren't as full of crops as I'd hoped, and I didn't see a lot of livestock, which made me wonder how badly the farmers had been hit by the raiders. Hunter shook hands with a few villagers and whenever a farmhand thanked him for coming to protect the village, he smirked at the rest of us. I wished that I could tell the villagers how evil he and Krull truly were.

"I know this sucks for all of us," Wes said, "but we're going to have to put up with Krull and Hunter."

"Fuck that," Marco said.

"I grew up being bullied by Hunter and plenty of other pukes on Bounty Hunter Island," Huck said. "Do you have any idea how it feels to be fighting side by side with my greatest enemy?"

"You're right Huck, but Wes is also right," Julia said. "It fucking sucks, but we need all the help we can get. Let's put aside our personal problems, kill the farm raiders, and then settle things with Hunter and Krull."

"We will kill them," I said. "If anyone asks, they died in battle."

We nodded in unanimous agreement. Krull and Hunter were off talking to the local war chief. It was going to be hard to make their deaths look accidental with others around. Maybe if we were lucky Krull and Hunter would get butchered by Santalonian soldiers, but you couldn't rely on anything when war was going on.

After an hour or so of patrolling the fields, a loud horn bellowed.

"A group of horseback Santalonians are approaching," the war chief said. "They're armed with fires, lances, and a few other weapons. It looks like they're all human, and they should be here in a few minutes. Get ready to kill."

Each of us drew our weapons. Even though I hadn't swung my katana since Sheri's death, I kept it at my side as a good luck token. My sword had saved me numerous times, and it had done wonders for Sheri, so maybe it could save me again.

"I wonder if any of the cavalry are soldiers who we've fought with in the past?" Hunter said.

"I thought you guys recently joined the war?" Wes inquired.

"Ha," cackled Krull. "Not too long ago we were fighting for the Santalonians. We decided to make things more interesting by betraying our comrades and joining the enemies; this way we get to slaughter on both sides of the battlefield."

"War gives us an excuse to kill, and nothing is more fun," Hunter said.

I wanted to slash Hunter, but a gang of raiders emerged from the sand dunes. Since the land was relatively flat and without many obstacles, the galloping horses were going to be in the village within moments. Most of the raiders were atop stallions, but a wagon loaded with troops was also being towed.

"I'll take the wagon," Wes said. "Genies, you guys should take to your magic carpets and blast the cavalry from the sky. The rest of you hang tight. We will be back here soon."

Wes took to the air. Hunter, Huck, and Marco followed on their magic carpets. Right when I stepped onto my magic carpet, I felt a sudden surge on my ring finger. Before I realized what had happened, I heard cackling. I turned around and saw Krull clutching my ring in his fingers. He'd used telekinesis to steal my ring while I'd been distracted, and I loathed him for it.

"I know you want to kill me," Krull said. "You might be wickedly powerful with this little treasure, but war is a good time to remind you that you're not as strong as you think you are."

I lunged at Krull. Trent and Bashar stepped forward, but Krull took off on his magic carpet before any of us could tackle him. Julia tossed her javelin, but Krull was already out of range and headed toward the oncoming terrorists.

Those of us without flight powers stood and watched our friends battling the approaching raiders. Wes enclosed on the wagon and blasted fire at the transport. The wagon burst like a volcano, and Wes had to fly at top speed in the opposite direction to avoid being incinerated. Burning soldiers blasted from the exploded wreckage. Flames demolished the horse reigns, letting the animals run free from the battle.

"The wagon must have been loaded with thithaleeth," Bashar said.

"Probably," I said. "It's what goons have been using to burn down villages."

"I'm happy the horses got away," Julia said. "It's totally wrong that animals have to die on account of human problems."

Though Julia had lost all ability to pilot a magic carpet, she refused to mount a horse. Instead, she trudged along the land though cavalry would have given her much more speed and strength.

Huck fired multiple stun rays from his ring. Four out of five of the rays hit target, knocking troops off their horses. Like the horses who'd escaped from the burning wagon, animals without riders retreated. The horses didn't seem to have any bonds with the jockeys, which made me wonder how the horses were treated at the military stables.

Hunter followed Huck's example and blasted down riders with force blasts. Of the five troops who Hunter dismounted, each one got stabbed in the back with a broadsword. I believed that most of these troops had died upon crashing to the ground, but killing wasn't enough for Hunter; he had to mutilate dead bodies to feed his viciousness.

Marco flew toward the last standing horseman. The jockey had been riding the smallest, slowest horse and had very much lagged behind the rest of his company. Since Marco shared Julia's viewpoints on animal ethics, he used his telekinesis to lift the rider off the horse. Marco dropped the troop to the ground with a thud. The horse joined the fleeing stampede.

Krull didn't attack a single Santalonia, which made me wonder about his motives. Hunter stuck within his shadow, but it looked like Krull was trying to outrun his comrade. It always seemed that Hunter was afraid to leave Krull's darkness. As enigmatic as Krull's evilness was, I wondered why he was trying to ditch the battle.

My attention reverted to Sid when she barked. Four Santalonian cavalry were approaching from the east. Each was within moments of attacking Bashar, Julia, Trent, and I.

Trent charged forward. Two horsemen galloped forward on opposite sides of Trent; each was armed with a saber. Right when it looked like Trent was going to get slashed from the left and the right, he clutched each troop by the ankle. The charging horses were galloping so fast that they lost their riders. Trent released his grip on the soldiers right as the horses zoomed away. The captured troops thumped to the ground with the wind knocked out of them.

A crossbowman took aim at Trent. Before the archer could pull the trigger on his weapon, Julia tossed her javelin. The javelin slid through the archer's torso like a harpoon digging into a seal. The archer spat his last bloody-bubble breath before falling to the ground.

A horseback-archer charged in my direction as if he wanted to trample me, though his arrow was aimed at Bashar. I stepped to the side and swung my katana right before the horse could boot me. The archer's upper half dropped to the ground, sprayed blood and dust, and covered me in death juice. I hadn't killed anyone with the katana since Sheri's death. Wielding such a gruesome kill made me wonder if perhaps I needed to stop relying so much on magic and go back to the basics.

"Don, look out," Julia shrieked.

A rider with a lance was headed directly toward me. Within a second or two, a lance was set to pulverize my head.

Krull flew toward my approaching killer, flung his cutlass, and chopped the rider into a corpse. The horse changed it's course to avoid a slaying from Krull. The jockey dropped to the ground with a thud and organs wept from the massive incision in his torso.

"Aren't you going to thank me Don?" Krull smirked. "I saved your life buddy."

"Give me back my ring," I barked.

"Someone has an ungrateful attitude," Hunter said as he approached us with Marco and Huck.

"Today's the first time I ever did something kind for Don," Krull said. "You'd think that maybe we could finally patch things up and get into one another's good books. Something lovely has to come out of war after all."

"Quit with the mocking pseudo-philosophical bullshit," I growled.

"Someone sure is jealous," Krull laughed. "You know Don, I can't recall having ever drawn blood from you, yet you and that little shit Huck have wounded me pretty bad a few times, even tried to murder me too."

"He has no manners," Hunter said, "and yet he thinks he's the peoples' hero."

"Both of you shut the fuck up," Huck yelled.

"And look at that little prick," Hunter said. "He's never had any respect for anyone and has always given me lip. I tell you Krull, I think we criminals are more polite than these so-called heroes."

"Take your stupid ring Don," Krull said as he chucked it at me. "You really aren't very much without it."

I felt like pointing out that I'd saved Bashar from an archer but kept shut. No one could win an argument with someone as incorrigible as Krull.

Some of the villagers came out of their homes. They applauded us, called us heroes and saviours, stated that we deserved medals, and offered to cook us a feast. While I was happy with their words of kindness, my hatred toward Krull still boiled. He had saved my life which was humiliating, but I felt like he'd almost planned the rescue considering he'd done nothing else in today's battle. The rider with the lance would have never approached me had it not been for Krull stealing my ring.

After getting hugs, handshakes, and snacks from the villagers, our troop had a meeting with the war chief to discuss what had gone on during the battle. The war chief was impressed with us, but that didn't make me happy.

Following the meeting, I headed to the clinic where many people were ill from malnourishment and food poisoning. I healed so many sickly folks that my blood felt deprived of magic. In order to boost my energy, Huck and I settled next to a pond, which had acted as a drinking hole for water buffalo. We drifted off with the pleasant breeze. It was surprising at how relaxing the land could be after such a recent attack.

Huck and I were awoken by screaming. We were without magic carpets, so we dashed toward the cries. I had my sword, but Huck was without his crossbow. The screaming died, but Huck and I continued sprinting toward the area of distress. We halted in our tracks when we saw Hunter and Krull. Each was carrying a bloody sickle. Three bodies lay on the ground.

"What the fuck is this?" Huck exclaimed.

"What does it look like stupid?" Hunter chuckled. "We butchered some civilians. It's our way of reminding the villagers that the war isn't over, and they're not safe after a relatively easy battle today."

"Ha," Krull said. "Don was the only one who came close to death today while the rest of us were nothing but safe."

I unsheathed my sword. Krull was going to die, Hunter too. I didn't care what the war chief said about working with your team. If I was banished from the army for killing murderers, so be it. I would win the war as a vigilante.

My sword clashed with Krull's. I wanted to use magic, but my energies felt weak, and I didn't think that I could fire off a spell in less time than it would take Krull to slash me with his word.

Hunter ran off, and Huck chased after him while mine and Krull's sword bashed at one another. I hated how my greatest enemy was my equal in fencing. Our blades flashed, smacked, parried, and clanked but neither weapon came close to slashing their rival down.

"You know Don, war is the best example of how people are such a sad and fucked up stupid species," Krull said. "Fools like you like to view yourselves as good. You kill yet look at yourself as a hero and saviour. How many good men have you killed in this war? I'll bet you've killed way more conscripted soldiers than you have criminals."

"Shut it," I growled as I swung my sword with much more ferocity.

"You're losing your temper because I'm speaking the ugly truth. At least I admit that I'm evil and love killing. For the record I'm not prejudiced since I'll kill anyone regardless of who they are; I'm an equalist. You love killing too Don. You're selective about which lives you end, and you need criminals like me to justify your love of action."

I didn't want to listen to Krull's words. They weren't true. They were impossible. Yet they made me reflect on myself. The thought of there being some truth in Krull's words was truly alarming.

Krull got ready to mock me again, but dropped to the ground before words could fall from his mouth. His eyes closed and his sword fluttered from his fingers. What had happened? I hadn't cut him or attacked him with magic.

"Halt," a voice barked.

The war chief approached. Eight crossbowmen were at his side. I lowered my sword. The sight of eight crossbows reminded me of Robin's death, and I wasn't ready to join him.

I turned to the right. Bashar was standing next to me. There was blood on Bashar's knuckles, and gore was seeping from Krull's temple. Krull's skin was paling, and I wondered if he'd died.

"I heard swords clashing and Krull talking a lot of crap," Bashar said. "When I saw the two of you fighting, I stepped in and punched him in the head."

"I owe you forever Bashar," I said.

"Knocking down this son of a bitch was rewarding enough in itself," Bashar said.

"Both of you stop," the war chief said. "Fighting among soldiers is strictly forbidden, and both of you will be punished severely."

"Krull and Hunter just killed these three civilians," I yelled as I pointed to the corpses. "They didn't come here to protect; they came here to kill. They've slaughtered soldiers on both ends of the battlefield, and you were nuts to have brought them here."

"How dare you talk back to your commanding officer," the war chief bellowed.

"Go fuck yourself boss," Bashar said. "If you can't see that Don was doing the right thing then you're as fucked as that twat lying on the ground."

The crossbowmen lowered their weapons. It was comforting to know that they'd sided with Bashar and I.

The angry silence was broken by screaming. Bashar and I ran toward an alley, which divided mud-brick huts.

The screaming led us to the backyard of a slaughterhouse. Hunter was trapped in a net, which was suspended by a rope tied to a tree branch, holding him several paces above the ground.

"You always thought that you were so much stronger than the people who you hurt," Huck said, "and you always acted like you were better than all the kids who you bullied."

Steam rose from Hunter's flesh as his screaming increased. I couldn't figure out what was going on, but Huck's ring was glowing.

"You harassed people to mask your incompetence, you worthless son of a bitch," Huck said. "You were too stupid to assert yourself without magic and weaponry, and you were always hiding behind that prick Krull because you were too cowardly to act on your own."

"You're using a heat ray," I said. "Huck, I didn't think you were that powerful."

The heat ray was a very advanced spell. I had never used one on an enemy, though had experimented with them and used heat magic to start fires. Marco had yet to learn how to use the heat ray despite being a more advanced genie than Huck.

"I hope this human garbage is the only one who I ever use death magic on," Huck said.

"Help," Hunter screamed as his blood boiled and his flesh melted off his bones. "This is homicide. This fucking guy is murdering a fellow soldier. You have to stop him."

Bashar and I watched the execution while Hunter squirmed without hope. The helpless weakling showed his true nature despite his previous malicious demeanor. Never had the death penalty felt so appropriate.

"Huck, you fucking horse, I will get you, you animal fucking cornhole," Hunter roared before being silenced.

Puddles and splats of boiling blood, melted flesh, and liquified organs spilled from the holes in the nets. Huck released his heat ray. The last of Hunter's melted body splashed to the ground. His bones remained in the net while fleshy liquid dangled and dripped from the ropes. I'd seen plenty of killings, but no other death compared to having been melted in a net. Flies buzzed around the slop which had once been Hunter's body.

"Why do we have to become evil in order to make peace?" Huck said as we walked to the hut which had been assigned as our bunker. "War and murder and all that shit shouldn't happen with a government that is supposed to take care of people. Society is made up of civilians, and civilizations are designed to be safe for everyone, hence the word civil. Why can't we all be kind to one another?"

"The most important questions don't have an answer," I said. "Maybe we're too stupid to find a solution."

Krull was healed by an army witchdoctor. While he was in delirium, he confessed to the medic that he and Hunter had escaped from Naflit Bayou with the help of other criminal genies. Once the fugitives had reached a point of safety, Hunter ended up slaughtering the rescuers out of rage due to the failure of the genocide plan.

Once healed, Krull disappeared from camp. We all wished that Santalonian troops would slaughter him in the jungle. It was the first time I wished for the Santalonians to kill anyone.

The war chief's threats of punishment for attacking fellow soldiers were dismissed. All other superiors thought we did the right thing by attacking Krull and killing Hunter. The farmers of Dadeaka had been supplying our army with food, so Krull and Hunter were committing sabotage against their own army. The war chief argued that we still deserved punishment, but Bashar threatened to expose this story to the public, and this warning shut the war chief up. War really brought out the worst in people, and it was really sad that our superior was a power tripping twerp who viewed heroes as criminals and crooks as innocents.

Three days after the fight with Krull, Trent learned that Larissa had given birth to their son Wiley. The birth had happened a few weeks back, but slow mail had delayed the news. Cyclops had much longer gestation than humans, and Trent had really hoped that he'd be home in time to become a dad.

"You have to let me take a vacation," Trent protested.

"Absolutely not," the war chief said.

"I'll come back."

"No, you won't. The only reason you're here is because you were threatened with jail if you didn't go through with conscription."

"But I'm a family man now."

"So are many other soldiers. If you want to live to see your family alive, then keep fighting. You're a tough soldier Trent. You'll live through this war, and you'll see your family. Now don't ask me for time off again, you're not getting it, period."

Trent was tempted to desert the army. His desire to flee was heightened when Wes was called up to O'Jahnteh. A council of strategists wanted Wes to work with them since Wes was a scholar and had come up with clever methods of fighting our enemies. I agreed with the council considering Wes always threw his brains into fights before his fists.

Sid was also banned from participating in the war. Lazox was angered by the slaughter of horses, elephants, and livestock so used his god powers to end all involvement of animals in the war. This caused much controversy among the council of gods and goddesses. Many cavalry troops were outraged and thought Lazox was trying to make combat harder for the soldiers.

Whenever we were out on patrol, Sid stayed in a kennel with the other dogs of war.

"I really admire Lazox's stance," Julia said. "It is really wrong to drag animals into war and have them die for the conflicts of people."

"It also means no one is going to give you shit for not riding a horse," Bashar said.

"As soon as this damn war is over, I'm going on a very long horse journey up in the northlands," Julia said.

In the following weeks, Santalonia lost more territory as the allies secured the entire jungle. The next push of the war was to take over the beaches on the south-west coast. Santalonian troops had much more experience fighting in sand dunes so would be at an advantage. Victory was in our grasp, but we still had a major stone to step over.

Our squad set up camp on the north side of the sandy shores late one afternoon. This was the first time our team had been to this area, and we were unsure of what lay ahead of us.

Marco and Julia erected our tent. Huck cooked dinner. Trent collected water from a stream. I set up a sump.

"You guys got to start working harder and faster so we can relax and go for a swim," Bashar bellowed.

"And what are you doing bossy Bashar?" Huck snorted.

"I'm supervising and delegating tasks," Bashar retorted.

"You're playing the role of babysitter," Huck shot. "We're all equal here so get off our lazy ass, quit playing the role of commander, and do something or you're not getting any dinner."

Even though Bashar was lazy and despotic, it was fun to laugh at the argument between him and others. It was funny how humour could be found in war.

Night fell faster than we'd anticipated. Huck served us peanut soup in the dark. After dinner, Marco took the first patrol. Julia went with him on his magic carpet. Since we were surrounded by many tall sand dunes, it was impossible to see what lay to the south of us. For all we knew, we could have been walled in and surrounded by enemies.

Julia and Marco returned to our camp unexpectedly soon. The rest of us had been washing our dishes in the sump. Everyone was responsible for their own bowl and cutlery, but Bashar had to clean the pot on account of being such a sloth while the rest of us had set up camp.

"We have to abandon our camp," Marco said. "There are legions just beyond the first sand dunes."

"I have never seen so many soldiers," Julia said. "I'm worried they might have seen the light from our lantern."

"The Santalonian government is probably hording all its soldiers in one area," Huck said. "They've lost so much territory that they had to do everything they can to protect their last lands."

"What are we just sitting around here for," Bashar bellowed. "Let's break some ass."

"Hell no," Marco said. "We'll be overpowered like nothing else. Running out there is suicide."

"Quit being a wimp," Bashar said. "Come on Marco, you were always the tough guy. Has this war turned you chicken?"

"I'm being sensible," Marco said.

"It's our job to kill," Bashar said. "We're all experts at guerrilla combat. We surprise the scouts with an ambush, slaughter them, retreat, come back, kill some more. I don't know why you're all being a bunch of chickenshits."

"Bashar I'm a family man now and I won't fight unless I'm certain of victory," Trent said. "Six warriors taking on a legion is mindless."

"If you guys are too pussy to fight some rangers then I'll throw you into a jam," Bashar said. "The faster we kill the Santalonians, the faster this fucking war will be over."

Bashar went to the tent, pulled out a war drum, and banged on it until he broke the skin. We'd yelled at him to stop, but our screams probably garnered more attention. Within minutes, an overpowering number of Santalonian scouts showed up at our camp site.

"Your stupidity is not going to kill us," Julia growled, "but you will pay for this dick move."

"Hells yeah," Bashar said. "My bravery will take us to victory."

"Shut your obnoxious trap and fight you son of a bitch," Marco growled.

I raised my ring and fired dozens of small silver rays. Each ray flashed to every enemy metal weapon as if the bronze and iron had magnetized the rays. Spearheads, axe blades, swords, daggers, and arrowheads turned to rust. Flaky ginger crust fell from arrow shafts, while swords turning to amber crumbs. Soldiers shouted in astonishment as their weapons disintegrated.

Bashar smiled at me, and then dashed into the crowd of disarmed scouts and started bonking them with his hammer.

Bodies with smashed bones fell to the ground. Julia joined in with her sword and cut defenseless troops to the ground. Even though it was dark out, I could see blood spilling into the sands. Huck fired his crossbow, taking down a troop who was armed with a wooden club. Trent joined in on the fight by punching and kicking Santalonians into the sand. Rays from my ring floored foes.

Marco smacked his whip at one troop. The troop managed to dodge the lashing. Before Marco could try again, a ranger snuck up behind him and tackled him to the ground. After some punching, shoving, kneeing, and elbowing, Marco wrapped his whip around his attacker's neck and strangled him. His opponent choked, drooled in the sand, and fell as a corpse.

A trooper armed with an axe dashed toward Bashar. I wondered why his weapon still had its axe-head intact. Right as the weapon was swinging toward Bashar's shoulder, I realized that the axe fighter was wielding a stone weapon.

Bashar jolted and then stood as still as a statue. His right arm fell from his shoulder, plopped into the sand, and sent up swirls of dust. His hammer fell from his fingers, resting next to his amputated arm.

Trent jumped in front of the soldier who'd disarmed Bashar, seized the ranger's weapon, snapped the wooden shaft in half, tossed the bottom end of the stick away, and slammed the axe-head into Bashar's attacker's face. The sharp stone axe-head pulverized the troop's brain. His corpse dropped right next to Bashar's amputated arm. This was the first time I'd ever seen Trent use a weapon.

I sprinted toward Bashar and healed his wound. While genies could heal a cut, our magic could not reattach limbs. Bashar didn't respond to anything which had happened so would need to be treated for shock.

An arrow landed next to me. Several more followed. We couldn't tell where the projectiles were coming from since the sand dunes acted as natural obstruction. Huck created a force shield, flew up in the air on his magic carpet, and quickly descended back to the ground.

"There are dozens of longbow troops approaching," he said. "Hordes of other soldiers are following. We have to retreat."

Marco and Trent ran toward Marco's magic carpet. Julia climbed aboard Huck's flying rug. I told Bashar to come along, but he was still catatonic. I ended up using telekinesis to transport him onto my magic carpet before we took off. Bashar's wound had scabbed and wasn't weeping, but I wondered if he'd been psychologically shocked to the point of long-term depression. Either way, his days as a soldier were over. Losing an arm would change one forever. Even though I felt like Bashar brought some of this upon himself, I promised myself never to mention his hubris attitude toward running into danger.

Huck fired his ring at the sand dunes and created a small windstorm. Dust scattered in the mini hurricane, temporarily masking us. Blowing dust stung soldiers' eyes and arrows were blown astray.

I felt an unexpected pain in my shoulder. The cotton on my shirt was ripped. Blood seeped from my flesh. An arrow had slashed my skin. It scared me how close I'd come to having been shot to death. I could have easily been hit in the neck, died, crashed, and killed Bashar along the way. I told myself to stop dawdling and heightened my speed.

I caught up with my friends. Once we were in the jungle, we took a break at a clearing. Marco healed my wound. Julia convinced Bashar to drink water and he slowly started responding. Huck checked Bashar's wound. Bashar's shoulder was clean, but his arm was gone for eternity. It seemed that if war didn't kill you immediately, it ripped you apart piece by piece.

We returned to base after our break. Huck told the war chief what we'd seen and what had gone on down at the dunes. The war chief had no idea how to solve our problem. It was terrifying to know that no one had any solution to enemies at the door. I wondered how long it would be until arrows were flying at our base.

Bashar was dismissed the next day and sent to Stodaneatoo in a convoy. Right after Bashar hit the road, a sexy woman walked into camp and Huck started flirting with her. The two of them soon snuck off. It was funny that Huck could still think about his libido when so much evil was going on. Seeing Huck flirt with a chick made me miss Sheri even more. I'd been telling myself to not mourn her until the war was over so that hurt feelings didn't put me in danger, but some things were impossible for the heart. I really hoped that Huck wasn't going to lose his new girlfriend when I saw them share a kiss.

It was kind of funny how Julia and I had each lost lovers while Huck had found one. The tricks of war never ceased to sneak up on you.

"This is Willa," Huck told us.

"Hi y'all," Willa said as she went around shaking hands with each of us. "Just to get it out of the way, I'm from Santalonia, but don't get worried about that. I totally hate the Santalonian government and all the evil things that it has done to its own people and everyone else in Sionia. I've been fighting alongside with the forces from O'Jahnteh, but I was recently reassigned to the coast because I was told that my wizard powers could be put to real good use down here."

"You're a wizard?" Julia said.

"Shit yeah, I understand that you're all pretty talented warriors so I'm sure we'll win this sucker real soon," Willa called.

About an hour after meeting Willa, Trent called a private meeting with Huck, Marco, Julia, and I. He'd politely asked Huck to not bring Willa along. It was always hard to separate Huck from his chicks, especially at the start of a relationship.

"I'm going to bounce out of here," Trent said.

"You're deserting?" Huck said.

"Yeah fella," Trent said.

"But we're so close to victory," Huck said.

"I know, and you are all going to kick a lot of ass, but I'm done," Trent said.

"Come on man," Huck pleaded. "Don't abandon your friends. You're putting us in danger by leaving."

"I'm sorry Huck, but my heart is calling to elsewhere," Trent said. "I can't centre my spirit on the war any longer, and if you can't do that you're a dead man."

I knew there was no talking Trent out of walking away. Although I thought he was doing the right thing, I also felt flustered. We had started out with the ideal team, but it was shrinking by the battle.

"I'm going off to meet my son and become a dad," Trent said. "I will not let this vague war stop me from being a family man."

"You're doing the right thing," Julia said.

"It's actually pretty inspiring man," Marco said. "You've always hated being here, and the most powerful calling in your life has gotten you away from all this terror."

"If anyone can escape, evade the rangers, and get home to their family and tribe safely, it's you Trent," I said. "You know the jungle better than anyone else."

"Thanks Don, thanks all of you; this is very important to me," Trent said.

"Just be sure to say hi to Bashar for all of us when you pass by Stodaneatoo," Huck said.

"Will do," Trent promised.

We each hugged Trent and he gave Sid a belly rub before disappearing into the trees. I wished each of us could abandon the war. Maybe the whole thing would be over if we all walked away.

The next day Huck called what remained of our troop to the beach. We didn't feel like a team anymore. Everyone was disappearing, leaving our team down to its minimal pillars. Not to insult Willa, but she seemed like an interloper. The last time new folks had joined our squad they'd been our greatest enemies. I couldn't help being a bit paranoid of Willa considering she was a Santalonian. She ranted regularly about how much she hated the Santalonian government, which made me wonder if she was trying to convince herself or the team that she was an ally. By all accounts she'd been a tough soldier who used her wizardly abilities to bring carnage to our foes. I was sure it must have been hard to live as a Santalonian among Santalonian enemies.

Zadohkoo appeared from thin air in front of Willa. The god of death never made random appearances. With all the killings that had been going on, I was sure he'd been very busy with permitting dead souls to enter the afterlife.

"I've called you guys here to witness the most audacious battle in Santalonian history," Willa said. "I know you're all lifelong combatants who have stories like no one else, but amid all the tragedy, I think you deserve an award.

"You see, this beach is the last obstacle between here and Santalonia, which is why there are so many legions here. Once these troops fall, Santalonia will be ours.

"Zadohkoo and I have a plan. We are going to raise several legions of dead soldiers and bring them here to the beach. We can take a step back and let victory come to us."

"Death is the best way to kill the living," Zadohkoo said.

Willa closed her eyes and raised her staff. The orb at the top of the staff turned purple and glowed like a lightning bolt before it rumbled. Many flashes of light shot from the orb, each one hitting Zadohkoo. Zadohkoo looked as if he was meditating while standing up. He absorbed the light flashes and then fired them from his fingers. When the light hit the ground, soldiers rose as conjured zombies. Each zombie soldier was armed with a spear, sword, axe, club, lance, or archery gear. Some of the soldiers were genies while others were cyclops, ogres, or humans. While many of the living dead soldiers were mangled corpses, others looked completely healthy. After twenty minutes, Willa and Zadohkoo had created an enormous army of living dead warriors.

"This is the most amazing thing I've ever seen," Huck said. "Death is the solution for life."

"What the hell does that mean?" Marco asked.

"Our lives are going to be saved by the dead," Huck responded. "The dead save the living."

"Not even the dead can rest" Julia said. "Is this how chaotic war has become?"

"Once the battle is over, the dead will return to the afterlife," Zadohkoo said.

The legions of dead soldiers marched south. We weren't far from where Bashar had been amputated. I really hoped that the dead outnumbered the Santalonians and that the zombies were in tiptop fighting shape.

"Why don't you climb on your magic carpets and watch the battle?" Zadohkoo suggested. "Your safety will be guaranteed as long as you don't wiz into battle."

"We will survive death," Willa said.

Marco stepped aboard his magic carpet while Julia and I stepped onto mine.

"You coming Huck?" I asked.

"I'll be there soon," he smiled. "I just want to thank my girlfriend for creating something so amazing."

"Hey don't forget me," Zadohkoo said. "I'm only the god of death."

Huck and Willa smooched while the rest of us took flight without looking back. The dead captured our eyes like magnets on iron. I wondered if the other gods and goddesses would get pissed at Zadohkoo for taking such a bold stance in ensuring victory for the allies, but now wasn't the time to get skeptical.

"I feel like I'm watching the mother of all gladiator fights," Julia said.

Countless bouts were going on beneath us. You couldn't look anywhere without seeing swords, clubs, spears, arrows, crossbow bolts, battle-axes, or staffs doing what they were designed for. Dozens of Santalonian bodies were dropping dead. The sand dunes darkened with corpses and gore.

The zombie soldiers had retained their fighting abilities, and they were oblivious to pain. You could smack them, shoot them, or stab them, but they kept fighting. Marching corpses with missing limbs, smashed skulls, torn torsos, and battered flesh swung blades and blunt weapons as though they were walking killing machines. Some Santalonian troops tried to run from the army of the dead, but the horde of zombies traveled southward, annihilating all Santalonian soldiers in their way.

"If it takes dead soldiers to win the battle, does that mean that the war will only end when we kill one another?" I asked.

"Don, stop thinking such morbid thoughts," Julia said. "I know we're staring at the dead, but if you think too much about death, then it'll get you killed."

Marco flew toward a shadowy area of palm trees. While the sand dunes had been loaded with Santalonian troops, none of them had journeyed beyond the trees. The shady sandy area of palms had almost acted as an invisible border so Marco was sure that he wouldn't be hurt and that he could get a closer look at what was going on. Julia and I followed him. We didn't know where Huck was, but we weren't at all worried about him.

"Don, let me off," Julia said.

I wasn't sure what she was talking about or why she had gotten so excited, but when I saw an albino dressed in red, I halted in my tracks. Marco's jaw dropped and his eyes dilated to saucers. Jason clubbed a Santalonian, turned away, and dashed toward Julia.

Julia jumped from my magic carpet, ran over to the shady area beneath the palm trees, and made out with zombie Jason. The rest of the zombie army moved south so the reunited lovers were safe. Since Jason was wearing his trademark red clothes, few death wounds were revealed. I wanted to talk with him, tell him how sorry I was that he was dead, and remind him of how much of a friend he had been to me. I also wanted to learn about the afterlife.

I hadn't seen Julia this happy since Jason had been alive. I wondered if perhaps he could come back to life and live among us once this battle was over. It didn't seem right that the dead were hauled from the afterlife, thrown into one battle, and then sent back to grave after a fight to the death.

If Jason could come back from the dead to battle the living, then it didn't seem right if Sheri couldn't return.

I ditched Julia and Jason and flew over the battle. There were hardly any female soldiers so finding Sheri wouldn't be too hard.

"Don, what the hell man?" Marco called. "Don't you want to talk to Jason?"

"Later man, help me find Sheri first."

We combed the battlefield back and forth. I saw few women, and none of them looked anything like Sheri. I stopped paying attention to all the carnage beneath me. I forgot about the horrors of war and was completely focused on love.

"Is that Ace?" Marco asked.

I hadn't even thought about running into him. It had been so long since I'd seen Ace, and a lifetime's worth of crazy events had happened since Frosher Volcano, so I wasn't sure if I would recognize him. Nonetheless, I saw a big dude flinging around a flail and taking down more Santalonian troops than anyone else.

"The spark that started it all," Marco said.

I really did want to talk with Ace, but I had to find Sheri first. Marco stopped to have a word with Ace while Ace was smashing soldiers with his flail along the shoreline.

Ever since Sheri and I had fallen in love, I'd measured all events in my life by before and after I'd met Sheri. It was really hard to measure new events by a timeline which consisted of after Sheri's death.

I continued to zoom back and forth above the marching zombie army but saw no sign of Sheri. Marco caught up to me. Neither of us needed to speak because he knew what the only thing on my mind was.

"You guys want to join in on in the march of the carcass," a familiar voice cackled.

Robin stood ahead of us. He was wielding his favourite sword. Six crossbow bolts hung from the wounds which had killed him many years ago.

"Are you guys so desperate to die that you have to hang out with a bunch of zombies?" Robin laughed. "Well good to see you too, say something assholes."

"Holy fuck," Marco said. "There are some things which not even death can kill."

"Yeah, me and my craziness," Robin cackled. "Are you guys too much of pussies to fight with an army of the undead? We're doing you a big favour, at least thank us."

"Robin," I said. "I'm really sorry about your death. I have always felt responsible and have never forgiven myself for it."

"Ah come on Don," he said. "I haven't seen you in forever and I don't want any boo hoo mushy shite. My audacity killed me, and mistakes are part of the human experience."

"What's it like in the afterlife?" I asked.

"I'm not going to spoil any secrets," Robin smirked. "You'll find out soon enough man, I promise you that."

"You're not a psychic, are you?" Marco asked.

"If I was, then I might have been a lot smarter and seen my own death coming," Robin said.

Robin dropped his shorts and mooned approaching soldiers. Upon seeing his ass, the soldiers backed away.

"Don't run away man, I didn't even fart on you," Robin said. "Toilet paper is in pretty short supply though."

Robin's sword flew forward and slashed a soldier who he'd mooned. The soldier dropped to the ground while blood squished out of Robin's old death wounds.

"That's what you get for not kissing my ass," Robin said.

Zadohkoo appeared, hovering above the battlefield.

"You guys got to say goodbye," Zadohkoo said to Marco and I. "The army of the dead has killed nearly all the Santalonian troops stationed on the dunes so it's time for them to go back to the afterlife."

"Wow, hold it right there," I said. "You can't make all of them disappear yet. I haven't seen my dead warrior girlfriend yet."

"Don, gods don't take orders from anyone," Zadohkoo said. "You of all people should know that. You've already got a pretty bad reputation among the deities due to your squabbling with I'magee."

The dead soldiers vanished by the dozens. Robin disappeared without getting the chance to say goodbye. Zadohkoo disappeared with the last soldiers and within a minute there was no one on the sand dunes but fallen Santalonian warriors.

"Didn't I tell you I was too old to die," a craggy voice spoke.

Keifer waved to us from the battlefield. He was dressed in sailor clothes and covered in Santalonian blood. His staff looked like it had taken a few licks from the fight. He vanished before Marco and I could say anything, leaving us as the only living among the battlefield.

"I'm sorry Don," Marco said. "It's totally unfair. I feel for you man."

"There really is no justice in death," I said. "The only thing nearly as insulting as death is everyone coming back except Sheri."

I turned my magic carpet northward and zoomed back to camp. Marco kept up with me but had a bit of difficulty. Unlike him, I had my eyes focused ahead while he kept eyeing the slaughtered squadrons.

I stopped to pick up Julia. Jason was gone. Had I known that I wouldn't be reunited with Sheri, I would have made more of an effort to talk with Ace, Jason, Robin, and Keifer; great friends who I sincerely wished were still alive. The fact that I hadn't stopped to talk with those guys made my futile effort to find Sheri even more hurtful.

Huck and Willa were still smooching. I figured they hadn't watched any of the battle. I couldn't fault them for that. Why watch others die when you could be with your lover?

Marco pulled Julia aside and told her what had happened. Julia came over and hugged me.

"I'm sorry Don," she said. "I would have loved to see Sheri too, and I know this hurts you even more. Know this though, Jason is extremely proud of us, and he has seen Sheri in the afterlife. You are still her lover for eternity."

Amid major heartache, I'd never been more thankful to have Jason as a friend. I'd had a lot of amazing folks in my life. It was queer how the war was making me realize how lucky I was.

Troops from O'Jahnteh, Stodaneatoo and many other northern communities quickly secured the area. There was one more military base between us and Santalonia. Once the last standing Santalonian troops fell, Sionia was ours. Many troops were excited about knocking down the last remaining forces while some feared that things would be extremely hard for the final step. There was paranoia that Santalonia was prepared for a siege, had put their best soldiers in front of the city, and set up traps.

Before any more troops could be transported south, a clan of dragons arrived. The arrival of such beasts alarmed many soldiers. Though the twenty dragons were animalistic, several of them were piloted by Tathika dragons. This shocked many as we'd thought that Wes was the only member of his race.

"I told you I would return to help win the war," Wes said.

"This is an amazing surprise," Julia said as she hugged Wes. "Not only you, but this whole army of dragons."

"Have you found a tribe of Tathika folks?" I asked.

"Dirotalo has been repopulating the Tathika race," Wes said. "There are two communities now, one north of O'Jahnteh and the other outside of Basbahti. We herded up most of these animalistic dragons from Basbahti."

"Did you bring all of these dragons here to win the war?" Huck wondered.

"Indeed, I had a talk with Dirotalo, and he agreed to lend us some dragons," Wes said. "Many of the dragons have jockeys who are Tathika dragons, and we have one human jockey named Krist who is a dragon rider with a circus. The generals really like this idea. Tomorrow we will fly over the last Santalonian base and burn it to crisps. All dragons will carry a few drums of thithaleeth oil to act as bombs."

"Wow," Huck said. "I can already hear the drum roll of victory."

"It's about time we won," Wes said. "By the way, I'm really sorry about Trent and Bashar."

"Trent is probably living the happiest days of his life right now," Marco said. "There are no reports of him being captured, and if anyone could hike home, it's him. He's probably not even thinking about the war cuz he's so happy to be a dad now."

"We haven't heard from Bashar," I said. "Once the war is over, we should visit him."

"One question though," Julia said. "How can these dragons be used in war if Lazox has banned animals from being used in combat?"

"Lazox does not have sovereignty over dragons anymore," Wes answered. "Dirotalo is the god of dragons, and he is completely alive, much to I'magee's dismay."

"His actions are definitely going to piss off many of the gods and goddesses," I said. "Man, I bet Zadohkoo is pretty unpopular after the battle of the undead."

Most of the soldiers spent the night relaxing around bonfires. While booze was banned throughout camp, authorities decided to ignore alcohol restrictions. Never had there been so much promise for a victorious battle. Everyone was completely confident that the dragons would descend from the sky and burn Santalonia to a crisp. Some folks were praying to the fire god Rahn in hope that the fires would burn like volcanoes. Troopers were happy that they wouldn't have to fight in the final battle.

"Wes, I want to be there for the dragon attack," I said.

"That's nuts Don."

"But you're going to be there."

"That's because I'm commanding the dragon horde."

"Look, if I fly around up in the air above the dragons, then I'll be safe, think of it as watching gladiator combat."

"This isn't like cheering your sister on in the coliseum."

"I think she might be at the raid too," Huck said after draining a mug of beer. "She and Krist are making out right now, and Julia isn't scared of anything."

I glanced toward the bonfire and saw Julia and Krist cuddling and smooching among the glowing flames. I hadn't spoken with Krist yet, but Julia was happy, so that was good enough for me. It seemed kind of weird that Julia was smooching with a stranger after having been reunited with her dead boyfriend, but perhaps Jason had encouraged her to find a lover among the living.

"If Don flies into combat tomorrow, then so will I," Marco said.

"Me too," Huck said.

"Huck, don't go," Willa said.

"You can come too," Huck said.

"I won't go," Willa said. "I know this battle is important for victory, but what if people I know are in that camp. It would feel wrong to watch them die as entertainment. Stay behind to keep me company, Huck."

Huck thought about this for a moment, sighed, and then agreed to stay behind with his girlfriend.

"Huck and Willa are the sensible ones," Wes said. "Marco, Don, both of you guys have survived the war. Why go down during the last battle?"

"I love Sionia and am doing this for my country," I said. "The government has done all it can to ruin this country, so I should do all I can to fix their shit."

"No offence man, but we really don't need your efforts," Wes said.

"Wes, I am the only genie who has the power to control dragons," I said. "My magic could be a real asset in case things get sticky."

"Okay, but don't try and use any of your magic to try and control me or any of the other Tathika dragons," Wes said. "They know what they're doing and are all pretty smart."

"Did Dirotalo resurrect them?" Marco asked.

"Yes, each of those dragons is composed from souls of deceased Tathika dragons in the same way that I am," Wes responded. "Numbers are slowly going up, and with hope and time, we will be an equally recognized species in Sionia."

The twenty dragons were mounted as light started to glow across the land and ocean the next morning. About fifteen of the dragons had Tathika jockeys. Krist was riding the biggest dragon and Julia was sitting behind him on his saddle.

"Wes, you still have four dragons that don't have riders," I said.

"Dragons are fairly obedient as long as you know how to communicate with them," Wes said. "They will follow my lead."

Marco mounted his magic carpet and floated upward.

"Don, where's your magic carpet?" he asked.

I took a deep breath and said, "I have a new trick to show you guys."

"You've really saved it for a crazy time," Marco said.

I jumped into the air, as high as I could. For several moments I floated above the ground as if I were a low-hanging cloud. Everyone gazed at me in surprise, wondering why gravity hadn't pinned me to the ground. I rose higher and higher.

"Don," Julia gasped. "You're flying?"

"It's a spell I recently learned," I said. "One of the privileges of the magic Dirotalo bestowed onto me."

"Man, why can't he give me any cool presents," Marco said.

"So, this was why you were sneaking off so much these last few days," Julia said. "You were learning to fly?"

"I can fly without wings or a magic carpet," I said. "Today is the last day of the war and I am going to fly to victory."

The twenty dragons took off, heading south. Marco and I followed behind. Every few moments Marco glanced from his magic carpet to see if I was still in the air. I'd always loved flying on a magic carpet, but I felt such an uncanny adrenaline when I flew without one. I knew Wes's wings sometimes got sore after much flapping, but whenever I flew, I never felt like much of the magic from my ring was being drained. Of all the magic gifts, flying was by far my favourite, even if healing was the most important one.

We approached the last standing Santalonian military camp. Since the morning was still young, not too many soldiers were awake. There were dozens of tents set up and the odd night watch guard bounced between them.

Without warning the dragons dove downward. Fireballs blasted from their mouths. Tents erupted in flames. The fences which acted as the makeshift wall around the camp caught fire, and the entire perimeter of the camp became a ring of fire. Smoke blinded soldiers as they tried to evade the flames. All weapons were useless against the dragons.

The dragons circled around the camp and then dove downward into a new location. More flames spat from the dragons' mouths. The inferno grew across the camp, burning new areas which had yet to be directly hit by the dragons. The dragon jockeys dropped barrels of thithaleeth oil which exploded like bombs, destroyed tents, and blasted Santalonian soldiers to immediate death.

Marco and I hovered above the glowing land. Neither of us said anything, but both knew what one another was thinking. We had to be here. We had to witness the end of the war.

Julia and Krist's dragon flew toward Marco and I. She looked a bit panicked, and I wondered if she was going to ask to be taken home.

"There are a few approaching ballistas and catapults," Julia yelled above explosions and flapping wings. "We've got to do something."

Killing a dragon was extremely difficult. I thought back to the ancient days when Aurelius had swallowed me, and I'd been forced into carving him up from the inside. Since the dragons had quick speed, agile maneuverability, and firepower like no other, it seemed a bit paranoid to think that an army on the brink of collapse could kill them.

"I'll handle this," I said right as my heroic compulsions kicked in.

I flew toward the approaching siege weapons, which were outside of the camp. The catapult and ballista operators were definitely brave, but sometimes bravery and determination weren't good enough. Marco followed me, unsure of what was going on. I trusted him to stay out of my way, so I didn't protest.

Wes continued to circle the camp with the dragon he was riding. The four dragons without riders tagged behind his lead. I pointed my ring at three of the dragons and fired a trio of rays. The dragons flew toward me after having been zapped by my magic. Through telepathy, I commanded the dragons to fly high and then dive down behind the catapults and ballistas. The siege weapons were pointed toward the dragons who were still scorching the camp, but since the dragons were moving quickly, the siege weapon operators were unable to secure targets.

My three dragons dove to the ground. Before smashing into the dirt, they flew up, dropped their jaws, and unleashed long waves of fire. The flames roared like spirals of heat. The siege weapon operators died on the spot. The catapults and ballistas crisped to ash before they even had an opportunity to burn. The danger was dead.

I released my control of the dragons, and they flew back to Wes. Wes flew upward and the squad of dragons regrouped. All twenty dragons were alive. None of the jockeys had perished along the way.

Wes took the lead and led the flight of dragons back to the camp. Marco got ready to follow them but then looked back at me.

"What are you floating around for?" Marco asked. "The battle is over."

"I'm going to take a joy ride over Santalonia," I said. "Do you want to come?"

Marco was surprised by my words but decided to ride along. A minute later Julia and Krist showed up.

"Don't you guys want to go back and party?" Krist asked.

"We'll be there soon," I said. "Marco and I have to take care of a personal note."

"Got you," Krist said. "Oh yeah Don, you pulled an amazing move back there."

"I'm really proud of you," Julia said.

"Be proud of yourselves," I said. "You kicked a lot of ass today."

"We've all done amazing things in this war," Marco said.

Krist and Julia rejoined the dragon air force while Marco and I flew into Santalonia. The city looked fancy but eerily different. There weren't many people out. Was it too early in the morning for people to rise? Were people too scared to wander the streets in fear of an invasion? Perhaps so many people had died from the war that the city's population no longer crowded the streets?

Marco and I flew across gardens, parks, businesses, homes, the city lake, recreational venues, and the circus grounds. We halted at Dadokoh Square and gazed at the national palace. I thought back to the long-gone day when Robin, Marco, and I had stirred up trouble and then come under Ace's wing. Kyle had surprised us with regicide though Shilotey's curse of Post-17 was the real game changer. I had seen some of the most important events in Sionian history yet all of them had been born from carnage.

"This is where it all started," I said, "and this is where it'll end."

"Don, I know you're the Lord of the Warriors and you might as well be a god of magic but are you seriously thinking of attacking the palace?" Marco asked.

"No friend. You know, I don't want to be the Lord of the Warriors anymore. Our lives as warriors were born here, and this is where our warrior lives should have closing, think of it as a circle story in which the circle stops spinning."

Marco and I each went quiet for a few moments as we reflected on things.

"Our lives have a new path now," Marco said, "and that path leads back to our friends."

We headed to our companions without looking back.

BOOK XIV:

BUILDING A NEW PATH

An hour after Marco and I returned to camp, the big news was made. Santalonia had surrendered. The city had lost most of its army and now had nothing to fight with. Qiami had given the news to our warlords who made the announcement of our victory public. Every soldier erupted in cheers and dance before any of the war chiefs could make any victory speeches. Words didn't need to be shared to express the emotions everyone was feeling. The warlords didn't bother trying to quell the audiences or offer congratulations because we'd earned our time to party, and no speeches could express how we felt.

We spent the rest of the day drinking and dancing around the bonfire. A nearby brewery gave away free beer. So much beer was drained that snakebites became the most common drink since there were many unopened barrels of cider lying about. A feast and a concert were also provided for us as a reward. The war chiefs must have known victory was close considering they'd timed the party so well. Everybody was cheering Wes, saying that he was the mastermind who'd won the war.

"Give yourselves' a pat on the back too," Wes said as he double fisted his drinks. "I brought in the dragons thanks to Dirotalo, a god you should all starts worshipping; give all the other dragons tons of thanks too."

"There would have been no zombie battle if it weren't for my babe," Huck said. "How about getting her a drink to show thanks?"

"You know Don, you did just as good a job as any of these heroes," Marco said at one of the quieter bonfires.

"We all did well," I said.

"I know that you wanted to be the Lord of the Warriors, and I know you feel like so many of your vigilante efforts have gone unrecognized, but you played a big role in some important battles, and you helped keep a lot of people safe."

"Thanks man."

I had saved many people and I'd done plenty to push the army south, but I'd been unable to save Sheri. Surviving war and saving your friends made you a hero in its own way, but I wouldn't be remembered the same way Wes or Willa would be, and that was okay with me. The war hadn't been about me. Maybe the title Lord of the Warriors was something I didn't need to strive for anymore. To be the Lord of the Warriors, you needed evil and chaos. You had to fight endlessly to prove that you were better than anyone who challenged you. None of that would ever give me tranquility. I wanted peace right now, nothing more.

The beer and cider flowed like waterfalls that night. Marco puked. Huck and Willa disappeared, passed out beneath a coconut tree, and had to be moved when the wind picked up. Julia and Krist spent most of the night making bonfire love.

"Don, you are so amazing, and your sister is a goddess," Krist said with drunken slurred words.

"You're a hell of a guy too Krist," I said, "just be careful with my sister. She can kick anyone's ass."

I stumbled out of my hammock the next morning and headed back to the party site. People were gathered all around bonfires that were still smoldering. Hangovers weren't enough to keep people in bed. There was a strange force coming from the clouds that was calling our attention.

The clouds broke away and Silotious appeared in the blue sky. The queen goddess didn't appear without a reason, so the news had to be big. It would no doubt be about the war.

"Congratulations, northern soldiers, you've won the war," Silotious said.

Everyone cheered, but something didn't feel right. Silotious wasn't smiling, and I sensed uncomfortable information ahead of us. Maybe she'd decided to let us have our party before telling us about the future of the nation.

"The capital of Sionia will be moved to O'Jahnteh," she said.

More cheering followed.

"It's time for all of you to know the truth," Silotious said, silencing all. "All of you were told that Santalonia started the war, assassinated prominent politicians from Stodaneatoo and O'Jahnteh, and planned to demolish the cities in hopes of mining precious minerals. You believed that you were fighting a land war, defending your homes, sticking up for your fellow citizens, and rebelling against greedy dictators.

"There are no precious materials located beneath either city. None of the politicians were executed. They have all been in hiding since the start of the war and have been working with generals and other bureaucrats in the war effort. Santalonia had no wish to destroy Stodaneatoo or O'Jahnteh. The northern cities which you fought for started the war."

I felt physically ill. How much more horrible news was the queen goddess going share?

"O'Jahnteh started the war in an attempt to become a more powerful city," Silotious said. "The plan was to make O'Jahnteh the political and financial capital of Sionia. Since you've won the war, that action will be carried out.

"All of you were lied to. I am very sorry for this. I am sorry for the soldiers who died and fought a war based on deception, and I am very sorry for the civilians who died because of the war efforts. Essentially you all fought a useless and stupid war based entirely on greed and deceit.

"I hope that some good will come out of all this conflict and that you will find peace even if you had to go through horror to achieve it."

Silence turned to grumbling. The mob grew and people were screaming indecipherable rage. It looked like a riot was going to break out.

I gazed at my friends. They looked as angry as I was. I nodded and pointed toward the trees, indicating that I wanted a place to talk away from the bedlam. Julia, Wes, Marco, and Huck followed. Willa and Krist wanted to come but Huck indicated that I only wanted to speak with my core friends. I would come to trust Krist and Willa at a more relaxed time.

"So, this is where the path of pathos took us," I said once we'd walked a considerable distance into the jungle. "We fought on the wrong side. We fought for bullshit reasons, and the criminals won. War of the fucking losers eh."

"Politicians," Marco scoffed, "bunch of professional criminals and liars."

"Let's get together and protest against them," Huck said.

"No, Huck," I said.

"What?" Huck gasped.

"So much damage has already been done, and things can't be repaired with fighting," I said. "Let's let the revolution take over. I don't want any more people to die in a futile scramble."

"I can't believe that for once in your life you're not being nosy and seeking to destroy evil," Huck said, "especially when the crime against the country was carried out by the government."

After so many years of living as a vigilante, I was surprised by my submissiveness. My life story had taught me that conflict was inevitable, but I'd lost faith in the idea that battle would bring peace by vanquishing evil with a sword. People didn't get along; it was within our nature to bout. You could be a good person with integrity who solved disputes through intellect, heart, and diplomacy, but there was always a monster who didn't share your virtues.

"Don't go chickenshit now man," Huck said, "this is our chance to get even."

"There will be a war later on," Wes said. "Once Santalonia re-grows its army, there will be bloody vindictive campaigns, that's how things go. Everyone is always trying to get on top and one-up others in our competitive world."

"Society is a very cruel and self-destructive creature," Julia said. "Nothing about it makes any sense, and I want nothing to do with it."

"What if something good comes out of all of this?" Wes said. "I know we feel like our country has reached its ultimate bathos, but maybe everything will get a lot better if O'Jahnteh becomes the national capital and the head financial district. Santalonia was always autocratic and run by kleptocrats who ignored the rest of the nation; maybe things will be better off now."

"Maybe things will be better in the future," Marco said, "but I'm not about to forgive the actions and lies of our government."

"Now is not the time to be hopeful for governments," Huck said. "I love all you guys, but I think right now we need a vacation from one another. For the next season, I think we should all go off, do our own thing, and then get in contact with one another once we're feeling a bit more relieved."

"I agree with you Huck," Julia said. "I'll finally get to go on my horse trip up north, but I wish that I was headed up there on account of better circumstances."

"War is dead," I said. "It's nothing, but the death of anything good."

Julia and Krist hopped aboard a dragon and headed north to Basbahti, where they set off on a long horse trek. After their journey by hoof, they flew by dragon to more remote areas of the north. My sister ended up being a pretty good dragon jockey, and Krist got her a job working in the circus.

Wes also went north, but with the other Tathika dragons. He could have settled in the Tathika community outside of O'Jahnteh, but he wanted to get as far away from the city of lies as possible. He got a job with a religious book publishing company and started rewriting the Alontae, detailing the biography of Dirotalo. I was included in the story of Dirotalo's rebirth. This story enraged I'magee since Wes made him out to be the most diabolical of all deities, while my good friend praised me as a legend. The true story of the genies' origin was finally made public by Wes.

Wes ended up finding a girlfriend named Rhea. Never had any of us been happier for him. We'd all spent way too much time worrying that Wes was going to spend his entire life as a celibate.

Trent was living the life he'd always loved and was happier now that he had a wife and son.

Bashar recovered from his injury. He decided to not let getting dismembered keep him from being a fighter. He joined an arm-wrestling club and won a bronze medal at his first competition. When Bashar found out that he'd written propaganda articles for a war based on lies, he swore that he'd never write another news article again. His shame toward being involved in irresponsible journalism was understandable, but he didn't stay away from the pen or paper for long.

A blacksmith in Stodaneatoo invented metal clothing called armor, and metal hats called helmets. Bashar wrote technical articles about these inventions. The blacksmith patented these inventions, started a factory, and quickly became a stinking rich tycoon. Bashar worked as his publicist. So many soldiers' lives would have been saved if armor and helmets had come into use before the war, but there was no future in fussing over the past.

Huck and Willa moved to Santalonia.

"I want to learn about city life," Huck said. "I've seen so many cool areas of the country and I will revisit all of them, but first I want to try something new."

"Living in the city will help us fall back in love with culture," Willa said. "It will also give us the chance to help rebuild civilization, and we can redeem ourselves for having fought on the wrong side of the war."

"You didn't fight for the wrong side," I said. "We were put on the wrong side, and we are innocent of any crimes."

"Thanks Don, but I will feel better about myself if I show altruism towards my hometown."

It took me a long time to accept that I'd been fooled, and that none of the problems which resulted from the war were my fault. I still felt guilty some days, but I realized that I did no one any good by being hard on myself.

Marco headed out to the west coast on the day the war ended. After a few days of wandering around aimlessly, I met up with him.

"I am part of the unknown," I said to him when I dropped by unexpectedly at his house in Raroaka.

"Stay here as long as you need to man," he said. "The ocean has been healing me."

I took up Marco's offer. If the ocean could heal him, then I was sure it could heal me. I found a hut to live in and got a job teaching sailing. It had been a long time since I'd enjoyed time on a boat. Returning to my old happy roots made me feel pretty good about myself. People on the coast were friendly, but I wasn't ready to start dating. It still bothered me that Sheri hadn't appeared during the zombie battle. Occasionally I wondered if she had been resurrected and I'd missed her.

"Hypothetical thoughts will destroy you," Marco said one night over a beer. "Sheri was an optimist, so worrying won't honour all the beautiful memories of her."

Marco started dating a navigator named Martina when he was on a scientific expedition to study kelp. Martina regularly invited me over to their house to hang out. Sometimes the three of us went sailing. Even though life sometimes felt strange, and horrible memories could be sparked easily, there wasn't much to complain about in Raroaka.

I didn't pay too much attention to national politics. I was focused on my community. Some folks thought that I should be more informed of things on a federal level, but I still felt like I needed a break from Sionia. There had been protests and demonstrations against the government, but thankfully none of them had led to riots or wars. O'Jahnteh was becoming quite a rich city, but my quiet life on the ocean had taught me that materialism wasn't wealth.

I had health, food, friends nearby, friends faraway who I still got to visit, and fun things to do. Could I reasonably ask for more?

I no longer owned a sword, and I didn't want to.

BOOK XV:

THE INEVITABLE

One afternoon, after having taught sailing lessons, I was relaxing on the dock. One of my favourite activities was to lay around like a lizard on the wharf until I got so hot my flesh felt like it was on fire. When I could no longer take the burning, I would jump in the ocean, swim around for ten minutes, climb back onto the pier, and repeat the process.

My peace and quiet was shattered when I heard several loud bells. I looked toward the land and saw an enormous amount of smoke coming from a warehouse. Flames traveled across the structure. I had to do what I could to save anyone who was trapped inside.

Without hesitation I flew toward the burning building. I flashed my ring in the direction of the fire and used my genie powers to conjure water. The stream of water I created entered the burning building, crushed a smoldering wall, but did nothing to the flames. Without hesitation I aimed my ring at the clouds and commanded rain. A monsoon plummeted to the burning warehouse, but the rain did little to the flames. The building must have been covered in thithaleeth oil. This seemed very strange considering the warehouse was normally used to store seafood.

I entered the warehouse through a window and flew around. Smoke blinded me, so I used my magic to create wind and blow the stinging clouds away. Though I could see, I still coughed a lot. Flames roared, and I was careful to dodge them, but the heat in the building scalded me.

Thankfully, I'd learned self-healing through advanced magic. I was constantly healing my body to make sure that heat waves and fire wouldn't take my life.

I passed from room to room and found no one. When I'd enter the burning warehouse, I'd hoped everyone had escaped the inferno and it looked like my hopes were going to be honoured.

Just to be sure of everything, I did another sweep through the building. There was no screaming or coughing. I couldn't find any injured people or burning bodies. Smoke grew thicker, flames became longer, and the heat singed every speck of my flesh. Since I was in grave danger and no one needed rescue, I decided to vacate the warehouse, which looked like it was going to collapse at any moment.

"Ha," a hateful and familiar voice cackled.

I looked up. Krull was flying on his magic carpet. He'd created a force shield to protect himself from the flames and heat.

"You always have to be the hero Don," Krull said. "You just can't let the world be as bad as it truly is. Your prying compulsions will be the death of you."

Ever since I'd moved to Raroaka, my opinion on the world had improved. Krull could only find happiness in evil which was why he couldn't understand good.

I flew toward a window. I wasn't going to be able to fight Krull and heal myself at the same time. The roof of the warehouse was going to collapse at any second but maybe I could beat Krull to the escape point. Hopefully he would die before getting a breath of fresh air.

Krull jumped from his magic carpet and landed on my back. I lost control of my flight and healing spells as I flopped downward. My body erupted in pain when I smacked the ground.

I was surrounded by flames. The smoke choked my lungs. My eyes went red. Everything became hazy. The roof of the burning building collapsed while I lay unconscious beneath it. Scorching coals buried my body, burned my flesh to nothing, and left me as a skeleton among fire.

I died.

BOOK XVI:

MY CAMPFIRE STORY

That's my campfire story. The life of Don of O'Jahnteh. Every death tells a different story, but every life leads to one place: death.

I wasn't sure how old I was when I died, but I reckoned that I lived for 907 seasons. A lot of the time I thought that I had eternal life since I was among the first wave of youth who never aged passed seventeen. Until recently, I had a real knack for escaping lethal situations, but whether you age or not, death is your destination.

I had yet to meet Zadohkoo. I was totally unsure of what was going on, and I was too confused to be upset. It was bizarre how I wasn't sad considering death was supposedly the most tragic thing of all.

"We share the dark side," a familiar voice said.

I looked around but couldn't find Sheri, the first person who I'd hoped to see when I reached the afterlife. Instead I'magee appeared. Next to Krull, I'magee was the last jackass who I wanted to see. Okay, I didn't want to see Rahn either; the fire god could go fuck himself.

"Welcome to the afterlife," I'magee said.

"And I suppose this makes you happy?" I grunted, "me being dead. Congratulations, you get to mock the dude who you've always had problems with. It must be rewarding to know that the best genie in Sionia is dead."

"You kidding?" I'magee laughed. "I've got to put up with you in the afterlife now."

"I'm glad to disappoint you."

"Don," I'magee said, and for the first time ever I heard kindness in his voice. "There are two spells I never taught you."

"And what good are they now? I'm fucking dead in case you haven't noticed that you bloody moron."

"They are spells which are only available to the dead."

Now I'magee had my attention.

"How would you like to get even with Krull?" I'magee asked.

"I'd like that fucking guy to suffer for eternity. He didn't just kill me, he was the biggest pain in the ass of my life, always showing up at the wrong time. To think that up until I'd met him, I thought Julia was the most annoying person ever. Rest assured I'magee, you were a colossal prick of the very highest order, and at one point I considered you my greatest enemy."

I'magee snorted and chuckled, "you have the power to banish Krull from existence."

"I don't totally want to kill him. I know that sounds strange, but I don't want his ass showing up in the underworld on the same day as me. Back in Raroaka, I was really happy to be far from battle."

"Banishing him for existence doesn't merely mean killing him, it means eliminating his soul. He will have no opportunity to reach the underworld if his spirit is destroyed."

"Okay, now I'm interested."

I'magee flashed his ring and a small portal appeared. Through the portal I saw Krull. I instantly angered and wanted to jump through the portal and strangle the son of a bitch to death.

"You can't walk through the opening," I'magee said, "but shine your ring at him."

I waved my ring and a green light flashed from it. The ray traveled through the portal and hit Krull. He disappeared upon contact.

"Congratulations Don, you've just killed an agent of evil. I agree with you by the way, Krull was a machine or terror. You might be dead, but you did Sionia one last vigilante favour by destroying the most wicked man ever."

"And who ever said revenge isn't sweet?" I laughed.

It was funny how I had to die to make amends with I'magee. It was even funnier that I'd had to croak to get vengeance against my greatest enemy. Maybe my second greatest enemy was really an ally against my biggest vendetta?

"I've got one more spell for you, and then I'll bugger off," I'magee said.

He created a second portal which I gazed through. I looked closely through the opening. A funeral was going on, my funeral.

"Why don't you visit?" I'magee said as he gave me a shove in the back.

I toppled head-first through the portal. A funny sensation shivered through my body. I became transparent as if I were a ghost. I still had a figure, but anyone could see through me.

There was no body to burn or bury at my funeral. Instead, there was a tombstone with my name on it. My epitaph read,

Born a Rebel
Died a Hero
Remembered a Legend

I was pretty happy with the inscription. I feared it would say something weepy or that I would be called the Lord of the Warriors.

My gift of youth had allowed me to be a hero for longer than mortality would have normally allowed. My participation in the curse of youth had truly been my calling.

I gazed at my friends. Huck and Willa were cuddling tightly, they looked the most upset out of everyone. Julia was giving Sid a belly rub; Krist was holding her other hand. Wes and Rhea had their heads bowed in my honour. Trent was carrying Wiley in his arms while Larissa was wiping her only eye. Marco stood closely with Martina; she was pregnant. Bashar gave me the thumbs up with his only remaining hand.

Everyone looked up at me. I'd never felt anything so poignant before. I'd been to tons of funerals, watched many die, and even seen an army of the dead, but nothing compared to what I was feeling right now. I was dead, but still had the chance to say goodbye. I was very grateful that my curiosity had given me one last gift of knowledge.

I tried to speak, but words couldn't escape my mouth. I couldn't hear what anyone was saying either. Tears fell from my eyes while I waved goodbye and slowly faded away. As I disappeared, I felt like I'd healed my mourners.

"Leave life," I said. "I am leaving life. I don't know where I'm headed. No one knows where they are headed."

I liked to think that life didn't end with death and that you could exist beyond death by living in the memories and hearts of others.

Green lights flashed in front of my eyes, and I felt like I was falling. Was I leaving the half-way house and being carried to the afterlife by Zadohkoo, or did I'magee have some more surprises for me?

When everything snapped back into clarity, I found myself lying in very warm water on a beach. The sky was very blue. There were nearby mountains. Palm trees swayed back and forth in the distance. I waded toward the whitish-yellow sand beach and wondered if the afterlife was a sister beach to Raroaka.

Jason was jogging down the beach with a dog. My albino friend didn't need to worry about the light. His red clothes were gone.

Keifer was sitting on a dock next to a sailboat. He had a beer in one hand and a fishing pole in the other.

Robin was building a sandcastle with some folks who I didn't recognize. They were laughing, and I felt they would welcome me as soon as I approached.

Ace was swimming through the water ahead of me. We waved at one another but then he pointed to the right.

Sheri was standing on the shoreline. I jumped out of the water and flew toward her. I was happy to know that my genie powers still worked in the afterlife, but that kind of happiness didn't compare to what I was feeling for Sheri right now.

We embraced tightly, kissed passionately, and elevated the power of romance.

One of these days, my living friends would feel a similar sensation, welcoming them to the afterlife. I didn't want them to die, but I looked forward to being reunited with them. I had a feeling that many strange adventures lay ahead.

I'd seen so much history through young eyes. When you had the fountain of youth, you were always the youth of the future. When I died, I was both young and old, but memories always outweighed age. Maybe I would finally grow old and return to a natural life of aging now that I was dead?

Even in death my spirit still existed.

About the Author

River Wolf first conceived a very rudimentary version of Lord of the Warriors for an assignment in Grade 4. After four failed attempts at expanding this four-page story into a novel, River Wolf eventually completed the first draft of Lord of the Warriors at age twenty-eight. Greek mythology, Robert E. Howard, the Arabian Nights, Tarzan, Batman, Star Wars, and anarchist ideology all played a role in the creation of Lord of the Warriors.

River Wolf enjoys the outdoor pursuits of traveling, hiking, and boating and the indoor hobbies of movies, collecting comics, and blasting heavy metal and punk rock.

River Wolf lives with his wife and daughters in the sovereign lands and seas of the Wsanec (Saanich), Lkwungen (Songhees), and Xwsepsum (Esquimalt) peoples of Victoria, British Columbia, Canada.

THANKS FOR
READING

LORD
OF THE
WARRIORS

PLEASE LEAVE A
REVIEW ON
AMAZON
OR
GOODREADS

UNTIL
NEXT TIME
HAPPY READING
AND
PEACE BE THE
JOURNEY

Manufactured by Amazon.ca
Bolton, ON

37522218R00205